THE DREAM SIFTER

Book One of the Depths of Memory Trilogy

CR BUNDY

Lusios Publishing, LLC

For my Son

CONTENTS

CHAPTER 1

GUARDIAN GRAEBER STOOD CLOAKED IN THE shadows of fading dusk outside the walls of the Zebio Sept's three-story masonry home. The scanner in his hand indicated the source of his focus resided under this roof. Although the Sept had locked things down like a fortress for their post-dinner meditation, as was proper and correct, the one hazard they could never protect themselves from stood on their doorstep.

Some thanked him. More had cursed him. The hunt used to drive him, yet he cared less and less every day.

Graeber slid the scanner back into place on his belt and pulled a lever next to the door. Chimes echoed within the halls of the Zebio Sept, alerting them to a late caller. The approach of light footfalls echoed from within, and then the loud slam of the door bolt thrown open no doubt indicated the mood of the person on the other side. The thick, wooden door with its steel reinforced frame swung open.

"I hope your purpose will make up for the timing of

this..." the butler's brusque words fell short. No doubt as he came face to face with a Guardian, the servant's thoughts drained from his minuscule brain. All Guardians wore distinctive variegated clothing made of perfect tones for blending into the native environment. The overlapping dark blue, green, gray, and brown colors shifted with just the slightest movement of the material. No one would have mistaken him for anything but what he was: an enforcer.

The matching cloak and raised hood obscured Graeber's face, but there could be no doubt as to his purpose.

"I doubt altering my timing would offer the Sept any degree of solace." The butler's face drained of color in reaction to the hard, dispassionate edge in the Guardian's voice.

"My pardon, Guardian. It's not my place to interfere." The butler stepped aside and bowed low, no doubt desperate for the protector's focus to pass over him. He never asked what this concerned; it could be only one thing. Graeber glided into the house and headed straight for the main hall, knowing the entire Sept assembled there at this hour. The butler closed and bolted the front door before trailing a short distance behind him.

At the end of the corridor, Graeber reached an ornate double archway, beyond which lay the main hall. The entire extended family consisting of the Sept proper had gathered for their post-dinner meditation.

He knew from his research that Zebio was a mid-sized Sept, consisting of a handful of first-degree children to the Chieftess, her sisters and brothers and their children, and various extended aunts and uncles related by blood or marriage. All of them skilled artisans in the family trade--earthenware, ceramic, and pottery creations.

He cared nothing for their craft, but it helped to study the trade of a given target as it indicated their aptitudes. For instance, potters would be good with their hands and have excellent attention to detail, and could be brawny through the upper body if they worked at the wheel. Therefore today's target would be a simple capture, no strain upon his skills.

A pity, that.

Most of the adults in the room sat in chairs, either around tables or in clusters, while others gathered on the floor with children on their laps or leaned up against them. Most of the small ones tried to make an effort at the meditation, but the practice was an academic one, and they were as yet unskilled.

The Az'Un had grown to learn the importance of daily calming exercises for maintaining optimal health, and the members of Zebio Sept appeared to be ardent practitioners.

The Butler rubbed his hands together next to him, eyeing the assembled thirty-odd members of the Sept. Then he gulped and took a step back, away from the scrutiny of the Guardian.

Graeber threw back his hood and surveyed the room, testing the undercurrent, prepared in case his prey might attempt to flee.

A collective gasp rippled through space as the Sept members took in the newcomer--and processed what his arrival--heralded. A few members trembled, some paled, while others slunk down in their seats, as if hiding was even a possibility.

"Who's that man?" little Solla asked. It took a child's honest inquiry to stir a verbal response from the stunned gathering. She didn't know the impropriety of disturbing the meditation or staring at a Guardian.

"Hush, child," Chieftess Taura replied, her surprise over the newcomer obvious in the strained lines etched on her face and the sudden taut muscles of her body. She straightened her back in her plush chair and flattened out her skirt before folding her hands in her lap. All of the faces in Zebio Sept turned toward the Guardian. Wide eyes and whispered words bared the naked anxiety of the crowd. Murmurs rose in volume, and mothers cradled their small children to their breasts.

"Silence," said Chieftess Taura. "Remain still." She shot a chastising look at the butler, who then took a seat near the hallway.

Even with her shock at this turn of events, Taura wasn't about to question Graeber or protocol. Her sharp gaze schooled all present, and those who'd moved quickly retreated to their seats. No one in the Sept would go against his or their Chieftess' will. "Zebio Sept welcomes your protection, Guardian. Please do what must be done."

Her tone belied the spoken welcome, but it didn't concern him. Graeber had a job to do--as long as no one interfered, everything would go smoothly.

Graeber pulled the scanner from his belt again and moved around the room. He touched every person one by one, each flinching at the brief contact. Some burst into quiet sobs at the contact, unable to contain their terror. He paid them no heed, intent only on his quarry.

In this case, the scanner only served to confirm what his honed senses detected in subtle amounts--an off stench he'd come to associate with the plague. After a lifetime scouring the planet for any living thing infested with the abomination, Graeber had to force himself to continue through the entire Sept to make sure he missed nothing.

He finished his circuit of the room and approached Taura, showing her the display on the scanner.

"This one has an active infection." His baritone, steady voice unaffected by the consequences this revelation implied and the emotional havoc it would wreak upon the entire Sept.

Taura's eyes widened, followed by silent tears as she struggled to keep her composure. "Zebio asks for your help in this matter, Guardian. Please bring cleansing to our family so we may sleep in peace again."

Taura rose and walked toward one of the windows in the corner and appeared to gaze out upon the street. Facing away from the group Taura's shoulders shook with silent sobs as her fingers gripped her arms.

"I'm happy to oblige, Chieftess Zebio." Graeber slid the scanner back into his belt.

As he pulled his hand out of his vest, Graeber grabbed an object from a satchel hanging from his belt. Moving faster than most would be able to track, he spun, flicked his wrist, and let fly a small metal dart at Terem, Taura's youngest son. The willowy sixteen-year-old cried out as it hit him on the side of the neck with an audible thunk. Terem's eyes met the Guardians with a shock that morphed into a murderous rage. He tried to stand, to back away, but the tranquilizer's immediate potency prevented even these simple tasks.

With the Guardian's target now singled out, everyone shied away from the boy, huddling along the walls and crying even harder. Danger and death marked Terem.

Graeber walked up to the teen with the grace of a predator, not a trace of fear evident in his posture.

"How dare you? I've done nothing wrong!" Terem slurred, his words forced out through now uncontrolled lips. He slid flat onto the ground, unable to hold himself upright.

Graeber squatted next to him, contemplating the boy. "Did you think no one would notice? Did you think that you were somehow immune and thus didn't need the drugs?" he snarled. He plucked the dart from Terem's neck and slid it into a vest pocket.

Shocked gasps replaced the earlier screams as the Guardian's admonishment rippled over the assembled family. Terem's illness wasn't due to the plague medicinals failing. No--for whatever reason he'd chosen to cease taking them, signing his death warrant, and placing his entire Sept at risk.

Terem tried to defend himself. He grunted, whined, and shook his head, pleading his case. He looked around the room, but the answering gazes from his Sept held no compassion, no sympathy. His betrayal had endangered them all. Guardians didn't make mistakes, and no one would start questioning them now.

Graeber took out a large black fabric bag and pulled it down over Terem's head past his midsection. He raised the boy over his shoulder. The body was now merely a limp, anonymous form.

"Your Sept may rest easy now, for no others among you are ill. Dwell in peace."

He walked from the room and down the hall, not waiting for a response from the shocked family. It took the butler a moment to catch up, and he followed along at a respectful distance. Graeber turned as he opened the front door, inclined his head, and then disappeared off into the shadows of night.

Echoing through the streets, he heard the distant sounds of Taura Zebio mourning her youngest son.

CHAPTER 2

Voices murmured through a soft fuzzy sea of near consciousness. Sensations washed through and around, leaving nauseating waves rocking through her gut. She needed the world to stop spinning--if only for a moment--and right now she'd be willing to barter almost anything to make it happen. Intense voices marked a critical event unfolding just beyond reach. Slowly draft and dampness eased their way in, calming the endless vertigo. This gave way to a single conscious action: breathing.

"That's it. Deep, slow breaths. You're doing fine." Someone held her hand and stroked her face, and she was grateful for the contact. "I'm Apprentice Mala, Temple Healer, and your nurse. You're emerging from deep-sleep. Can you nod your head, Rai?"

Rai? The name didn't fit quite right.

Rai nodded her head. She sensed calm and reassurance from Mala, and this, in turn, allowed her a small amount of comfort. She wasn't sure why she'd awoken so anxiously, but it gnawed at the pit of her belly, so she focused inward on the thought. The smell of sweetwood hung in the air, an obvious attempt to mask the antiseptic smells of medicinals. Among these odors, something felt out of place, a discordant harmony, but Rai was unable to pinpoint the source.

"Can you open your eyes for me?" Mala asked, interrupting her focus.

Rai opened her eyes and blinked, despite the dim light in the room. She surveyed the expansive space, her eyes refusing to focus with any significant clarity. Her sleek, black, egg-like deep-sleep crèche was one of many, but only the immediate area was illuminated. Regularly spaced units stretched out into the surrounding darkness of the womblike cave. The other crèches status lights blinked, their greens and blues pulsing in the darkness, indicating everyone else rested soundly.

Her crèche's lid stood open to the side, and the comfortable underlayment cradled her body with the ease borne of off-world Juggernaut engineering. The sidewalls were high, wide, and long--constructed with much larger creatures in mind. Mala placed fluid lines, cables, and other equipment from Rai's birthing crèche onto a small table next to them. Her tanned face held chestnut-brown eyes framed with matching dark-brown hair, which flowed down her back in a single braid. Mala's calm demeanor as she worked radiated confidence.

"Your vital functions are regulating on their own again, so I'm going to finish disconnecting your lines. Please let me know if the nausea or dizziness gets worse."

Rai wondered how Mala knew she'd been feeling ill,

but realized this must be a common reaction to the crèches. She couldn't help but smile up at the Apprentice, grateful for her care.

Despite her still blurry vision she caught sight of a robed figure at the back of the room. The face of this Priestess, along with the rest of her, remained obscured behind floor-length, dark-brown robes--the station of an Elder Priestess.

Mala wore the blue, sleeveless, floor-length Apprentice-level robes of her station. Why would an Elder be troubled with such basic administrative duties as overseeing an Apprentice?

Mala removed the last line from Rai's left forearm and a brief but intense moment of painful pressure brought her focus back to her body. At the insertion site a small wound remained--large enough that it would take the next few days to heal. More troubling was the bright cerulean blue triple-moon tattoo on the back of her left hand--devoid of any accompanying stars.

The triple moons marked her fulfillment of her Temple duties and subsequent discharge after that, according to Az'Un law. To wear the mark indicated your status as a citizen in good standing with the Temples. All women above childbearing age displayed the colors in some form--even if death in childbirth meant the ink saturated cold, stiff skin destined for a funerary pyre.

A twinge of sadness overcame her as Rai surveyed Mala's tattooed left hand. The expected blue triple moons indicating temple service gleamed in the dim light, but in addition, seven stars surrounded them--five red for boys and two green for girls.

Rai knew she should be disappointed or upset by her own lack of stars, but instead, an enveloping emptiness threatened as she recognized her tattoo, minus the stars, as a symbol of her failure to her people, especially her Sept.

"The Temple must be proud of you. Few women are so lucky."

Mala ignored her compliment, perhaps focusing on the hollow sentiment underneath. "Now, don't dwell on that which can't be changed. You should thank the Divine Spirit you're here at all. You suffered a severe miscarriage and almost bled to death. We felt future pregnancy attempts posed too great a risk. Thus, the Temple declared you barren. You've spent the last few weeks in recovery.

"Be reassured, there are many ways you can continue to serve our people, and others will expand our colony, this plague be damned."

Rai nodded, upset she hadn't contributed to the colony, and that she could have died, yet relieved over not being a mother. How odd. "Thank you for helping keep me alive."

"You're welcome. Rai, can you tell me what you remember before today while you sit up for me?" Mala asked. She triggered an opening in the front middle of the crèche, which lowered the sidewall, allowing an easier exit.

Rai sat up, taking her time, holding the nausea and dizziness at bay for the time being. She turned and placed her legs down the proffered exit step while she considered the Apprentice's words. Mala's question evoked fear and panic where memories and recollections should lie.

"I know my name, and the names of everything here, but I don't remember my time before I woke up, Apprentice Mala," Rai replied. "I assume what I should remember. Memories of my stay here at the Temple, my past with my Sept, my friends, you know. I'm afraid nothing's there."

Mala glanced toward the Elder in the shadows, and then looked back to Rai. "The increased medicinal dosage used during your crisis has been known to cause temporary memory impairments. Usually, this lasts for a few days or weeks, but sometimes it takes longer to resolve."

Mala's happy demeanor vanished, replaced with a placid, emotionless expression, which conveyed little. Her movements as she cleaned the fluid lines turned abrupt and jerky. Even without her full faculties, Rai suspected Mala of not being honest.

Rai raised a brow. "I'm sure all things will become clear in time, Apprentice Mala?"

"Let's focus on your present needs," Mala replied. "Let me help you to your room. With some warm food and proper rest, you'll be back to yourself in no time at all. Oh, and please just call me Mala."

Standing slowly, Rai soon felt her equilibrium return. Mala led her out of the unadorned room, past the rows of undisturbed crèches, her arm around Rai's waist to steady her. Hobbling past the occupied crèches made her want to move faster, to escape the cavern and all of the women in stasis. When they passed out of the dark cellar,

Rai breathed deeply, only then grasping she was free of her confinement.

Despite her foggy state, the Temple corridors appeared vacant to Rai--unlike what she'd expect for any Temple, which were the lifeblood of the cities. As they rounded a corner, the narrow corridor opened into a wide passage with colorful tapestries depicting vibrant, outdoorsy scenes to liven up their underground surroundings. Doors were spaced along the left wall while the right wall contained many large windows hewn through the stone, through which a magnificent natural-appearing amphitheater was visible. The rock in the amphitheater included many horizontal swirls of color gradients within the green, gray, and black ranges, demonstrating the varied geology of the planet. Several Novitiates prepared the amphitheater for the mid-morning meditation. Their beige robes appeared to glow in the hazy mid-morning sunlight.

"Which city are we in?" Rai asked.

"This is Raven's Call, the largest settlement next to Barrow's Grove," Mala answered, with more than a hint of pride in her voice. Raven's Call had grown to just under twenty thousand under the current Matriarch, so Mala had reason to be proud to serve here. The weather was fair, if humid, at this inland city and farming wasn't a challenge. There were worse places on the planet when all held the same threat. At least the city walls afforded some degree of protection.

"Shouldn't the Temple be more crowded?"

Mala laughed. "This is an underground facility, so it's difficult to gauge who's here. We have about three hundred and eighty women in Service right now, and the staff capacity to care for twice that if needed.

"We'll have as many as twenty girls in transition, either in or out. Our team is large enough to handle it, with three dozen Priestesses of varying levels assigned to the Birthing Quarters.

"Still, you won't see our staff in large groups. We all have our specialties. Most of us spend our time dedicated to the girls in Service or the Medicinal Vaults. However, plenty of other functions the Temple offers citizens keep the Priestesses occupied. This is a very well structured Temple."

Mala opened the third door down the hallway and ushered Rai into the room. The room was adorned in beige tones and contained a bed, table and chair, and a rounded natural stone bath at the far end. The oblong tub stood hip-height with a set of stairs carved around the front facing, and a utilitarian bathroom with a full-length mirror was located on the far end of the room beyond the curve of the pool. Inviting wisps of steam curled up from the swirling whirlpool, beckoning Rai to enter. The pool was the only source of warmth in this otherwise cold room.

"This room is for your use. Please bathe, as it will help purge the crèche medicinals." Mala motioned to a set of packets on the shelf next to the bath. "Use these soaking herbs and salts for your bath. They're quite good at leeching out toxins. Sometimes your body can lose control over its homeostatic balance in the crèche. Considering the crèches' superior ability to maintain and control bodily functions, your system isn't always prepared to work as hard at removing cellular waste products when you first awaken."

"And this is all normal?" Superior technology should leave you feeling better, not worse. How long had she been in the crèche to make her body so dependent?

"Don't worry." Mala stroked her arm. "Your hepatic, renal and respiratory systems will catch on quickly--returning to normal capacity within a few days. Let me go get you some food, so you'll have something to eat after your bath."

When the door clicked shut, Rai shed her clothes. Thinking two packets were better than one, she opened two of the folded parchment packets and poured them into the water. Stepping into the bath Rai felt the contents of the packages fizzing against her calves. After grabbing a washcloth from the shelf, she moved into the waist-deep water in the middle and on impulse submerged fully. Much to her delight, the fizzing bath salts resonated through her ears.

Rai located a submerged ledge toward the far end of the bath and lounged on it, taking ease in the neck-deep water. Alone in the quiet room, the disjointed distresses of the day flooded her thoughts. Her entire body ached, an apt reflection of her state of mind. The amnesia, when she focused on it, caused anxiety to tingle from her scalp all the way to her fingertips. Rai remembered so many ordinary, day-to-day things, just nothing about herself. The frustration galled her.

However, Mala had said the amnesia would pass, and only existed because of the drugs the Temple staff had used. The knot in her stomach said otherwise.

Rai ran a hand over her belly, the slight curve betraying no hint of either the trauma or the history her body had lived through while she'd slept unawares. Would she feel more connected to the tiny life she'd lost if it had been born first? If she'd had a chance to hold it in her arms? She'd never know for sure, but Rai was relieved: her instincts told her she wasn't natural mother material.

The distant murmur of chanting voices and rhythmic drumming sounded from the mid-morning meditation. Still drowsy from the crèche medicinals and comfortable in the water, Rai closed her eyes and relaxed into the sound, intending to wait out Mala's return with the food. As the drumming and chanting grew in volume, Rai nodded off into a trance-like sleep.

With sleep came a dream.

Rai stood in a forest full of ancient trees, so tall the crowns were lost beyond her vision. The smallest shimmer of light shone through the dense canopy, not enough to burn away the thick morning fog lying in the valleys. A melodious trickle pointed the way to a nearby stream. Gliding deep into the large grove, she took in a landscape dotted with immense ferns growing out of rocky outcroppings and long-dead fallen trees. The trees had split into great building block sections, as if formed into massive tables and benches laid out for a feast. Moist humus squished between her toes. Rai felt like a mere trog bug dwarfed by her surroundings.

Blisters covered the soles of her bare feet. She wore a long brown cape over a simple dress--mud caked the areas around the knees and forearms. Her waist-long red curls contained bits of fern and dirt within their tangled mess. She gasped at the cool, humid air, trying to slow her breathing, then stilled in fright when the rustling fronds of ferns moved in the distance.

The sound of muted voices grew, echoing off the ancient trees. The meaning of the words escaped her, but their tone was all too clear. They were coming to punish her, but where could she go? The voices became a thundering force pushing down upon her, relentlessly pressing her to either run or face their malicious threat.

Filled with terror, Rai ran away from the voices. The forest fought her, fern fronds whipped her in the face, branches ripped at her clothing, and gnarled roots caught at her toes and twisted her ankles as she fled. She caught glimpses of hooded figures in her peripheral vision, and her fear drove even faster. Running through fog and fern the voices pursued, getting closer with every step. She stopped to gauge her path through the dense fog, and the voices abruptly ceased. The entire forest stilled. Something brushed through her hair, took hold, and pulled. Rai let out a desperate scream, striking her fists against her unseen attacker as she fell backward ...

Mala's voice delivered Rai back to consciousness for the second time that day. Rai laid in the bath, Mala leaning over her, Mala wrenching Rai's wrists in the air between them, her grip burning against Rai's skin.

"Stop it!" Mala cried out. Her grip on Rai's wrists tightened.

Shaking in residual fear, Rai relaxed her arms and tried to regain some composure. "Yes, Mala, I'm all right."

A red mark on Mala's chin stood out against her tanned skin. "Oh, I'm sorry! Did I hurt you?"

"Be still, Rai. It was just a nightmare." Mala released her grip and stepped back, and then straightened her skirts. "You must be more tired than usual from the crèche. It happens sometimes. Still, for your own safety, don't nap in the tub."

Rai sat up, bristling over her mistake. "It won't happen again."

"I brought some food for you."

Rai climbed out of the bath, the mention of food twisting her empty gut. She stopped to grab a robe and throw it around herself, not bothering to dry off her still dripping skin. The chairs were wooden and waterproof, which was good because water from Rai's hair and body continued to drip, forming a small puddle on the floor as she took a seat at the table.

The food was bland and tasteless, but she didn't complain because it sated her hunger. Sliced, roasted fowl accompanied with an assortment of root vegetables and some brown bread and butter entertained her eyes if not her palate.

"Get some proper sleep after you finish eating. You need it." She poured Rai a glass of water and then pulled a packet from her pocket, tore it open, and then dumped it into the glass. "This should help you to sleep more ... soundly. Don't get back in the water until after you've slept off this sedative. I'll check in on you from time to time, just in case." Mala turned to leave.

"What happens now?" Rai asked. "When do I return to my Sept?"

Mala hesitated, looking back at Rai with her calm, controlled face--the one Rai now dubbed as the 'withholding information' look. "Today you rest and recuperate. You'll meet with the Matriarch tomorrow, and all your questions will be answered." Mala left and closed the door behind her.

It occurred to Rai for the first time that she had no idea what her life might become, and to her great concern, what it ever had been.

Although she'd lost her appetite, Rai tried to focus on the steaming hot food in front of her.

CHAPTER 3

Rai awoke from a dreamless sleep. A dim light shone in from under the door, and Rai realized this room had no windows. It seemed odd to her, but she remembered that the sections she'd walked through with Mala was part of an underground cave complex. Perhaps they didn't bother with windows because they'd only provide a view of the hallway? Rai touched a rectangular metallic plate on the wall next to the door, eliciting a soft glow from the recessed lights in the ceiling.

A breakfast tray sat where last night's dinner tray had been. Today's breakfast contained an assortment of sliced native red fruit and spotted melon and adapted Earth grapes and pears. Two slices of toasted egg bread framed the plate. Rai poked at one of the yolks, confirming the eggs semi-soft perfection nestled atop the toast. A fresh glass of water and a medicinal packet sat in the corner of the tray.

Still foggy from the crèche, Rai decided on a quick bath to help clear her head. The bathwater had become transparent again, so the medicinals and soaps from last night must have circulated out while she slept. This morning's cooler bathwater made for a more invigorating experience than the previous evening, and the fogginess cleared from Rai's mind.

New clothes lay out on the bench next to the bath, and Rai slipped into the beige dress, long vest and sandals. Rai dried her hair and regarded herself in the full-length mirror in the back of the room.

Her bright auburn hair tended to clump into tight ringlets. It was the long hair from her dreams, just cut at chin length. Rai studied her body, understanding she somehow knew that she was petite and short. The crèche appeared to have kept her body in decent shape despite the months she'd lain flat, judging by the still toned state of her arms.

Her gaze again fell upon the blue triple-moons tattoo on the back of her left hand. It had healed completely and must have been administered days or even weeks ago. Perhaps when Rai had first arrived for Temple service? That memory was lost with all the others, at least for now.

For a moment, the unfairness of it all burned within her. How she could remember the names of fruit and how to work the lights, but not remember her own Sept or name? Or losing a child? Wouldn't she have been awake for a miscarriage, if it had happened?

Rai stared at herself in the mirror in frustration and sensed a brief surge of recognition in her light-hazel eyes. However, beyond her eyes, the rest of her face brought no such recognition. She liked her high cheekbones but was less than impressed with her overly thin lips. Her current expression came across as either critical or harsh; Rai couldn't quite decide which. Neither appeared an appealing or pleasant demeanor to project to others.

She tried to soften her expression but still found herself facing a shorter than average stern-looking teenager. Rai figured some would see her as attractive, if the light caught her face just right, and at the right angle. Rai decided the intensity of her eyes made her whole face appear stern, regardless of her expression.

Realizing studying her physical appearance wouldn't yield any clues to her past, Rai sighed and walked back to the table and sat down in the chair. She took a bite of bread. Something was wrong. The bread lacked flavor and aroma; it was ... well ... missing somehow. She picked up a slice of red fruit and sniffed it, and then took a tentative bite. It also had hardly any smell or taste. Rai got the disturbing impression she, and not the food, might be the problem.

Had something muffled her sense of smell and taste as well as her memory?

Remembering how Mala had said the medicinals helped to cleanse her system, Rai opened the packet and emptied its contents into her glass of water, hoping this might also help her nose return to normal. Waiting for the medicinal powder to dissolve in the water, Rai picked up the empty packet and sniffed it--and sneezed. Rai dropped the packed and grabbed a nearby towel. She wiped the powder from her face and stopped sneezing at about the same time. A momentary feeling of dizziness came over her, no doubt from inhaling the powder.

Rai picked up a slice of spotted melon and took a cautious bite, expecting its signature tang. Instead of the usual tart flavor, this slice was so bland it was nearly flavorless. Picking up the bread again, Rai smelled it and took another bite. The flavor of the bread had faded further. If anything, breathing the medicinal had caused her taste and smell to fade further.

She ran her tongue over her teeth, stretching her jaw uncomfortably.

She took a small sip of the medicinal water, followed by yet another bite of the bread to confirm her suspicions. As she consumed more of the medicinals, the flavor of the food was nonexistent. The medicinals dulled her senses of smell and taste. Could they be contributing to her mental fog as well? The thought wasn't a comforting one.

Although Rai couldn't fathom why Mala or the Temples would give her something that would dull her senses, nevertheless she decided to forgo the treatment. Rai looked at the empty packet more closely, but it lacked any identifying markings. She had assumed that it contained more detoxifying medicinals, but it could have been anything.

Rai poured the remaining water from her glass into the bathtub where it would filter out with no one the wiser.

When Rai heard the door unlock, she realized they'd locked her in the room all night! Why would they lock her inside? She set her empty glass back onto the tray and picked up another slice of melon. Rai did her best to seem only mildly interested in the opening door. Mala opened the door, cheerful and smiling as ever. With a mouthful of melon, Rai nodded her acknowledgment, wondering to herself if Mala knew about the medicinals' ill effects.

Mala walked into the room and left the door open behind her. "Good morning, Rai. I trust you slept well?" Her eyes moved to Rai's water glass and the empty medicinal packet next to it.

Rai noted Mala's jaw line and the bruise she'd inflicted yesterday was already a vivid, mottled purple with red tones around the edges. The raw power of Rai's blow must have been considerable. Rai's head ached, knowing she'd done such a thing to another person, however unintentionally.

Rai forced a smile. "Yes, thank you. No more nightmares, either. I awoke just a little bit ago."

"That's good to hear. I had some concerns after last night." Reconciling Mala's caring eyes and soft expression with the suspicions Rai carried in her mind gave her stomach twists. Did Mala know what she was doing, or was she simply handing out medicinal on a schedule set by a Priestess, or Elder?

"I would appreciate some additional packets of that sedating medicinal for tonight, if it's not too much trouble," Rai asked, not intending to take it.

"I'd planned for you to have extra anyway."

"Thanks, Mala. What was in this one?"

"Oh, that's a unique antiviral treatment we give to women who are postpartum. It helps them to heal more quickly while also preventing the spread of the plague."

"How long will I need to take it?"

"Just a few days. You have an appointment with the Matriarch now, so we need to leave."

Mala's cheerful mood was in stark contrast to Rai's own. The Matriarch oversaw the fate of the entire city. The prospect of having her fate handed out to her galled. "I just finished up with breakfast. I guess I'm ready." Rai stood and smoothed the front of her dress.

"Let's go then." Mala walked out the door with Rai following behind her.

The hallway overflowed with brilliant morning sunlight streaming in through the arches along the left wall. As Rai walked a few steps behind Mala, she took in everything around her, anxious to fill the void left by her memories and study her surroundings in detail.

The corridor they passed through encircled the amphitheater she'd admired yesterday. The upper rim of the amphitheater climbed an additional story above the hallway. The base appeared to be one to two floors below them. A walkway surrounded the structure at the base, allowing attendees to move freely. Arched, regularly placed doorways allowed passage into the corridor a floor below them. Although morning observances had passed, a few devotees still lingered in meditative thought. The bright blues, yellows, reds, and browns of their robes brought contrast to the otherwise dull space. Semi-circular, terraced rings of stone seating radiated out from the northern altar to the southernmost side of the amphitheater. The rectangular unadorned altar cut from pure white marble -- the centerpiece of the theater. The space resounded with the quiet murmurs of the devotees. Rai imagined with a few hundred parishioners filling the space the noise reverberated into the nearby city streets.

They progressed down the corridor until it forked and a separate set of stairs framed by a graceful arch opened to the sky, leading left to the upper rim of the amphitheater's bowl. A simple waist-high railing was all that separated them from the wide-open space below. With the amphitheater now below them, Rai followed Mala along the path into a series of large, verdant gardens. Some plants held produce in differing stages of ripeness, while others appeared to be grown for their flowers or unique beauty alone.

"Well, at least now I know where breakfast came from this morning," Rai mused, recognizing a plant bearing spotted melons.

Mala looked back at Rai, and she decided the Apprentice's pleasant expression was beginning to grate on her. "The Temple has these gardens to thank for breakfast, lunch, and dinner, all year round."

Rai could believe it. All around them were fruits and vegetables of every kind. "It's a beautiful technique, combining produce with the more aesthetic plants."

"Most of the non-fruiting plants here have medicinal purposes, aid in the health of nearby plants, or promote soil regeneration," Mala informed her. "Priestess Vartrell oversees these gardens, and with her insight and leadership, the yields have doubled. These fields grow a variety of crops year-round, allowing for a constant supply of fresh produce." Various workers were scattered through the gardens, tending the plants and nurturing the rich soil in which they flourished.

"Raven's Call Temple is indeed lucky to have such a gifted Priestess," Rai replied, even more in awe of the gardens.

"Indeed we are."

The gardens gave way to lush orchards. Rai recognized the red fruit, but trees bore many other fruits as well. Rai wondered if meeting in the Temple gardens was standard for the Matriarch. She'd assumed the Matriarch had an audience chamber. Strolling through the gardens was a peaceful and meditative act, and Rai could imagine using the space for quiet contemplation, whether wandering or tending the plants. She recalled that Raven's Call, one of the planet's three original settlements, had the unique gift of soil amendments and fruit trees from humanity's home world. These orchards were the only places on Az'Unda where purebred Earth stock could grow. Because of this, the orchards stood as a reminder of the power the Temples, and thus the Matriarchs held.

The humid environment provided the precious trees with significant annual growth and fullness of leaves, but the plague held their fruit production to only a fraction of its potential. The sickness of the planet seemed to hinder their natural fertility, despite their size and otherwise good health. Az'Unda's crushing disease left no part of the world untouched, not even this sacred ground.

The trees were in full bloom covered in cascades of pink, rose and white clusters of aromatic flowers. The canopy of blossoms all around Rai drew her into something of a meditative state of her own. They walked past a line of trees when the bright white robes of the Matriarch interrupted her reverie.

Like the Elder who had observed Rai's awakening, this ornately-cloaked Matriarch stood motionless. A large, white veil obscured her face, leaving the Temple leader unreadable. It hung down past her shoulders, managing to conceal even her hair before blending into rest of the Matriarch's bright robes. It was semi-opaque so Rai could sense the vague outline of the form beneath. Rai wondered if anyone ever saw the Matriarch out of the glittering white robes.

A woman stood next to the Matriarch, and Rai gathered she served as the Matriarch's assistant. The woman's bright yellow robes were a simple, floor length sleeveless garment, revealing willowy and delicate arms. Swirls of amber and orange adorned a scarf wrapped around her waist-length braid and contained her black hair away from the otherwise bright color scheme. The woman's hands moved in short jerky movements, taking notes on her data tablet without even breaking eye contact with Rai. The assistant's stern expression suggested the notes were none too flattering.

Mala and Rai stopped a few feet before the pair. Rai followed Mala's lead and bowed, going first to their knees and then lowering their heads to the loamy ground. Due to her proximity, Rai could smell the ground. A cacophony of images flooded her mind. Leaves, flower petals, grass, pebbles, moss -- every element of the soil's aroma became full of detail as they forced their way into her consciousness and then slipped away the next instant, fading into numbness. The brief intensity of the sensation overwhelmed her, and only the deep, powerful, melodic tones of the Matriarch's voice brought her back to reality.

"Rise, my children." They stood, and Rai realized the Matriarch had a smooth and calming voice. She was at ease with this enshrouded yet powerful figure. Even so, she didn't dare bring her eyes to meet such an impressive figure. Rai kept her gaze down, circumspectly studying the line between the perfect whiteness of the Matriarch's robes and the decomposing humus beneath them.

"Dear Mala, thank you for bringing your charge all this way. I'm sure you understand my desire to sweeten this day in any way possible," the Matriarch continued.

"Agreed, Mother. The walk was no burden. We are lucky to have the gift of this day and the bounty of the spring in these orchards. Your request to meet here is a gift to our senses." Did they drill ceremonial speech into Apprentices? Mala had a gift for it.

"My dear child, you understand that you have been found barren, yes?" the Matriarch asked, her voice soft and melodic.

"Yes Mother," Rai replied. The Matriarch's question filled her with a stark reality: she would never have children of her own. Children for her birth Sept. She fingered her tattoo for a moment, lost in a brief wave of panic, and then clasped her hands behind her back. Rai's gaze returned to the ground at her feet. She should feel regretful about the loss, her failure to her Sept, but instead, she felt powerless in this situation. Dread ate away at her hopes for her future.

"And you understand that by Az'Un law, your Sept is

under no obligation to welcome back barren women?" Rai nodded her understanding. "To avoid the scandal of having you return to them in this circumstance, your Sept has formally refused you re-admittance. In situations such as this, it is my duty to attempt to find a suitable placement. Will you accept my judgment in this matter, my child? I will warn you that if you do not, I will be forced to send you to one of the Sept-less work houses."

An image of living amongst the lowest caste on Az'Unda, taking whatever work the shift managers doled out to her, living in bunk dorms with other women and hoping nutritious meals occurred at least once a day flashed through her mind. Sure, it kept the Sept-less alive and engaged in society. The only reason they didn't revolt was the omnipresence of the Guardians and the dependence everyone had on the Temples to remain healthy from the plague. Rai shuddered -- that option was no real choice.

The fact that her prior Sept had turned her away didn't surprise Rai, but it was nonetheless disturbing. No respectable Sept welcomed back into the fold someone who'd failed them -- even through no fault of their own. Moving on to a new house afforded her the chance to start over without fear of shame or retribution, although she'd never hold rank or title within the new Sept. A ball of anxiety rolled in her belly over her uncertain future -- so much was out of her control. Still, there wasn't much alternative to accepting the Matriarch's placement, unless she wanted to become a social pariah.

"Whatever future you have laid out for me, Mother, I will strive to embrace it," Rai replied.

"Wonderful, child! I've taken the liberty of placing you with the Durmah Sept. Are you familiar with the Durmah?"

"Revered Mother," Mala interjected, "Rai suffers from amnesia related to the treatments for her ... time in the crèche."

"Ah, is that so, my dear?" Rai nodded to her query, wondering just how much the Matriarch knew beforehand of her situation. The Journeywoman furiously took notes; Rai heard the staccato tap-scratch-tap of her magnetic pen against the tablet.

"Well, my dear, perhaps you should consider that a blessing," continued the Matriarch. "After all, it will be easier for you to move into your future when the past isn't there to hold you back, yes?" Rai nodded again, hoping the Matriarch's wisdom held true. "I will finalize things with the Durmah, and they will pick you up this evening. I think you'll fit in well with them. I can tell you the Durmah are a Merchant Sept, a large family, and there is some urgency in their need for you. Do you have any questions?"

"Did the Durmah request me?" Rai asked, unsure how the Sept expected her so quickly.

The Matriarch laughed. "Oh no, my dear. They know no specific details concerning you. We don't permit shares of information between Septs. Rather they have been awaiting a new adoptee for some time, to help them expand their business."

Rai didn't think it sounded like this placement had

much to do with her best interest at all. The Matriarch's job was to serve her people, and Rai's placement did satisfy needs on both sides. Rai doubted that her own desires outweighed the greater needs of the populace. With her amnesia, she didn't know what she would have preferred, had she had any real ability to choose. On the upside, she wouldn't be waiting for weeks waiting for placement. It was a lot to take in at once.

"Is there anything you need from the Temple or from me before you go? You have but to ask," the Matriarch offered.

Rai glanced up at the Matriarch's assistant to find her meeting her gaze, clinical interest giving way to a slight smirk. Her eyes held a predatory glint, such that Rai imagined her with that same expression spending free time pinning and arranging insects for display.

She had hundreds more questions racing through her mind now--about her memory, about the effects of the medicinals on her, about her life before two days ago--but none she thought wise to ask the Matriarch just now.

"Do you know what role I'll have in the Durmah Sept?"

For the first time the stony-faced assistant spoke; Rai wasn't surprised to find her tone gratingly unpleasant compared to the smooth, round tones of the Matriarch. "Your new Sept will fill you in on everything you need to know. It's not our place to divulge internal Sept workings to the adoptee."

"Do you have any other questions?" the Matriarch inquired. By the somewhat impatient tone in her voice, she had other things on her agenda.

Rai sensed unease welling within her but from where? She felt urged to action and had to restrain herself from moving.

"My humble thanks for your wise counsel in this matter. I owe you my future." Rai managed another deep bow, touching her forehead to the line between the hem of the Matriarch's robes and the orchard's pungent floor. This time Rai cautiously breathed out as she neared the ground, lest the smell overwhelm her again.

"We leave you in Mala's capable hands. Good luck in your future life," the Matriarch said, and then turned and walked away from Mala, Rai, and the Temple, moving deeper into the orchards.

Rai rose and smelled something beyond the garden floor and the countless pink blossoms on the trees.

She smelled fear. Profound anxiety. Bordering on what an animal might sense off its prey.

Was she the fearful one? She had anxieties about meeting the Durmah, sure, but not this fear.

No. This was from the Matriarch.

Why this situation made someone of such high status so scared, Rai had no idea. Nonetheless, there it was, as real for her as the ground itself.

The Matriarch disappeared out of sight, and the sensation subsided. The meeting left Rai filled with questions about her future, about her past, and about this power of perception she held.

Rai was lost in thought on the long walk back to her room.

CHAPTER 4

#BEGIN TRANSMISSION#
*#ROUTING CODE: CHIEFTESS
RAZA, GUARDIAN SEPT,
BARROW'S GROVE FROM
GUARDIAN GRAEBER,
GUARDIAN SEPT, ROAMING
COM H3-29Y#*
#ENCRYPTION: HIGH#
*GRAEBER: I need to update you on a
special project. Do you have time?*
RAZA: I'll make time. Hold a moment.
*RAZA: You have my full attention. By
your reference, I'm already
disappointed--although not surprised.
Be honest, how far have things gone?*
*GRAEBER: I know I'm acting against
your wishes, sister, but I've joined
with the Veil. She set the course, but*

couldn't carry through on her own. I'm acting as eyes and ears.

RAZA: Please know that I cannot support you. Rest assured the Anemoi won't find out from me, but I'll make no attempt to defend you from them either.

When they find out, and they will--it's only a matter of time--it will be the end for both you and the Veil. Have you stopped to consider what losing both of you will mean for our cause? The repercussions for all the people who've sacrificed to get us this far? The public may not know your name, but you would be missed by those who work with you. On the other hand, the Veil will not go unnoticed into the night. The repercussions of her absence will not go unnoticed and will cause some eyebrows to raise amongst the populace.

You may not understand this from your emotionally charged perspective, but their decision was the right one. Their rules--our laws--were broken. Their sentence will be carried out with or without yours or the Veil's assistance. This may be hard for you to hear, but I supported their decision, just as I also understand your point of view.

You have another option--to simply walk away and let her take sole responsibility for what's happened. The Veil promised them she'd carry out their sentence--and therefore she must take the fall. You could deny any knowledge of the Veil's actions, and they wouldn't question you.

It's not too late to get rid of the problem. If you act quickly enough, they might be none the wiser and at least hold you blameless if you cleaned up her mess. Consider this possibility.

GRAEBER: *Do you think I haven't considered all of this before? You will drop this line of discussion if you wish to remain in contact with me.*

RAZA: *I had to try.*

GRAEBER: *I understand. On another note, although it may be impossible for you to imagine a traitor within the Anemoi, I've been suspecting one for some time now. I don't know who it is yet, and I don't think I'll have any time to find out, considering what I'm taking on. I'll have to rely on you.*

RAZA: *I'll look into your concerns regarding security within the Anemoi. I doubt I'll find anything to flag--this issue aside, we all more or less agree. If you have anything*

> *further for me on this, for example,*
> *specific evidence of a security breach,*
> *please let me know.*
> GRAEBER: *When I can give you more*
> *details I will do so.*
> RAZA: *Very well. I will continue to send*
> *you assignments. After all, if I'm not*
> *sending my top man routine work*
> *requests someone will suspect*
> *something. Like I said, I can't support*
> *you along this path--and I won't be*
> *implicated either.*
> GRAEBER: *I can handle both. I'll*
> *maintain regular contact with you.*
> RAZA: *Here's hoping I see you again*
> *soon, alive.*
> GRAEBER: *Stay safe yourself.*
> #END TRANSMISSION#

LATE IN THE AFTERNOON, APPRENTICE MALA escorted Rai down a new hallway to a small meeting room. With only the clothes on her back and simple leather shoes to call her own, Rai couldn't wait to get out of the Temple, and hoped the Durmah didn't change their minds at the last minute.

"This is where I say goodbye. Chieftess Durmah awaits you inside."

"Thank you, Apprentice Mala."

Mala opened the door and held it open. Rai hesitated

only a moment, mustering her courage before she strode through, chin up, shoulders back, and hands clasped in front of her. The room she entered contained a couple of simple, dark-brown couches arranged around a central low-set round wooden table containing a delightful arrangement of blue and purple-colored blossoms as its centerpiece.

Chieftess Durmah wore long robes, not unlike the style used in the Temples, except these were bright swirls of green and yellow hues. She'd aged well beyond her mid-thirties, with wrinkles creasing the edges around her eyes and streaks of silver ran through her long blond hair.

"Welcome, Rai," said the Chieftess.

"It's an honor to meet you, Chieftess Durmah." Rai remained standing, unsure what this process would entail.

"I understand you've been turned away from your birth Sept. Is this right?"

"Yes, ma'am," Rai nodded.

"Durmah needs a new member, but not one who will cling to their past. You'd need to make a fresh start of things if you join us. No contact with your old Sept. No mourning over the separation. A clean break. Can you commit to this, here and now?"

Rai fought the bitter laugh that threatened to surface. How much had the Matriarch shared with the Chieftess? "It won't be a problem. We've done our parting of ways. What's in the past is best left there."

The Chieftess pursed her lips into a wry smile and then inclined her head in acknowledgment. "So be it. Our Sept is a merchant guild. Some of our members travel between the cities on Az'Unda in wagons, transporting goods for sale. You may be involved with these trips, outside of the safety of the city walls. Does this concern you?"

Rai knit her brows. "Have you ever lost a member on a trip?"

"There's been a rare injury, but no. No deaths." The Chieftess' face remained impassive.

Had the Chieftess turned away others who'd exhibited cold feet? Rai wouldn't blame the woman -- she needed citizens of higher than average quality. For whatever reason, the concept of being outside the city walls felt liberating, not terrifying.

Rai shrugged with a nonchalance rooted in her solar plexus. "Every Sept house has a chosen trade they ply, and I'm sure each has elements they consider dangerous to their chosen craft. At least with the travel, although it has an element of risk, I'd get to see more of Az'Unda."

"You have fortitude, Rai. I can see it in your eyes, in the way you comport yourself. It makes an impression, especially for one so young. You'd be a good fit for Sept Durmah, if you're willing?"

Rai worked to not be too obvious as she let out the breath she'd been holding. "I'd be honored to join your Sept."

The Chieftess nodded and rose. "Although you enter our family as a full member, your barrenness dictates that you cannot marry or own property. Within my Sept only your vision and your work ethic limit your opportunities. We welcome you to this journey into our now collective futures, and we look forward to meeting new challenges one Durmah stronger." Despite the formality of the speech, her eyes shone with warmth.

"Thank you, Chieftess. I won't disappoint you." Rai couldn't help smiling along with the Chieftess.

"I know you won't fail us. Let's go to the Sept House. I believe they have a feast awaiting us."

They exited the Temple where the Chieftess walked up to two men, who took after the Chieftess in their features.

"Rai, these are my eldest sons, Stoi and Meik Durmah. Boys, this is Rai, our new adoptee."

"Good to meet you, Rai," Stoi shook her hand. "It's about time the Temple came through for us," he said to the Chieftess.

She gave a curt nod. "Let's head home. We can discuss further there."

They walked through the streets of Raven's Call as dusk settled over the city. A long scar ran vertically along Stoi's face, passing close to his left eye. The injury notwithstanding, the family resemblance between the two brothers was evident. They shared a stocky, muscular build, both of them taller than average, and both had curly, brown hair. The laugh lines on their roundish faces spoke of sunny demeanors, though there was an element of strain in their eyes when they hovered over Kait and helped her across intersections.

Rai didn't recognize the city streets, and yet it fit familiar patterns within her mind. She expected the market section when they passed it and yet couldn't remember ever being there. The stalls had all closed for the day; tarps tied down beside the frames, baskets empty and stacked in an orderly fashion for tomorrow.

They sauntered down sidewalks made from sheets of gray stone, while Rai observed a farmer's wagon led by a single horse and laden with a variety of ball fruit from local orchards stop in front of a stall. The wagon wheels fell into grooved tracks in the hard stone of the street, a testament to the frequency of use and age of the city itself.

"Any Ence's pears ripe yet, Aden?" Stoi asked, and they stopped to talk to the vendor.

The young man paused in his work, a cautious grin playing at the corner of his lips. "You know they aren't in season yet."

"I know the time is about right and it's been a hot growing season, so I'm betting they might be early. Am I right? Your Sept also has the most protected grove in the valley..." Stoi replied.

Aden threw up his arms in good-natured defeat. "You're right, Stoi, they're ripening early."

"Fantastic." Stoi rubbed his hands together. "I bet you have a few with you today, don't you?"

The farmer shifted on his feet, kicking at a seam in the stone beneath their feet. "Not yet, but in two days I'll have a bushel for you. I can set it aside for Durmah."

Stoi sighed, his shoulders slumping. "Yeah, you do that. Thanks, kid."

He was so upset; Rai couldn't help reaching out to Stoi. "Hey, it's just a day. I'm sure whatever you need them for can wait."

He gave her a brief hug around the shoulders. "But

tonight is your induction feast. You only get one of these, and Ence's pears are such a delicacy... I'd thought it would be such a treat."

"No worries, Stoi. Durmah puts out an excellent feast," the Chieftess said.

"You guys are brutal, and you know it." Aden broke in, holding out one single roundish-grey pear. "I saved this single ripe one for a girl I'm courting, but she'll never know otherwise. Since it's your feast night and all, congratulations."

Rai reached for the pear, but he held it back a moment longer, his gaze pinning Stoi. "We've upped our par five percent this year, on all produce. Agreed?"

Stoi ran a thumb across his chin. "You're authorized to negotiate for your mother now?"

"I know her intent, and this looks like an opportune time."

"So it does, and you have a deal, now hand over the pear and send over the paperwork in the morning." Stoi held out his hand.

They continued down the city streets, Rai with a spring in her step and an Ence's pear clutched between her fingers.

When they reached the end of Bennon Lane, their destination, the size of the Durmah Septhouse surprised Rai. Three stories hall and a full block deep, she couldn't tell how long the building ran in the fading dusk. They passed a large stable yard at the end, fenced in by sturdy timbers a good ten feet high and made their way to the main entrance. Grey rock sheeting encased the entire structure except for the windows, doors, and roof. The windows and roof pale-beige hardened plasticine components allowed ambient light in and out, and some windows even appeared to slide open.

Meik knocked on the front door, a thick wooden structure ribbed with steel reinforcements, Rai heard bolts thrown, and then it swung open wide. A butler, wearing a simple brown tunic and black pants, bowed low and ushered them inside the foyer.

The Chieftess, head held high, led the way. Meik, with a steady palm to the small of Rai's back, urged her forward.

"You next," he whispered in her ear.

She wouldn't have been able to keep the glimmer of anticipation out of her eyes if she'd tried.

Rai followed the Chieftess down a wide hallway, her brothers right behind her. The far end of the hall opened into a large kitchen, but they turned to the left and entered a large dining hall. The ceiling arched to the roof with exposed timbers and four large fireplaces lined the outer walls. The far wall contained large double doors, which appeared to lead to the stables, based on what she'd seen from the outside the building.

Around the dozen or so tables inside the hall sat Sept members of varying ages and platters of all types of food covered the tables. The staff ran back and forth, bearing pitchers of wine, water, and juice for the crowd of three dozen huddled around eight tables lined up in a grid across the room. Kait's presence registered through the group, and she came to a stop amidst the tables, pulling Rai to her side.

"Sept Durmah, let me introduce to you our newest member: Rai. Please welcome her with open arms."

A round of hellos and clapping followed the Chieftess' short speech, and then they sat at a central table. The rest of the night passed in a frenzied blur. The flurry of names and faces was overwhelming, far beyond her capacity to absorb. The Chieftess further introduced herself as Kait, short for Kaitlynn. Instead of standing on ceremony, Kait took it upon herself to name those present and explain the family dynamics to Rai herself. Although Kait was only 32, she had aged well beyond her years. Wrinkles covered her hands and spread out from the corners of her eyes, and streaks of white marked her dull blond hair. Kait's premature aging went hand-in-hand with motherhood, although Rai didn't know why she was so confident of that fact. Many of the Sept women, those who were mothers, were aged well beyond their years, while the men didn't suffer the same ill effects.

Motherhood on Az'Unda was a mixed blessing.

Between the savory meats, sweet fruit juices, and herbed bread, the feast surpassed anything Rai could have imagined. The Durmah was a happy, loving family; the interactions of the various Sept members gave no indication of a strict rule or caste system. They doted on the children during the feast with special desserts and sweet juices. Many stayed up late into the night, their parents in no rush to hurry them off to bed. The servants lavished attention on the children--which was unusual for a society that kept hired help at an emotional distance from the families they served.

Rai also discovered the Durmah' trade earned them more than a modest income. They also owned and operated a series of Waystations, one in each city, where Durmah merchants and other travelers could eat and spend a night or two. The hazards of travel on Az'Unda, many Durmah reiterated to Rai, were considerable. Rai didn't want to ruin the festive mood by inquiring tonight, so she made a mental note to ask about it later. The expense of overnight shelter had become prohibitive; hence, the Durmah built the Waystations. In effect, this extended the reach of the Durmah Sept house to all the cities.

As the evening wound down, Rai stood chatting with a pair of Kait's sister's by marriage, Cerna, Sacha, and Prish next to the fire while they enjoyed glasses of spiced wine. Out of the corner of her eye, she saw Kait draw her two eldest brothers Stoi and Meik into private discussions at a table in the corner, where no one else had gathered.

Rai continued her discussion, sipping her spiced wine, but kept an eye on the trio in the corner. When Stoi's eye flickered up and caught hers on them, she gave him a quick wave, unable to contain her flush of embarrassment. His reassuring nod let her know she'd done nothing untoward.

Rai welcomed the distraction when a short, impish woman approached a few minutes later with an air of authority. She couldn't help it: Kait's sisters were a tad dull.

"Evening, Mistress Rai. I'm Nimma, one of the house butlers. Would you like me to show you to your room for the night?" Her short, bright-white hair glowed in the candlelight.

"That'd be wonderful, Nimma," Rai replied, rising and walking along with Nimma. "But when you say 'for the evening,' what do you mean?"

"The Chieftess asked that I set you up in one of the guest quarters. I'm sure you'll be given a permanent room in the next day or so," Nimma explained as she escorted Rai across the dining hall.

As they walked to the sleeping quarters, she overheard her name mentioned by Stoi and wondered if they were discussing her future within the Sept. Yet she was too exhausted from the events of the day to be concerned. Rai wanted to stay and learn more about the Durmah as if she somehow needed to hold on lest they slip away into the night. She dismissed this as her own anxiety and resolved to worry about the Durmah history on another day.

Nimma stopped at the far end of a long, low-lit corridor, unlocked a door, and motioned Rai inside the room. In sharp contrast to her sparsely furnished Temple room, Rai observed beautiful tapestries on the walls, intricately designed rugs on the floor, and large plush-looking pillows on the bed. Nimma had laid out a night shift for Rai, along with neatly folded clothes for the following day.

"The bathroom is down the hall to your left. Sleep well, and you'll be awakened before breakfast." Nimma closed the door, not waiting for a reply.

Rai changed into her nightclothes and was about to climb into bed when a thought occurred to her. She walked to the door and turned the knob. To her great relief, she found the door unlocked, and the hallway empty. Jesse allowed her to move freely about the property, unlike her stay on the Temple grounds. Rai sighed, relieved that The Durmah trusted her, and for the first time Rai felt comfortable in reciprocating that trust with their collective future.

The warmth, kindness, and generosity she'd sensed from every Durmah she'd met were no illusion. She was full of questions, but the emptiness of her past wasn't something she'd have to face alone. She was one of them now. Rai closed the door and slipped into the soft, warm bed, feeling a tremendous sense of relief and security.

CHAPTER 5

MATRIARCH BAULEEL WOUND HER WAY UP THROUGH the caverns toward the refuge of her private chambers and once again doubted her own judgment. Would she later regard this day with regret? The girl Rai showed no signs of her memory returning. Perhaps things would work as planned after all.

Desperation was a powerful force, and the path she'd chosen held the power to save or destroy them both. At that moment, Bauleel wished that her mind could be as quiet as the hollowed out stone cavern walls in which she now walked. She decided to join the evening meditation, in hopes of regaining the focus and clarity she'd lost over the last few hours. She also needed to catch up on her paperwork, and late evenings were perfect as they usually drew few unscheduled visits.

Bauleel came to a door in the corridor and passed her hand over a small metal plate in the wall. She heard the accepting click of the door lock click open and she entered the room. The lights were on, and as Bauleel looked up and tried to remember if she'd left them on; her eyes came to rest on an unexpected visitor.

Much to her chagrin, Guardian Graeber looked quite at ease as he lounged on a couch in her private audience chamber, helping himself to a crisp red fruit. For a moment it sounded more like he crunched bones rather than fruit, but that was just her gloomy frame of mind. Graeber's blue eyes glittered at Bauleel's consternation through locks of raven-black hair, which hung altogether too long across his tanned cheeks. His sprawled-out position on the couch revealed his tall, lean, muscular frame.

She considered revoking security privileges to the entire Guardian Sept and realized the pointlessness. A simple door lock couldn't prevent a Guardian's entry when they had access overrides to most of the locks on the planet. Perhaps having a door lock on her private chambers was pointless anyway. The Matriarch's room was one of the few in the Temple complex to have one, besides the Medicinal Vaults.

Graeber had managed to maintain a constant state of arrogant self-confidence since his youth, which had never ceased to amaze Bauleel throughout their long-standing friendship. He excelled well beyond the skills of other Guardians, which made it difficult for Bauleel to fault his enjoyment in the often gruesome tasks of the profession. Enjoying your job took on an entirely different meaning within the Guardian Sept.

No other Guardian would have the raw nerve to enter uninvited into the quarters of a Matriarch. However, their unique relationship existed as stated peers and not the usual Matriarch to subordinate roles.

Before speaking to Graeber, Bauleel closed and locked the door. On the rare occasion she talked to someone in her chambers, it was here, and thus she'd take great care to project confidence and minimalism. The two austere black couches framed a low-set matching black rock table, which held a basket of fruit from the Temple orchards. Ball lamps resembling Az'Unda's moons hung in the corner and provided a glowing, ambient light versus the typical harsh overhead lights elsewhere in the facility. She'd even had a special woven thatch mat installed to distract from the usual rough-hewn stone floors. Bauleel had intended the combination to calm the mind.

Although he sat across from her, Graeber's presence consumed the room, setting her teeth on edge.

"I didn't expect you back so soon."

The situation with the girl was just as much his problem as it was her own. However, it gave Bauleel little consolation to think she wasn't walking this ill-fated path alone.

She knew his journey on horseback from the Far Reaches to the Temple here in Raven's Call had been a long one, and yet he showed no signs of weariness. Although he wore his guild's variegated standard leathers, she noticed the number of pockets he'd outfitted were those of a traveling Guardian. No doubt, they contained additional weapons, various scanners, and supplies the city stationed Guardians wouldn't require.

Knowing Graeber, he never removed the excess gear.

There was no dust or dirt on his cape or his travel bag, which lay next to him on the couch. Bauleel wondered if he'd taken the time to shower and shave before returning from his task to report in. His face appeared clean and smooth, as if freshly shaven. Perhaps he'd been in town a few days, and had just now decided to check in with her. She hadn't been traveling, and yet she still felt a distinct need for a shower. However, a simple shower would wash the day's actions from her conscience.

"I took my time and did some stargazing along the way. Do you remember how clear the sky is up there?" Graeber picked at a piece of red fruit skin stuck between his teeth, affording her no measure of courtesy, nor waiting for an answer to his rhetorical question. "Besides, the trip to the Far Reaches and back is like vacationing on Walhan Prime."

Bauleel knew otherwise. The journey was, in fact, a difficult and treacherous one, but she also was in no way surprised to hear Graeber speak of it with such ease. She held her tongue while he continued, lest she give in to his deliberate taunts.

"I even took the time to handle some unpleasantness at the Zebio Sept before coming to visit you. You might say I took my time returning to report you. After all, I know how much you like new toys for your Technicians to research. How could I resist?"

She ground her teeth together, clinging to her composure. "Did you deliver this newest toy in pieces too?"

By the tone of her voice and the slight tensing of Graber's frame, she hadn't managed to keep her irritation hidden. He loved pushing her buttons, and now he had every reason to strike out at her.

Yet the possibility he'd delivered the subject unusable always existed -- she never liked hearing those stories -- but she had to know.

"No. I handled him delicately as a flower in mid-bloom." A flicker of emotion graced Graber's lips, and Bauleel snorted in laughter. He sat forward on the couch, elbows on knees, frowning. "I swear the boy's unharmed. He's at the Technician's Guild now."

Bauleel made a mental note to visit the Technicians soon for details. "Apologies. It's just the image of you, with a flower. Moons preserve us!"

"You find humor in the oddest of places."

"I've learned to do so. I see you've made yourself at home. You could have let Camille know you were waiting for me."

"I thought it best to keep this off all formal records. I know you trust her, but she does annotate your every movement."

"Good thinking. Uh, why did you leave my quarters unlocked and sprawl out upon my couch?"

Graeber shot her a mischievous smirk. "I thought it best to make my presence more evident after I frightened off a poor Novitiate who was cleaning your chambers. She jumped out of her skin when she noticed me meditating, and then she ran off like a scared breacat, chittering to herself all the way down the steps."

"Well, what did you expect? It's not as if people see Guardians coming around for social calls. You should have hidden in my solarium and let her finish working."

"Oh, I'm not the one running around hiding behind a disguise today, my Esteemed Matriarch. Or perhaps I've mistaken you for one of your Elders?" Graeber pointed out, eyeing the brown robes Bauleel wore. Graeber tossed the gnawed red fruit core into the trash can across the room with a resounding plunk.

Bauleel had forgotten she wore Elder robes, all the better for spying on the girl as she met with the Durmah. That Graeber had witnessed her falsehood only served to increase her annoyance with him.

Graeber, infuriating as he was, had correctly pointed out her transgression. Regardless of the hour, it wasn't unusual for the Temple staff to seek out the Matriarch for guidance. She should change before anyone else arrived, in particular, Camille. If Camille found out she wore Elder robes on occasion to avoid her incessant schedules, she'd never be able to move around without an escort again. With an exasperated sigh, Bauleel passed through her small and uncluttered private office, through the spacious bedroom in gossamer whites, and into her bedroom's large closet.

Graeber followed at a respectful distance, standing just outside the closet so they could continue talking. She removed the dark brown elder clothes and hung the items next to her traditional sets of white Matriarch's robes.

While removing her shoes, she decided to try to shift the conversation back on topic. The cave floor was cold beneath her feet, as she stood clad only in her under shift. Bauleel looked over to Graeber, who now stood in the closet doorway.

"If your trip was as successful as you say, can I, therefore, assume that the package is hidden away?"

For the first time since his arrival, his tone took on a hard edge. "The package is safe. No one will find it." Perhaps out of habit, his body had become tense, mirroring his mood.

Bauleel emerged from the closet and Graber backed out of the doorway just enough to let her pass. "If you don't mind talking through the sound of water, I feel the need to bathe."

"Whatever you need to do."

"Where is the package?" Bauleel walked into the bathroom at the far end of the room. It was open with no doorway.

Matriarchs didn't entertain visitors in this section of their quarters. She kept no bathing pool, having no fondness for them, but instead had a walk-in shower, which functioned more like an indoor heated stream, which poured from a sluice overhead. Within seconds of activation from the wall panel, the flowing water had billowing steam clouds surrounding her.

"I should know, in case something happens to you."

"No, Bau. I alone must bear the burden of its care. I agreed to do so to its rightful keeper, and I won't pass that responsibility off to anyone else." Bauleel heard granite in Graeber's voice; he would not argue further. "Besides -- think about it. If anyone, even you whom I trust, knows of the location, there's the chance the rest of the Anemoi might find out. I can't allow that to happen."

The fierce look in his eyes made the hair on the back of her neck stand on end. She felt naked and exposed before his thinly veiled wrath at the other Anemoi. Bauleel realized she preferred Graeber's usual cynicism to this harsh intensity.

"But then if you die, what we've done, it can't be undone."

"I won't die."

Bauleel sighed. "So be it." She moved into the shower, hoping to diffuse the tension. Once inside she hung up her shift on one of the hooks along the wall. Graeber again remained just outside the stall, within comfortable speaking range. Bauleel stepped under the hot water she tried to let go of the strain from the last few hours.

"How have things gone on your end?" Graeber's voice echoed off the shower walls, muffled by the water sluicing over her head.

Did he detect the self-doubt welling up within her? She did her best to quell the rising emotions. "As expect-ed." Bauleel worked a generous quantity of refreshingly newcedar-scented soap to her hair. Would that she could clean her conscience so easily. "The girl woke up disori-ented from her special medication..."

"So she remembers nothing?"

"Fortunately for us, no. With the drugs in her system, it would have been impossible for her to hide any residual memories. She's genuine and honest, if upset about the amnesia."

"Then the plan moves forward?"

Was that regret in his voice? The shower hadn't done a thing to ease her own worries, yet she turned off the water and began toweling dry.

"Yes. I finalized placement of the girl with the

Durmah Sept today. Her induction feast is underway as we speak. According to the adoption petition the Durmah's presented, they need immediate assistance with a new Waystation they've opened in Kiya's Grace. Therefore, I expect they will want to move her to address this need."

"I wasn't aware the Durmah had built a Sept house in that town."

After slipping back into her under shift, Bauleel emerged from the steaming shower while toweling her waist-long auburn hair dry. Graeber stood outside, cleaning his nails with a short dagger while he awaited an answer. His eyes were hard and determined, but the earlier rigidity was gone. She stood close to him, unintimidated despite his size.

"Like I said, it's new. Besides, Kiya's Grace is off your routine patrols. The new Waystation is to be both a Sept house and a traveler's Waystation."

Her voice took on a more serious tone as her green eyes looked up into Graeber's. "Regardless, your task will be to follow the girl and watch her for any sign of repressed memories surfacing. We must keep her hidden and inconspicuous. If she does regain her memories or skills, things could get ... messier than anticipated. We wouldn't want the Durmah's at risk. You'll have to kill her if things get out of control. Or, if possible, you can always bring her back here and put her in stasis for the short term while we come up with some other solution."

"Let's see, I watch her. When I determine the whole 'hidden and inconspicuous plan' isn't working, I bring her back here. If things deteriorate, I kill her. Is that about the right level of messy for you?" Bauleel's skin bristled from the harsh heat in his tone. He might as well have hit her, his violence was so near the surface, but she wasn't about to call him on his underlying rage.

"Yes. You need to keep a low profile too. You never know who in the Anemoi will be keeping an eye on you. We are named 'as the wind' for a reason." Bauleel retreated to her closet and donned her Matriarch robes.

"Why place the girl with the Durmah? Do you think they might be connected to the growing unrest in the populace?" Graeber asked.

"I'm loath to blame the Durmah. They've always supported our initiatives. They travel across the continent--exposed to more dissent within the settlements via their business associates due to their trade. It's hard not to wonder about their loyalty to the Temples. Placing the girl there, well, if we need to we can always extract her and learn what she knows about the family business and politics of their associates. It's not as if we're planning to leave her with them long-term, even if things are optimal. We can't leave her anywhere for too long."

"Don't you think using her for information gathering could draw too much attention? Make her too visible?"

"I think she's been gone long enough no one's looking anymore. Everyone assumes she's dead. Since we changed her appearance, it should be impossible to recognize her. You'll be the fail-safe, hidden away in the shadows and keeping an eye on things. Making sure no one comes looking. Like I said, if things don't go as planned and we need to come up with another solution, we can always put her back in stasis."

After a few moments, the Matriarch emerged clad head to toe in pure resplendent white, her face just barely visible through the white veil.

"I trust your judgment in this, Graeber. You will be close enough to know if she's becoming dangerous." The Matriarch's grave tone was clear: they couldn't afford any mistakes. If anyone discovered who this girl was before the amnesia, what she'd done and who she'd been, his or her lives would both be forfeit.

Graeber nodded in understanding.

"If you need anything, it's obvious you know where to find me. Lock up when you leave."

Matriarch Bauleel left her chambers without another word.

PICKING UP HIS CAPE AND BAG FROM BAULEEL's couch, Graeber worried if her nervousness would complicate their plans. He'd expected her to act with more composure in a matter of such importance, regardless of the stakes in play. Despite the tight control she'd tried to keep on her emotions, Graeber had noticed her exasperation throughout their discussion. It wasn't that Bauleel poorly cloaked her feelings; he just excelled at reading the finest traces and clues.

Knowing Bauleel, Graeber predicted that she'd spend a great deal of time soon in meditation, no doubt hoping to clear her mind and catch any possible flaws in their plan. Once she came to terms with her choices, she'd need to re-solidify her inner shields to mute her thoughts and feelings from detection by other members of the Anemoi.

The possibility of outright failure crossed his mind daily. Perhaps the difference between them was in his acceptance of the imminent utter destruction of their plans from the start. The fact that they'd been able to keep the girl hidden and their actions unnoticed from the other Anemoi for this long shocked him. He recalled an old saying among his Sept: 'If there's something to hide, there are a million things to fall through the cracks.'

Their plan was destined to fail. Therefore, Graeber wasn't counting on Bauleel's plan in the slightest.

Locking the door on his way out, Graeber pulled the tracking device from one of his many hidden vest pockets. The coordinates of the package remained stable and none of his security measures within a five-mile radius showed any tampering either. He returned the scanner to his pocket. Bauleel was out of her element with her end of the plan--whereas this kind of thing was second nature for him. He expected at least some security measures to fail and therefore used every monitoring device and trick he could think of to safeguard the package. Graeber believed in, and practiced, systems redundancy.

He checked his communications device for new transmissions and found none. Although it was possible that Raza hadn't read his last message, he thought it unlikely. Raza was his sister, but also the Guardian's Chieftess; and for both of these reasons he knew she must have been monitoring his feed. Graeber knew better than to take the absence of a response as tacit approval of his handling of the situation. Her loyalty to him meant she wouldn't betray him, but she didn't have to approve of his choices either. Raza had agreed with the Anemoi's mandates, and abiding by their verdicts would have been safer and kept them appeased. However, they had wanted everything--everyone-- destroyed.

The problem was Bauleel had lied to the Anemoi, assuring them they'd eradicated the evidence. Only Bauleel, Graeber, and Raza knew the truth, and Bauleel had gambled they could hide it from the rest of the Anemoi. If they were to discover the truth, the removal of the evidence would be the least of their problems. Raza had done nothing to aid their defiance besides keeping quiet. Graeber hoped that knowledge, if discovered, wouldn't earn his sister a death sentence.

The shadow government of the Anemoi didn't abide dissent--much less traitors. There wouldn't be discussion or debate with the group at large. No, once the lies were uncovered he and Bauleel would be lucky if they saw death coming.

Striding out of the Temple compound, Graeber decided to pay a visit to the Guardian Sept house and check on Durmah travel permits. If the girl went to Kiya's Grace, then she'd need Guardian projection for the journey. Who better to give it to them?

He caught his reflection in wall mirror next to the front door, placed so the Matriarch could check her garments for correct placement before heading out the door. His lips were set in a grim line and his eyes reflected back a haunted, vacant expression.

Jarred by his own feelings so blatantly displayed, he

paused. Surely, things were not this desperate. Bauleel's plan to control the girl had a chance of success.

The utter sorrow lingering in his eyes told another tale. Bauleel had kept the girl alive so far. Now he'd have to hide and protect her from the other Anemoi, and more importantly, herself.

CHAPTER 6

MATRIARCH BAULEEL LEFT HER QUARTERS IN SUCH A rush that she all but ran straight over Journeywoman Camille, keeper of the Matriarch's appointment book, historic accountant, and personal assistant. From the tapping of her foot and belabored sigh at her emergence, Camille emphasized her prolonged waiting period. Camille was privy to a good portion of the Matriarch's dealings, and always got irritable when she felt she'd missed something.

"Good evening, Camille." The Journeywoman held a pile of documents awaiting the Matriarch's consideration. The loathed daily paperwork had taken a back seat today to the processing of the girl Rai, but Bauleel could avoid it no longer.

"I'm glad to see you're still up, Mother. Do we have time to review some outstanding items this evening, or do you have other commitments?" Camille tapped her pen on her trusty notepad.

"I've committed the remainder of my time tonight to

returning to my offices and reviewing paperwork with you, Camille. Where else would I be going at this hour?" The Matriarch ignored Camille's evident vexation. Bauleel expected Camille to record '11:15 pm - Matriarch returns to the office to complete paperwork' in her notepad. Although Camille could at times be high-strung and detail-oriented, Bauleel knew she couldn't hope to perform the duties of a Temple Matriarch without her. Above all else, a Matriarch had to have a complete schedule of what was coming, along with a record of what had been. Camille's seasoned skills provided both.

Bauleel walked around Camille and continued her march toward her formal reception chambers in the central section of the Temple. The Matriarch's personal quarters were toward the rear of the Temple compound, joined via a long, narrow hallway with the Temple's main sections. It wasn't the shortest walk, but Bauleel preferred the peace and quiet in this relatively empty section.

"I was concerned, Mother. I hadn't been able to find you these past few hours, and you missed an appointment with Priestess Parthe. She wished to discuss issues regarding the purity of medicinal components."

"Did you speak to her in my stead?"

"Yes. Priestess Parthe dropped by and spoke with me about an hour after your allotted meeting time. She said the issue is of broader scope than she at first realized. I rescheduled her for tomorrow morning." Although Camille talked openly in private with the Matriarch, she always refrained from doing so in front of others. This level of detail discussed in the public hallway alerted Bauleel that Camille considered Parthe's needs critical.

They continued down the long hall, and Bauleel heard the door to her private quarters open behind them. Cringing, Bauleel listened to the sounds of Graeber's steps fading away in the opposite direction. Who knew what Camille would make of it: an unannounced late-night meeting between the Matriarch and a Guardian in her private quarters?

"I...I'm sorry Matriarch, if I'd known you had a...scheduling conflict...I'd have avoided you this evening." Camille's widened eyes and pale face revealed her shock at the Guardian's appearance.

Reaching the corridor hub leading to the central Temple section behind the amphitheater, they turned the corner and lost sight of Graeber walking off in the other direction. Bauleel rolled her eyes behind her veil thinking she should have had Graeber wait a few minutes before leaving. Although Guardians posed no risk to the average, law-abiding citizen, their reputation kept most from even meeting their gaze, and the possible consequences of any additional scrutiny. Apparently seeing one when you weren't expecting it was enough to cause even the ever-controlled Camille to lose composure.

"A problem arose that required my immediate atten-tion. Be assured, Camille, for the most part you know more about my schedule than even I do. My duties to the Temple and to our city always come first, even before meetings with Priestess Parthe."

"Oh, I'm sorry, Mother. I didn't mean to question

your priorities. I know you devote yourself to our well-being foremost, and we are all indebted to you because of it. I trust everything is quite all right?"

"Don't worry. I'm quite sure the Guardian's issue will soon be resolved," Bauleel replied. Approaching the doors to her public offices, Bauleel paused. "Camille, could you fetch Apprentice Mala for me? I require a brief audience with her before she retires for the evening."

"Yes Mother, I'll go get her immediately," Camille replied in an even tone, having regained some semblance of composure. "I've placed some critical papers on your desk for review. Do you think you'll have time to address them tonight?"

"Yes, child, I'll do my best," Bauleel replied.

The Journeywoman set out in the direction of the Birthing quarters and the Matriarch swung open the thick, weighty wood door and entered, leaving the door open behind her. Passing through the front audience room, she opened a smaller door toward the back and entered her main office space. Sighing at the sight of a stack of papers two full hands high, she pulled her chair up and got to work. The Matriarch wouldn't want to disappoint her aide, after all...

The top item read from Priestess Parthe concerning contaminated luna berries from the bogs northeast of Kiya's Grace. Bauleel remembered reading the initial reports questioning the purity of the milled berries a few moons ago, but Parthe now claimed to have conclusive chemical evidence of the contamination. The luna berries played a key ingredient of the medicinals, acting as an inhibitor of the growth of the plague virus itself. Any problem with the precious fruit was of great concern to Bauleel. Paging through the notes, the source of the contamination hadn't yet been determined. According to the tests, fifteen to twenty percent of the berry supplies contained the toxin. Parthe ended the report on a bright note, at least as bright as could be hoped. The medicinal mixtures containing the contaminated berries had been isolated, as had the few unlucky people who had taken them. These poor souls had been afflicted with nerve damage, and research continued to cease or even reverse the damage. The nerve damage, she reported, was not only severe but also continued to advance as the affected nerve cells passed along disordered signals to healthy cells and increased the scope of the damage. One of the patients had already died-- mild arrhythmias had rapidly progressed to full-blown coronary arrest, and another was in critical condition.

Bauleel set the report down, overwhelmed with the findings. It broke her heart that something supposed to protect people from illness had instead taken a life. The plague was bad enough; taking the cure shouldn't be hazardous also.

Bauleel made a mental note to reaffirm the safety of the Temple's medicinals publicly, lest any rumors relating to this contamination spread and panic the populace.

Just as Bauleel wondered where Camille was with Mala, she looked up to find them both standing awaiting her attention. Bauleel again noticed the bruising on the left side of Mala's jaw and wondered how that had transpired. It hadn't been there when Mala had awoken Rai out of the birthing crèche, but Bauleel had noted it during her discussion with Rai and Mala earlier today in the orchards. The vivid blues and greens spoke of the force behind the impact she'd taken.

"Thank you for coming, Apprentice Mala. I trust I caught you before bed?"

"Yes, Mother. I was practicing my solitary meditation before retiring for the evening." Mala replied, her eyes respectfully cast downward in the presence of her Matriarch.

"I wanted to make sure Rai Durmah is in good health. The Durmah were in something of a rush to get her, and I wanted to make sure that we didn't miss something during the transition process." Bauleel eyed Mala carefully, hoping she would be at ease to disclose any concerns.

Per Temple protocol, Mala's eyes left the ground now that the Matriarch had addressed her. "I was transferred to Rai's care just a few days ago, so I can't give you the full details of her recovery history. However, I will do my best to summarize what I have learned since I assumed responsibility for her care."

Bauleel knew this fact. She'd been the one who ordered the reassignment. "I understand, Apprentice Mala. Please continue."

"The nature of her amnesia perplexes me. She remembers nothing before two days ago. I have seen cases of short-term, transient amnesia, but this instance is different. I, therefore, doubt her memory will return anytime soon, if at all. The absence of any memories of her birth family, however tragic, will make her move into the Durmah Sept easier. She's leaving nothing behind."

"I did have a concern you may find interesting. Rai needs higher levels of medicinals than usual for her size and weight. This became evident on her first night outside the birthing crèche. She slept poorly and had a rather fitful nightmare. It must have involved lashing out at someone, whoever that someone was in her dream, in the real world it was me." She pointed to the bruise on her chin.

Camille, who until this point had been quietly taking notes, looked up and studied Mala's chin. Bauleel guessed she'd find a full description of Mala's bruise someday in Camille's records.

"Do you think it's a memory from her past?" Bauleel asked.

"She didn't discuss any details from the dream with me. Nightmares of that intensity are often the result of some major event or past trauma. This might even explain her loss of memory. Trauma-induced amnesia is rare, but it can happen. The dream could have been the result of the unique medicinal formula we gave her. Its effects on the psyche have not been researched.

"This nightmare notwithstanding, however, she seemed in good spirits, though I can't say what the eventual return of her memory will reveal." Apprentice Mala once again fixed her eyes on the floor, awaiting any further questions from her Matriarch.

Bauleel contemplated all this with furrowed brow. Could the girl's past be returning to her in her dreams? Thinking of this possibility sent an icy chill down

Bauleel's spine; she'd risked everything to keep Rai's memories hidden. Bauleel had to take every conceivable precaution to ensure those memories didn't resurface. Considering what she knew of the girl's past, the increased levels of medicinals required for effective dose delivery didn't surprise her.

"Well, I doubt there's anything to worry about, but it wouldn't hurt if she had a few additional routine exams," Bauleel replied. "The Durmah indicated that the girl will be relocated to their new Waystation in Kiya's Grace. Why don't you contact the Temple healers there and make sure she gets the follow-up care she needs? Make sure they contact me when her amnesia fades. That's something of a curiosity, after all. Make sure they get enough of this new medicinal to administer to Rai for at least the next few days after her arrival at Kiya's Grace." Camille's head nodded as she scratched away at her notes.

Mala hesitated before answering. "But Mother, what of any side effects that could result from this medicinal? Without further testing, we have no idea what will happen to her. Should the girl not be made aware that there could be unforeseen side effects?" Apprentices were encouraged to question things they didn't understand. Even so, Bauleel sensed the girl's trepidation in asking the Matriarch herself.

Bauleel understood Mala's concerns and nearly sighed in agreement. Mala had, even more, cause for concern than she knew! This medicinal formula contained some controlled ingredients that had the unfortunate side effects of drowsiness, mental fog and diminished sensory perception in the extremities. The reputation of these herbs was exactly why Bauleel had ordered them for use with the girl.

"This is indeed a possibility," Bauleel said. "But the only way to ensure a full recovery for the girl is to keep her on this formula, despite any potential risks. Hers is an unfortunate situation, and there are no easy answers. Keep a close eye her situation so we'll be alerted to any potential issues before they become a problem for her or her new Sept. Please send word to Kiya's Grace as I requested. Also, I'll need regular progress reports on the girl's health forwarded to the local Matriarch at Kiya's Grace. I'd like a copy of each update to her medical notes as well," Bauleel concluded. The edge in her voice made it clear there was no further room for discussion.

"Yes, Mother," Mala replied. Bauleel thought she heard the doubt in her voice, but she knew that Mala would carry out her orders. "I will convey the message this evening before retiring. Do you know when the Durmah will be moving Rai to Kiya's Grace? I want to make sure she has an adequate supply of the new medicinal on hand."

"In two days at most, potentially even tomorrow. They delayed one of their shipments specifically to reduce the trip cost by relocating the girl at the same time. I don't know if you could find more astute business folk than the Durmah on all of Az'Unda! Regardless of when they're leaving, you could deliver the medicinals first thing in the morning to the Durmah Sept house. I'm sure they'd appreciate your speed and attention to detail."

Bauleel noted that the implied flattery brought the ghost of a smile to Mala's lips.

Mala bowed. "Yes Mother, I will heed your wise directives. Is there any other way I may assist you tonight?"

"No, child, that is all I require of you tonight. Go mindfully with joy."

Mala sank lower in her bow, and then arose and left the room, a pleasant but tired look on her face.

"Is there anyone else you need to speak with tonight, Mother?" Camille queried, still jotting down notes from Mala's visit.

"No dear, my remaining plans for the evening are to finish this paperwork. You may retire for the evening. I doubt staring at me doing paperwork in the middle of the night will be entertaining," Bauleel said, not wishing to overtax her indispensable--if somewhat quirky--aide.

"Oh, it's no bother, Mother. I'll just get a head start on some letters for your review tomorrow." Camille sat at her smaller desk in the corner and picked through her own stack of papers. The quiet company would be a boon through the long night after such an emotionally draining day.

EVEN BEFORE THE BUTLER NIMMA HAD A CHANCE to wake her, Rai awoke from her peaceful slumber to the sound of activity and bustle from outside her room. Rai got out of bed and changed into the clothes laid out the night before. They included heavy boots and a cloak--did it mean she'd be sent on the road already today? The idea filled her with excitement and let her know, once again, that she truly was a member of this family--if a new one.

Venturing from her room, Rai got a few steps when she encountered Nimma in the hallway. Nimma gave a hearty laugh.

"Ah, a true Durmah! Out of bed before I have a chance to wake you!" Rai couldn't help smiling back at the woman. Rai continued down the hallway toward the source of the commotion.

At the end of the hall, Rai dodged a pair of young girls running around the corner screaming in delight. Straight from the kitchen with steaming hot sweet rolls in hand and mischievous grins on their faces. Now they have the right idea.

She continued in the direction they'd come, her diminished olfactory sense nevertheless sufficient to guide her around another few turns to the kitchen--and the delicious scents of breakfast therein.

She'd found the source of the activity that had awakened her: the Sept's huge kitchen. The complexity of preparing just one meal at the Sept house amazed her. She saw a plate of the sweet rolls like the ones the girls had absconded within the hands of a scullery boy on his way out the door to the main dining hall.

Three cooks worked furiously over hot stoves and took no notice of her arrival. A few feet away from her, a cook placed the final touches on an egg and cheese casserole; he looked up at her, with a frown on his heat-reddened face. Either the cook had been expecting someone else or he just perpetually wore that sour expression. He placed a dish on a long counter filled with platters of food appeared ready for serving. As she watched, another scullery boy attempted to juggle two large trays at once. Walking over to the counter, Rai picked up a platter of fried sausages and headed for the door to the main hall.

She popped a hot, juicy sausage into her mouth and opened the door to the main entrance. This was just as busy as the kitchen had been, if not more so -- apparently set up as the staging area for the morning's activities. In the light of day, Rai could now make out the details of the room's structure. The great hall was twice as long as it was wide, large enough to hold three tables across and six tables long. Along the length of the room, there were two fireplaces on each wall. There was one fireplace at each end of the chamber. Family members sat and ate breakfast in groups across the room. A group of children hovered around the large fireplace at the far end of the hall. Their happy laughter echoed with the high ceiling. Rai couldn't help but join in until her chest ached and her cheeks felt stuck, full and rosy with joy.

At this end of the room near the large fireplace stood a larger, round table, which served as the hub of activity within the large dining hall. Stoi gave orders to various Sept members while Meik scribbled down notes and reviewed a large map spread out upon the table. Rai noticed plates on the table holding half-eaten chunks of food. It appeared Stoi and Meik had too much to do to devote themselves to their breakfasts.

A Sept member stopped next to Rai on his way into the kitchen. She recognized him from the feast the night before.

"You're the new adoptee?"

"That's me! Rai Durmah, at your service," she replied with a proud smile. Wiping her slightly greasy hand against her pant leg, Rai offered it up in greeting.

"Yarron Durmah," he said as they shook hands.

"What's going on out here?"

"Oh, just the usual daily travel preparations. Kiya's Grace is the destination for today. I can't remember whose all going." He pointed toward the far end of the room. "Those are travel packs. We assemble them here and then carry them out the side door into the courtyard outside. Then they're loaded onto the wagons. If you listen, you can hear the wagon wheels' creaking as each pack is loaded. I LOVE that sound!" As if on cue, Rai detected the noise of the wheels of a wagon creaking and groaning.

Yarron smiled and clapped her arm. "Welcome to Sept Durmah! I'm sure I'll be seeing you around," he said, and then headed into the kitchen.

Rai approached the table Stoi and Meik were working at, and Stoi turned to her, his greeting radiating genuine warmth. "Our new girl has some initiative!" His voice boomed through the rafters. "Up with the rays of dawn and already providing us with sustenance. Meik, I believe this one's a keeper."

Meik laughed. "Good thing, she's stuck with us either way." His easy smile didn't quite match the challenge in his eyes, letting Rai know she'd have to prove herself to him.

"We're discussing the plans for our trip today, Rai. Why don't you have a seat and join us?" Rai saw Stoi was still quite handsome, despite the scar running down his face.

"Sure." Rai handed Meik the sausage platter and sat down opposite Stoi. Stoi and Meik both grabbed some of the sausages. She noticed for the first time how profoundly the scar had affected Stoi's visage. The deep purple welt puckered the healthy skin around it, giving his face a puffy and round appearance.

"Wait, you said 'our.' Does that mean I'm coming along on this trip?" Rai asked.

"Yes," Stoi replied. Rai just looked back at him in confusion. It's not as if anyone had taken the time to explain this to her yet. "Oh, I'm sorry. I guess things have been so busy I'd figured someone told you you're stationed at Jesse's Waystation. She's Kait's eldest daughter, and runs the Waystation in Kiya's Grace."

The travel clothes she'd been given to wear now made more sense. "I thought the Durmah were traders?" Rai asked.

Rai felt a twinge of disappointment. The Durmah life of travel appealed to her, and the letdown of an assignment to a single location stung.

Rai took the opportunity to have a closer look at the maps, and she recognized the overall shape but nothing specific. The amnesia wasn't letting up yet. Still, Rai didn't know how excited she should be over identifying the familiar landmasses of Az'Unda and city locations.

"Are those maps of the routes between here and Kiya's Grace?" Rai asked because Yarron had mentioned the city just a moment ago.

Meik finished swallowing a bite of sausage and answered, gesturing to the large, hand-drawn map. "They are indeed! Here's the lowland route, straight east from Raven's Call. It's the faster of the two possible routes by about two days when the road's passable. With the moons in their current alignment with high tides and it being the rainy season, the chances are 50-50 that it's not--well, with anything less than a swamp boat anyway. Besides, the red fruit flies would drive us insane this time of year if we tried."

"Alternatively, the highland route starts out east but then veers due north, past the Baris Spine. Navigating the spine takes about a half-day all by itself, including the ever-interesting Baris Pass. The pass can be hazardous, what with the switchbacks and all the loose rock. The Vaagaren Sept has a small house up there, and this time of year, they have plenty of Zander moss to sell us. Do you know how much it goes for in Kiya's Grace? We'd make a par of twenty to twenty-five, and we'd still get there in six days, vs. four--if we're lucky--via the lowland route. Knowing all this, which way would you recommend, Navigator Rai?" Both gave Rai amused looks.

"Let's see," Rai said. She looked at Meik's notes and considered his question. She knew the question was rhetorical--to everyone but Rai.

Rai was about to answer him, but then she saw the second map under the larger one. She pulled out one labeled 'The Northeast Coastline.' At about the midpoint along the coastline the map marked a city circle labeled 'Resounding Cliffs.' As Rai read the words, an image flashed in her mind of pounding surf against white and gray marbled rock, with city walls rising in the distance. A thrill of joy surged through her, curling her lips. A memory at last! The amnesia didn't hold total sway over her. However, remembering what a place looked like wasn't useful without also having some context around the memory, but at least it was a start.

Raising an eyebrow, Rai queried, "What about this map? Is there a trip in the works here too?" Rai realized that she didn't know which city Jesse's Waystation was located in, and thus which trip, and which route, she needed to study.

Meik nodded with a shrug. Her ability to make sense of the facts at hand seemed to please him. "I have a separate shipment due to Resounding Cliffs in just under a fortnight. My trek will take eleven or twelve days, depending on the weather and the condition of the roads. Unfortunately, there are no passes over the Baris Spine in that direction, so the coastal route is the only option."

"You're going to Resounding Cliffs, while Stoi's headed to Kiya's Grace? Is it wise to split up forces?"

Stoi shrugged. "That's what we always do. As long as we're under Guardian escort, there won't be a thing to worry about. This reminds me, we'd better get the paperwork for that filed soon, Meik. You still haven't answered the question. Which route to Kiya's Grace should you and I take?"

Placing the route to Resounding Cliffs back on the table, Rai wondered what the Durmah transported in trade along that route. "What's the cargo for Kiya's Grace?"

"Raw wool for the weavers," Stoi responded. "The Weavers of Kiya's Grace are amazing, and their goods fetch a nice sum at the markets, so it's well worth our efforts." Regardless, wool wasn't perishable, and Rai had her answer.

"Everything you've said indicates that we'd be better off taking the highland route."

"Indeed Rai, that's the conclusion Stoi and I came to as well. Do you have any experience with wagon travel? If not, you're in for a challenge!" Meik said. He grabbed another sausage. Rai believed him. Eating like Meik did and still being as wiry and muscular as he was, there must be a lot of work involved.

"I'm not sure. I'm afraid I'm still suffering the after

effects of the Temple medicinals," Rai answered. She didn't know how to bring up the subject of her amnesia. Hadn't the Temple already informed them of her condition?

Stoi and Meik shared an anxious look. "What do you mean, after effects?" Stoi asked.

"Well, I don't remember a thing before two days ago," Rai admitted, smiling wanly. I mean, I can recognize the cities on this map and some of the other geographic features, but I can't tell you of any time before now that I've even looked at maps like these," Rai explained.

The brothers glanced at her and at each other, the concern in their faces deepening with her every word. Something about Rai's amnesia disturbed them. "Apprentice Mala said it wasn't uncommon for the medicinals to bring on a temporary amnesia, and that it would fade over time," Rai continued, trying to assuage their fears as well as her own.

"But you can't remember anything? I've heard of girls not being able to remember their stay of service at the Temple, or being tired in the days afterward, but never amnesia from before their stay at the Temple. I wonder what they're hiding his time," Meik grumbled, his eyes still fixed on Rai.

Stoi grabbed Meik's arm. "Now, have a care there, Meik. Rai is our sister now, whatever she remembers or doesn't remember. The Temple might not even have anything to do with Rai's amnesia. Keep in mind, this condition isn't her fault. At any rate, the past is over. Right now we've got cargo to deliver."

"I didn't intend to..." He cast his eyes to the floor.

"We've had a history of problems with the Temple. I get so upset sometimes I can't think straight. Still, I should know better than to cast blame in your direction. I'm sorry, Rai."

"That's okay Meik; it's plenty frustrating for me too."

Stoi released Meik's arm and turned back to Rai, brows knit with concern. Even though they directed their distress at the Temple and not herself, it still made her nervous to watch her new Uncles so upset by her amnesia. Apprentice Mala had portrayed it to Rai as no big deal, but with their reaction, she now knew it was a larger issue. She wanted to know more about what they knew of the Temple--but now was not the time.

"Well, Meik's right about one thing: amnesia doesn't happen every day--not even among those who've served in the Temple." He considered for a moment. "Do you remember anything else about your stay in the Temple that you thought of as unusual or strange?"

For a moment Rai wanted to avoid the discussion altogether; this was not the way she envisioned her first day with the Durmah going. Then it dawned on her that Stoi and Meik were the first people she'd met with whom she had something in common: an apparent distrust of the Temple, and likely so did the entire Durmah Sept. Luck had paired her with a family who shared her point of view. Rai lowered her voice to a whisper.

"One of the medicinals they gave me dulled my sense of smell. Even now I can't detect things right, and everything tastes off too."

"Well, that's unusual, but it could just be a typical

side effect too. It's hard to say. We're not Healers," Stoi replied.

"I don't think so. I faked taking the meds yesterday, and my sense of smell has started to recover."

"You stopped taking the medicinals? Didn't your nurse notice?" Meik queried.

"Well, I dumped the medicinals in the bath water before Mala came to check on me, so she never knew. She told me the Temple would send more of that unique mixture here to the Durmah house to aid in my recovery, but I do not intend to take it. I'll take the regular anti-plague meds like everyone else. Don't worry about me, I feel fine."

Stoi looked straight at Rai. "Look, as long as you're healthy, then that's all right with us. Please understand, our Sept's dealings with the Temple have a history, and I for one don't trust them with anything. If we could get plague treatments from another source, well, I'd gladly pay for it, whatever the par. You'd be better off not putting your trust in them. Anyway, we're your family now, and I want you to keep me apprised of any further interactions with them, understand?"

Rai nodded.

"Regardless, the Temple didn't inform us of any damage to your memory. They're supposed to disclose all illnesses and injuries of potential candidates, so I do wonder what they're doing. I wouldn't be surprised if they somehow damaged your faculties and just didn't want to admit it, assuming we wouldn't question them."

Stoi sighed, and then turned to Meik. "Well, I know you wanted to get out early today, but we need to stop by the Temple and at least leave a message for the Matriarch and let her know that Durmah won't stand for this. Hopefully, we can get the story on what happened to Rai here."

"Do you think there's something wrong with her they didn't want us to know about?" Meik replied, casting a sidelong glance at Rai. Rai took offense to the implications and his tone.

Stoi frowned back at Meik, also appearing annoyed with his tone. "No, Rai seems healthy enough. You feel fine otherwise, right?"

"Oh yes, just fine, like I said before." Rai didn't like the direction this discussion could go. Others could think of her as sickly or otherwise unable to pull her own weight. Stoi nodded back at her reassuringly.

"Well then," he continued, "I agree. We have to make a point of it." Meik said.

"Okay. Let's visit the Matriarch and hear what she has to say about Rai's amnesia. I think it's worth setting off a couple hours late," Stoi replied.

"Do you think we need to tell Kait? I mean, wouldn't she be the more appropriate person for such a visit?"

"No, we can tell Kait all about it when we get back from the Temple. I want to hear the Matriarch's excuse for this with my own ears. Assuming her Revered Excellence even condescends to give me an explanation, that is." Stoi rolled his eyes.

Stoi picked up a thick scroll from the table and handed it to Rai. "Well, since we need to run this errand, why don't you familiarize yourself with the goods being packed for this trip and make sure nothing gets missed?

Also, complete the packing by midday. I'm confident that we'll be back by then at the latest. It shouldn't be too hard, everyone around here knows the drill and it'll give you a chance to see how it all works."

Stoi stood and placed a firm but gentle hand on her shoulder. "Don't worry, Rai, one way or the other, we'll find answers for you. Besides, we don't like the Temples thinking they can get away with treating Durmah poorly, all right?"

Rai thought his motivation might be more about Durmah's treatment at their hands then her particular situation. "I understand. Don't worry about the wagons. I'll make sure everything's in order before you get back."

"That's the spirit! Oh, and if you need help finding any supplies, just ask the head cook. See you soon!"

Watching them leave, Rai's head filled with questions about the upcoming trip, her sister Jesse, and the Waystation in Kiya's Grace. She figured there would be ample time on the journey to discover. So much escaped her knowledge--about the Durmah, about the Temple, about her past. She only hoped the answers would come soon.

CHAPTER 8

Rai and Kait were pouring over the route maps over a cup of tea when Stoi stomped into the main hall, sweat beading on his brow. Laan, Stoi's cousin by Kait's sister Nele and long-time traveling companion, sat next to them, whittling away at a small woodcarving of a squirrel. From the tense draw of his features, Rai could guess how the meeting at the Temple went. She steeled herself for his news, reminding herself it had been a slim chance at best, anyway.

Laan glanced up, nodding acknowledgment of Stoi's arrival. He remained keenly aware of what was going on around him, despite his quiet demeanor. Kait had told her he could be entirely focused on something or someone, yet be aware of all the conversations taking place in the background--even in a crowded room.

"Everything looks well in order in the stable yard. What'd you do girl, give everyone the afternoon off? I mean, don't you know you have to drag the work out, to keep everyone busy?" Stoi asked.

Kait and Rai both chortled. "Your brother thinks he's funny, doesn't he?" Rai asked Kait.

"Here we thought you'd forgotten about the trip, you've been gone so long," Kait said to Stoi. She leaned back in her chair, a flicker of pain passing over her features. "But in all seriousness, Rai managed to load the wagons before noon, so I sent most everyone off on errands."

"Yes, and now I'll have to hitch the horses myself!" Stoi hung his thumbs from his belt, clucking his tongue in disapproval.

"As you do many times a day on the road, Stoi. Don't give the girl a hard time over it," Laan replied.

"Oh, Rai knows I'm joking, don't you?" Rai gave a quick nod, although his demeanor didn't relax the knot in her belly. She didn't have the courage to ask how his morning's errand had fared.

"Why didn't Meik return with you?" Laan asked.

"I sent him off to arrange for our Guardian escorts. It's late notice, but I doubt it'll be a problem. Besides, he got pretty worked up at the Temple, and I figured he needed the time to walk it off."

Laan nodded, and a lull in the conversation hung in the air. As they'd suspected, Stoi's news wouldn't be positive.

Kait sighed, resignation painted across her features. "Your wife decided not to wait for your return and headed off to visit with her birth-Sept for the afternoon. She bade you goodbye and a safe and quick return."

"That sounds like my Chirey, all right. Can you tell her I should be back within two weeks?"

While Stoi was away, Kait had grumbled to Rai how Chirey, against custom, maintained strong ties to her birth Sept, the Genneb, after her marriage to Stoi. Many husbands in the same situation would have demanded their wives commit to their new Sept entirely, but Stoi doted upon Chirey and indulged in her needs. Rai guessed it stemmed from guilt to his extended absences away from home while he was on the road.

"Sure. I had the cook prepare a late lunch for you, so you'll have something warm and fresh on your way out of town. Both Laan and Rai have already eaten. They figured you'd want to leave immediately," Kait continued.

"Thanks, Sis," Stoi said. He pulled up a chair. "Are you feeling better today? You looked a bit exhausted after the late-night feasting. We were worried about you."

"Yes, sorry. I was just a little worn out. You know how it is."

"Yeah, I suppose I do," Stoi replied.

Kait, as Chieftess for the Durmah Sept, should have been the one to confront the Matriarch but was unable due to her poor health. Both Stoi and Meik blamed the Temple for Kait's suffering. Kait had left for Temple service at fourteen, the picture of good health, having never been sick a day in her life. She'd returned six years later after having a respectable four children but a shadow of her former self, her vitality stripped from her like the colors of a flower. Their mother, Chieftess Marra, had passed while she was away, and Kait had stepped into their mother's shoes as Chieftess when she returned, but continually fought against overwhelming fatigue.

"How did your meeting at the Temple go? When I woke up and heard that you and Meik had run off to the Temple before your trip, Rai filled me in on her amnesia and your desire to find out what the Temple staff knew about it."

Stoi shrugged. "Meik was fortunate, I suppose, as the Matriarch herself agreed to meet with us without an appointment. As you'd expect, she wouldn't talk much about it, except to deny any wrongdoing by the Temple healers. She claimed when her birth Sept brought her to the Temple for service, Rai already had amnesia. They were tight-lipped on when or how it happened, and the healers felt no obligation to question them further. The Matriarch assured Meik and I her staff did nothing which contributed to Rai's current state."

Rai processed this new information, trying to understand how it might fit into the puzzle.

"A girl, with amnesia, left on the steps of the Temple for her years of Service by her Septmates? Why didn't they question them over what happened to Rai, or research her background first? The Matriarch's story doesn't ring true," Kait replied.

"That's what we thought too. Meik wondered, afterward, if you could have gotten anything more out of her, but I doubt it. Anyway, the Matriarch further assured us Rai is healthy in every way. She hadn't considered amnesia a significant illness or limitation and therefore didn't disclose it to us. She also thought Rai's memory of her service in the Temple would return, but couldn't say when that would happen with the memories she had before her Temple service."

"I don't believe a word of it. Wouldn't you think the Temple staff would at least be a little curious as to what would cause such a strange phenomenon in a person as total loss of memory? Prying into an adoptee's past and associated Sept business is held private and sacrosanct, and thus a prohibited practice--but situations like this warrant exceptions. Perhaps the Temple's just too busy these days to care much about the welfare of every girl they care for. It's horribly negligent of them. How could we rely on the Temples to find an eventual cure to the plague, if they can't get a simple adoption right?"

"I may never know." Rai couldn't hide the bitter disappointment in her voice.

"Don't worry about it, child. You can put your faith securely in Durmah, right where it should be. I know the Temple's not going to follow up on this, but I will," Kait said. "My health may be poor, but I do have a network of contacts I can ask and see if anyone's heard of any recent incidents of amnesia. However, you could have been in service anywhere from months to years, so it's possible that it's been too long for people to remember."

She turned to Stoi. "Keep your ears open on the road, too. This has Temple incompetence written all over it, and if they did it to Rai, then I imagine they'd do it to anyone. It might not be an isolated occurrence. My girls Blethe and Marra are in Temple service right now! What's going to happen to them? The side effects of the fertility treatments are bad enough!" The last sentence sent a chill down Rai's back. She knew Kait was referring to her own state of deteriorating health.

"I'll do that. We'll be discreet. The laws against

looking into the histories of adoptees are clear. The penalties for breaking them are on the stiff side."

"I never said we should ask about Rai's past in particular, I'm going to send letters to my contacts and ask if they've heard of any cases of amnesia. That's innocent enough. Who knows, one of them may even know of a folk remedy to try. Anything would be worth a shot since the Temples are no longer investigating these themselves. If I happen to discover a little more about Rai along the way, well it'll be a complete coincidence." Kait winked at Rai. "Well, I can't have you all sitting around all day just keeping me company! Stoi, why don't you go grab that bite of food the cook has ready for you. Rai and Laan can get the horses hitched up."

"Yes, ma'am. We'll get right on it," Laan replied. He pocketed his animal carving, sheathed his knife, and then headed out the door.

Rai turned to Kait and took her hands in her own. "Thanks, Kait. This means the world to me." They hugged briefly, and then Rai followed Laan out the door. "We'll be ready in ten minutes," she called on the way out.

CHAPTER 9

After a quick lesson on handling the horse-drawn wagon, Stoi handed the reins to Rai, and they set out on their journey. Laan followed behind them in the second wagon. It was the most exciting moment that Rai could remember, but she guessed that wasn't saying much. Rai turned around and looked at the Durmah Sept house one last time. She felt a twinge of sadness, knowing it would be a long time before she would see Kait, Meik, and the others again. Something inside of her told her to look forward, not back, and she once again focused her gaze on the road ahead.

The city streets were nearly empty in the heat of the late afternoon sun, so all was quiet and serene as the two wagons made for the city's western gate. The temperature had combined with the morning rain to form an oppressive haze that reached as far as the eye could see. Rai looked around; this was the first time she'd actually seen the city. As they moved toward the outskirts of Raven's Call, the large Sept houses gave way to multiunit dwellings as they moved toward the periphery of Raven's Call.

"Who lives in these buildings?" Rai asked. "They don't look like the other Sept houses we've passed."

"That's where the Sept-less live, the workhouses. The Temple's provide them those meager living units in return for day labor."

"But I thought the Temple placed people like me with Septs?"

"Yes, child. In cases like yours, they try to do so, but it doesn't always work out. Not every Sept is open to taking on new, non-blood members."

Rai cringed inwardly at the thought. Had the Temple not found a home for her with the Durmahs, she might well be staring out the small window of one of those dilapidated little dwellings even now.

"Some become Sept-less for other reasons," Stoi continued. "Sometimes, the plague has killed off their families or reduced their numbers such that they can't afford to run a proper Sept-house anymore. Others disgraced their Septs and soon after that turned out onto the streets to fend for themselves. Whatever their offense, the Temple feeds and houses them in return for their labor. The Temple won't turn anyone out of the cities."

Approaching the outer wall and western gate, Rai noticed the block housing gave way to large buildings that huddled under the span of the outer wall. They looked different from the tenement quarters, dirtier and somehow more industrial looking. They had no windows, and many of them had wagons and equipment in front and along the side.

"What are those buildings used for?"

"Those are the Temple's factories where the Sept-less work. They mill grain, butcher meat, produce simple clothing and shoes--pretty boring stuff actually."

"Sounds like it," Rai replied in agreement. It seemed a cold existence to Rai, working only to fill the Temple's pocket and having no connection to those around you.

As they came to the gate at the city wall, a Guardian emerged from the gatehouse to meet them. She was of average build but above-average height, with long dark hair. Rai pulled back on the reins to stop the horses and shot Stoi a quick glance.

Stoi gave Rai a wry smirk. "They always have us check in, to make sure we've been properly processed," Stoi said. "The Guardians are ever so courteous that way." Laan halted his wagon and waited behind them.

The Guardian stopped about three feet from the left side of the wagon. "Sept and destination?"

"Durmah Sept on route to Kiya's Grace via the Highland route," Stoi replied. "We filed travel papers this morning."

"I'll inform your escort of your departure." She turned and reentered the gatehouse. After a few seconds, the Guardian popped her head of the gatehouse door motioned to the guard at the gate. He opened the gate and allowed them through. Neither showed any expression. Rai urged the horses forward, perplexed with the impersonal nature of the Guardian's behavior. Were all Guardians so stiff and formal?

"Now was that a rousing send-off or what?"

"And I thought Temple folk were unnerving to be around," Rai replied.

"You'd be wise to avoid provoking them. The Guardians may be our protectors, but don't forget they'll take you out in a second if they think you're getting sick with the plague."

"But isn't that a good thing that they're here to protect us from the plague? I mean, we're not sick, so they're not any danger to us, right?"

"I'm all for them tracking down plague-infested menaces, as long as those Guardians stay away from Durmah, you know what I mean?"

"Ah, the enemy of my enemy is my friend, eh?" Rai found certain wisdom in his viewpoint. However, Stoi's anxiety around the gate Guardian puzzled Rai. As a Durmah and traveler, Stoi should've long since become used to dealing with Guardians. They were just another Sept with a job to do for the good of Az'Unda. Even with her amnesia, Rai knew the fight against the plague took priority over all aspects of life on Az'Unda.

Rai turned back to look at the city one more time. She could just make out a few Sept houses through the mist, dwarfed now by the outer wall of the city. The rounded roofs of the houses looked for a moment like a multitude of fish scales all layered upon each other, the hot sun glinting off their dark stone tile shingles. The city's circular, concentric rings of houses rose higher with the innermost ring of houses set close to the Temple. The main Temple structure towered above everything, at the literal and cultural pinnacle of the city. Beautiful as it was, Rai again felt an inexplicable need to put the past behind her, even her recent past in Raven's Call, so she turned to face the landscape before her once again.

The road ahead faded into the mist, but Rai made out the approaching tree line of a vast forest. They'd cleared all forest growth around the cities in the early years following colonization on Az'Unda to make it easier for the Guardians to defend against approaching threats.

The few narrow roads gave way to a dense forest, with a few spans to each side so travelers wouldn't have to overnight within the woods proper when out of range of city walls. Kait had explained this to Rai earlier, and now Rai understood she had been trying to reassure her of the safety of traveling these roads.

Near the forest line, the road split in two. From Rai's recollection of the maps that Stoi and Meik had shown her back at the Sept house, she remembered that the left fork traveled through the forest to sea level along the coastline. The other fork turned to the right and followed the tree line, vanishing in the haze where the hills rose a few miles off.

"We take the right fork, correct?" Rai asked Stoi.

"You should know. You're the navigator on this trip as I recall." Stoi chided, shaking his head. Stoi's fatherly ribbing was a genuine comfort.

"Oh yeah, I mean, we're taking the right fork," Rai tried to let his mood infect hers. "How far do you think we can get before dark?"

"Hmm, let's see. Usually, if we start first thing, we can

make the Baris Pass by early afternoon. We didn't start until late so we won't hit the pass until after sunset."

"Well, at least the heat will have subsided by then. I bet the view is fantastic from up there!" Rai said. Looking back to check that Laan was still behind them, Rai could just make out the circular walls of the city through the haze. They were going uphill now, and the mist was thinning, allowing Rai a clearer view of the dense forest surrounding them.

"The view from the Pass is indeed something to see. You can see everything--the ocean, the hills, the coastline, and the farms. Everything. You could even see to Raven's Call, assuming the enshrouding lowland mists blew off for a few hours. Wait 'til you get a view of the Zairne Spine from up there! Those mountains to the north are positively staggering in height."

"Perhaps the view will jar my memories."

"Maybe, but I doubt that, Rai. Few people your age have been outside the safety of the city."

Not what she wanted to hear, but he was probably right.

Stoi sank into a pensive silence, scanning the road and checking to make sure that Laan was still there behind them. Watching him watching everything made Rai nervous, so instead, she focused on the passing scenery.

Rai looked at them and noticed a lone rider on horseback following close behind Laan's wagon. "Is that our escort?" Rai asked.

Stoi turned around. "Yeah, about time he showed up. I hope that he won't annoy us this trip. I prefer it when they keep quiet. Usually means there won't be any trouble on the road."

They continued along the trail, gaining slowly but consistently in elevation and the landscape around them changed. First, the low shrubs in the plains on the right grew more frequent while the trees thinned along the forest line on the left. Even the birds appeared thinner and less substantial. Rai also noticed an improvement in her distance vision at this height and realized that they were climbing above the haze. She could see farther up the road, and back toward where the city would be, except for those mists.

As they rounded a turn in the road, Rai was surprised as a ridge of mountains appeared, towering in height.

"Wow!" Rai said. "Those mountains are incredibly tall."

"And that's just the Baris Spine," Stoi explained. "There are much taller Spines north of this one."

"Like that Zairne Spine you mentioned before?"

"Exactly. People who just stay in the cities don't get a genuine appreciation of the mountain ranges. It's one of the reasons I love the travel, despite the risks."

The road ahead twisted and folded back upon itself up the rise, forming a series of triangles upon the otherwise steep face of the Spine. The sun was now low on the horizon, and Rai counted no less than a dozen switchbacks along the rising trail before them. Stoi was right; they'd never make the pass before nightfall.

Approaching the first switchback, Stoi took over the reins, which was good because the wound in her arm was beginning to itch and ache. "You've done a great job so far, Rai, but I'd better take over now. This part of the trail gets a little rough."

"Thanks for letting me drive this far. Laan looks as though he could use some company back there. What do you say I ride with him until we make camp for the night?"

Rai was desperate for conversation, for reasons she couldn't quite express. She wanted more of everything from her senses; she wanted to see more, feel more, and hear more. Her mind was a gigantic void, a void she desperately wanted to fill as quickly as she possibly could. With Stoi so focused on the road, it was hard to keep him talking.

"Are you getting bored?"

Rai flashed him a guilty frown. "I'd love a chance to stretch my legs. Walk around a bit."

"I guess I should have warned you how slowly these trips can pass. I concentrate so hard watching for trouble that I don't have much left over for conversation! I guess we travelers just get too used to the solitude of the road. I'm so used to going alone, with all of my focus on the path ahead of me."

"I'll chat with you when we stop to make camp."

They reached the first switchback and Stoi reined in his horses, bringing the wagon to a stop. Rai disembarked, taking her cloak and travel bag with her. As soon as Rai was off the wagon, Stoi urged the team forward, handling the horses expertly. He took a slow but steady pace around the first turn, giving the horses' adequate time to pull the wagon up the dirt-packed trail.

Rai watched Laan's carriage approach and looking at the road behind them for the first time, realized just how far they had come in this short period.

Laan had a perplexed look on his face, likely due to Rai's sudden exit from the lead wagon. He slowed the wagon as he drew near and he moved over to the left side of the wagon's seat to make room for her. Rai shouldered both the pack and cloak, and then jumped up onto the running board and climbed up. She stowed her belongings under the seat and then sat down next to Laan.

"Stoi get too quiet for you?"

Rai laughed. "Yeah, you could say that. What's he worried about, anyway? Don't we have all the protection we need from the Guardians?" Rai turned around. Their escort followed a short distance behind them. Was the Guardian within hearing range?

"His wagon was attacked a few years back. He's never been able to relax on journeys since."

"No wonder he's so careful!"

"Yeah, but his 'carefulness' goes beyond the norm. I swear he thinks there's a Terror in every shadow. It borders on paranoia. I'd hoped having you along for the trip would make him more social and less anxious, but no such luck, I'm guessing?" The frown on Rai's face was all the answer he needed. "Perhaps we'll have some luck getting him to talk over dinner tonight. It's always worth a try, right?"

Rai shrugged. "I guess so. I'll try asking him to tell me a story. Something about Sept history to distract him. Did he get that scar on his face during the attack?"

"Actually, that scar is an altogether different story. I'll

let Stoi tell you tonight, if he can be persuaded. His injury happened as an isolated incident, but he did watch a Guardian take down a Terror before he got into the safety of his wagon. When he got back home from that trip, he couldn't sleep for days because of how deeply the creature had disturbed him. I hope we never come face-to-face with any Terrors ourselves. Hearing them in the distance is more than enough for me." Laan shuddered as he took the next switchback.

Rai wondered what the Terrors resembled, even though knowing might give her nightmares too.

"Have you seen them?"

Laan stared straight ahead. "No, I haven't had the misfortune of seeing a Terror." He paused, and Rai sensed a deep fear within him. "I doubt I ever will, either, with the Guardians doing their job."

"I know Stoi would prefer it if we didn't need the Guardians; they tend to make him anxious. I'm glad they're there. If I didn't know for sure that the Guardians were there to protect me, I'd probably be fighting you for that Waystation job, 'cause there's no way I'd travel!"

For the first time her excitement came with a twinge of fear. The light continued to fade, and she remembered the brothers saying it took a good half-day to make the Spine. They had only made four of the turns so far, and Rai knew they had another six or more to go before they reached the top.

"Will the daylight last until we hit the pass?" She didn't think that Laan's answer to this question would be any different from Stoi's earlier, but as with Stoi, she felt some comfort just hearing Laan's voice.

Laan looked up, and then back over the plains as if judging the light. "No, we'll get three-quarters of the way up before dusk starts to fade."

"Could we stop midway up the trail?"

Laan just shook his head. "This is one pass you don't stop on if you can help it. There's not enough space to turn these wagons around up here. We'll finish the last hour or so in the dark. It won't be so bad, you'll see. All three moons will light our way here soon. 'Dark' depends on the moonlight and cloud cover. Having all three moons up at once is a sign of good luck!" Laan flashed her a winning smile before returning his attention to the road ahead.

"Now on any trip where I'm lucky enough to have a riding partner, I'd have us take turns telling stories. I guess that your amnesia might make it hard for you to return the favor, but perhaps I can manage to keep us both entertained?"

Rai sighed, grateful for the suggestion. "That sounds like a perfect idea. Besides, being as I'm new to the family, I must have plenty of tales to catch up on! Who knows, maybe hearing your stories will help me to remember some of mine."

"That's the spirit! Let's see now, which tale to regale you with first..."

CHAPTER 10

JUST OVER HALF A DOZEN STORIES LATER, THEY reached the Baris Spine's northern pass. Laan ceased telling stories once night fell and advised Rai to remain silent, which she had done without question. Stoi and Laan directed the wagons down a short trail off the main road, and presently they came to a flat, established camp area with a ring of blackened stones in the center. Rai wondered if this campsite had been there since the original settlement of Az'Unda. Stoi and Laan unhitched the horses from the wagons, removing their saddles and harnesses, and then fit each with feed bags filled with grain.

As the men set about the nightly ritual of grooming the horses for the evening, Rai tried to get a feel for the surrounding terrain. Under the bright moonshine of Az'Unda's two largest moons, Meerius and Bruoh, Rai saw the pass was broad and flat at the top. She could just begin to make out the dark forms of the rolling hills to the northern side of the pass.

Looking up, Rai's breath caught as she took in the clarity of the stars at this height. Even the farthest of them seemed close enough to touch. Walking across the road, Rai noted how the steep walls on both sides of the road flanked both the road and their campsite. This pass is no place for the claustrophobic. The only exits were either direction on the road itself, either eastward from whence they'd come, or westward toward Kiya's Grace. Everywhere else was a sheer wall; it reminded Rai of the caves in the Temple. Then Rai thought she heard the sound of horse hooves, and she stopped and peered ahead, trying to pierce the darkness.

Just when she thought she imagined the sound, Rai caught a slight movement to accompany it and focused in on the image of a lone rider rushing toward her. Rai spun around and then ran back to the wagons.

"The Guardian just caught up with us."

"It's about time! I thought he was right behind us," Stoi replied. "I'll see if he has any news of the road. Why don't you stay in Laan's wagon tonight?"

Rai climbed into the wagon and slid into the small sleeping cubby to the left of the door. Laan entered the wagon a moment later. He closed and bolted the door. He lit a small lamp which provided little light inside, but it was enough once her eyes adjusted.

"Doesn't look like it would hold back a Terror, now does it?" he asked Rai, gesturing toward the door. Rai shook her head, although she couldn't say, never having seen a Terror before. "Well think again. This door lock is a geared system," Laan explained. "Just a half turn of this lever bolts the door on all four sides.

Rai glanced up at the air vent in the ceiling. "And I guess a Terror would be too big to fit through that?" Rai asked.

Laan nodded. "And even if it weren't, it'd never get into the cage." Rai was confused. She looked more closely at the vent and understood what he meant. Thick metal mesh lined the walls and ceiling of the wagon. "Nothing with more than two legs has ever gotten into any of our wagons."

"Indeed? Only city walls could make me feel safer! How will we keep the horses protected? Aren't they still exposed?"

"Yes, they are. One of the many reasons we don't make these trips without the Guardians watching over us."

Rai could hear the sound of the approaching rider much more clearly now and strained to listen. It seemed to her that the Guardian was moving at a leisurely pace. The sound of approaching hooves grew louder, their ringing echoing in the high pass.

"State your business, Guardian!" Stoi's voice boomed. Rai thought Stoi's greeting a bit harsh; the Guardian was their protector, after all.

The sound of the hooves ceased. "I am your escort," a smooth, masculine voice stated. The Guardian's horse snorted. Could Guardians train their horses to display indignation?

"What news have you of the road?"

The Guardian ignored his question. "I wanted to make sure you'd made camp for the evening. Nighttime travel is ill advised, as I'm sure you're aware, but now it would be suicide. This road is under a travel warning. Our scouts have been tracking an Iron Wolf pack in the area, although they haven't been able to locate their exact position yet. Also, I've been noticing Terror sign, fresh by the look of it too. You are to stay inside the wagons from dusk until dawn. Do not venture outside for any reason, not even to tend the horses. Remember, no more travel after dark, under any circumstances."

"The Guardians at Raven's Call didn't mention any of this when we left. The last thing we heard, the road from Raven's Call to the Baris Spine's northern pass was marked clearly."

"It was. I have just told you that the status of this road has been changed, from 'clear' to 'warning.'"

"And now that your scouts are tracking these creatures, they'll be able to exterminate them?"

Rai sensed the apprehension in Stoi's voice--and she detected no sympathy in the voice of the Guardian. What was going through Stoi's mind right now? What was it about Terrors and--what was it the Guardian said, Iron Wolves--that could so frighten a seasoned traveler like Stoi? Rai marked that Laan now wore a dark, worried look on his face and she wondered what he knew about iron wolves or terrors.

"Just follow my directives, and you'll be safe." The Guardian didn't answer the question. "Get what sleep you can, and set out again at first light. Stay on the road, and don't stop for anything."

"Very well. We'll do as you say."

Rai heard Stoi climb into the other wagon and bolt the door. The Guardian dismounted and walked his horse across the campsite to the other horses. After that, Rai heard nothing, save for the occasional whinny of a horse.

Laan dug through the supplies and handed her some bread, sliced sausage, and cheese to eat. There would be no campfire tonight.

Rai rolled uneasily in her sleeping cubby. She hadn't bargained for dangerous creatures roaming about while on this journey. Rai understood now why Stoi was so severe and vigilant. Although she loved being on the open road and away from the city walls and Temple, the ever-present dangers of travel dulled her enthusiasm. At least at a Waystation, she wouldn't worry about what beasts might attack her out on the road.

Rai heard the deep, regular breathing of slumber from Laan, and though it took longer, sleep finally found her as well.

RAI WOKE TO THE SOUND OF BIRDS CHIRPING AND wondered how long she'd slept. Although it was still dark in the wagon, Rai reasoned that the birds wouldn't sing in the middle of the night. Rai emerged from her sleeping cubby and put her ear to the air vent for a minute or so, listening for any activity outside. All she could hear were the wind, occasional snorts and whinnies from the horses, and the songs of birds. Rai pulled down on the door mechanism's lever as quietly as she could, and the bolts retracted into the door with little sound. She opened the door a foot or so and looked outside.

Although the sun hadn't yet crested the horizon, the first light of morning touched the land, and the trees and vegetation were wet with dew. Rai pulled on her boots, swung the door open, and stepped out. She used the latrine across the road Laan had told her about the night before, and then looked out across the southern horizon, waiting for the sun to rise.

Rai turned around just in time to watch Laan climbing out of the wagon. "Sleep well?"

"Yeah, you?" Laan fished around in the wagon, pulled out a water jug and poured some over his head. He vigorously shook his hair, sending water droplets flying in every direction. Rai burst into laughter and backed away from him.

"Your turn?" He offered her the jug, his brow arched in challenge.

"Thanks, but I'm holding out for a nice, warm bathtub at the Waystation."

Laan shrugged and poured more water over his head, repeating the process. Rai laughed again.

At that moment, Stoi emerged from his wagon. "No time to waste. We should be on our way." He started getting his horses hitched and ready for the day's travel.

Laan walked past Rai, dripping water. "Well, duty calls. Ready for another fun-filled day sightseeing?"

Rai nodded, and then she assisted Laan in preparing their horses.

Stoi seemed to consider for a moment, then turned to her. "Like I said yesterday, Rai, the view from up here is something to behold. Why don't you have a look around? Laan and I can do our parts without much time lost from your help. I'd wager you won't be back this way for some time."

"Thanks, Stoi, but just this once."

Rai walked back to the road and saw what Stoi was explaining. From the far side of the road, the entirety of the valley they'd been traveling in yesterday was visible and cloaked in a thin haze. As she looked down onto the trail far below, a quick jab of vertigo coursed through her. She found the feeling an unpleasant one, and she decided that if she ever had to travel that road again, Rai'd make sure she was inside the wagon for this stretch of it.

Deciding she'd had enough of the dizzying view, Rai turned and faced the other direction, where the sun was just beginning to crest over the distant hills. Vast plains rolled softly ahead of her, giving way to dense forests in the distance. She saw rivers in the southwest. The early-morning sunlight reflected from their winding surfaces, shiny ribbons draping across the green of the woods. Rai wondered why the Az'Un hadn't chosen to develop cities in these northern ranges. The land was more fertile and most likely easier to farm than the swampland they currently had to deal with.

Startled by the voice behind her, Rai recognized it as the gravelly Guardian's from last night. "The view is indeed lovely, but we should be on our way now."

Rai turned to face him, annoyed that she hadn't noticed his approach. Despite the fact that he was at least a head taller than she was--or any Az'Un she'd yet met, for that matter--she didn't find him intimidating in the way Stoi did, despite his station, height, or lean brawn. A look of intense curiosity emanated from his pale blue eyes, half hidden behind locks of dark black hair. A brief look of something borderline predatory passed over his face. It hit in the pit of her stomach, but Rai wasn't scared in the least. If anything, it felt like an unspoken challenge, although Rai couldn't begin to imagine why.

"I'll see if they're ready." She turned and walked back toward the campsite. What in the world had gotten into her?

Stoi observed her as she approached, having noted her exchange with the Guardian. "You look a little shaken?" Laan also seemed keenly interested, and again Rai noticed their mutual distrust of the Guardian.

"He strikes me as a consummate hunter."

"That's how they're trained," Laan placed a firm hand on her shoulder. "Don't worry, he's not after you."

"Did he say anything?" Stoi asked.

"He suggested we get moving as soon as we can." Stoi relaxed at this, as did Laan.

"Well, I think we're about ready, but if he wants us to move then, we'll have to eat our breakfast rations on the road. How about you Laan, everything ready to go?"

"Sure, ready when you are, boss."

Stoi turned to Rai. "Choose your wagon, kid. Personally, I'd pick mine. That guy over there looks shady to me."

"Well, how about I ride with Laan this morning and with you after lunch? We ARE stopping for lunch today, right?"

Stoi clapped her on the shoulder, guffawing. "Hah! Not eat lunch? Don't be ridiculous! Besides, the horses will need to eat and rest too. We travelers need our sustenance, after all. We don't want to push the horses too hard either." He frowned in the direction of the now mounted Guardian. "Well, our hero appears ready to go, so let's mount up!"

"Right!" Both Laan and Rai replied in unison. Stoi climbed into his wagon and took the reins, setting his team into motion. Laan and Rai were not far behind.

Today the Guardian rode a few feet in front of them. Rai wondered how bad Stoi's mood would be after staring at their escort's backside all morning.

CHAPTER 11

THE MORNING PASSED QUICKER THAN RAI HAD expected, even though they'd awoken with the sun and traveled past noon already. This was just her second day of the journey with the Durmah, and already she felt an uneasy edge accompanied their journey. Stoi made no signal to stop; he just pulled off to the side of the road, and Laan followed.

When they stopped, their Guardian escort came around a moment later and stopped as well. He pulled a device out of his pocket, scanning the area around them. He must have found something of interest, because he turned and rode off into the forest, disappearing from their view. Knowing that there were possible threats along this road, Rai would have preferred having the Guardian stay by their side.

Laan lead the horses to a nearby stream to drink, and Stoi readied their feedbags with a mixture of oats and grain. It was already past lunchtime, so Rai tended to their own lunches: bread, cured salami, hard cheese and fresh fruits. Laan unpacked three stools from the cargo area of the wagon, where the trio sat and ate lunch in silence. The forest was quiet around them, so much so that Rai took note of it and wondered about the lack of bird song.

"I remember the Guardian asking us to travel at a fast pace, but did he also ask us not to talk? Is there some sort of prohibition against talking that I don't know about?"

"Well, well, no he didn't." Stoi looked apologetically at her. "Sorry for the silence, kid. I guess we're just a bit more stressed than usual this trip, with the travel warning and all. I've been going this route for close to a decade. It's rare to have problems on this road."

"I wouldn't take that windbag too seriously. I'd bet he's just making it all up so he can feel important." The two of them chuckled in agreement. She didn't believe the Guardian would do such a thing, but she'd prefer to think of the Guardian as making up stories rather than there being any real danger.

High-pitched shrieks in the distance cut their laughter short. Immediately Rai remembered the Iron Wolves and Terrors that the Guardian mentioned last night, and by her cousins' reactions to the ominous screams, she feared one of those options was likely the source. All three scrambled into motion. Rai tossed the stools into the wagons, Stoi removed the feed bags from the horses, and Laan hitched the horses to the wagons.

"Shouldn't we just retreat to the safety of the wagons?" Rai remembered Laan's confidence in the safety the offered.

"We could hide away in the wagons, but the horses don't have that luxury," explained Stoi.

"Are you sure the wagons can outrun ... whatever those are?" Rai asked.

"No," Stoi answered. "I'm sure the Guardian will get them before they get us, so we'll have nothing to worry about. However, I'm not about to wait around and watch."

"Do you know what they are?"

"There are a few possibilities," Laan replied. "A number of predators call these forests home. The Guardian mentioned Iron Wolves last night, so maybe that's them. You can bet whatever it is isn't friendly. I've never been chased by something friendly on the road." Laan didn't mention the Terrors as an option.

Another shriek poured from the forest, and all three of them piled onto the wagons, Rai riding with Stoi in the front. With the reins of the horses in one hand, Stoi reached under the wagon seat with his other hand and retrieved a hefty crossbow. He set it between his legs, arrow down, leaving his hands free for the reins.

The high-pitched shrieks continued, coming from behind them. Even over the noise of the creaking wagons and the horses, the hideous sounds got closer. The terrified horses ran down the road, away from their pursuers, needing little prodding from their handlers.

Although Rai kept looking back toward the direction of the shrieks, she hadn't yet seen their escort reemerge from the forest line. The roadside had a good thirty feet of cleared ground on each side of the road, lending plenty of visibility to the travelers.

Looking back and listening intently, Rai searched for the source of the sounds. Her hearing focused on the beasts' barking. The sounds of the wagons and horses faded as if muted by a great distance. From the different timbres and styles of the yelps, she somehow knew the shrieks came from at least two, potentially three sources. All were in close pursuit of their wagons but still out of sight. The beast's voices held a ravenous, desperate quality to them. Focusing harder on the sounds, Rai heard the animal's claws scraping over rocks and ripping through the wood in their frenetic pursuit.

This awareness confused Rai and for some reason reminded her of the time she'd met the Matriarch and smelled fear on her. This assumed that they'd be able to escape the howling beasts without incident.

Still astonished from what she'd just experienced, Rai turned to look at Stoi--wondering if he'd also had the hearing shift and if it wasn't just her alone having these odd sensory moments. From his hardened expression and keenly focused gaze on the road ahead, it was evident to her that he hadn't shared in her bizarre episode.

"See anything?" he asked. Stoi's scar stood out prominently, an angry red color against his ashen face.

"Not yet." Rai turned again, watching the road and wondering if her attention in that direction would once invoke the super-attuned hearing, but it did not. The beasts had ceased their shrieking and were making a strange hooting sound. Had the creatures scented them?

As if to confirm Rai's fears, Stoi said, "Sounds like they're getting close now."

"How long can the horses run for?"

"Long enough, I hope."

Laan was following close behind them, and Rai saw he had a crossbow of his own.

"Shouldn't the Guardian be showing up about now?"

"He should indeed, unless he somehow got lost." The eerie hooting sounds were now quite loud behind them. "Why don't you get in the wagon, kid? Kait will have my head if I let anything happen to you."

"Sure--provided these things chasing us don't end up having both our heads."

"Don't worry too much ... this isn't the first time we've had trouble. I'm sure the Guardian will handle it. For the time being, you get into the wagon and bolt the door. I can climb in with Laan if things get rough. Don't open it until we give the all-clear."

The thought of leaving Stoi locked out was unnerving, although she took some small comfort in knowing he had the crossbow. Rai told herself that he was just extra careful with her welfare.

"Whatever you say, Stoi." Rai reached around, grasped the side rail on the wagon, and walked carefully along the lower step-rail toward the back of the wagon, gripping the upper handrail.

After she had reached the back end of the step-rail, Rai looked up just in time to see a large animal burst out from the tree line behind them. The beast was a giant, four-legged thing covered in scales from its head to tail. Two more emerged from the trees a moment later, loping along on all fours, close to the ground. At the sight of their prey, the three creatures let out a fresh round of triumphant hooting. They were no more than five hundred feet away, and Rai realized that on a flat road, they'd catch up to the wagons in mere minutes.

Laan's eyes caught hers; he'd been watching her, fear evident on his face. Guessing he wanted to know how many followed, Rai held up her a hand displayed three fingers. She had no idea what to call the breasts, and so didn't even try to explain them in sign language. Laan turned pale in response to this information and fidgeted with the grip on his crossbow.

Rai flung open the back door, effortlessly swinging inside. One of the pursuing beasts let out a terror-filled shriek that quickly changed into gurgling and plaintive whines. Somehow, Rai knew that once one of the three animals was now on its way to the grave. Had she heard that death rattle before?

Rai reached to close and bolt the door, when her eyes fixed on the array of weapons Stoi kept mounted along the ceiling of the wagon toward the rear. At that moment, something emerged from the darkest reaches of her mind, some force that wouldn't allow her to hide away in the back of the wagon. She grabbed a dart gun and a crossbow from the weapons rack, and then quickly secured the gun under her belt. Mounted on the sides of the crossbow were six shafts, each with a sharp steel tip. She loaded a shaft into the crossbow.

Rai closed her eyes. This is crazy. The last bray from the beasts sounded like a kill shot. Thus the Guardian must have returned and killed one of them already. Still, she hadn't yet seen the Guardian--for all Rai knew she'd imagined the noise and its meaning. There were two more beasts on top of Laan.

With grim determination, she said aloud, "Stoi and Laan need me. I'm not about to just sit here and hope everything turns out all right!"

Clutching the crossbow in her left hand, Rai climbed back out onto the step-rail. She was now right back where she'd been a minute ago, except now she was well armed. Laan gaped in surprise at her and pointed frantically toward the wagon door as if to say, "Get back in there!" Rai held up the crossbow for him to see, hoping its presence would communicate her resolve. Besides, she was right at the door. Jumping back inside was always an option.

Moving to her left along the step-rail, Rai reached the back corner of the wagon. Looking back at their pursuers Rai's heart sank. The beasts were much closer now, traveling nearly half again as fast as the horses. Confirming her previous interpretation of the creatures' sounds, only two of the animals continued their pursuit. She'd come to the correct conclusion before. The noise had happened when one of the beasts fell.

Beyond the beasts, Rai spotted the Guardian on horseback. He was in hot pursuit of the creatures, but Rai wasn't sure he'd catch up in time to deal with both of them before they overtook the wagons. Steeling herself, Rai turned her full attention to the beasts themselves.

She understood how these animals had earned the name 'Iron Wolves.' Rai searched for possible vulnerabilities--but there weren't many. They were covered with apparently impenetrable scales--each about the size of a man's fist. Around the legs and face the scales form-fitted around every inch of hide, leaving nothing exposed. The slighter of the two was as high as a horse, with the larger beast being a few hands taller. Despite their size, they moved gracefully, their long claws and razor sharp teeth gleamed silver. Rai bet only a direct shot between the scales or in the face had any real chance of hurting such a formidable foe.

The wolves, now less than twenty feet away from the back of Laan's wagon, focused their full attention on Rai. Rai mused that they must be pleased to view their prey perched so invitingly on the back of the wagon, holding on with her right arm hooked through the handrail.

She swore they noticed the crossbow in her hands and hooted to each other about it. This caused Rai a moment of panic. Would it make them go after her? She glanced down at her crossbow, and then looked back at the Iron Wolves. Are they smart enough to recognize this weapon as a threat? The smaller of the two surged forward, toward Rai. It was now just five feet from Laan's wagon. Rai caught a glimpse of The Guardian, he was close but still too far behind to lend any real aid. Sheer, unbridled anger eclipsed her panic as she looked towards their would-be protector with dismay.

Rai raised the crossbow to shoulder level and pulled the trigger. The shaft hissed through the air, destined for the closer beast. To Rai's great chagrin, the wolf anticipated the move and lunged to the side. The bolt glanced off the monster's back. Its thick scales served their protective task. Rai was stunned. She'd underestimated the intelligence and foresight of her adversaries.

Rai swore under her breath and threw the crossbow into the wagon, not willing to take the time to redraw the string, especially with only one hand free. She drew the dart gun from her belt instead, just in time to watch the lead beast jump forward and latch onto the back of Laan's wagon. It clawed itself up, relying on its curved, long claws seemingly designed for just such climbing feats. Reaching the top of Laan's wagon, the beast's eyes fixed on Rai and her dart gun. For a moment, Rai imagined it was somehow evaluating her ability to fire the weapon. The wolf's muscles rippled as it crept toward the front of the wagon, digging claws in with each step. For his part, Laan was beside himself with fear. His face was pale white, his eyes were widened, and a thin sheen of sweat had enveloped his skin. Laan kept looking back to try to see what was on his wagon, but from his seat, he couldn't yet glimpse the approaching Iron Wolf.

Rai aimed the dart gun at the creature's head. She had no idea what impact this weapon would have on such a massive beast, but it was all she had. She did have one big advantage this time. The wolf was now confined to the roof of Laan's wagon. It had minimal room to elude the dart, the way it had dodged the crossbow's bolt. If Rai's aim was true, that is. If.

Rai knew she wouldn't get a second shot, considering how close the beast was--it would reach Laan any moment now! The two wagons very were close to each other at this point, no more than twenty feet apart.

Both adversaries seemed to decide at once that it was time to act.

The wolf crouched down to spring, a deep growl reverberating from its throat. Never breaking eye contact, Rai took careful aim and pulled the trigger. The gun kicked a little and the dart hit the creature's right eye, burrowing deeply into its skull. The Iron Wolf held eye contact with the left eye for a brief moment, frustration pouring through its gaze as blood gushed from the now empty eye socket. The creature gave out a final, agonizing shriek, and slumped onto the roof of the wagon. Its lifeless body slid off the wagon's roof, hitting the ground behind it with a dull thud.

Rai's eyes met Laan's, and she forced a smile at him, for lack of a better way to communicate the wolf's death. Soon enough they'd both be cleaning a large amount of blood off his wagon. Surely, he'd thank her later.

A high-pitched whining sound from behind them signaled the fall of the last Iron Wolf. Rai looked back just in time to witness the Guardian astride his horse, gazing at the last wolf. A bloody streak down its back was ample evidence of the mortal wound it'd just sustained.

Rai yelled at both Stoi and Laan to stop. Both brought their wagons to a crawl and then pulled the teams to the side of the road. Laan looked shaken from the ordeal -- his pallor an unhealthy shade of pale compared to his natural tan. Rai's gaze turned to the approaching Guardian, who was lowering a gun of his own and bringing his lathered horse to a stop. She could be angry but instead was only grateful. Rai doubted she would have been as lucky taking down the last wolf on her own.

The wounded wolf regained its feet and turned to face its attacker. The Guardian dismounted from his horse and walked toward the beast, raising his weapon once again. The beast roared at the Guardian in anger, charging at him in a bloody rage.

Zzzt! Zzzt!

The Guardian pumped two more shots into the Iron Wolf. Rai hadn't seen anything exiting the weapon, but the two gaping holes in the creature's chest were evidence enough to the raw power of the armament. The beast stumbled forward in a motionless heap.

The exhausted horses pulled the wagons back toward the Guardian. Rai saw a thick, black smoke pouring from the dead wolf. The Guardian had set fire to the body and was now watching it burn--something Rai found a bit disquieting.

Black blood smeared the Guardian's leather clothing. Even his travel cloak, which he'd thrown over the back of his horse, dripped the thick ooze onto the ground below. That blood hadn't come from the wolves. Their blood was red.

As the Guardian turned toward his horse, Stoi vaulted off his wagon, running toward the Guardian and shaking his fist. His scar was dark purple against his skin. "What the blazes was that? What do you think you were doing, wandering off like that, leaving us to fend for ourselves? You almost got us all killed!"

The Guardian turned to face Stoi. He said nothing.

"What? You can't be bothered to explain yourself!" Stoi shouted, grabbing the Guardian's shoulder.

The Guardian's response was swift. He grabbed Stoi's wrist and brought it around to his back, and at the same time pulled a dagger from his belt, holding it up to

Stoi's neck. Both Rai and Laan gasped, though neither made a move to interfere with the Guardian's actions.

"You need to calm down."

Stoi seethed in a bright red flush but he fell limp in the Guardian's grip. After a warning look at Stoi, the Guardian retracted his blade and took a step back.

"I did not 'wander off.' You stopped your wagons at lunchtime, so I circled the surrounding area in search of, shall we say, unwanted guests. I came across the Iron Wolf pack. They were already onto your scent and I proceeded to dispatch them. There were eleven of them and I was able to kill eight of them." He paused, waiting for the full impact to hit. Rai was sure she wasn't the only one to connect the copious blood covering The Guardian with this news. "When the other three continued their hunt, I pursued. As you know, I then dispatched two of them. The third was dealt with before I got to it." He shot her a look, and Rai stood up taller and stuck her chin out in defiance. He shook his head, a hint of a snarl curling his lip.

"Rai shot it?" Stoi asked.

"Sure did. Rai was cool as iced melon," Laan replied. "Had to have been a one in a million shot, too."

"If you recall, I did warn you that this area wasn't safe. The good news is these packs keep vast territories and we've dealt with the wolves in this zone. Now the rest of the trip should go more smoothly. Now if you'll excuse me, I need to make sure all the bodies burn." He mounted his horse, paying no attention to the smears and streaks of both red and black blood--even when they came into contact with his clothing and hands on the reins. She mused that the Guardian's fight with the Iron Wolves must have included some close encounters to spill that much blood.

Stoi continued to glare at the Guardian. He'd lost the argument but appeared set to fume over the circumstances, and so said nothing. The Guardian rode off and Rai breathed a sigh of relief. She now understood why Stoi and Laan were so uncomfortable around Guardians.

They inspected the horses and wagons for any damage or injury. Laan looked at the scratches on the back and top of his wagon where the Iron Wolf had been. They were superficial but still an impressive reminder of how close the beast had gotten. Beyond this minor damage and the exhaustion of the horses, nothing would prevent them from continuing in safety to Kiya's Grace. After watering and rubbing down the horses, they fitted them with feedbags. They would go no farther today.

Satisfied everything was in order; they retrieved the stools from Stoi's wagon, along with some bread and dried cheese, and sat down to complete their lunch. After a few minutes, they saw smoke and a few small fires in the distance. The Guardian had begun the process of burning the other dead Iron Wolves.

"Do you always have this much fun on these trips or are you just trying to keep me from getting bored?" Rai queried. Both men laughed weakly. "That way station job is starting to look real nice right now."

"I have to tell you, Rai, that shot was one in a million! Our fearless Guardian took the credit for saving the day, but from where I'm sitting, you saved my life--maybe all our lives," Laan said. Rai saw the gratitude in his eyes, and it filled her with a warm sense of accomplishment. He said this as if he were thinking about something else.

Rai had a good idea of what it was he was thinking. She knew he'd seen her take the shot, seen how calm and steadily she'd held the gun. The answer lay in the dark void of her mind, far beyond her present memory. Have I had training in the use of weapons like this? The thought gave her a shiver, which she hoped Laan and Stoi hadn't noticed.

At that moment, Rai realized she still had the dart gun in her belt. It felt natural somehow. Like it was a part of her. She wasn't eager to give it up.

"Hah! That'll be the last time Laan gives me grief about keeping all my weapons loaded! See!" Stoi basked in his cleverness.

Laan shot Stoi a smug look. "No. I guess I'll just have to find something else to pester you about!"

Rai's mind churned, trying without success to see beyond the barrier of her amnesia. Looking down at the gun at her waist, Rai wondered what other hidden talents she might have within her. You never could tell, maybe it had just been a lucky shot.

CHAPTER 12

Rai sat next to Stoi on the afternoon of their fifth day of travel to Kiya's Grace. To her great relief, there had been no other encounters with Iron Wolves or any other of the 'local wildlife' (as Stoi had come to refer to them). They were just a day out from Kiya's Grace, and Rai was growing anxious about meeting her new sister. Rai's future lay at the Durmah Waystation and in the hands of its Innkeeper, Jesse Durmah. Rai had spent the rest of the journey wondering how best to make a good first impression on Jesse, considering that it sounded like she'd be staying with her indefinitely. However, to Rai's vexation, no good ideas had presented themselves.

The wagons passed a small rise in the road, and Stoi pulled back on the reins, bringing the horses to a quick stop.

"Is something wrong?"

"Underneath that tree up ahead," Stoi replied. "Do you see it?"

Rai saw nothing at first, nothing but the winding dirt road in front of them. Then her eyes found the tree Stoi was looking at; it looked no different from any other tree they'd seen so far. Then she focused on the shade under the tree and saw at once what Stoi meant. In the tree's shadow lay a four-legged animal of some kind. From the lack of movement, it was either sleeping or dead, but it was hard to know at this distance. Stoi contemplated it as though it were very much alive.

Laan pulled his wagon up alongside them and scanned the road ahead.

"Look in the shadow of that tree at the base of the hill," Stoi said.

Laan nodded, and at once took on the same anxious look that Stoi wore. Rai was curious as to why a dead animal should be of such concern to them.

"Iron Wolf?" asked Laan.

"Nope, too small," replied Stoi.

"What do we do?" Rai asked.

"Well, we do nothing. We wait here while the Guardian takes a closer look," Stoi replied.

Rai became aware of the sound of horse hooves on quick approach. Rai turned to look. It was the Guardian, who she'd noticed had been following them at a much shorter distance since their encounter with the Iron Wolves. He noted their pause and was coming forward to investigate. The Guardian reached them and brought his horse to a stop just in front of them.

"What is it?"

"There's an animal of some kind under that tree. It's not moving."

"Stay here." The Guardian ordered, and then urged his horse into a gallop down the hill.

Rai watched him go, curious to see how he'd handle the unknown animal.

The Guardian stopped at the bottom of the hill. Rai watched him pull out one of his the devices from his belt. He keyed the controls as his horse shifted beneath him. The Guardian held the device out and panned it back and forth. Apparently satisfied with the results, he motioned for them to approach.

Rai looked back at Stoi and Laan, who had both relaxed now that the Guardian thought the animal wasn't a threat.

Stoi looked at Rai and Laan. "It's safe. Glad he didn't have to work too hard this time, right?" He urged his horses forward.

Laan followed, and they continued down the road to the bottom of the hill. Throughout their descent of the hill, the Guardian gathered nearby fallen wood into a pile a few feet away from the animal. Rai scrutinized what she could now see as a dead animal under the tree. It appeared wasted away. It's skin leathery. The savaged and torn apart neck had nearly severed the head from the body.

"Swamp deer?" Stoi asked the Guardian. He hadn't even bothered to look up when the wagons had arrived.

The Guardian flashed Stoi an irritated glance but didn't deign to answer the question.

"I guess this poor fellow didn't fare as well with the Iron Wolves as we did," Rai said.

The Guardian sighed. "Wolves eat what they kill, girl."

"What was it then?"

"I'd guess it was a Terror. Nothing will touch what they've come in contact with." The Guardian sized up the woodpile and collected more sticks and small logs from the ground.

Although this didn't appear to upset the Guardian, the revelation disturbed Rai. Having another dangerous beast along the road with them wasn't good news to any of their ears.

"Do we need to modify our travel plans at all to avoid it, assuming it's still in the area?" Stoi asked.

"No. You will follow this road to the next hill. That's about a quarter of a mile away," he said, pointing up the road. "That spot has a good mile of visibility in any direction. You will pitch camp for the night, eat a quick dinner, and lock yourselves in your wagons for the duration of the evening. I will alert you when it is safe to exit your wagons in the morning."

"But if we traveled through the night, we would be safe inside the walls of Kiya's Grace by early morning."

"Whatever killed this swamp deer is lumbering around this forest, looking for other animals to kill. It could have already infected a few dozen other creatures, but it's hard to know for sure without a thorough sweep of the area. No other Guardians are patrolling this sector today, so I'm obligated to root out the beast and keep the road clear. While you're locked away for the night, I will ensure your journey can continue tomorrow."

"We'll do as you say, Guardian," Laan replied. He

gave the reins a flick of his wrist and his horses surged forward, as if eager to be away from the dead deer. Stoi guided his wagon behind Laan's as they set out again down the road.

"What do we do if morning comes and you haven't yet given us the all clear?" Rai called back to the Guardian.

The Guardian enigmatically swept his gaze over her in response before turning and walking toward the swamp deer's corpse.

As their wagon climbed the road before them, Rai tried to keep the fear from welling up within her. What if the Guardian couldn't find the Terror? What if there were too many of the beasts for him to handle? He'd said himself that he was the only Guardian in the area. Rai found herself looking in all directions for more animal corpses, for movement, for anything out of the ordinary. There was nothing but endless road and endless forest against the dusk sky.

Laan's wagon pulled farther ahead of Stoi's, and by the time Stoi drew his horses to a stop at the top of the hill, Laan was unloading some feed for the horses. Stoi stopped their wagon and jumped down to start tending to his team as well. Rai opened the wagon door and was pleased to find that the lids on the food bins in Stoi's wagon had remained secure despite their bumpy escape from the Iron Wolves. She now extracted some jerky, dried cheese and a handful of dalnuts, and served it on the folding travel table. Rai ate some jerky as the brothers finished hobbling the horses for the evening so they wouldn't stray too far from the wagons.

A plume of smoke rose from the wood gathered around the swamp deer. Once the deer was engulfed in flame, the Guardian mounted his horse and rode into the forest.

"Don't worry, Rai, he'll find the beast," Laan said.

"What did he mean when he said the Terror would kill and infect animals?" Rai asked. "How can it infect something that's already dead?"

"He meant that corpses killed by Terrors carry the plague. Left alone, they will rise again, and seek out our human settlements. That's why they burn the bodies, to prevent the creation of new Terrors," Laan explained.

Rai knew there were crematoriums in the cities for burning the corpses of all Az'Un, plague-infested or no. It was just another necessary safety measure to slow the progress of the disease.

"How do we know the Guardian will be able to kill the Terror even if he does find it?" Rai asked.

Laan patted her reassuringly on the knee. "Because that's what Guardians do. They train all their lives to protect the Az'Un. They have toxins and weapons that can knock down the largest animals on this planet. They learn a variety of fighting techniques, to protect us from our own people, should that become necessary. Some even say that Guardians have an almost supernatural ability to find and protect us from dangers ... from the way they're able to detect risk well in advance to their amazing ability to fight off multiple threats."

"Surely you can't be serious?" she asked. "People actually think they're gifted in some way?"

"No, the only thing at all 'supernatural' about them is

their use of machines and computers," Laan said. "Such technology is off limits on Az'Unda, and rightly so. The first Az'Un settlers felt strongly enough about it that it was even a stipulation in the original planetary charter. The Guardians only have it because they keep arguing it'd be impossible to protect us without it."

"The Temple, too," Rai replied. She remembered the birthing crèche she'd awakened in within the Temple. "But if we allow them to have it, then it must be for the greater good of Az'Unda."

Stoi finished with his horses, pulled up a stool and sat down. "That's what they'd tell you, anyway. I imagine that's what the Temple healers did tell each other, back when they were doing who-knows-what to your memory, Rai." Rai and Laan's eyes met his, each considering Stoi's grim words. "What's to keep the Guardians from behaving any differently? If a Guardian were to stroll into the Durmah house tomorrow and tell everyone that Kait had the plague--with only his precious technology for evidence--who'd argue with him? Who could argue with him? No. The more we assume they have only our best interests at heart with all their gadgets and machines, the more likely they are to get away with misusing them for their own purposes. Besides, they flaunt their use of technology, which is offensive to our ancestors' ideals."

"True enough," Laan replied. "The sun's starting to set. We'd best get locked up in the wagons for the night."

"Good idea," Stoi replied. "If a Terror is around, we'd make a pretty good target just sitting around here!"

They quickly ate the remainder of their dinner, then

folded and stowed the table in the wagon. As per usual for the trip, Rai stayed in Stoi's wagon while Stoi and Laan bunked in his. Rai locked herself in securely, grateful for the safety of the wagon. It took Rai some hours to fall asleep, as every chirrup from a squirrel or hoot from a northern owl brought her awake.

A LOUD RAPPING ON THE DOOR OF THE WAGON brought Rai bolt upright. "Wake up! It's time to get moving!" yelled the Guardian. Whispers of sunlight crept in around the edges of the door.

"Did you kill it?" Rai croaked out, still half asleep.

"I'm back, aren't I?"

Rai was infuriated. She'd worried about the Guardian's welfare while he was off fighting the Terror! What drove him to his consistent flippant state of mind? Had he even cared if he made it through the night? Considering the sarcasm-laden in those icy-blue eyes, why did she even care?

Rai didn't want to get up, didn't even want to move because she knew doing so would force her to interact with the man. She knew the sooner they left, the sooner they'd be in Kiya's Grace, and away from this loathsome Guardian.

CHAPTER 13

Matriarch Bauleel left her formal reception chambers in such a rush that it took her two hallways and a staircase to notice Journeywoman Camille following behind her.

She'd resolved to visit with Priestess Parthe today, regardless of the hour. Bauleel had canceled another appointment with Parthe yesterday due to an emergency council meeting concerning an unexpected spike in the plague victim count in the city's northern district. Bauleel hoped this wouldn't put the Priestess in too sour of a mood tonight, but whether or not; there was no helping it now.

The location of the Medicinal Vaults and Formulary led them on a long walk down to sub-basement two--deep within the bowels of the Temple. She and Camille navigated through the seemingly endless corridors and stairs.

Priestess Parthe presided over the Medicinal Vaults and Formulary in the role of Chief Pharmacist. Only the

Matriarch herself outranked the importance of the Chief Pharmacist position in the Temple. Parthe presided over the creation and manufacture of all of the Temple medicinals. This made her the last line of defense against the Plague in Raven's Call.

Bauleel approached the Formulary door and passed her hand over a metal plate on the right side. Only Temple personnel could use this entrance. It led into the bottom--and most secure--level of their three-floor high quarters. The Formulary had a second entry via the Temple's outer wall two floors up where they dispensed medicinals to the city proper.

The door slid open, and the pungent smell of many herbs and plants that hung in the air rolled out, overwhelming Bauleel's senses. Several Temple apprentices scurried this way and that, carrying plants or bags of medicinals.

An apprentice, unknown to Bauleel but identifiable due to her pale, blue-tinged robes, approached them. "If you please, Matriarch, I'll fetch Priestess Parthe for you?"

"Thank you, Apprentice. I'd appreciate that," Bauleel replied.

The Apprentice dashed off and was lost amongst the hubbub. Although Bauleel knew her way around this section, it saved time to have Parthe's Apprentice ferret out the Priestess instead of searching for her in this melee of yellow-robed Journeywomen and blue-garbed Apprentices. Much to Bauleel's satisfaction, no beige-robed Novitiates were present in the Formulary--per Temple policy. It was best to keep the untrained out of critical areas. Any mistakes in mixing medicinals endangered the populace.

Priestess Parthe joined them, accompanied by her Journeywoman. Her deep red robes swept along the ground as she walked, and a crocheted burgundy and gold hairnet captured her dark hair high on her head. As they approached, Bauleel tried to think of the Journeywoman's name. Revon? Klavun? Divun, that was it. The friendly look on Parthe's face appeared a bit forced to Bauleel, and with the luna berry problem and Bauleel's delay in meeting her, it wasn't hard to understand why.

"Matriarch Bauleel, I'm so glad you could make the time to meet with me," Parthe said, tucking a loose strand of hair behind her ear. Her flinty eyes and thin lips spoke volumes to her mood.

Bauleel held her ground. "It is my pleasure to meet with you, Priestess Parthe, as my schedule dictates. However, my apologies for keeping you waiting." A crowd of Apprentices had begun loitering around them, trying to catch snippets of conversation.

"Let's retire to my offices, my Lady? There we can discuss business in a less hectic atmosphere."

"Let's do that."

Parthe and Divun bowed slightly in acknowledgment. "If you will follow me?"

Bauleel inclined her head. Parthe led them through rows of various bins and shelves to the far wall of the Formulary. This place had always held her in absolute awe. The responsibility for supplying the entire city of Raven's Call with anti-plague treatments, as well as other standard malady medicinals, was no small order.

Without the Formulary, Raven's Call would cease to exist, for there would be no people alive to populate it.

They approached the far wall and came to two sets of double doors. The leftmost set led to the Priestesses offices. The rightmost resulted in the all-important Medicinal Vaults. Besides the Matriarch herself, only select Priestess' and Journeywomen had access to open these doors. Keeping the anti-plague supply safe was of paramount importance, so much so that Bauleel required her personal review of every person with access to this chamber.

Divun walked ahead, opened the leftmost door to Parthe's offices, and held it open for the three to walk through, bowing as they passed. Parthe's unpretentious conference room included a large wooden table surrounded by eight matching chairs. Ordered stacks of paperwork lay on the far end of the table, evidence of Parthe's heavy workload.

Divun closed the door, and Parthe motioned for Bauleel and Camille to take a seat. "Please wait here a moment while I gather the reports." Parthe retreated to her office, where Bauleel watched her digging deep into her desk drawers.

Divun shifted nervously in her chair while they waited. She asked tremulously, "Can I get you anything?"

"No, thank you, Apprentice Divun," replied Bauleel.

"Oh, well ... I better go see if the Priestess needs my assistance." With that, she retreated to the back office.

Bauleel and Camille looked at each other across the table in silent agreement: a Journeywoman should behave with more decorum. Bauleel recalled seeing

Divun once or twice before, and she didn't remember the girl seeming quite so nervous on those occasions. Bauleel remembered Divun had been serving with Parthe since late last year, so apparently, the Priestess was content with her performance, or she would have reassigned her.

Parthe and Divun returned and sat down at the table across from them. Parthe placed a lengthy report down on the table in front of her and folded her hands on top of the document as if wanting to keep the information hidden or protected.

"Many thanks for taking the time to discuss this in person. I know you must be very busy," Parthe said.

"I'm never too busy to look into such matters. My humblest apologies for not attending to this sooner, but I had another emergency on my hands this week." Parthe softened a bit toward Bauleel upon hearing her apology.

Bauleel took a deep breath. "I assume I don't need to stress upon you how disturbing it is that someone would deliberately taint luna berries. This, in turn, impacts all medicinals in which the berries are used -- most importantly, they are the key ingredient of the anti-plague treatments." Concern reflected from the faces of those present. "My first and most important question: have any other Temples received contaminated luna berries, as we have?"

"Yes, my Lady. All of the other Temples have also received some of the tainted luna berries." Camille's eyes widened a bit, and Bauleel's face flushed in surprise. The implications were not lost on anyone in the room. In one stroke, someone had threatened Az'Unda's entire supply of plague medicinal -- their only defense against the horrifying disease.

Parthe quickly continued. "But as I'm sure you're aware, Temple policy requires that older supplies of all medicinal constituents be used before the fresh supplies. We identified and removed the contaminated luna berries from circulation. Hardly any of it has found its way to the public."

"How did you discover the contamination?" asked Bauleel.

"A few of the citizens reported some ... difficulties they had with one of our eczema medicinals. We tested the medicinal and all the ingredients used to produce it, and thus found the luna berry problem. Fortunately for Raven's Call, few here suffer from chronic eczema so that medicinal batch was small and few were exposed. Soon after realizing that the taint didn't show up on our routine tests, we shared our testing methods with the other Temple Formularies to aid in detection. Our plan is to continue testing each and every new shipment."

"If the older supplies of medicinals are used first, how did the newer ones get into the hands of citizens so quickly?" Bauleel asked.

It was Parthe's turn to blush. "A clerical error allowed some of the fresh supplies to be used in the formulation of the eczema treatment." At this revelation, Divun also grew a bit red in the face, and Bauleel now guessed why the Journeywoman had been tense. She may well have assumed this meeting would include punishment for her clerical errors, but Bauleel could care less about Divun's derivation from the protocol.

"No need to concern yourself with that now. The error was fortuitous, as it has helped to protect our people from further harm. Regardless, aren't all goods checked for potency on arrival?" Bauleel said.

"Indeed they are, but only spot checks. Considering a number of goods that can arrive, we rarely check every bag due to the time involved."

"In that case, please evaluate work needs based on testing of every parcel delivered and submit to my office by the end of the week. I will make sure appropriate resources are made available to you." Out of the corner of her eye, she caught sight of Camille nodding her head in agreement. She'd have headcount charts put together today on who might have the available personnel to spare.

"Many thanks, my Lady." Parthe replied. "I must also note that the tainted berries were evenly distributed amongst all of the Temples. We found each Vault received four bags. We use one bag per batch of anti-plague treatment. Four full batches of contaminated treatment would affect most of the population for about a month's worth of doses at each city. If the other Temple's followed the typical usage patterns and had average amounts of luna berries on hand, I'd estimate that the tainted berries would have been incorporated into formulas within a matter of two to three months from now." Parthe left unsaid the likelihood that this was not a simple mishap or random corruption.

"I understand the implications, Priestess Parthe," Bauleel answered, trying not to sound too distressed."

This was an act of genocide, hitting each of the colony's three cities at once. But by whom?

"Have you been able to determine what the luna berries have been contaminated with?" asked Bauleel.

"It's most curious, Matriarch. Some kind of heavy metal was ..." Parthe struggled for the right word. "... infused with the berries themselves. The metal isn't common on Az'Unda, and it's not healthy to ingest in any quantity. The amounts are so minute. There's no detectable difference to the berries themselves. It causes irreparable and irreversible nerve damage to the recipient, directly proportional to the amount one has eaten."

"Infused? How is this possible?"

"We don't know, my Lady. It's something we've never seen before," Parthe replied.

Though Parthe's words troubled her, Bauleel experienced a moment of tremendous pride for Parthe. She'd handled the situation brilliantly, having first discovered the contamination and a way to detect it, then alerting the other Temples' Formularies, keeping the entire crisis quiet in the process. She'd made a fine choice in selecting a Priestess of Parthe's fortitude for this role.

"Were only those treated at our Temple for eczema exposed to this poison?" Bauleel asked.

"That's correct."

"How many ill, and what effects have they suffered?" She had to know.

"Eighteen individuals were exposed to this medicinal, all had differing levels of illness depending on the amount of tainted medicinal consumed. An older man who succumbed to the poison had the worst case because he had ingested the highest amount of the contaminated treatment. Before we identified and retrieved the poisoned medicinals from the other seventeen, another four had ingested enough to cause death. Seven others had minor exposure, but will not experience long-term problems or effects. Six are still under observation in the hospice."

"What is their prognosis?"

"They will most likely survive, but with varying degrees of nervous system damage including reduced motor skills, tremor, and the loss of sensation in the extremities." Parthe held a forlorn look on her face.

Bauleel closed her eyes for a moment, trying to imagine what that would mean for these unfortunate souls. Could they still pick things up with their hands? Could they still do their jobs? Even as these questions haunted her, she knew it could have been so much worse.

I am their Matriarch, thought Bauleel. I am their mother and their protector. I have failed them. Though it was a struggle, she managed to maintain her composure. At least since this was limited--only eighteen people--and not at all to similar plague symptoms, the city folk wouldn't panic thinking it was a disease outbreak.

"I will visit the hospice and witness the effects myself, Priestess Parthe. Please do keep me informed on their individual progress. I am saddened to hear of their suffering, but also glad others will not have to face this fate," Bauleel replied, heart aching for her charges.

"As am I, Matriarch."

"If I remember correctly, Priestess Parthe, luna berries grow only in swampland..."

"That's correct, Matriarch," interjected Divun. "There are only three sources of luna berries in all of Az'Unda. The swamps west of our city, south of Resounding Cliffs, and northwest of Kiya's Grace." Icy stares caused Divun to flush with shame. Even lowly Novitiates knew that interrupting the Matriarch was never appropriate. She shrank back in her chair.

Bauleel took it in stride. "Thank you, Divun. Have you been able to ascertain which of these locations the tainted luna berries originated from and who shipped them?" Bauleel knew of a handful of Septs that specialized in trading goods. Each tended to cover different territories and types of products. It shouldn't be too difficult to identify the location.

"The Kiya's Grace swamplands, as far as we can tell," replied Parthe. "All the tainted berries have appeared in shipments originating there. All deliveries occurred within the past month. All were shipped via the Durmah Sept." Parthe paused, waiting for Bauleel's response.

Bauleel considered this new information. During the hundreds of years the Az'Un had used luna berries as an anti-plague treatment, never had there been such contamination. She couldn't blame the Durmah for the tainted luna berries just because they'd shipped the product. Neither could she seek to blame those Septs that farmed the swamplands. She knew the Durmah were not very fond of Temple practices. They were in a position to notice things, but might not be willing to report what they saw.

"Priestess Parthe, you have proved your value threefold, and your record will reflect commendations for your efforts." Parthe accepted the compliment gracefully. "I have the utmost confidence in your abilities and initiative, and I encourage you to continue researching as your intuition guides. With that said, I want to caution against jumping to conclusions. We don't know what the cause is. Many farmers harvest luna berries. It's possible some new fertilizer or ground treatment is to blame. We must first assume the cause is entirely accidental.

"Kiya's Grace is where we must begin our investigation. Camille, I need any information you can get me on the farmers in that region. Start with farms that have changed management over the past cycle or two. Also, I want to know all of the trade routes that the Durmah have used in that region over the past few cycles. I'm specifically interested in any instance in which the Durmah have changed from one trade route to another, particularly when food and plant shipments are involved." Camille furiously wrote it all down on her tablet.

Bauleel addressed Parthe. "For now, continue accepting luna berries from Kiya's Grace." Divun appeared shocked at this, but Parthe nodded calmly. "Test every luna berry batch you receive from anywhere, twice, for contamination. Do not speak of this matter to anyone outside the Temple, for any reason. Assuming it is an intentional poisoning, whoever's doing this probably doesn't think that any of the Temples have discovered the contamination. This assumption can work to our advantage. The longer they continue shipping poisoned berries, the longer we will have to track them down. I want weekly reports from each of you on this. Complete reports, mind you. No detail is too small.

"Camille, draft a message to all Matriarchs and their respective Chief Pharmacists, informing them of our findings. Make sure they are all 100% proficient in administering the luna berry test, and tell them, as I've told you, not to speak of this to anyone outside their respective Temples, and as few as possible within the Temples. Have it ready for transmission within the hour."

"Begging your pardon, my Lady," Parthe broke in, "I'm afraid a number of my staff already knows about the contamination."

"That's alright, Priestess Parthe. I'm doubtful it's someone from the Temples responsible for this. After all, they'd have to have access to all of the tainted bags, which couldn't happen with the Temples so far geographically removed from each other. I'm sure if we stifle the rumors now things will quiet down. Perhaps it is best to spread the story that only one bag was contaminated by some strange swamp mold?"

Nods served as replies all around.

"Are there any further questions?" All were silent. Bauleel rose to leave, Camille in tow. "Then I must visit the hospice ward, where I can witness the damage firsthand."

"Many thanks, my Lady, for your attention to this matter. We trust in your wisdom and value your guidance." Parthe and Divun bowed deeply.

Bauleel left the room without further comment. Once in the corridors on the other side of the main

Formulary floor, she headed in the direction of the hospice.

"Camille, I'm sure you have plenty of reports to catch up on. I'll be in the hospice if you need me."

"Yes, my Lady. I will bring you that letter within the hour, as requested." Camille bowed and left without another word.

Bauleel's heart ached. Was someone trying to kill the entirety of the Az'Un population? Hadn't life always been precarious enough for them on this planet without some maniac working against them? Who could possibly want to make things any harder? A desperate laugh escaped her lips, accompanying the tears welling in her eyes.

CHAPTER 14

Rai, Stoi, and Laan shared a palpable sense of relief when the walls of Kiya's Grace materialized through the haze that permeated the low-altitude areas of Az'Unda. The Guardian had left them a few minutes before, much to Stoi's obvious delight, but with her eyes fixed on the rising walls of the city, Rai scarcely noticed their escort was gone.

Rai knew this journey was likely her last and the thought troubled her. She knew she'd be working at the Waystation for as long as Jesse and Chieftess Kait wanted her there, likely the rest of her days. She surveyed the land around them, knowing that it might be the last view she would ever have of Kiya's Grace, from outside it at least.

This city was perhaps a third of Raven's Call, but it made up for it in bustling activity and color. People's clothing contained vibrant colors which should have clashed but didn't. Sept houses painted their stone walls in alternating stripes and segments, foregoing the dull gray of plain rock sheeting. An occasional mural even stood out, displaying the artistry of the inhabitants. Moreover, wildflowers in every color imaginable surrounded the city walls. Raven's Call had abundant plant life surrounding it, but nothing like this. Had the citizens planted them on purpose, or were they native species? Why did they paint the walls of their homes here? Rai didn't know, but she liked the change and the character of the place.

An image floated up in her consciousness: a prison with stone walls and thick iron bars and cold, hard floors. She had no idea where or when such a place entered her mind, under what unfortunate circumstances, but as the large city gates came into view, she suspected why the image surfaced now.

Rai looked wistfully at Stoi and Laan. They'd be on the road again by this time tomorrow, whereas Rai would be stuck behind the great walls of the city. Again, she hoped Jesse and she would hit it off. Rai cringed, fearing she wouldn't live up to Jesse's expectations.

She glanced at Stoi, who was only now relaxing. The main gate of Kiya's Grace was bustling with activity, with a steady stream of carts and wagons arriving and departing. It was much more active than she'd seen at Raven's Call. They slowed their wagons and joined a long line of Az'Un waiting to enter the city.

"Kiya's Grace is foremost a farming community, so you get a lot of traffic between the city and the fields and swamps around here," Stoi explained. "It can be difficult traversing the gates morning and night, not that you'll have to worry about that, I suppose."

"No, I guess not."

"Look, I know how alone you must feel right now, but trust me. Jesse's the only friend you'll need. Once you meet her, you'll see what I mean."

"It's just happening so fast. I've barely met you and Kait and everyone, and after you and Laan leave I may never see the Raven's Call Sept house again." Stoi had no reply for her.

Eager to change the subject, Rai pointed to the cart ahead of them, filled with fish. "Do those fishermen have a death wish?"

Stoi looked confused for a moment. "What do you mean?"

"Don't fish have enough toxins in them to kill an iron wolf, much less a person?"

"Only the deep-sea fish. These must come from the swamps to the north, or from one of the aquatic farms. They don't have near the problems that the ocean-bound ones do."

"Uh huh. Well, don't expect me to eat any." Why would anyone take the risk?

Stoi thought a moment. "But the question is ... how do you know about fish?"

"Memory!" she beamed. "Not something about me, but it's a start!"

"Hey, today fish, tomorrow -- who knows, right?" Stoi turned to her, narrowing his brows. "Fish are quite a staple around these parts. I guess that rules out Kiya's Grace as your hometown. Otherwise, you'd think nothing special about eating fish."

"Eminently logical," Rai replied, pursing her lips.

Despite the stress along the road to Kiya's Grace, Stoi still focused on helping her discover her past. This touched Rai deeply.

"Let's run with this a bit, O Well-Traveled One. Where do people eat fish?"

"You need swamps for fish harvesting, and only this city and Resounding Cliffs have swamps. So I guess really just those two places eat fish. Now I suppose there's a chance that someone in one of the smaller coastline townships has found a way to harvest ocean fish safely, but I'm not aware of any. We'd need to ask my brother Meik about that one, as he runs those trade routes."

"So that leaves Raven's Call and Barrow's Grove as the two largest cities that consider fish unsafe to eat?" Stoi nodded in agreement. "Well, it's not much, but it's something. I guess you can tell Kait that Raven's Call and Barrow's Grove may be good starting points."

"Indeed I will! But don't you worry. Kait won't stop until she figures out this puzzle." Stoi lowered his voice before continuing. "I know Kait has some Temple Healers as friends, and she finds out all sorts of gossip from them. Perhaps they will help fill in the details on your past or amnesia." Rai wondered how Chieftess Kait had managed to gain the confidence of these Temple Healers but was grateful for the advantage nonetheless.

The line moved forward and a short, blond Guardian at the head of the line greeted them. "Sept and cargo," he asked, eyes roaming over the wagons.

"Durmah, Gatemaster. Our cargo is woolens," Stoi replied, staring straight ahead. His curt tone was even more clipped than he'd been with the Guardian who'd accompanied them on their journey. Rai had no idea of knowing if this was his typical treatment of their Sept or a reflection of the past few days. Although she didn't understand his full discomfort around the Guardians, Rai suspected his distrust came from his concerns the Sept shared regarding the Temples.

The Gatemaster wrote down this information on a small tablet in his hand and then continued to survey their wagons. His eyes caught the deep claw marks on the side of Laan's wagon and he frowned, examining them more closely now. "Did you encounter any ... problems on your journey?"

Stoi looked him straight in the eye, and to Rai's great surprise, he lied. "Not a one. A rather mundane trip, actually." He turned straight ahead again, breaking the Guardian's intense gaze. The Guardian turned to Rai for confirmation, but she took Stoi's lead, dropped her gaze, and also stared straight ahead, saying nothing.

The Guardian arched a brow, ignoring Stoi's explanation. "In that case, I'll discuss the matter with your escort instead. Have a pleasant stay," he said, motioning them forward. He moved on to the next cart, which was brimming over with some sort of brown mossy-looking plant.

Once inside the city walls they navigated through the main corridor and turned onto a side street. They came to an open courtyard and pulled inside. Attached was a two-story building Rai assumed was the Waystation. From the outside, it looked nearly as big to Rai as the Durmah Sept house. The stable at the end of the courtyard was in fact much larger than at the main Durmah stable. Rai counted over twenty stalls. A man emerged from behind two of the mounts on the opposite end of the stable.

"Master Durmah! A warm welcome to you on this bright afternoon!" The man beamed toothily and his short, dark hair stuck out in all directions. He walked with a slow, odd-looking swagger.

"Hey there, Markel! I trust you've been keeping things in good order around here since I've been gone?" Stoi asked, smiling back at the man as they dismounted the wagons.

Rai remembered what Stoi told her about the staff at the Waystation. Jesse was the only blood Durmah here. All the other Waystation workers, including Markel, were Septless hired help.

"Yes, Sir! You know Mistress Jesse keeps things in order, never fear about that Sir." Markel answered, nodding and smiling all along. He stepped forward and unhitched Stoi's horses.

"I'm sure she has, Markel. Our girl Jesse's got a good head on her shoulders, no doubt about that."

A hearty laugh rang out from the archway leading from the stable to the Waystation. Rai knew this must be Jesse from Laan's descriptions in his stories. She was the spitting image of her mother Kait, just a few inches taller with straight, chin-length brown hair and a well-proportioned figure. Her olive complexion, coupled with her brown leather pants and loose nutmeg-toned shirt, gave her a sultry yet commanding presence. She looked no more than seventeen or eighteen, yet projected confidence and maturity well beyond her years.

"I don't suppose you'd put that in writing, would you Uncle Stoi? Perhaps a letter to my mother, recanting all your doubts about appointing me Innkeeper, and admitting she was right all along?" Besides Jesse's forced smile, there was no mistaking the cutting edge in her voice.

Stoi approached Jesse with open arms. "Now Jesse, you know I think you're doing a fantastic job out here, regardless of what may have happened in the past. Truce?"

Jesse gave in and approached Stoi, accepting his big bear hug. There was clearly a lot of affection between them, whatever might have happened.

Pulling away, Jesse turned to Laan. "Cousin, happy to see you again." She hugged him too.

"And you, Jesse," Laan replied. "It looks like Kiya's Grace is treating you well?"

"Yes it is, quite well," Jesse answered. "Can I assume this one is why you're overdue on the wool shipment?" Jesse cast Rai a penetrating glance that made her feel weighed and measured. "The Weavers Sept has been sending little Velin over twice a week to check on the delivery. Do you know much I dislike dealing with that brat?"

"Sorry, Sis. Jesse, this is Rai Durmah, newly inducted adoptee of just one week now." Stoi introduced, emphasizing the word Durmah. "Here's a letter from Chieftess Kait, posting Rai at the Waystation, to be of any aid you require." Stoi handed the folded parchment envelope to Jesse, who slipped it into a pocket on her belt as she appraised Rai. "Why don't we head inside and bring you up to date over dinner? It'd be a bit more private."

"Good idea," Jesse replied. "Let me just get someone to unload these wagons." She looked toward the wagons, and similar to the Guardian at the city gates, her eyes widened at the sight of the deep claw marks in Laan's wagon. "Looks like someone already tried to unload them. Someone of the four-legged variety?"

"You might say that, yes," said Stoi. Jesse waited for him to elaborate, but he said nothing further.

"Well, we'll have lots to talk about over dinner. I'll arrange to get someone out to fix your wagon too, Laan. Grab your stuff!" Jesse led the way inside.

Through the archway, a half-rise of stairs opened into an immense dining hall. People sat at two of the tables, but no one took more than a passing notice of the Durmahs walking through. In the corners of the room were alcoves containing tables, for those who wanted a more private dining experience. At the far end of the dining hall, a short hallway lead to a private dining room. Rai, Laan, and Stoi entered the room and sat down at the large oblong table in the center. Jesse lingered in the main hall for a moment. Rai heard her instructing her staff to unload the wagons and place an order with the kitchen.

Jesse arrived a few seconds later carrying a tray with four mugs and a pitcher each of beer and water. She poured mugs of the thick, dark liquid for Stoi and Laan, and then raised a brow to Rai. Rai nodded and Jesse filled her mug. Jesse sat down with a cup of her own, and they sipped beer in silence for a time. The thick, dark brew was surprisingly sweet in flavor and stronger than Rai would have guessed.

After another few short minutes, the head cook appeared with a platter of freshly roasted meats and roots. "Mmmm. This looks fantastic!" Stoi exclaimed, his expression finally relaxing after the long and trying trip. The head cook placed the platter on the table and withdrew, oblivious to their conversation. A kitchen boy followed behind her with some plates, a loaf of fresh dark-grained bread, and few chunks of sweetened butter. The intensity of the food's aroma was nearly overpowering to Rai, and she surmised that whatever dulling effects she'd experienced from the Temple medicinals were gone. She buttered a slice of bread, and Stoi and Laan eagerly did the same.

The three travelers feasted voraciously, having eaten nothing but travel rations for the past several days. Jesse waited patiently, but after about fifteen minutes, her curiosity got the better of her.

"So, are we starting with the adoption, or with the claw marks in the wagon? No offense to you Rai, but those claw marks look like a far more interesting story."

Stoi leaned back in his seat and pushed his plate away. Jesse leaned forward and refilled his glass. He took a long pull before filling her in on the past few days. Rai watched for Jesse's reaction to her amnesia or to her expert use of the dart gun during the Iron Wolf encounter, but if either of these fazed Jesse, she didn't show it. Just then, Rai realized that she still had the dart gun at her side, and she did not intend to give it up. Something about Jesse told Rai she wasn't one who missed much. Once Stoi finished, Jesse looked pensive, as if trying to digest it all.

"Iron Wolves! Who'd have thought? You're the first travelers to suffer an Iron Wolf attack around here since-- you know, I can't even remember when! Well, that's why you have Guardian escorts, eh?" Jesse exclaimed. Rai expected an angry diatribe from Stoi at any reference to the Guardians, but none came. "Anyway, please tell me you're going to stay here at the Waystation a few days before you take the fabric shipment to Raven's Call? You both look exhausted, likely from losing so much sleep on the trip here."

"No can do, sis. We leave at dawn tomorrow morning." Laan shot him a surprised look. "We'll file papers and get the wagons reloaded tonight. Besides, the Iron Wolves that attacked us are now ashes."

"You sure I can't persuade you to stay and rest up some more?" Jesse asked.

"Hey, if it were up to me, I'd stay for the food alone!" They all chuckled. "But Chirey's been feeling lonely again, and I'd like to be back with her as soon as I can." The disappointment on Laan's face spoke volumes. Only one night savoring the protection offered by the thick city walls and the Waystation's hot food was less than he'd expected.

"Are there just the fabrics to take back, or has that brother of yours delivered more of the herbs from up around the swamplands? The Temple in Raven's Call asked when they can expect their shipment." Stoi asked.

Jesse sighed and shook her head. "No, Ponar's overdue by over two weeks on this last shipment. There's been more flooding in the swamps this month, so I'm guessing that's been holding him up."

Stoi looked exasperated. "Ponar is overdue on most of his shipments these days. It makes Durmah look bad; to say nothing of the money it costs us. When he does bother to show up, perhaps you can mention my ... concern for him. That boy has to shape up and start pulling his weight. If he were here, I'd give him quite the talking to."

"Hey, don't tell me, tell him. Perhaps if you didn't push him so hard..." Jesse began.

Stoi held up his hand. "No, Jesse. I haven't been pushing him that hard. Kait's best at that. I've begun to wonder if these delays are just excuses to keep him away from her and from choosing his future spouse." Jesse frowned at this last remark, but he said nothing further.

"See what I put up with around here, Rai?" Jesse asked. "Now what about you? Amnesia? Wow, that's rough. You'll recover your memory, right? Anything come back to you on the trip or here at the Waystation?"

"Unfortunately no, and it's been over a week now. A few little things have come back, but it's slow going," Rai replied. "I'm beginning to wonder if my full memory will ever return."

"Don't lose hope, girl. I'll let Kait know what's happened to date, and then when I'm out this way again I can tell you what she's discovered," Stoi replied. "In the meantime, settle in here and get used to life at the Waystation."

Rai nodded in agreement. "I'll do that. Hopefully the

quiet of this town will help me relax enough to remember."

Jesse's shook her head. "Well, the city might be quiet, but this Waystation rarely is! Whether you want to work on remembering or not, I doubt you'll have the time. By the way, a Temple Apprentice delivered a unique formulation of the plague treatment two days ago. He said it was for the new Durmah stationed here. Is there any reason to think this stuff will be any different from the last medicinal batch they gave you--the one that dulled your taste buds?"

"None that I can think of. Apprentice Mala was quite insistent that I continue the treatments," Rai replied. "I can have a look at it, but I think I'd still prefer to take the standard medicinals if that's ok with you and you have enough?"

"That's no problem. The Temple keeps us well stocked since we harbor travelers. Once we're finished with dinner, I'll go get some for you."

"Hey, I don't suppose Somnu is in town now, is he?" Stoi asked.

"No, the Tinker's not here right now, but he's due within the next day or two," Jesse replied.

"That's a shame. I was hoping to prod him for information about locals getting amnesia. I'd wait around and ask him about Rai's amnesia, but I can't lose the time." Stoi let out a big yawn.

Rai remembered Laan mentioning Tinkers picked up bits of gossip and had incredibly ornate and colorful clothes and wagons. Their storytelling and bardic skills had wide fame, and everyone relied on them for their ability to repair antiquated machinery--even the old pre-colonization machines. The Temples weren't too fond of them. Fixing machinery that old was a talent that the Temples reserved for themselves.

"I'll ask him when he gets here, and fill you in next time you're back," Jesse offered.

Stoi nodded. "I'd appreciate it. However, don't mention any names. No use manufacturing suspicion if we don't have to." Now it was Laan's turn to yawn, and he did so noisily.

Jesse looked around the table, assessing their obvious fatigue. "I'll do that. Look, I can take care of loading and provisioning the wagons tonight. Why don't you all make an early evening of it?"

With everyone's agreement, Stoi and Laan hugged Rai goodbye and good luck in case they missed her on their way out in the morning, and Jesse led Rai to her new room. Stoi and Laan grabbed a couple of guest rooms for the night, as the Waystation wasn't full.

Jesse led Rai up a flight of stairs and down a hall toward the back of the Waystation. She swung open the second door from the end of the corridor and stepped inside, motioning for Rai to follow. "This is your room now, mine is the one on the end. We share the bathroom on this end of the hall. Everyone else in this wing is staff and shares the other bath."

"It's very nice." This room was equal in lavishness to the one she'd overnighted in at the Durmah Sept house. About twelve feet deep and eighteen feet across, the room gave enough space for a large bed, a writing table and chair, a wardrobe, three lamps and two full sets of windows. A variety of wall hangings and carpets broke up the otherwise plain gray stone walls and dark wooden floors.

"Thanks, I just had it refurbished about a month ago when I first heard we'd be getting a new adoptee to help out here. The staff sleeps two to a room, but we owners get the spacious, private rooms," Jesse confided. "There are a lot of things we need to go over, but tonight you rest. Is there anything you need before tomorrow?"

"If there is, I can't think of it. Thanks so much, Jesse. You've been so kind to me, all the Durmah have, and I truly appreciate it."

Jesse gave Rai a soft look, her gaze filled with compassion. She held her left hand up next to Rai's. Rai was confused for a moment but then understood. Jesse had a bright blue tattoo on her hand, with three moons and no stars. Matching Rai's. "You're not an outcast here, Rai."

Rai was speechless. No wonder Jesse had accepted Rai so quickly. They shared a common loss; neither could bear children. The pain Rai felt about being barren had only been with her a week, since she'd awoken; she could only imagine what Jesse had been through. Rai realized Jesse had walked a much harder path than she, having stayed with her birth Sept even after being declared infertile. What had it been like for Jesse, eldest daughter to the Chieftess, to know she'd never inherit her mother's role?

"You get some sleep, and I'll see you in the morning. If you need anything, you know where I am." Rai nodded, and then Jesse shut the door. Rai locked the door.

Rai looked around the room, feeling overcome by a sense of deep satisfaction. Whatever the future had in store for her, at least for this moment, she was home.

CHAPTER 15

Matriarch Bauleel swept out of the hospice wing, grateful for her veils, which hid the stream of tears, which were drying on her cheeks. She'd spent all night reviewing the cases of those harmed by the poisoned luna berries. Bau had witnessed their infirmaries, held their hands, bolstered their will through kind words, and--most importantly--let each of them know she cared enough to listen for as long as they'd wanted to pour their hearts out to her.

Grateful her enhanced constitution allowed her to skip sleeping Bauleel headed towards her office chambers, ignoring the women rushing out of her way and bowing in deference along the busy corridor. The Healer's and Medicinal wings were the two areas of the Temple, which were hectic no matter the early hour. Despite her gloomy mood and the curious glances shot in her direction, Bauleel entertained no discussion, knowing Camille, no doubt, awaited her presence with an impending stack of paperwork.

Duty alone kept her overseeing the health and welfare of Raven's Call. Bitterness had long ago swallowed her joy for any aspect of the work she completed at the Temple. Bauleel ached to move on, but there was too much at stake. The Anemoi would replace her, and she didn't know if the evidence of her ploy to hide the girl had been entirely eradicated. Not yet.

Only one thing of late elevated Temple life beyond the day to day monotony: Terem Zebio. His existence gave her one bright ray of hope amidst the daily tedium of signing off on marriage dowries, allocations of workable land amongst the differing farming Septs, and settling disputes, often over verbal agreements made months earlier where neither side quite had the facts down right. Drudgery, the lot of it.

As she passed a side corridor in the Service section, Bauleel overheard a muffled sob from down the hall, which gave her pause. Changing course on a whim, she sauntered down the carpeted corridor on nimble feet. There were few Healers in the Service section at this hour, which made sense. Only those overseeing an encounter would be present.

Again, cries erupted from behind a closed door up ahead, but this time Bauleel pinpointed the exact one. A moment later she stood outside, hand hovering over the doorlock as she listened.

"I'm sorry, Elder. If I'd acted more quickly, this never would have happened."

"Perhaps you failed to get the dosage correct. Have you checked your records?"

Bauleel recognized Natre's clipped tones and activated the doorlock, striding in without hesitation and closing the door behind her. Facing the other Anemoi, she forced her emotions under tight control, a feat she'd congratulate herself for later, considering the circumstances.

Natre, in her brown Elder robes, faced off against Journeywoman Iella--Natre's raw anger buffeting against the wisp of Iella's raw nerves in the room filled with shadows. A naked female, perhaps sixteen or seventeen years of age, lay on the bed, unconscious and covered with bruises and a few lacerations. Bauleel noted her labored breathing -- as long as she made it back into a crèche reasonably soon the damage shouldn't be permanent. A man, also unconscious, lay sprawled out upon the floor next to the bed, also naked. Blood laced his fingers, mouth, and spattered down his chest. None of it appeared to be his own.

No wonder Iella wept. She'd never be able to wipe this day from her mind's eye. Bauleel would speak to Camille later about transferring Iella to the Orchards, Medicinal Vaults, or well, any other station in the Temple the girl wanted.

"I spent the night in the hospice wing and happened to hear you two in a heated discussion as I was on my way to my office. Perhaps I can help sort things out." By her tone, Bauleel made it clear the 'perhaps' was a pleasantry.

"We about had things sorted out here, Matriarch," Natre spat the words out. "There's nothing of import for you to contribute."

Iella's eyes grew wide as saucers. The pale orange

tones of her robes appeared brown in the dark, the effect giving her a waifish, Sept-less quality. Bauleel noticed with no small amount of joy the Journeywoman had ceased weeping, distracted no doubt by their open conflict.

"Journeywoman Iella, your records, please," Bauleel held out her hand for the woman's terminal, which she returned without question. The files for the encounter in question were already on display on the handheld unit, which Bauleel used to scan and confirm the identities of the unconscious individuals out of habit. "Tell me, in your own words, Iella, what transpired here last night. I'll confirm with system records as you go."

Iella took a deep breath, which rattled as it passed through her. "The girl, Riuth of Sept Taz, is seventeen. She's been in Service with us since she turned fifteen, per standard protocols. She bore her first child at sixteen, no complications, and this was our first attempt at an encounter to breed her for another. She's been in the crèche, stable and in stasis until we flooded her system with fertility drugs about a week ago. Tests confirmed she responded positively to those treatments."

"All via crèche?" Bauleel asked. This would isolate the girl from the plague as much as possible.

"Yes. I brought Riuth here and gave her the standard dosing schedule of relaxant within two hours of the encounter, per protocols."

"Nothing incorrect so far. What about with the man?"

"He's Phen of Sept Gileen. He's performed Service three times before without incident. He arrived yesterday, per summons. His attitude, as noted in the report, was receptive. His unfortunate selection today due to a complete lack of genetic crossover with Sept Taz's lineage. Once he arrived, I placed him in a crèche to flush his system of all medicinals for twelve hours. After this process completed, I gave him his usual dose of relaxant, placed him in a waiting area for two hours, and then led him in here."

"And..." Natre asked, pointing to their bodies.

"And for many hours I observed the encounter passing quite ... regularly, as such things go." Iella had the grace to blush. "Then they both slept for a while, which also appeared ordinary to me, but I allowed it because sometimes such encounters get a second wind. Anyway, he talked in his sleep a bit, which I didn't have on file, but I didn't assume it meant a problem."

"Per your training, any unusual behavior is to be treated as a threat and acted on immediately!" Natre's voice climbed an octave.

"Sleep talking is a common human condition, Elder Natre. Not an assumed sign of illness. Please continue, Iella."

Iella's eyes flitted back and forth between the two of them, but then she gave in and continued despite the tension in the room. "I kept my watch. After an hour or so of Phen muttering in his sleep, he awoke, moving slowly. I figured he was under the influence of the relaxant or simply tired. Whichever, his focus shifted to Riuth, and he climbed atop her."

"To what, breed her again?" Bauleel asked.

"No." Tears returned to Iella's eyes, and Bauleel had

to fight to keep her empathic emotions in check, especially after her recent trip to the hospice ward. "He straddled her, and then he hit her, over and over. I grabbed my tranquilizer and ran into the room; he didn't even notice I was here. By the time I'd arrived and shot him, he'd bitten her on the face, chest, and arms. Do you think she'll scar?"

"If she does, it'll be your fault, Iella," Natre replied.

"Elder Natre. You will fetch two gurneys and prep the crèches needed to heal these two? I appreciate your help."

Natre's anger rolled off her in waves, but she wouldn't defy the Matriarch in front of a Journeywoman. "I'll return right away. We've spent enough time discussing this sad event. The sooner these two are healed, the better." She stomped out of the room, almost scraping against the door as it slid open in her rush to leave.

Bauleel doubted Iella could see anything through the haze of her redoubled tears, poor thing.

"Did you shoot both of them with the tranquilizer when you returned to the room?"

Iella wiped tears from her cheeks. "Yes, Matriarch. That's the protocol. I shot him twice, and her just the once."

"Very good. There's a short acting amnesiac in the tranquilizer, so most likely, she won't remember a thing, and he won't remember very much. Hopefully, he'll assume it was just a nightmare."

"Good. I mean, not good, but it helps a little to know that."

"Also, you need to know that what happened to Phen is not your fault. You followed all of the correct protocols." Bauleel keyed in the necessary changes via the med terminal. Phen days of service had come to an end.

"But why? I don't understand what could have gone wrong?" The lost look in Iella's eyes, her upturned hands, nearly broke Bauleel. She'd heard the same question so many times over the past few hours.

"The process we use, Iella, is very safe most of the time. However, sometimes a person develops a resistance to our treatments, and the protocols fail. It's not your fault. It's not their fault. It's biology. The biology of Az'Unda."

She nods her head. "Do you mind if I go? I should file my report."

Bauleel understood what she asked, on so many levels. "Go ahead, Iella. I'll make sure they get to the crèche's safely. You've had a long night. Go get some rest now."

"Thank you, Matriarch." She bowed and left the room, but Bauleel caught the sounds of her sobbing echoing off the corridor halls as she fled.

Looking down at Riuth and Phen. Bauleel cradled her face in her hands under her veil in frustration. Riuth's scar would be permanent, no matter how long she spent in the crèche.

How much longer can we keep this up? How many more will be maimed in an effort to prove the colony is viable and maintaining sustainable growth?

How could she fight the will of the Anemoi, and live?

CHAPTER 16

Rai lay in her room the next morning, stretched out luxuriously in the soft, supple bed. After only one night, the various kinks and cramps in her legs and back from sleeping in the wagons were already gone. Rai walked over to the room's far window and observed considerable activity on the street. It must be at least mid-morning. Jesse must have let her sleep in. Rai crossed the room to her wardrobe and opened the door. Inside were three pairs of identical freshly pressed pants and shirts. She grabbed one of each and slipped them on. Rai debated wearing her well-earned dart gun but hoped there'd be little use for it within the safety of the city.

Rai left her room and crossed the hall to the bathroom. This bathroom was a veritable private grotto, and Rai felt honored Jesse was willing to share it with her. It held an immense bathtub that was at least ten feet in diameter. A wide assortment of plants adorned the walls, draped over the large sink, and partially covered the wall mirror behind them.

Rai wondered what hardships and pain Jesse faced over her life. Rai knew the firstborn usually assumed the role of Sept Chieftess by birthright, but until last night, she'd never considered what might happen to a firstborn who'd suffered the shame of being unable to bear children. Rai wondered if Jesse's placement in this Waystation as caretaker had been anything more than an alternative to casting her out of the Sept altogether.

Rai washed her face and brushed her hair, then headed downstairs. She walked out of the family and staff quarters through a doorway and entered the main upstairs hallway separating the two sections. Rai passed the hall leading to the guest rooms section and walked down the main staircase. She looked around the main floor and spotted Jesse behind the bar.

"Sleep well?"

"Are you kidding? Babies don't sleep that well! Sorry I slept so late though."

"No worries, Rai. Besides, I figured if I let you sleep late I wouldn't feel so bad saddling you with the night shift tonight."

"By myself?" Anxiety gripped her stomach. "I've never worked in a Waystation before, at least not that I can remember ..."

"Oh, it's nothing. It involves receiving late-night visitors, showing folks to their rooms, and getting them a little food. It's nothing you can't handle."

"I'll trust your instincts, Jesse. So am I the official night person around here?"

"Nah. I'll switch the shifts around from time to time.

I do want to expose you to each shift, though, to make your training go quicker."

"Makes sense to me."

"You hungry?"

"I am, although I didn't think I'd ever be hungry again after that marvelous dinner last night."

A glint of amusement flickered in Jesse's eyes. "Well, let's head over to that alcove table and see if we can't top it."

Rai followed Jesse to one of the four alcove tables in the dining hall. "If I'm anywhere in the dining hall, this table is where you'll find me." Rai understood why. The table offered the most privacy in the entire room, yet also afforded an excellent view of the kitchen, the bar area, and most of the dining area. They even had a clear view of the stable yard through the south window. Jesse motioned to a waiter who hurried off to the kitchen.

"I imagine Stoi and Laan have already left?"

"Yes, just before dawn."

"Well, I hope their trip home is less stressful for them than the last one." The waiter arrived, placing a plate of steaming food and a fork in front of Rai and some wine mixed with melon juice for both of them, and was gone before she had a chance to thank him.

"Oh, I'm confident Stoi will find some way to make it stressful," Jesse replied. "You, on the other hand, appear much less frazzled by the trip here. A cool head will do you a world of good around here during the busy times."

Rai chuckled. "A cool head, eh? An empty head, anyway. That's what my amnesia feels like. I don't know what to make of anything. Something happens, somebody says something, and I don't know whether I should be happy about it, sad, stressed, angry--I just don't know." Rai fell silent for a moment, hoping that Jesse hadn't heard the desperation in her voice.

"Well, I suspect you're handling it better than I would."

Rai's lips formed a thin line. "Thanks. The only thing that keeps me going is that occasionally a part of a memory will appear out of nowhere. Every time it happens, I get another small clue, another tiny bit of insight into who I once was." She took a small, tentative bite of the food. The taste reminded her of the smell she'd detected from the fish wagon they'd encountered on their way into the city, and she guessed she was eating some kind of fish stew.

"Do you keep a journal of these moments?" Jesse asked. Rai shook her head.

"Well, it may not be a bad idea. Sort of a 'Who am I?' clue book, you know?"

Rai laughed. It was a good idea. "I like that. Between you and Stoi, I'll have my memory back in no time! He's been supportive of me. Oh, that reminds me. I meant to ask him about that scar on his face. Now I'll have to wait until the next time they're in town."

"You're probably better off. You don't ask Stoi about that scar unless you have a few hours to spare listening to him rant about the Temples."

Rai stared in disbelief. "What does the Temple have to do with Stoi's scar?"

"Everything. I'll tell you the story myself if you promise never to say who told you."

Rai remembered Laan's unwillingness to tell her the story, and she doubted Stoi wanted any outsider knowing what had happened. A twinge of guilt touched her, but she cast it aside--she wasn't an outsider after all. She was Durmah now and knowing the family history was necessary.

"I promise."

"It happened some eight or nine years ago. Stoi was 21, I know that. He was preparing for a trip to the Baris Spine. The day before he was supposed to leave, he received a 'request' to serve at the Raven's Call Temple. Again. He'd been called for service two or three times already, so he wasn't too happy going in. Men have to serve a few days when they're called, but Stoi knew it meant missing the trip, which went beyond a minor inconvenience. You can just imagine the not so minor impact to his temper. But Temple service isn't exactly a voluntary thing. You serve without question or your Chieftess answers to the local Matriarch." Rai nodded. "Stoi had one of his cousins, Felmar I think, handle the trip while he reported to the Temple for service."

"Now you might not remember with your amnesia, but men's service in the Temple is much different than women's. We, women, start our service the moment we become fertile--around fifteen to seventeen, and then women stay for as long as we can bear children, up to seven or eight years in some cases. Some very prolific girls end up sequestered there for over a decade--I swear their Sept's must forget all about them! Unless you're barren, like the two of us, then you only have to serve a year at the most, maybe less. It's funny--infertility is viewed as this terrible thing, but it meant giving up less of my life to the Temple, so I don't see the problem!" Rai chuckled at Jesse's wry comment, but also she knew what Jesse's infertility had cost her. Was Jesse trying to find some meaning in their shared condition? Still, a decade was a very long time to be away from your Sept and friends.

"Anyway, men only go in for two, maybe three days at a stretch. Some men are then called back after their initial round, while others don't. I'm not sure why this is, and when it comes to the Temple, believe me, I don't ask. Not that the men ever have any complaints, mind you. In fact, according to the drunken bragging, I hear around the bar at night, the more times you're called, the better-- or at least the more the manlier if you catch my drift?"

"Yeah, I think I do. How juvenile."

"Hey, a good number of fertile women flaunt their stars too, so it's not just a man thing. Anyway, Stoi hastened off to the Temple to serve his time, no problem. Three days passed, then four, and still no Stoi. Shipments started piling up and being delayed, and Kait got understandably anxious. So Kait sends one of the butlers to the Temple to inquire when they'd be releasing him."

Jesse paused to refill their wine glasses. "Nectar of the gods, sis. Never doubt it." Rai hadn't even noticed they were empty, as she was so engrossed in Jesse's story.

"The Temple said he was receiving medical treatment for injuries sustained while under their care and they expected him to return home in another week or two." Jesse drew a finger down her face, mimicking the line of Stoi's scar.

Cold fingers of fear radiated from the center of Rai's chest. "That's it? That was their explanation? That scar runs almost the entire length of his face! What could he have been doing in the Temple that would have caused that kind of an injury?"

"The official word from the Temple was that he'd suffered an accident and that they were doing their best to treat him. Nothing more. Stoi returned home two weeks later. You think that scar looks bad now? There aren't words for how it looked the day he walked in the door. The initial cut must have sliced down to the bone! That's why the scar is still so purple, so vivid, it's like it happened yesterday." Jesse sat back in her chair.

"Did Stoi ever talk about what he remembered of his accident?"

"That was the eeriest part, the way he always refused to talk about it. The Temple has laws against talking to anyone about their experiences while in Temple service. You wouldn't think that someone who'd just had his face sliced in two, courtesy of the Temple, would be really respectful of Temple law, right?"

Rai shook her head, unable to believe what she was hearing.

"Yet Stoi's never said a word to anyone but Laan. When Laan asked him about it, maybe a week after he got back from the Temple Stoi raged about how Laan should mind his own business. Believe that? Stoi raging at Laan?"

"Was that the end of it?"

"Not entirely. Laan kept right on pushing, offended Stoi wouldn't tell him. They're best friends after all.

Eventually, Stoi admitted that he didn't remember the details clearly, but he swore to Laan that he'd been attacked by a monster!"

"A monster? In the Temple?"

"Yeah, I found it pretty hard to believe myself. I mean, someone besides Stoi would have reported something, wouldn't you think? Anyway, Stoi's story astounded Laan, and he pressed for specific details on the alleged 'monster,' but Stoi couldn't recall anything more about the beast or the supposed attack resulting in his injury. He said he couldn't remember clearly and then just stormed off. Laan never got any more details out of him. Was it real or hallucinations due to fever? We'll never know.

"Personally, I suspect the Temple somehow wiped the experience, whatever it was, from his mind. The Temple Healer warned us that he might be a bit fuzzy due to his 'head trauma' as she called it. What better way to avoid answering for your mistakes? No memory, no answers."

"So, that's why Stoi is so suspicious of my amnesia and is convinced the Temple is at fault."

Jesse nodded. "Precisely. Stoi won't go near any Temple now unless he has to. He sends staff members to make any deliveries to the Temple, and I think he'd die before he'd do Temple service if they ever called him again, not that they would at his age. So if Stoi appears a little ... distrustful when it comes to Temple dealings, now you know why."

"This is unbelievable. I appreciate you confiding in me."

"No problem. Better you hear it from me than from Laan or someone else. Just remember, you didn't hear it from me."

"I understand," Rai agreed. "I guess sleeping in wasn't such a bad thing after all. At least I didn't get the chance to make a fool of myself asking Stoi about the scar."

"I agree, it's better you heard it from me."

Rai's chest constricted, but she forced the next words out of her mouth. "Since we're on the topic of forbidden subjects, can I ask how your period of Temple Service passed?"

Dark shadows gathered in Jesse's eyes. "Sure. Why not?" She took a long drink, draining her glass. "As I've said, my time there was blessedly short due to my infertility. Sadly, unlike you, I remember everything all too well."

The anxiety in her chest slipped and plummeted like a rock into her stomach. "What do you mean?"

"You understand our time of Service is just a glorified term for breeding, right?" Rai nodded, albeit slowly. "When I was summoned to serve, I knew what to expect, more or less. No girl knows the specifics going into the Temple. Anyway, I got there, and a Temple Apprentice placed me in a crèche. I woke up after some indeterminate period, and a different Apprentice led me off into this quiet, dark little room. She gave me a unique medicinal, telling me the time would pass more quickly for me. I got very relaxed after taking it. I about passed out on the bed. She was wrong--I remembered everything." A look of disgust passed over her face, her downturned lips forming a sneer.

"What do you mean?" Rai's brows rose. Torn between needing to know and demanding her sister quit the chilling tale, she refilled Jesse's glass.

"To this day, I remember each of the three times they tried to get me pregnant. My memories of lying there while a man whose face I didn't recognize used me while I watched, barely able to move, have been etched into my brain forever." Her eyes, glistening with moisture, held one emotion. Rage.

"I don't understand," Rai replied softly. "Why did they drug you?"

"For a while, I thought they didn't want me to remember what had happened. Not that I'd care about the specifics, I mean, we all know we're there to produce children. I think all girls, going into Service, know what's expected of them." Jesse took a long drink, the banked anger in her eyes simmering beneath the surface.

"With the technology available to the Temples, why even involve sex? They could reduce the process to a series of clinical steps, and the partners involved would never need to meet."

"I suppose they could, but you forget, sis, our societal hatred of technology--using the crèches during gestation might be pushing the boundaries far enough. On the other hand, perhaps it's too expensive or takes too much time. Who knows? The men in service with me spoke in slurred words, so no doubt they'd had the same drink or one like it?

"Still, what you're describing ... it's barbaric, Jesse."

Jesse rubbed her forehead with her fingers. "Sure, the drugging is weird, but it's not what I'm getting at. I assumed I couldn't talk about who I'd been paired with-- it made the most sense at the time." She shook her head, frustration pouring off her in waves. "No, there was more to it. From the time I stepped out of the crèche the first time until I left the Temple, the most unusual sensations built inside of me."

"What do you mean?"

Jesse's expression pleaded with her to understand, the frustration plain in her eyes. "I felt anger. The medicinals they gave me calmed me down, they helped, but over the few days and weeks they had me awake I developed this hatred of everyone around me. It's completely unlike me to behave that way."

"How bad did it get?"

"I remember lashing out at one of the Journeywomen, I think I hurt her arm, but it's not altogether clear. They had me so drugged up, I'm not certain. After that, they sent me home, declared barren."

"Were you still angry?"

"No, that's the weirdest thing. I came out of the crèche the final time, happy and carefree. I have no idea what got into me while I stayed at the Temple." Her frown intensified until her brows almost touched.

"I have to say I'm with Stoi on this one," Rai sighed. "Something isn't right in the Temples. Be glad you've done your Service, and you're free of them. For my time there, Apprentice Mala had some secret, and I'll never know why she drugged me either."

Both quieted for a moment. Once again, the depth of her new familial connections moved Rai. They complemented each other well. Satisfaction washed over her, and for the first time since her awakening, she suspected she might actually fit in here. She almost felt home.

The front door opened and all sound ceased in the room. As she and Jesse turned simultaneously to look, she understood why. A Guardian closed the door behind him and looked around the room. Rai felt the tension in the room wick through like sparks from a fire.

He withdrew a device from his belt, and walked around the hall, passing it over at each individual as he neared. Rai recognized both the device and the Guardian using it. It was the same Guardian from their journey, and the device was the plague detector he'd used on the dead swamp deer. Each person he scanned breathed a sigh of relief after he'd moved on. Rai wondered if this was a common occurrence or something out of the ordinary. She had no way to know without asking Jesse but didn't want to bring it up while the Guardian was still in the building.

The Guardian approached their alcove table and stopped in front of Rai. He leveled his device at her and passed his hand over it. When he lingered for longer than the usual moment, Rai realized something was wrong. *This Guardian was with me yesterday. He knows I'm clean. What gives?* The Guardian locked her in an icy stare for a few seconds and turned his attention to Jesse.

"Jesse Durmah?" the Guardian asked, placing his device back inside his cloak.

"The same. You need a room?" Jesse offered. The Guardian did not appear amused.

"You have the flu. You'll have to come with me to the Temple so the Healers can treat you."

"Are you sure? I feel fine." Jesse voice trembled but she rose to follow him.

"The bio-scans don't lie. Left untreated, the flu will reduce your ability to fight off the plague. We don't want that, do we?" Did she detect sarcasm in his voice?

Jesse let out a resigned sigh. "No, or course not." She looked at Rai. "How long will this take? I do have a Waystation to run here."

"That's up to the Temple healers, not me. From your bio-scan, I should think an overnight stay at the Temple should be sufficient."

Jesse frowned. Turning to Rai, she shrugged. "Well, Sis, I guess it's all yours." The Guardian cleared his throat.

"Okay. I'm sure we'll do just fine," Rai replied, trying to display a confidence she didn't yet feel.

Jesse took her hand and gripped it firmly. "You'll be fine, Rai, I promise. Hilse will take good care of you. I'll be back before you know it."

Now there's a laugh. Jesse comforts me while being dragged off by a Guardian. Rai managed a slight smile, though she now felt sick to her stomach.

Jesse reciprocated the smile, though it lacked the confidence Rai had come to expect. "See you tomorrow." She walked out the door with the Guardian in tow.

We both hope, Rai thought soberly.

Hilse emerged from the kitchen and hurried over to the alcove table where Rai sat. "Where did he take Jesse?" The other diners kept glancing over in their direction.

"The Guardian is taking Jesse to the Temple Healers for flu treatment. She should be back sometime tomorrow." She wished she could be more certain of that herself.

Hilse relaxed and adjusted her hair, pulling it back loosely into a long braid. "We'd best get busy. There's much to do around here. You're Mistress Rai, are you not?"

Rai nodded. "It's good to meet you. I presume you're the Head Steward Hilse?"

"That I am. Come on, I have quite a bit to show you!" Rai didn't doubt it.

"Indeed. First, can you get me a journal of some kind, one I can take notes in as you show me things?"

"There's an extra in the kitchen office. Right this way." Rai arose and followed Hilse.

Rai's head spun as they walked to the kitchen. Everything had been under control an hour ago. Now she'd have to endure her first day at the Waystation without Jesse.

It just doesn't pay to get too comfortable.

CHAPTER 17

After a full day of training under Hilse's expert tutelage, Rai relaxed behind the bar, surveying the empty dining hall. Now in the wee hours of the morning, Hilse and the other staff had long since gone to bed, and Rai sat finishing notes in her journal.

The last guest had retired not long after dinner, leading Rai to wonder if Jesse's claim that the Waystation was busy at all hours was valid. Setting the journal aside, Rai wished for something, anything, to happen to take her mind off the boredom. She'd need to ask Jesse what she did to entertain herself through the long nights.

The faint sound of a wagon pulling into the stable yard broke her train of thought. Shoving her journal into a cubby behind the bar, Rai strode to the stable yard, glad for the distraction.

Rai opened the door, and a lean yet muscular, plainly dressed man was unhitching two tan horses from his wagon. The dim light emanating from the single wall torch in the stable was insufficient to reveal the man's features, apart from his short, sandy blonde hair, so Rai lit two more torches and placed them in sconces along the wall. Now she saw him more clearly, with her immediate attention drawn to the wagon. Whereas the Durmah wagons were traditional and dull on the outside, this one was colorfully painted, and Rai made out ornate carvings in the wood. This wagon was so much more ornate from the Durmah wagons she'd seen, so she knew this must belong to the Tinker Stoi, and Jesse had mentioned, although she couldn't quite remember his name. The man finished unhitching his horses, and now his attention turned to her.

"Well, well, well," he said, looking at her with a rakish smirk, his gaze openly roving. "I know I would have remembered if I'd met you before. You must be the new girl." Rai moved to take the horses into the stable, as Hilse had trained her that afternoon. He kept the reins on one of the horses, indicating they'd take care of one each.

"Yes. My name is Rai. Jesse said we should expect you." Rai wished she could remember his name, but dared not ask lest she offend the Tinker. They each walked a horse to an open stall in the stable, neither of them speaking for several seconds. She felt the heat of his gaze as they walked.

"Ah, so she's been telling stories about me?"

"No, I mean I know a little about you, but not much. I've only been here for a short time myself. How long will you be staying with us?"

He sighed. "Just overnight, I'm afraid. Time waits for no one, least of all travelers."

"No, I suppose not." Rai frowned. Stoi had asked

Jesse to speak to the Tinker about any other recent cases of amnesia the man may have heard about. Stoi couldn't have foreseen the Tinker would be back this way again so quickly, and that the two might not even get an opportunity to talk. He caught her frown and frowned back at her, and Rai laughed. After they had finished brushing the horses down, Rai walked out of the stable, wondering how Stoi and Jesse would want her to handle the situation. He had stopped not long after Rai and joined her near the wagon.

"Thanks for helping me with the horses, Rai. Is Jesse awake tonight? I should talk to her before I head out in the morning."

"Actually, Jesse's in the hospice with the flu at the moment," Rai explained. At this, he raised an eyebrow in concern. "Don't worry. She wasn't even sick when she left. She should be back tomorrow afternoon, but I'm afraid you won't have a chance to speak with her if you leave early tomorrow."

"Well, that's a relief. I'd never hear the end of it if I don't stay and say hello to her, so I guess I'm here until then."

"Are you hungry at all? I can get you something to eat?"

"Yes, I'm famished. You can survive on jerky and dried fruits for only so long." They entered the dining hall, and he looked around. "So, you're new on the job, and Jesse leaves you with the night shift? That hardly seems fair."

"Well, Jesse wanted me cross-trained in all areas. A trial by fire, I guess you might say. I have no complaints."

Rai felt somehow at ease with this man, though she wasn't sure why.

He laughed. "That sounds like Jesse all right."

Rai motioned to the table closest the bar. "Have a seat, and I'll get you some real food." She walked toward the kitchen door and glanced up at the mirrored wall behind the bar to her left. He watched her walking away with blatant interest. His eyes traveled down her legs, and an electric thrill ran through her.

Rai swallowed hard as she entered the kitchen. She filled two bowls with stew from a large pot on the stove and placed them on a tray along with two wine glasses. As she opened the door to return, Rai blew out a long breath before returning to the dining hall. Perhaps she'd misread his look, or was she truly that attractive to him?

She walked by the bar on the way to his table and grabbed a bottle of wine, deftly balancing the tray in her other hand. He warmly regarded her as she approached. She placed the bowl in front of him, poured the wine, and took the seat across from him.

"Mmmm, venison stew, and wine! How can I repay you this exceptional hospitality?"

Rai laughed. "Think nothing of it. I'd consider it a great favor, though, if you'd tell me a little about Kiya's Grace. I'm new here, and I haven't had much time to get familiar with the place."

"Say no more, my lady! You are looking at the eyes and ears of this city." He winked at her conspiratorially. He regaled her with all things Kiya's Grace, from the layout of the city to the people, the Temple, all of it. He even covered the politics, right down to the recent feuds over water rights in the farmlands surrounding the city walls. Rai grew more and more comfortable with him as the morning hours drifted by, and she was amazed he'd discuss the town with her in depth when he so obviously was in need of rest.

"So where do you hail from? A great distance, if this is your first time in the city."

Rai hesitated a moment. "I don't know."

He stopped in mid-drink and laughed at the absurdity of her statement. "What do you mean, you don't know?"

Rai just stared blankly at him, and his laughter melted away. "You're serious?"

"Yes." Hearing herself say it to a stranger, she realized how crazy it sounded, and laughed.

"So you just appeared here yesterday out of nowhere? Hello, I'm the new girl? Did you come in with a fishing boat?"

"No, I'm a bit adverse to fish, so no boat for me. I have complete amnesia from my time before Temple service. The Temple staff was tight-lipped too, not revealing anything about my former family since they'd given me up. Before that time, there's nothing."

"Well, now I've heard everything. Does Jesse know about this?"

"Yes. In fact, she's the one who suggested I ask you about it because you travel so much. I don't suppose you've run across any other cases of mysterious amnesia?"

"Sorry, you're the first. You see some memory loss in the elderly, but nothing like this." He must have seen the disappointment on her face because his expression softened and he leaned forward. "Tell you what. I know some people close to the Temple. I can make some inquiries and see what I come up with."

"That's most kind of you. I'd appreciate it."

"It's the least I can do. This must be very hard on you. I mean, not knowing who you are ... I just can't imagine."

"Everyone I've met has been terrific about it. All I can do to repay the Durmah is to do the best job I can. Yet I feel like--I don't know, I'm failing everyone somehow." She paused, shaking her head. "I'm sorry. I didn't mean to ramble. I guess I haven't had much of a chance to talk to anyone about this."

"No, please, rattle on! I can understand your worries about living up to others expectations. My family never lets up on me either. Besides, this is fascinating! Do you have any clues at all as to who you are?"

"A few guesses here and there, but they're based more on supposition than anything else. I've found that sometimes I just know things. Not things based on a memory or a feeling--I simply know them. However I have no actual memories of my life."

"Well, not to worry. I'll help you get to the bottom of this, any way I can." He reached forward and touched her hands. A surge of energy, attraction, and raw sensuality passed between them. Shocked, Rai stood up, unable to believe that such a sensation arose from a simple touch.

Rai's mind raced back to the day of her first meeting with the Matriarch. That day she'd smelled the soil, and her mind was flooded with images of flowers, trees, grass, and everything the soil contained. She stared at her hands in disbelief. Was it more than just smell? Could she somehow sense the emotions of another simply by touching them? The thought chilled her to the bone.

The man stood, shocked by her reaction to his touch, his expression turned sheepish with consternation. "I'm sorry if I made you uncomfortable."

"No no, it's not you," Rai replied softly, still trying to get a handle on the sensation.

"Did I trigger a memory of some kind? A good one, I hope?"

His eyes were full of concern for her, and at that moment Rai knew what she'd sensed when they touched was accurate. There was no mistaking it. How could that be possible? It was so much to absorb, Rai suddenly wanted the night over and done with.

"No, it's not that either. Look, I've kept you up long enough. It'll be daylight soon. Let me clean up these dishes, and then I'll show you to your room." She picked up the plates and walked to the kitchen.

She returned to the dining hall a moment later and retrieved a room key from the top drawer of the front desk. "This way." He followed her up the stairs to the best suite in the Waystation. The casual banter they'd enjoyed in the dining hall had been replaced with an air of uncertainty, and neither of them spoke while they walked. She unlocked the room, and he entered.

"Have a nice rest, and I'll see you around midday. With any luck, Jesse will be back by then, and the two of you can talk." Rai rubbed her hands, the intensity of his touch still electrifying her skin.

"Very well. I appreciate your hospitality, Rai."

For a moment, she considered telling him of the phenomenon that had passed between them but then thought better of it. Rai wasn't ready to discuss this newest discovery with anyone.

Rai left him there, trying to make sense of it all. She passed Hilse's room, and the door opened. The steward stepped out--already dressed and ready for the day. Rai hoped she appeared less shaken by the events of the past few minutes than she felt.

"Good morning, Mistress Rai. How was your first night?"

"Just fine. No problems to speak of. That tinker fellow--the one Jesse and Stoi talked about the night I got here. He arrived early this morning. I put him up in suite one."

"Ah, that would be the Tinker Somnu," Hilse replied, and Rai immediately recognized the name from her conversations with the Durmah. "Mistress Jesse will be so pleased!"

"Indeed. Now if you don't mind I'm a bit tired, so I'll be retiring. I'll be back up and around by lunchtime, I'm sure."

"Good rest, Mistress. Oh, and I can take that room key back to the desk if you'd like."

Rai rolled her eyes. She'd forgotten to give Somnu his room key! "That's okay, Hilse, it's the Tinker's. I'll take it to him now."

"Very well. Off I go!" She hustled away to her work. How anyone had that much energy, at any time of day-- much less the predawn hours--was quite beyond Rai. She shook her head in wonder and made her way back to Somnu's room.

She knocked on his door and waited. Had he already fallen asleep in the short time since she'd left? She heard footsteps just before the door opened.

Somnu looked a bit puzzled at her return. He'd already taken off his boots and shirt. Standing there in only his leather pants, Rai's eyes took in his lean body and powerful shoulders.

His eyes lit up at her unexpected reappearance. "I don't remember asking for a wake-up call."

Rai held out the room key. "I forgot to give you this. My apologies."

He reached out to take the key from her. "My thanks." His hand brushed against hers and again his thoughts coursed through her body. This time the sensations held more intensity, and Rai closed her eyes, trying to regain some level of composure. She wobbled, and he reached out and held onto her shoulders to keep her from falling. The additional contact only compounded her attraction to him.

"Hey, steady there." At this range, his masculine scent surrounded her. Astounded, Rai discovered the scents he emanated registered as feelings. She smelled his anxiety, his desire, and his yearning for her. She didn't pull away this time, but let the experience flow through her, wash over her. It was intoxicating.

She opened her eyes and looked up at him. "I'm not sure. You have a certain ... electricity about you."

"Funny, I've been thinking the same thing about you." He lifted a hand to her cheek and stroked it, and Rai let the sensation draw her in, tingling across her skin. Soon her response moved further, manifesting itself as an intense desire fluttering in her belly.

Catching her breath, a haze of tingling static and the smell of his sweat took shape within Rai's mind, and she found a deep empathic awareness inside herself. His emotions and hunger flowed through her, and she struggled to not let them consume her. The difficulty in winning the battle lay in progressively desiring to give in with each passing moment. Somehow, her awareness of his needs made admitting her own easier.

He sensed something in this silent exchange, and he responded to her receptivity, sliding his hand from her cheek to the nape of her neck, cradling her head. He leaned into her, breath hot and quick, their eyes locked into a dark, penetrating gaze. Rai no longer distinguished his emotions from her own and had little desire to try. His hunger urged her forward, pursuing the solace his touch offered. Their lips met, and Rai lost all sense of time and space. She transformed from a physical being into pure, raw desire, lost in the consciousness of her skin.

He pulled her into the room, kicking the door closed behind them. The room key hit the floor with a soft clink. Then her world melted away. As if outside of her own body, she felt lifted from the floor, carried across the room, and then laid down gently upon the bed. Rai gave into the man's embrace, allowing herself to drown in the sensations of his flesh and thoughts.

Clothes peeled away, shedding layers of inhibitions along with them. Flesh upon flesh, lips, the graze of teeth, fingertips delving into hidden centers. Her entire body aflame, she writhed beneath him, then desperate in her need, rolled their bodies until she was on top, driving the action.

Rai opened her eyes and confusion reigned when the eyes meeting her own, his blond hair, and the pallor of his skin jarred her consciousness. Her heart sank, instinctively knowing there had been another, now buried deep in her memories, deep in her past life before the Durmah. She closed her eyes, trying to regain the image of her lost lover, but the moment had been fleeting at best.

"Is everything all right?" He stroked a light caress down her flank, back up her thigh, gently cradling her knee. There was no urgency in his voice, only concern.

Rai leaned into him, pressing her breasts against his chest as she grasped his fingers in her hair. "I'm fine. I just needed a little breather, I suppose. Where were we?"

"Here." He pulled her down into a mind-numbing kiss, claiming her mouth not just with his lips but his need to comfort her. She felt it seep through to her very core.

It was the last conscious thought she would have that morning.

CHAPTER 18

Bauleel read Graeber's latest message in the solitude of her personal quarters. Deciding to reply later, she placed the message terminal back in the hidden drawer in her desk. Few Az'Un owned such devices, as they were reserved for emergency communications use between the Temples and other purposes at the discretion of the local Matriarchs--and the Anemoi.

Bauleel rose from her desk and paced the length of the floor. This wasn't something she wanted to hear, considering her limited options. If Graeber was right and the Anemoi had them under surveillance, they must suspect some level of foul play on her part. If Graeber could keep the girl hidden until the heat of their scrutiny passed, not all was lost.

However, if anyone in the Anemoi suspected, wouldn't both she and Graeber already be dead? Her friends within the Anemoi had been there for the staged execution, and not a one expressed any doubts concerning its veracity. Yet Graeber's stance of vigilant caution was reasonable. Better to assume the worst than to ignore the possibility, lest she ends up attending her own execution.

The clock on the opposite wall read just past midnight. Bauleel's body ached for sleep, but there was one more stop for the evening. She donned her signature veil and left her quarters. She locked the door behind her and set it to quiet mode, just in case she wasn't back by morning. Bauleel didn't want to torment Camille by not being in the proper place and schedule.

Bauleel headed for the Technicians wing of the Temple, which was well separated from the main complex. The long journey down the tunnel connected the main living quarters with the Technician's area via a hub of four service corridors. Bauleel approached the passage sealed by a large, metal door, and removed one of her long, white gloves. She tucked the glove into her belt and placed her right hand on a metal plate next to the door. A small light just below the plate blinked green as the lock mechanism actuated. A moment later, the door swung open. She instinctively looked down the corridors for any movement, but at this hour, all was quiet. She quickly passed the security door, which swung shut once she'd walked through.

She approached another locked door at the end of the corridor, identical to the previous one except for the lock plate which contained an imprinted hand shape with a small hole in the fingertip of the middle finger. Bauleel placed her right hand down onto it and centered her finger over the depression in the metal. She held steady as a needle pierced her skin and collected a few drops of her blood. A short beep signaled the end of the collection process, allowing Bauleel to withdraw her hand. Sucking the fingertip, she waited impatiently for the door to open. Would she surprise Technicians by her late arrival? She was long overdue for a visit.

Similar to the other Septs, the Technicians Sept consisted of birth members and adoptees. There was one key difference: the Technicians only adopted children with marked aptitudes in math and sciences. Trained from childhood, those selected completed their schooling at the Temples. Rank and status in this Sept were determined wholly by accomplishment and contribution rather than by birth order. Technicians had the distinction of having a few male Chiefs in their history in an otherwise entirely matriarchal society.

The birth Septs might not like the idea of giving up their most gifted children, but they had little choice in the matter. Their only comfort lay in knowing their child would work in one capacity or another toward the continual effort to find a cure for the plague. In return for their sacrifice, they received the thanks of the citizens of Az'Unda and the Temples got what they wanted: the smartest minds on the planet.

This door protected the Technicians from outside influences and distractions. This controlled information leaks and maintained their focus on their ever-present goal. Two communities of Technicians existed, one at Raven's Call and the other at Resounding Cliffs. Both groups boasted no more than three to four dozen members. The Temple complex raised their children so they wouldn't disrupt the research process by their presence. The girls attended advanced Temple schooling until their time of service, and then joined the main group after that time. The boys transitioned over in their mid-teens once completing Temple education. Once they'd joined in the plague research teams, they left the facility only for rare field research assignments. The Technician's Guild required a lifetime commitment. Once a part of the Sept, the members never left their protected facilities, living separately with their technology from the rest of Az'Unda.

The door before Bauleel slid open and revealed the main arboretum of the research facility. The ceiling rose in a wide arc, dotted with a variety of plants cascading from hanging lighting fixtures. The room was active given the late hour. Groups of Technicians appeared involved in serious discussions, some in heated debate, and still others ate a late dinner at one of the sitting areas. *By the moons, these people work more hours than I do!* What pleased her more was the level of intensity and dedication they displayed. *Surely someday they'd discover a cure.*

Bauleel headed straight for the testing labs at the far end of the room. The conversations among the various techs grew hushed as she walked by each group. No matter how hard she'd tried to emphasize they not stop on her account, they always treated her with the deference of her status.

She reached the laboratory facilities and entered a room filled with tables full of beakers and assorted glassware. Computer terminals adorned the countertop running along all four walls of the room, most of them running test models. A handful of techs stood in the chamber; some pored over the monitors, but most ran tests at the tables. Bauleel walked to the left wall and viewed the displayed varieties of charts.

The Techs worked to counteract the effects of new mutations by minimizing their spread and adjusting current plague treatments to include new variants. Although they'd made no significant headway on possible cures, according to the charts at least they'd contained the new variants quickly.

After a little searching, she found the section labeled 'New Plague Variants.' It contained only a single chart. Surprisingly the plague virus had thrown but a single new curve at them in the last few weeks. In the past when Bauleel came by this section, she'd discover a wall covered with a multitude of charts, notes, and memos--a living monument to the virulence of the dreaded disease.

Bauleel plucked the chart from the wall, aware of Journeyman Rilte's approach. He was a tall, dark-haired man with a pleasant, helpful demeanor she appreciated. He had a unique ability to explain complex technical concepts for the layman to make them feel insightful, rather than ignorant, for having asked the question. Rilte was one of the few from the Technician Sept who grasped that non-techs might still be moderately intelligent.

"It's good to see you again, Matriarch Bauleel. May I be of any assistance?" Bauleel smiled from under her sheer, white veil, despite herself.

"It's good to see you as well, Journeyman Rilte." He smiled in response, no doubt flattered someone of her status took the time to remember his name. "I've come to review the status of new viral mutations. I understand a new one presented about two weeks ago?"

Rilte frowned. "Indeed, and we've been monitoring it ever since." He paused as if debating his next words. "We haven't finished our preliminary reports yet. Otherwise, we would have sent those along to you. How did you hear about this case?"

"From the Guardian who reported it to you. He'd noticed something odd with the victim's strain of the plague. You're always so good about doing a complete analysis before alerting me, but I had a free moment so I decided I'd come and have a look for myself."

Rilte's cheerful demeanor shifted, losing his relaxed posture. "Let me just fill you in on what we've found so far. First, the subject is still alive."

Bauleel raised an eyebrow. "That's unusual!"

"Yes, isn't it? For some reason we have yet to determine, this one is holding on. He's in one of the holding cells in the containment area. Would you like to observe him?"

"I'd love to."

At the far end of the room, a secured entrance led to the containment area. Bauleel passed her hand over the plate next to the door but didn't hear the lock release.

Had they locked the door, or simply shut it? Surely it wasn't routinely left unlocked.

Bauleel and Rilte stepped through the doorway into the containment area. Along each wall, there was a row of four large floor to ceiling windows made of a shock-resistant yet clear plastic compound. An observer looked into each of the eight small holding cells. Access to these cells was through service corridors behind each cellblock, also secured through separate doorlocks. All but one of the cells was dark. Bauleel slowly approached the lighted cell, not sure of what she'd find inside.

Bauleel stood in front of the cell in amazement. "This is Terem Zebio? The one with the mutation?" Bauleel lifted her veil and folded it back, exposing her face so she could get a better look at Terem. If her unusual behavior shocked Rilte, he hid it well, neither reacting nor commenting.

"I'm afraid so," he sighed. "For this to happen to someone so young ..."

"And he's had the plague for two weeks now?"

"It's been over two weeks, two days, and fourteen hours since he was brought to our facility."

Bauleel scarcely believed it. She'd never heard of a plague victim surviving--in any condition--for more than a few days. Yet here was an absolutely normal-looking teenager, if a bit thin and gaunt. His eyes were red and swollen, which Bauleel surmised was from crying. He sat in the corner of his cell, staring off apathetically into space. From the stringy appearance of his hair, Bauleel guessed he hadn't bathed despite the shower facilities in the cell. A platter of food sat untouched near the door at the back of the cell. From his vacant gaze Terem apparently took no notice of their arrival.

Yet here stood Terem Zebio, infected with the plague--yet he displayed not one visible symptom of the disease.

"How can he have been here for two weeks and still look so healthy?" Bauleel couldn't take her eyes off the boy.

Rilte ran a hand through his hair. "Frankly, Matriarch, we don't know. We've run all the standard tests. His blood samples show record highs of the pathogen in his blood, and yet he's not progressing per the usual course. Normally by the time Guardians get to plague victims, they're within hours of symptoms, but he's never progressed. There's been no dementia, violent outbursts, or hallucinations."

"Is the mutation responsible?" Their eyes met, and Bauleel felt exposed. She hadn't spoken with anyone face-to-face without her veil for longer than she could remember. The Anemoi meetings she attended unveiled, but that was an altogether different matter. The Temple Elders and Journeywoman Camille wouldn't even recognize her face. Despite worrying about her identity being revealed, Bauleel realized she trusted Rilte. Besides, he had no reason to suspect anything unusual in her appearance.

"It's a possibility. If it is, it's far different from any variety than we've ever witnessed. Compared to other mutation subjects there are no further signs of the disease.

By now, the victim should be showing signs of profuse cellular breakdown with internal bleeding, necrosis, and hemorrhagic petechiae. We'd usually expect death within three weeks or less, although we euthanize and burn their bodies long before that point. If not for the scanners the Guardians use, I doubt anyone would have known Terem was sick. I'd almost venture to say this mutation is stable."

Bauleel stared dumbfounded at Rilte. A stable mutation? If so, his blood might open the doorway to the development of a vaccination and thus protection for the Az'Un. There had never been a single stable mutation since the Az'Un colonized this world over 600 years ago. Were they lucky enough to have found one in Terem Zebio?

"Only time will tell, Journeyman Rilte. What symptoms does he display?"

"Well, he's distraught, depressed, and anxious. He asks for his Septmates and mother daily, but that's expected for a boy his age separated from everyone he's ever known. So far, no signs or symptoms of the plague have presented themselves. We test his blood four times a day, and the viral counts continue to increase, but they're the only symptom at this point."

"He appears so disconnected and unaware of his surroundings."

Rilte shrugged. "He knows he has the plague, and he's resigned to the death awaiting him. Do you want to speak with him?" He motioned to the communication panel at the side of the cell.

Bauleel nodded. "Perhaps I can rouse him."

Rilte activated the communications speaker, and instantly Bauleel heard the boy's soft breathing.

"Terem Zebio?" Bauleel asked, not sure what she could say to jolt him out of his apathy. He sat motionless, his breathing the single sound defying his statuesque state. "Terem?" Bauleel demanded, louder and more insistent this time.

Terem turned and met her eyes, his breath quickening. Bauleel raised a gloved left hand to the transparent barrier, splaying her fingers in a gesture of acceptance and friendship. Terem got up from the floor and shuffled toward the Matriarch. Rilte looked on in amazement.

Terem came up close to the barrier and in imitation of the Matriarch, raised his right hand and aligned it with hers. He appeared to crave the contact, despite their separation by the thick plastic.

"How are you, Terem?" His gaze was eerie. Had he gone mad?

"You can't be the Matriarch. The true Matriarch wears a veil across her face." Terem's hand slid down the wall, and he looked downward. Bauleel thought he might start crying again.

"I am the Matriarch, Terem. My veil is drawn back so I can see you more clearly."

He brought his face close to the barrier and pressed his nose to the surface, fogging the wall under his nose. "You're beautiful," he whispered. Terem's eyes remained fixed on hers. He appeared unaware of Rilte's presence.

"Thank you Terem, but right now I'm just concerned about you." She rarely received compliments on her looks, due to her veil and her position of power, but in this context, his words disturbed her.

"Oh, don't worry about me, my Lady."

Bauleel frowned. Did he appreciate the gravity of his situation? "Why shouldn't I worry about you, Terem?"

His dazed eyes stared at nothing as he spun around the room, arms high in the air, head thrown back in apparent ecstasy. Bauleel glanced at Rilte, whose confused look mirrored her own.

"Terem?" Bauleel asked, unable to form a more cogent question.

Her voice jolted him out of the dance, and for a moment, his eyes became quite lucid. Terem looked back and forth between the Matriarch and Rilte, walking back toward them. An odd look came over his face, a mix of confusion and sarcasm. "You shouldn't worry about me, Matriarch Bauleel, because I am already dead. Isn't that obvious?"

"You're not dead. Very sick, but hardly dead ..." Bauleel explained. Terem held up a hand and shook his index finger at her, casting an accusing stare at her.

"I'm dead. I'm here, aren't I? I will never again see my family, never again see the moons rise, never again run with my brothers in the fields. Everything I ever took for granted is now gone." His voice broke, and Bauleel feared he might soon slip back into his earlier catatonic state.

"You need to understand a few things, Terem. First, you're not dead. Second, you don't appear to be dying anytime soon. Third, if you're infected with a new variant of the plague, one we've never seen before, the Techs may be able to find a cure for you--or at least a treatment for your symptoms. In fact, the unique nature of your case might reveal a cure to the plague for everyone."

The anger melted from Terem's face, filled instead with the shock of hope. "You're saying there's a chance for me?"

Bauleel took a deep breath. "There's a chance, yes. For this to work, you need to cooperate with the Technicians. You need to answer their questions, and submit to whatever tests or procedures they demand of you."

"So I might be able to go home to my Sept again someday?"

Bauleel paused. No one with the plague lived, much less returned home. Still, keeping him cooperative would ease the testing process for the Techs. "If a treatment can be found and you recuperate, you can return home," she promised, knowing that the likelihood of this happening was slim to none.

"I'll hold you to it," Terem replied. "How long will it take, do you think?"

Bauleel shrugged. "It's impossible to know, but most likely a few months." Considering the ridiculousness of such estimations with this unprecedented case, if he lived that long they'd deal with the repercussions of her promise.

Terem said nothing for several seconds; he must have been trying to take it all in. "Can I get some books to read? I've been so bored."

Bauleel managed a thin smile. "Sure you can. I'll make sure the Techs get you a few. Even a few of my personal favorites." Clearly, the Techs rarely had subjects healthy enough to ask for entertainment beyond the next narcotic dose. Bauleel would call for new procedures from the Sept to help maintain their charges sanity.

"Perhaps you send someone to talk to me sometimes? I don't want to take up a lot of anyone's time, it's just it gets so quiet in here." Terem's voice wavered on the edge of tears.

"Oh, you'll have plenty of company, I promise," said Rilte, and Bauleel believed him. Terem was the patient of a lifetime, especially for the younger techs who'd never witnessed a plague mutation firsthand.

Terem approached the barrier and gathered his composure, as well as any teenage boy in his position could. "Many thanks, Esteemed Matriarch. I apologize for my earlier behavior. I'll help you and the Techs in any way I can."

Bauleel hoped her presence gave some comfort beyond mere words. "Know you're in my thoughts daily, Terem. I'll return to check up on you soon."

Journeyman Rilte turned off the comm, and they walked together back into the central research lab. Once inside, Bauleel turned to Rilte. "I trust you'll honor his request for books?"

"It's the least we can do. Keeping Terem's morale up will make him easier to work with. I'm ashamed we didn't think of such palliative measures earlier."

"It's a rare case. You couldn't have anticipated he'd have lasted this long." Bauleel adjusted her veil to conceal her face.

Rilte sighed. "The boy's right, you know. You are

quite beautiful, Esteemed Matriarch. It's a shame you have to wear that veil all the time."

Bauleel stiffened. An age-old panic slipped through her bones. "As you well know, it is Az'Un custom for the Matriarchs and Elders to remain faceless, so we can better guide our people." The real reason for the veils was an entirely different matter, but she wasn't about to share that with Rilte. "I trust you won't share that aspect of this encounter with anyone."

"Never, Esteemed Matriarch."

"What I want are answers, Rilte, not compliments. Find out what makes this boy tick, and for all our sakes, make sure nobody else gets infected with Terem's mutation. We can't know how stable or dangerous it proves until it runs it's course."

Bauleel didn't wait for a reply, but instead fled back to her quarters, wondering what secret Terem Zebio's infection harbored, and how long it would take to unearth them. She only hoped they had enough time.

#BEGIN TRANSMISSION#
#ROUTING CODE: GUARDIAN
GRAEBER, GUARDIAN SEPT,
ROAMING COM H3-29Y TO
MATRIARCH BAULEEL,
RAVEN'S CALL TEMPLE,
RAVEN'S CALL#
#ENCRYPTION: HIGH#

GRAEBER: *I have informed my sister of my choice to assist you. She stands neither with nor against us. She's willing to keep things quiet, but she won't cover for us either. I hope you weren't expecting any more from her.*

BAULEEL: *I expected nothing less. I'm shocked you shared our plans with her. Can we trust her to be discreet?*

GRAEBER: *She promised to remain neutral, but tried to convince me to back out and end my involvement with you. You can't blame her, can you? There are days I can scarcely believe what we're doing. Consider the costs to both of us should we fail.*

BAULEEL: *You think I haven't? Do you regret the path we've chosen?*

GRAEBER: *I had a moment today where I almost ended this charade. Fortunately or unfortunately, depending on your point of view, I didn't. I'm not ready to finish it yet.*

Anyway, here's our status. The girl is adapting to her new Sept, and I've observed no problems any of the Sept members have had with her to this point.

BAULEEL: *That's ideal. Perfect even.*

GRAEBER: *All the news isn't good. During an unfortunate altercation with Iron Wolves along her journey to Kiya's Grace, she managed to fire a sidearm and kill one of the beasts. Her two Durmah Septmates may wonder how a teenage girl managed to bring it down. I have only myself to blame for this incident. If I'd been a few moments faster, she'd never have had the chance.*

BAULEEL: *Don't blame yourself. I'm sure you of all people would have managed to avoid the situation if you could. It's unfortunate, but doubtful they'll attribute the episode as anything but sheer luck on her part.*

It appears things are relatively well on track then, in your opinion?

GRAEBER: *From what I can tell, yes. I will continue to monitor for signs of her other unique 'talents' resurfacing-- though my limited exposure to her may make this somewhat difficult. I hope that this was merely a fluke, but we should hope she has no other incidents that trigger further awareness.*

Watch your back. It's best to assume the Anemoi are watching.

BAULEEL: I am ever vigilant, old friend.

#END TRANSMISSION#

CHAPTER 19

RAI STOOD IN A FOREST FULL OF ANCIENT TREES SO tall she couldn't make out their crowns. A whisper of light filtered down through a thick fog clinging to the valley floor. The only sound was a melodious trickle pointing the way to a nearby stream. The landscape was dotted with ferns as big as boulders growing out of rocky outcroppings in between sections of fallen trees. She was an ant dwarfed by her surroundings.

Rai looked behind her, out of breath. Mud caked the bottom of her long, brown cape and blue tunic, and bits of fern and dirt tangled through her long red curls. The cold, humid air tore at her lungs. She tried to slow her breathing, afraid to make any sound at all. She froze, sensing movement nearby.

Muted voices echoed from the ancient trees. They spoke menacingly in a language she didn't remember, yet somehow understood. They accused her of trespassing, of going where she was not welcome, of committing atrocities. They called for her death.

Rai ran through fog and fern, terrorized by the voices. They pursued her relentlessly, unwilling to give up on their prey. Fleeting images of faces and forms haunted her through the fog, but she was too petrified to turn and face them. Suddenly the voices ceased. Confused, she stopped running and listened, but the forest was silent. Sharp claws dug into her shoulders and neck, and her essence, her very soul, drained away from her.

Rai let out a desperate scream, clawing against her unseen attackers, falling backward into the mists.

Rai woke with her hands wrapped firmly around the neck of Tinker Somnu. Both bathed in sweat, Somnu fought to dislodge her grip. She released his neck, and he gasped in air. He pinned both her arms to the bed, and she let him. Unable to move, Rai took stock of his injuries, which included a bloody cut on his right cheek, bruising along his right shoulder and up to his neck where she must have been gripping it.

How had her dreams yet again manifested themselves so violently in the real world?

He continued to hold her while he caught his breath. His eyes held a mixture of suspicion, anger, and curiosity. The electricity that had coursed through her body at his touch previously shifted into a sensation of nausea.

"Are you awake now?" Blood from the cut on his cheek ran down his face, dripping down onto her.

"Yes." She wasn't wearing any clothes. A single sheet separated their hips, but her breasts were fully exposed.

"I trust you won your dream battle?"

"No, I'm afraid not."

"Well, it wasn't for lack of trying. That must have been one heck of a nightmare?"

"Yeah, terrifying. I'm sorry I hurt you."

He stared at her for a long moment before he released her hands. He slid off the bed, pulled on his pants, and picked up a washcloth. He wet it in the washbasin on the dresser and wiped at the still oozing blood on his cheek. "You have these nightmares often?"

Rai sat up in bed, rubbing her wrists. "Now and again."

"Well, I hope your other victims have fared better than I." He turned back to Rai, reappraising her as he held the cloth firmly to his cheek.

"I hit my attendant healer in the jaw at Temple a few weeks ago. So I guess not."

"You'll be glad to know your fingernails are every bit as effective as your fists." Confusion filled his gaze.

"I'm sorry ... I'm so sorry." Rai arose from the bed in tears. She threw on her clothes, not meeting his gaze. "I don't know what's wrong with me." Rai headed for the door.

Rai stopped and looked at him one more time when she opened the door. She needed him to say that it was all right. Instead, he stared back with an expression of vexation. With tears still running down her face, Rai ran out the door and closed it behind her.

Rai walked through the quiet guest corridors she

reflected on the night. Although sleeping with an unmarried male was acceptable in Az'Un culture, she guessed that attacking a hotel patron--for whatever reason--would be anything but acceptable to Jesse. How could Rai possibly explain herself? She should never have allowed such a turn of events to take place to begin with.

Rai passed by the staircase leading to the main floor and heard the voices of numerous people moving around downstairs. She quickened her step. It must be early afternoon by now. Most patrons would be either socializing in the dining hall or, more likely, out in the town conducting business. She'd better clean up before Hilse came looking for her.

Once back at her room Rai removed her clothes and hung them over a chair next to her dresser. Naked and alone with her thoughts, she assessed her situation. She still had no memories of anything before three weeks ago, and she now could look into a person's emotions at the slightest touch. What did it all mean?

On her first night in charge of the Waystation, she'd managed to sleep with and attack a customer and good friend of Durmah. Dark red drops of his dried blood still marked her chest and belly, serving as wordless reminders of her transgression. Not wishing to remain bloodstained, Rai rummaged through the wardrobe, located a bathrobe, and wrapped it protectively around herself.

She dashed across the hall to the bathroom, but not before Hilse could find her. "Good afternoon, Mistress Rai! I bring good news: Jesse has returned, and she wishes to catch up with you. Once you're dressed, that is."

"Ah, excellent, Hilse. You can tell Jesse I'll be down in a moment." Rai opened the bathroom door.

Hilse shot her a penetrating stare. "Is anything wrong, Mistress? You look pale."

A thin smile was all Rai had to offer. "Bad dreams."

Hilse looked at her a second longer. "I see. Perhaps the Temple could provide you with a medicinal that also helps you sleep. It's amazing what they can do these days."

Amazing indeed, Rai thought to herself. "Thanks for the suggestion. I'll look into it. Can you please tell Jesse I'll be downstairs once I've cleaned up?"

"Very good, Mistress," Hilse replied.

Once inside the bathroom, Rai slid into the tub, anxious to remove the Tinker's smell and blood from her skin. She submerged under the water for a few seconds, taking in the underwater silence--the only pure silence she'd known since her awakening--and then emerged, feeling refreshed. She was so sensitive to smells she could tell every place he'd touched her flesh.

Rai climbed out of the tub and dried off. Still frustrated with her inability to remember the details of the newest dream, she decided to try a new tactic: she reviewed every aspect of the dream she'd had back at Temple, and then focused her thoughts on the dream this morning. To her surprise, it worked! The particulars of the dream came flooding back to her, the voices, the landscape, the fog, the dirt and leaves in her hair, everything. She remembered it all, and she froze.

Her hair.

She remembered that in the Temple dream her hair was long--as she had it when Rai'd awoke in the Temple, but in last night's dream, it was short, as she currently wore it--a reminder of her unmarriageable status. She couldn't believe that this was at all significant, but she decided to write it down in her journal. When it came to her past, she couldn't afford to make assumptions about anything. A dark thought then came to her: what if these dreams were somehow related to her past. She shivered for a moment, wondering what she could possibly have been running from in her past that would compare with the malevolence that had haunted her dreams.

A dark thought came to her: what if those angry voices in her dreams were real. Most likely, her dream metaphor represented the disappointment she brought to her Sept by being barren, and thus why they cast her out. What if they were something else? Something darker, malevolent? Whatever, or whoever could she have been running from?

She wondered, not for the first time if she should forget about her past.

BY THE TIME RAI EMERGED ON THE MAIN FLOOR, the dining hall was bustling with activity. She looked around the room for Jesse but didn't locate her. She walked over to the front desk, where Hilse was dealing with a patron.

Hilse called over to her. "Jesse's out in the stable yard."

Rai walked toward the staircase leading to the stable yard, stopping only to retrieve her journal from the cubbyhole behind the bar and stepped out into the yard, and saw that the Tinker's wagon was still there. She had half-hoped he'd left by now, but perhaps she'd have another chance to patch things up with him. The afternoon sunlight filled the yard with a rosy warm glow.

Markel emerged from the open storehouse sporting his trademark grin. "Mistress Rai! Greetings this fine afternoon!"

"And good afternoon to you, Markel." Rai returned his smile. "Have you seen Jesse around?"

At that moment, Jesse appeared from behind the wagon carrying a large bag over her shoulder. "Oh he sure has, but he woke up at a reasonable hour and didn't sleep the day away, unlike you." Rai chuckled at Jesse's usual sarcasm and was glad she was in good spirits, but also made a mental note to have Hilse awaken her a bit earlier from now on. Her face must have given the thought away, because Jesse said with mock amazement, "Wait, I'm gone for a day, and people don't get my jokes anymore? What's the world coming to, Markel?"

Markel responded with laughter and then disappeared behind the wagon to fetch another load.

Rai fell in with Jesse in the direction of the storehouse. "How are you feeling?"

Jesse rolled her eyes. "I'm fine! I wish people would stop asking me that! After spending a lovely evening with the Temple healers--who are about as lively as hibernating toads, I might add--I feel exactly the same as I did yesterday." She paused, contemplating for a moment. "On second thought, I do feel a bit different somehow. Ah yes--I'm a bit surlier, that's it." Laughter erupted from Rai and Markel.

They entered the storehouse, and Jesse shouldered her bag onto a nearby shelf. The large space was separated into sections, allowing a range of goods to be stored. From her orientation with Hilse, Rai had learned the rear few sections were for the Waystation's operations and held long-term storage products, while the front sections kept the short-term items. Despite Jesse's carefree attitude, she maintained an organized Sept-house.

Jesse turned to Rai. "You, however, don't look to have gotten much sleep. Perhaps a Temple visit might be in order for you as well. I'm told they have some premium sleep aids."

"Oh, I'm fine. Does the Tinker always bring this much stuff with him? His wagon was almost overflowing." This elicited a perplexed look from Jesse.

Markel came in and dropped off the last bag of goods. "That's all of it, Mistress Jesse. Can I help with anything else?"

"No, I think we're done here," Jesse said.

"Excellent, Mistress." Markel headed inside.

"I'm sorry, Jesse. I should have gotten his wagon unloaded last night."

"Rai, did you even talk to the Tinker last night?"

"I did. I also got him some food and showed him to his room." The confusion on Jesse's face morphed into laughter. "What's so funny?" asked Rai.

When Jesse finally calmed down, she said, "By the moons, Rai, this isn't Tinker Somnu's wagon. It belongs to your newly adopted brother, Ponar."

"It ... it, can't be. This is a Tinker's wagon." Rai argued, remembering how Laan had described the Tinker's wagons as colorful and flamboyant in style.

"Yes, it does belong to him. Ponar traded with the Tinker Sept for it years ago and refitted it to maximize the storage capacity."

Brilliant, she thought. Uncle Stoi and cousin Laan are suspicious of me, and now I've attacked my brother Ponar--after sleeping with him. She wondered if maybe it would've been better for all concerned if she'd left the Temple Sept-less.

"I can't believe that you didn't even exchange names with him! Were you completely asleep?" Rai blushed in response.

A somber Ponar joined them in the storehouse with a fresh dressing over the cut on his cheek. He was dressed in a high-necked shirt that hid the marks on his neck and shoulder from last night. Jesse looked at her brother, laughter renewing over their predicament.

"Hello, Jesse. I understand the Temple healers have restored you to your usual, jovial self." He nodded toward Rai. "No need for proper introductions, by the way. Hilse just brought me up to date. I'm afraid I assumed you were just another of our hired staff. Regretfully, I didn't know they'd granted our request for a new adoptee. It usually takes years, after all. My ... apologies."

Jesse wiped tears of laughter from her cheek. "I'd have told you about Rai ahead of time if you'd sit still long enough, but you're always on the road." Jesse pointed to his scratched cheek. "You run into Iron Wolves on the road or something? Like Rai did?"

Ponar dropped his gaze. "No, no trouble on the road at all ... though I might have fared better with them." His voice trailed off. Rai steadied against the wall, wishing she was anywhere but here right about now.

Jesse looked from Rai to Ponar and back to Rai again. "So ... Rai hit you?" Jesse asked, turning on Rai. "Why in the world would you hit him?" Rai blushed deeper, the heat from Jesse's anger overwhelming her senses.

Rai answered in a small voice. "I had another nightmare, like the one at the Temple, only worse. Remember me telling you about how I hit Apprentice Mala?" Ponar's gaze caught hers, and Rai knew he would have covered for her, had she lied.

Jesse's eyes widened. "Wait a minute. The two of you didn't ..."

They nodded in unison, each looking a little sick.

"And then she hit you?"

More nodding.

"Bright moons! I'm away for just one night, and this happens?" Jesse exclaimed. It was Ponar's turn to blush.

Jesse caught the look in Rai's eyes and softened a bit. "Oh, cheer up, you two. You especially, sis. If you can take on an Iron Wolf and win, you can survive this. Besides, you can't feel bad about something this funny!"

"Wait, you took down an Iron Wolf?" Ponar asked. Rai shrugged her shoulders. "Well, I guess I got off light." They all chuckled a bit.

"Ah, there are the smiles!" Jesse said. "Now, I'm sure I

don't have to tell you to not to breathe a word of this to anyone. I'll keep an ear open for rumors among the staff here, but I'm assuming no one else knows?" They shook their heads. "Good. Oh, and the two of you will keep your distance for the duration of Ponar's stay here in town, and there will be no sappy pining crap. Mistakes happen. Agreed?"

"Agreed," Ponar and Rai replied in unison.

"All right. We're starting over as of now. The herbs Ponar brought from the Barrow's Grove swamplands need to get up to the Temple today. Rai, I'll have Markel help you, so you know where and who to deliver them to."

"Sounds good to me," Rai replied. "It'll be fun to get out and see more of the town."

"Wonderful. That'll give my brother and I some time to catch up with family business before he leaves for Raven's Call in the morning. I'm sure you're looking forward to getting back to the Durmah Sept house and reconnecting with the family. I'm sure Kait can't wait to hug her eldest son again."

Ponar groaned. "Yes, if only to get me to commit to marrying one of her chosen candidates."

"Oh, buck up! I bet marriage will suit you just fine," Jesse said.

"Sure, easy for you to say," Ponar replied.

"Yeah, it sure is." Jesse clicked her tongue at him. "Besides, you can't put it off forever." Ponar frowned, and Jesse shrugged him off. "Rai, I'll go find Markel to help you with the load. Ponar, why don't you show Rai what bags need to be delivered, and then come find me inside.

Now play nice, but not so sweet." Jesse left, her laughter bouncing off the stones.

Ponar turned to Rai, rubbing the back of his neck. "Well, this isn't awkward, or anything is it?"

"Oh, I think we'll get past it. Not that we'll ever live it down with Jesse. I hope we're good?"

"Don't even worry about it," Ponar replied, but Rai sensed the trepidation in him. She hoped that one day soon she'd convince him otherwise.

"Anyway, the luna berries are over here." He motioned to a nearby stack of large bags. "They were gathered from various sources, so the bags have different styles depending on the farmer, but they're all labeled luna berries."

Rai stared at them. "That's a lot of berries."

He nodded. "Yes. They're a key ingredient for a variety of medicinals."

Rai walked among them but detected a difference in one. "This smells different from the others. Are you sure these are all luna berries?"

Ponar checked the tags on the sacks, including the one she'd pointed out. "No, they're all luna berries. How can you tell the difference? They all smell a bit foul to me."

"You're probably right. I guess my nose is just a bit off." The peculiar, acrid odor must only be evident due to her enhanced sense of smell. Ponar must not be able to perceive the difference at all.

"Well, I'm going inside. My apologies again."

Rai nodded, despite the awkwardness in the air. Although they'd chatted these last few minutes, an electric charge still hung in the air between them. "No worries, it was an honest mistake. Besides, it's not as if we'll let it happen again."

"No, never." Was that a note of melancholy in his voice?

Ponar brushed past her on his way back inside. Rai sensed that despite all the reasons why last night shouldn't have happened, Ponar didn't regret it. She doubted things would ever be simple between them.

Soon enough Markel returned and they hefted the bags onto a cart destined for the Temple. All Rai thought about was the look on Ponar's strangled face and the nightmare that led her to it.

CHAPTER 20

Meik waited in line at the Temple Formulary of Resounding Cliffs Temple with his regular shipment of luna berries and swamp moss. Journeywoman Teirna handled the long line at the Formulary's dispensing counter today. Her lush lips tantalized him, not to mention the slight flush she got in her cheeks while she ran back and forth filling orders.

Journeywoman Teirna looked up and smiled at Meik in recognition, and he reciprocated. "I'll be right with you," she called over the crowd. In the morning light, her long blonde hair swished as she retrieved medicinal packets for an older man, who leered at her with a bit more than simple gratitude.

Meik maintained many such harmless crushes where his regular travels took him, and the fact that he was married didn't deter him one iota. Due to the amount of time he spent on the road, he deserved a small distraction here and there. Although rather attractive in her own right, his wife Jeri, a match made by his mother and hers, was less than the ideal mate for Meik. She held her own in conversations but she wasn't very bright, and when they did talk, she usually lamented his time-consuming trips.

As a result, Meik had been driven to attain many lady friends over the years, and he'd become friendlier with some than with others. Teirna was someone he'd like to know better, but things hadn't yet progressed beyond the casual conversation level. Still, he liked to think she admired him.

Teirna finished up with the man and walked over to Meik, giving him a moment to take in the graceful sway of her hips. "Good morning, Journeywoman Teirna. I trust the health of the city fares well under your watchful eyes?"

Teirna blushed. "Ever the charmer, that's our Meik Durmah. What do you have for us today?"

"Luna berries and swamp moss, a dozen bags of each." Her sunny disposition clouded over as she peered over the side of the cart at the bags. "Is something wrong? Don't tell me you don't need lunas and moss anymore? I've been carting these things around for miles."

"Oh, no it's not that. It's just that we have plenty of luna berries now, so we can only give you four credits a bag. Is that alright?"

Something about her statement didn't ring true. Meik had never known the Temple to have 'plenty' of anything. "So, you don't want them?"

"Oh, we do, but we'll put them in a different area this time." Teirna smiled, but it didn't rest easy on her features.

"That'll be okay," he said. "I'll help carry the bags if you'd like."

"Please do." Teirna heaved a bag onto her shoulder and led the way.

Meik followed her into the Formulary. They headed toward the back, walking down rows of shelves that held organized groupings of medicinal packets. They reached the back of the room, and Teirna plopped her bag down against the wall.

"Can you put them here?" Teirna asked.

"Will do," Meik replied.

It took a number of trips, but at last all of the bags were moved into the Formulary. As Meik set down the last bag of berries, he peeked around a shelf and overheard Teirna talking to a Priestess, recognizable by her long, elegant burgundy robes.

"This is the Durmah you spoke of?" the Priestess asked Teirna.

"No mistake, my lady."

"Very well. Don't let anyone touch them. The berries must be tested at once."

Tested for what? Why his luna berries? Apparently, they'd been waiting for them.

Meik moved on, afraid they'd notice him standing around. He retrieved the last bag, dumped it onto the pile and walked over to the two of them as nonchalantly as he could. "That's the last of them."

"Thanks so much, Sir Durmah. If you wait for me outside, I'll bring your payment," Teirna replied.

"Begging your pardons, I couldn't help overhearing

you just a moment ago, saying these had to be tested? Is there something wrong with these luna berries?"

The two women exchanged a quick glance. Meik wondered if asking directly had been the right thing to do.

"We're not sure, Sir Durmah," answered the Priestess. "The Temple at Raven's Call had some problems with luna berries recently, and so we're just being careful and testing all luna berries."

"Problems?" asked Meik.

"Yes, some individuals became sick after being treated. One died," the Priestess replied. Was it just his imagination, or was she watching his face for a reaction?

"Surely you don't think Durmah's responsible?" Despite the day's heat, a cold chill traveled up his spine. Would the Temple's stop buying from Durmah because of a bad batch of berries?

"At this point, we are reviewing all possible options and testing all batches." Her eyes were icy, as were their trade options if their products were poor quality.

"Priestess, I can assure you that Durmah is in no way responsible. All we do is transport the product; we never alter them in any way. We don't even open the bags!"

"Then I'm sure you have nothing to worry about. If what you're saying is true, I'm sure our investigation will release Durmah from any liability. Now, if you'll excuse me, I have other things to attend to." She walked off, quickly disappearing around one of the many storehouse shelves. Teirna followed close on her heels.

Teirna reappeared after a few minutes, carrying a small pouch. "Here's your payment. As always, we are grateful for the service to the Temple. A safe journey homeward to you." Her previous playfulness was lost, replaced with stiff formality.

"Until we meet again, Journeywoman Teirna." He couldn't help but feel that she was more polite than usual, not at all her usual self.

Meik pocketed the money and took his horse's reins, wondering what to make of what had just happened. He decided to leave for Raven's Call at once so he could share with Chieftess Kait what he'd learned. Any suspicion upon Durmah needed quick resolution, lest their Sept suffer the wrath of the Temples.

***

AFTER RETURNING FROM AN UNEVENTFUL SHIPMENT drop-off across town, Rai spent a quiet evening at the Waystation with Jesse and Ponar. Jesse relayed Sept news to Ponar, whose travels often kept him out of the loop. After Jesse and Ponar had headed off to bed, Rai focused on writing down the events of the past few days in her journal. She recounted the details of the dream, as well as her newfound empathic abilities.

When dawn broke the next morning, Rai didn't notice, she was so engrossed in the journal. She heard, rather than saw, Jesse approach the bar where she sat.

"Morning, Rai. I won't even ask what sort of vile things you're writing about me in there."

Rai laughed. "I'm afraid I'm too busy trying to figure me out to write about much of anyone else."

"I hear you. Ponar leave?"

"Yes, about an hour ago. I heard one of the wagons leave, so I can only assume it was him."

"Everything good between you two?"

Rai pursed her lips. "I still feel sorry for what happened."

"He'll get over it. You both will. I've never known him to hold grudges. Oh, I almost forgot." Jesse held out a small bag.

"What's this?" asked Rai, taking it from her.

"Only the finest powdered faown that money can buy. Guaranteed to deliver a restful night's sleep--or in your case, a restful day's sleep. It even suppresses dreams."

Rai looked the bag over. "I appreciate the thought, Jesse, but you know about my experience with medicinals. What if this has some kind of side effect only the Temple understands?"

Jesse laughed. "Oh no, you won't find this in any Temple I know of. I get faown from a particular vendor."

"I thought only the Temples distributed medicinals?"

"People medicine, yes. This is formulated for horses." Rai shot her a dubious look. "Faown is an animal sedative, but it's perfectly safe for humans. We've all used it from time to time here at the Waystation, what with the odd hours we work. Trust me; this stuff should be just the ticket for you."

"Look, I believe you when you say it's safe for me to take, and I do appreciate it. The nightmares I've been having ... I don't think they're random, Jesse. In fact, I believe that they're clues to my past. Something happened to me, or something I did before I became a Durmah."

Jesse pondered this. "Intriguing." She pocketed the faown. "So you think these nightmares have some use?"

"Believe me; I'd rather not have to endure them. If there's even a chance, they might help me to remember who I am. Then yeah, I'm stuck trying to figure them out," Rai replied.

"So what happens in these nightmares?"

Rai described the nightmares to Jesse. She was surprised how comforting it was to have someone to confide in.

"And you have no idea who the people chasing you are?" Jesse asked.

"No, there are no faces. It's maddening because I have no way of knowing if they're people from my past, or from the Temple after I woke up, or just unknown strangers."

"Perhaps the next time you have that dream, you should try focusing on who's coming after you, and see if you recognize them?" Jesse said.

"I'll try that, but it is a dream. I'm not sure how much control I'll have," Rai said. Still, Jesse's idea held merit. If she could overcome her fear, perhaps she could see who was chasing her.

Rai yawned, and Jesse chuckled. "Looks like all this dream talk is getting to you. You'd better turn in."

"I'll do that," Rai replied. As tired as she was, she was nevertheless apprehensive about the dreams that may come to her.

"Oh, I almost forgot, Hilse's on duty tonight, so you've

got a night free. However, I do have a small errand for you after you sleep."

"What's that?"

"There's a weaver Sept on the far end of town, the Torers. I want you to check in with them and see if they've completed the order for our new blankets. I figured that would give you an excuse to learn more about the town."

"Perfect," Rai said. "Have a good morning."

"I'll be here. Sweet dreams sis," Jesse said. "Ah, on second thought, just try not to break anything in your room, Okay?"

Rai rolled her eyes and kept her comments to herself.

RAI WAS UP AND DRESSED BEFORE SHE EVEN realized her sleep had been free of nightmares. As much as she detested the nightmares, Rai was also desperate for any clues they might bring. Frustration tore through her at the lost opportunity and yet she sighed in relief.

Rai returned to the dining room and spotted Jesse in her usual alcove poring over a large piece of parchment holding a full-color map of Az'Unda. A superb hand had etched the coastlines, spines, cities, towns, rivers, bays and forests with intricate detail.

"Sleep well?" Jesse asked.

Rai pulled up a chair next to Jesse. "I did, for once. What's with the map?"

"Your dream got me thinking about forests, and I decided to get an idea of where some of the major ones are. Most of what passes for forests around here are little more than heavily wooded swamps, but this one caught my eye." Jesse pointed to a forest area on the map, near the town of Barrow's Grove.

"Why that one?" Rai asked. She was intrigued by the idea of pinpointing the location of her dream. "You think my dream happened in this forest?"

Jesse nodded. "Many travelers have described the trees here as massive. I don't know that they're the size of the ones in your dream, but they're colossal by the sound of it."

"But we don't even know if the forest from my dream is real. It could just a metaphor for an unknown scary place."

"It's possible, but I can't shake the idea that these nightmares are trying to tell you something. Especially for someone like you, who has had no memories before a month ago. This is just absurd, and it has the Temple written all over it. Or the Guardians. Or both."

"Speaking of the Temple, you never did tell us about your visit to the Healers. Hilse and I were worried about you." Rai said.

"You and everyone else," Jesse said with a smirk. "You should have seen the look on people's faces as the Guardian and I walked to the hospice. They thought the Plague had gotten me for sure. It was rather touching."

"So, what happened when you got there?" asked Rai.

"Trust me, not a lot. He had me wait at the entrance while he whispered something with the Healers. They were distant toward me after that, even for Temple Healers. Then the Guardian left and I haven't seen him since."

"That had to be a relief. I swear, there's something that bothers me about that man," Rai said.

"I can't argue with you there. I feel that way about all of the Guardians," Jesse said.

"Yeah, but this is something different, I just can't quite put my finger on it, but he irritates me," Rai said. "Anyway, what happened then?"

"Well, they stuck me in this tiny, windowless room, alone, for at least an hour. Eventually, this kid comes in-- an Apprentice by the look of him--and has me drink a cup of this thick, dark, nasty-tasting brew. He then he tells me it'll knock me out a while, but that my flu would be cured when I wake up."

Rai thought of the medicinals that the Temple had given her and their effect on her olfactory sense. She wondered, with more than a little discomfort, what other things that dark brew might have done to Jesse.

"Within maybe ten or fifteen minutes I'd fallen asleep on this small cot they'd provided. I couldn't have kept my eyes open if I tried. Next thing I know some Healer is waking me up, telling me it's morning and that I'm free to go."

"That must have been a little scary," Rai said.

"Oh, it gets better. I asked her if the flu was cured, and she said 'Well, we wouldn't let you leave if you were still a threat to the populace' and then turns and walks away as if I'm some sort of idiot!"

Rai stared aghast at her. "Well, that's not what I expected. Remember the Healer I mentioned back at

Raven's Call, Mala? She was nothing but sweet and kind to me. I'd never imagined that a Healer could behave so coldly toward their patients."

"All I know is it's a pity that I don't have nightmares like you do, that way I could have gotten away with smacking this Healer upside the head when she woke me up."

Rai burst out laughing and was genuinely relieved that Jesse could come away from a Temple experience, any Temple experience, and joke about it.

"Look, I'm telling you it was nothing. I'm still the same old Jesse, and I'm still your boss. I'm ordering you to get out of here and go see the town!" said Jesse, mock concern knitting her brows while her eyes sparkled mischievously. "You've been at the Waystation for two days straight, and you need a break."

Rai sighed, giving into Jesse's enthusiasm. "You did mention that earlier. Where's this Torer's Sept?"

"Here are the directions." Jesse handed Rai a map of the city, which she studied and then folded, and placing it into her pocket.

Focusing back on the map, Rai considered the possibility of her dream being from a real place. She made a mental note to keep her journal at her bedside, so when the nightmare recurred, she could write everything down while it was still fresh in her memory. Perhaps that way she'd be able to remember some landmarks or faces from the dream.

"Speaking of maps, what's the name of that forest, anyway?" Rai asked.

"It's an odd one. Harper's Sorrow," Jesse replied.

"How far is it?" Rai asked.

"Oh, about two days out of Barrow's Grove, though you'd have to cross the Gorath Spine so it could take longer. I'm afraid I don't know anything about that passage. Also, Barrow's Grove is about a week from here, so it'd take say, eight or nine days each way," Jesse mused.

"Hmm, somehow I doubt Kait wants me, a newly inducted adoptee, and the only other Durmah here to help you, running off for a few weeks on a wild frendar chase!"

Jesse pursed her lips. "True enough. You're correct to assume she'd have to authorize the journey. Right now the only Durmah who travels between here and Barrow's Grove is Ponar, and somehow I think you might want to wait a little while before taking a trip with him."

"Eh, you think it might happen?" Rai asked.

"Sure, if Kait agrees, and if I can spare you around here, and if Ponar's willing to risk the journey. It's more dangerous to travel off of the usual trade routes."

Rai shook her head. "I'm sorry Jesse. I just arrived and here I am talking about running off into the far reaches. I hope you know I'm not trying to make things harder for you."

"Don't stress about it for now. I'm sure a time will work out. Now enough! Get outta here! If we chat away the afternoon, I'll never get my blankets!"

Rai stood. "Thanks, Jesse. I'll be back before dark." With that, she headed for the stable yard.

She couldn't stop thinking about Jesse's experience at the Temple and why it should be so different from hers. It was as if this Healer had something against Jesse. Was there some kind of history between them? Had Jesse had other altercations with the Kiya's Grace Temple before?

Nothing she'd heard had helped to ease Rai's fears about the Temple and about what occurred within their walls.

CHAPTER 21

RAI WALKED ALONG A BUSY STREET IN KIYA'S GRACE in the warmth of the bright mid-afternoon sun. Jesse had been right. It felt good to be away from the Waystation for a while. Jesse had also warned her that the city was often cloudy and drizzly, but today was a welcome break from the norm. She took in everything, the houses, the shops, and the jewel-toned clothing worn by the many city dwellers who passed by. The Durmah Waystation was located toward the outskirts of the city, but Rai's business was in the center of town.

Rai came upon a park filled with lush grass and dotted with tall, shady trees. At the boundary, a wooden sign read "District 3 Schoolyard." All around children laughed and played, supervised by two schoolteachers. At the far end of the park stood a large, long building, which Rai surmised, was the school. One of the schoolteachers noticed her and approached, stern-faced yet not intimidating. A brief glance up and down the street revealed no other passers-by, so Rai chose to wait for him.

Rai shifted, unsure of what to expect from this stranger. He wore a simple beige tunic and pants under a bright orange longvest belted loosely around his waist. Thin and middle-aged, flecks of gray peppered his long, black beard and short-cropped scalp.

"Good day, ma'am. What is your business here this fine afternoon?" He glanced down at her left hand, taking in her tattoo, and thus her social status as well. She'd noticed this less at the Waystation, but then, everyone there knew the Durmah women and their history.

At this distance, she picked up the metallic-tinged musk of his scent and thus understood elements of his emotional state. He was protective of the children playing behind him. Was he their teacher? No, he was their headmaster. She needed to reassure him.

"I'm Rai Durmah, of Sept Durmah. I just arrived in town a few days ago. I'm on a Sept errand, and now I'm having a look around this beautiful city."

His face softened. "Nice to meet you, Mistress Durmah. I'm John, Lead Historian and Headmaster of District Three here in Kiya's Grace, at your service." He extended a hand to her.

Rai grasped it, and his emotions intensified. It was as if she'd focused her eyes on something that had heretofore existed only within her peripheral vision. "And you as well." Rai released his hand, overwhelmed with the intensity.

"I've eaten many excellent dinners at the Waystation. It's nice to meet someone who works there in a new setting. You know, if I may be so bold, at times young ladies terms of service to the Temples can disrupt or delay their schooling. We do offer adult education classes for those who have an interest in completing their studies."

What level of education had she received? She'd understood most the Temple and Durmah's conversations since her awakening, but just how much training she'd received to a point she had no way of knowing. However, going back to school might jog some memories. The idea intrigued her. However, unlike her episode with Ponar, she decided to think before acting.

"I'm kind of busy with my duties at the Waystation right now, but I'll keep it in mind," Rai replied.

A bell sounded from the school, and the children ran toward its open doors.

"Very well, our doors are always open. Good day." Without waiting for a response, he marched off toward the school.

Rai tried to make sense of what had just happened. There was no denying it now: she could read the thoughts, or at least emotions, of others. A part of her had believed her episode with Ponar was a fluke of some sort, an isolated incident, one related to the intimacy of the moment. This time there was no mistaking what had happened with John. His thoughts had become hers! Or, perhaps she could only read his emotions? Rai wasn't so sure.

About all she did know was that neither Ponar nor John appeared to have sensed that she was reading them. Thank the moons for small favors. Still, she needed more information about this ability of hers.

More practice.

She continued down the street. The park soon gave way to houses, and then shops and businesses. Presently Rai found herself a food market with shops on both sides of the street offering all manner of loaves of bread, produce, and sweets. The streets were busier now than they had been when Rai left the Waystation, and every shop had a line of people in front of it. Perfect.

Rai spent the next hour reading people, first one, then another, and then another. With every individual she knew, she became more and more comfortable with it. Rai discovered that she could only read surface thoughts, something Rai had suspected after her encounter with John. She only knew what the person was thinking at the exact moment of contact, nothing deeper than that. Often Rai detected the person's overall state of mind--anxious, happy, impatient, angry, or whatever. She learned how to brush against someone as she walked by so that he or she didn't notice, to strengthen her contact with the person.

Most of what she read from people she found dull and mundane, though there were a few entertaining moments. She discovered that a red fruit vendor in the market had his eye on the attractive operator of a fish store across the street. A single moment's touch across the fish hawker's skin informed Rai she didn't reciprocate his interest.

Critically, she'd found no indication from anyone that they recognized she was in contact with them. This had concerned her from the start, so it was a great relief for her to discover that she had nothing to worry about in her empathic snooping.

At dusk, Rai decided to return to the Waystation, not yet interested in wandering about the city at night. As she moved through the bustling crowd, she debated whether to tell Jesse about her empathic ability. Jesse was the only one she trusted. She was her senior and her sister within the Sept, and it would be improper to keep secrets of any kind from her. Yet this was more than just a secret--it was a phenomenon, an ability no Az'Un, or human for that matter, should have. What if Jesse felt obligated to tell Kait or other Sept members about it? Rai couldn't take that risk.

Halfway back to the Waystation and before the crowds thinned too much, Rai decided to perform one more foray into the mind of a stranger. The crowds were thick here, making it easy for her to brush her hand up against a random individual. Rai's mind fogged and she was unable to delve into this person's mind as she had the others. To her horror, Rai sensed he not only knew what she was doing but also seethed over the invasion of his privacy.

"Not everyone appreciates ... intrusions." The words slipped into Rai's mind. The message carried a harsh yet familiar masculine tone.

An intense tingling sensation rolled over her, and she staggered a few feet to a lamppost and clung to it to steady herself. Her head slowly cleared, and she turned around to get a closer look at the man, but he was already gone, having disappeared into the throng of people. She didn't even remember the last few faces that had passed her by, so she had little hope of remembering his face out of the masses.

Rai's head swam. Did this man have the same empathic ability as hers? If so, how had he blocked her attempt to read him while also sending her such a clear a warning laced with malice? A chill of fear ran down her spine. Had he known what she'd been doing in the marketplace too?

Rai looked around one more time, but she didn't notice anyone watching her. At least, no one was staring at her, but she knew that didn't mean anything. Rai wanted to find the man; perhaps he'd answer some questions about her past. Then again, his silent message hadn't been at all friendly either.

Rai made a hasty retreat to the Waystation, and along the way couldn't help wondering if there was an entire Sept who had this empathic ability. Rai wondered if there was a casual way of asking Jesse about it, but knowing Jesse, that would only pique her already abundant curiosity.

About halfway to the Waystation and after the sun had set, Rai decided to take a detour down a dark, deserted street. None of Az'Unda's three moons had yet risen, adding to the shadows of the night. Rai'd kept looking for anyone following her and hadn't caught sight of anyone, but she didn't want to take any chances. The Waystation was the one safe place for her in the city, and if someone was after her, she didn't want to lead him straight to it. She ducked into a dark doorway and waited.

She didn't have to wait very long. The soft sound of footsteps on the cobblestone street alerted her, and she pressed her back harder against the door. She reached and tried the doorknob, but it didn't budge. The footsteps slowed as he approached her hiding place. He'd followed her! Her heart raced, and sweat trickled down her cheeks. A hooded, cloaked figure passed slowly by, and she held her breath.

By the moons, I wish I could disappear through this door.

After the man had passed her location, he slowed and stopped. He stood still, and Rai didn't move a muscle, lest she alert him to her location. Abruptly he turned and backtracked along his previous course. She was convinced he'd notice her, but instead, he passed by. She poked her head from the doorway in time to watch him disappear down the street in the darkness, his robes flowing behind him, much like those of Temple folk or those of Guardians. Why would this man be clad so?

After a few more minutes, Rai convinced herself that he wasn't coming back. She emerged from the doorway, and Rai felt her shirt catch and rip on the wooden door. Wasting no more time, she rushed off toward the Waystation, resolving at that moment to resist any more urges to explore her newfound abilities.

CHAPTER 22

It took Rai nearly an hour to find her way back home along the dark side streets. When she arrived back at the Waystation a man's loud, gregarious singing filled the main dining hall, spilling out through the windows with gut-busting volume. Rai hoped it would distract from her late entrance. Rai swung open the door and encountered a laughing and somewhat intoxicated man leaving the establishment. He laughed harder, very amused at almost walking right over Rai. He stepped aside and held open the door for her to walk through. Rai entered the Waystation and found the hall filled with raucous laughter. No one noticed her entrance.

The source of the entertainment was immediately apparent, despite the smoke-filled space. A dark-skinned man sat on a stool at the far end of the hall, the bright motley colors of his clothing contrasting with the natural light woods in the instrument he played. Rai recognized it as a ukulele and considered it an odd choice knowing they were considered rare. He sang a familiar song, an old dark comedy about a couple that tries to consummate their attraction, but they kept misunderstanding the agreed upon meeting times and dates until the entire town knows what they're up to, including their now aware and irritated spouses. The patrons sang along, drinking more ale, and laughing as the man sang. Rai realized this must be the real Tinker Somnu.

Rai felt a draft behind her--a reminder she needed to change her shirt. Rai headed to her room with only a quick wave to Jesse, who sat in her usual alcove. Jesse raised a curious eyebrow in reply, and Rai waved in quick acknowledgment and shot up the stairs. She locked the door behind her and changed her clothes, selecting a dark blue shirt and matching skirt to wear for the evening. As soon as she finished donning the clean outfit her attention turned to the shirt she'd just removed.

Rai found a small hole in the back, just large enough for her thumb to fit through, roughly aligned with where her right shoulder blade had been. Inspecting the hole, Rai found wooden splinters embedded around the edge of the tear in the fabric, as if it had been ground into the wood. In the back of her brain, an odd tingling sensation grew. Something significant had happened, but she had no words for this. The tear in the fabric signaled an alarm deep within.

A knock on the door startled her, and she had to remind herself that she was safe from the stranger she'd dodged only a short time ago. Answering the door, she found Hilse waiting.

"Mistress Jesse inquires if you will still be eating

dinner with her tonight, Mistress Rai." Hilse's face was full of curiosity.

"Tell her I'll be right down, Hilse."

She glanced at the shirt Rai held and noticed the hole immediately. "Did you need that mended, Mistress? I can have it done for you by morning." She held out her hand.

Rai didn't want to hand it over but decided it might seem odd if she refused the offer. "Thank you, Hilse." She gave Hilse the shirt.

"Now hurry downstairs, Tinker Somnu is too funny to be missed!" Hilse took off down the hall, eager to enjoy his antics herself.

Closing her door, Rai walked to the mirror, pulled off her clean blue shirt and took a good look at her back. There were no marks or scrapes. How had she torn the shirt, without marring the skin? It just didn't fit together.

Rai suspected that things would get much more complicated since she still didn't feel comfortable discussing these strange revelations about herself to Jesse or the other Durmah. She put her shirt back on, and Rai resolved to rely only on herself. With the amnesia, the empathic and scent senses, and her skills with weapons, and this newest...whatever, Rai was nervous the Durmah would turn their ever suspicious natures toward Rai. The plague took the blame for all odd or bizarre ailments, and those afflicted always suffered harshly. Thus, she should hide her issues. She'd keep the knowledge of these gifts, or curses, to herself. Perhaps after she'd resolved new newfound abilities, she'd share what she knew. However, not now, not when there was so much to lose. She'd just have to wait and keep quiet until she made sense of it all.

Rai returned to the dresser and pulled her dart gun out from under a stack of under shifts. She placed it in the pouch on her belt along with her journal--it had just enough room. Putting it behind the larger form of the journal kept it hidden so that no one would know it was there. After her run in with the man in the market, she just didn't feel as safe, even being at home in the Waystation.

Rai realized the person who'd followed her definitely got a better look at her than she had of him. During her attempt to elude him, she'd walked down roads with street lamps. Since he'd followed her, he had known her hair color, build, height, the way Rai walked, as well as what she'd wore at the time. She hugged her arms to her chest, yet shivered despite a lack of chill in the air. What other kinds of advantages might her opponent have?

Rai's disquiet followed her back down the stairs, and she tried to act cheerful, but there was no fooling Jesse. Tinker Somnu sang a tale of lament now, bringing a frown to Rai's lips and brow. Rai joined Jesse in the alcove, and seconds later one of their young wait staff, Zibe, presented her with a plate of mashed tubers and sausages along with some wine. Jesse sat and openly studied her while she ate.

"Sorry I'm back late," Rai said between bites. "The town is bigger than I'd expected."

Jesse met this comment with a raised eyebrow. "So you had a fun if lengthy walk?"

"Yes. I spent some time talking with Headmaster

John and surveyed the goods available at the market. The silversmith's work is quite impressive."

"Don't the markets still close at sunset?"

Rai had returned two hours past sunset. "Like I said, it's a big city." Rai avoided meeting Jesse's probing gaze and felt her own cheeks flush with heat.

Jesse snickered and then poured herself some wine. "So you got yourself lost?" Well, it was a convenient charade. "Did you at least get a sense of how the streets run, or do I need to send you out with an escort the next time so you can find your way home again?"

Rai blushed, not comfortable lying to Jesse. "I think I have a handle on the town layout now, but I'm sorry I didn't make it to the Weaver's Sept. I went down every street at least twice so I can remember them from here on out." Jesse laughed along with her, and Rai breathed a sigh of relief, happy she'd smoothed over her absence.

Applause filled the hall, accompanied by shrill whistling and occasional hoots, and soon the Tinker took his bows and walked toward them. Jesse rose to greet him, extending her hand in welcome, which he grasped before pulling her into a hug. Rai also stood, observing the easy intimacy between the two. Rai realized he must have been sitting with Jesse earlier. A travel cloak hung over one of the chairs in the alcove, and a small pack and case sat in the corner. The Tinker's clothes were even brighter up close, with yellows and oranges predominating. An odd lime green accented at the belt, shoes, collar, and buttons. The overall effect left Rai a tad nauseated and dizzy. Only as an afterthought did Rai note his deep laugh lines grooved through his dark-skinned face, framed by white, light tufts of hair. Rai thought he looked something of a clown, not that she'd say such an impolite thing aloud.

"Well, I presume this is your wayward sister, finally returned?" Somnu greeted them, picked up his case, and carefully stowed his long-necked, hand-carved lute inside it, latching it shut. Rai disliked Tinker Somnu, surprising herself. Perhaps it was her mood, but something about this man set her on edge.

Jesse nodded in response. "Thanks for bringing joy and laughter to our guests, Somnu. This is indeed my sister Rai, newly arrived from Raven's Call. Please sit, drink some wine, and share conversation with us."

He placed his ukulele case back in the corner and pulled out a chair across from them. "Good to meet you, Mistress Rai." He tilted his head with deferential respect. Tinkers held a proper Sept all their own, only very spread out and without large houses in any of the cities. "I trust your meandering was enjoyable?"

"Yes, thank you, I think I have a good grasp of the city now." Rai busied herself eating, hoping he wouldn't engage her if her mouth was full.

"Jesse and I talked a bit earlier. I understand you have some sort of amnesia?"

Rai honestly didn't care for this man. Mouth full of sausage, Rai nodded, looking around to see if anyone could overhear them, but she doubted their voices traveled outside the alcove walls. Still, she kept eating and refrained from further affirmation.

"Odd, that amnesia. Jesse asked if I'd heard of it happening anywhere around and about, but I'm afraid it's news to me." He sounded sincere and helpful, yet Rai resisted falling for his natural charms. She didn't understand the drive behind her caution but trusted her instincts. "Are you sure this isn't the result of head trauma or some other accident?"

Rai swallowed hard. "I'm afraid I don't know. I don't remember my time before the Temple service after all. I didn't have any bruises or scars that indicate an injury."

"Well, you might not have. Those sorts of marks may have healed during the time you spent at the Temple. You haven't had any glimmers of memory surface in the time since you left the Temple?"

"I can shoot a dart gun well, but that's more skill than a memory I'm afraid," Rai offered a bit too pointedly. Jesse shot her a penetrating look, and Rai wasn't sure if she disapproved of her tone or the information she shared.

"That's not helpful, is it?" Somnu replied, not offended but instead lost in contemplation. "I can do my best to ask around. Sometimes the Septs in the far reaches encounter odd health effects of the plague treatments, and they often don't complain to the Temple healers for fear it's the plague and that the treatment didn't work. I do think the most likely scenario is head trauma, just from what I know of field medicine."

"Anything's possible, Somnu. That's why it'll be so helpful for us if you can keep your ears open," Jesse spoke up. "We'd want to know if one of our own had been harmed, intentionally or otherwise. Especially if the Temples are involved."

"When aren't the Temples involved?" he replied with

obvious disgust. "Don't you worry though, I'll be discreet. They'll never even know I'm poking around."

"Many thanks, old friend," Jesse replied. "How long will you be staying in town this time?"

"As always, until the Tinkering is done," he replied with a sly wink. "Seriously though, I won't be in town long this trip as folks don't appear to need me as much as usual. That's all the better for you because I'll be off and be nosing around for you even sooner." He winked and raised a glass to them.

"We appreciate your efforts," Jesse replied, also raising her glass. Rai raised her glass as well, although her heart wasn't in it. The idea of this man hunting around for information about her past and her amnesia didn't fill her with enthusiasm.

Rai finished her meal and decided to excuse herself. "I'm sorry, it's getting late, and I'm afraid my feet are hurting a bit from all the running around. I hope you can forgive me, friend Tinker?"

"Oh, dear girl. Please, call me Somnu. We'll have plenty of time to talk over the next couple of days, don't you worry." Could he sense her innate dislike of him? Then she chastised herself; thinking that way was just fostering her paranoia.

"That sounds great, Somnu. Good night to you both," she replied.

"You going to be alright, or do you need something for that headache?" Jesse asked.

"I'm sure a good night's sleep will take care of it," Rai replied.

"Okay. I'll make sure no one disturbs you until midday tomorrow, so you have plenty of time for sleep."

"Thanks, Sis." Rai headed upstairs to her quarters, glad for the distance from the Tinker. How she'd manage to avoid him over the next few days, she wasn't sure, other than she'd find some way. Something about him grated on her, but she couldn't quite place it. Until she could, she had better keep on good terms with him, lest she damage his relationship with her Sept. Not to mention he might prove helpful, and find information concerning her amnesia. Yet, the idea of him knowing the answer to her mystery unnerved her. Rai tried to shake off her anxiety, hoping it was just the stress of the day. After all, he hadn't done anything to earn her suspicion. At least nothing she remembered.

Somnu appeared lost in thought after Rai took off upstairs. Jesse chose not to disturb him and instead focused on her patrons, monitoring the mood of the crowd, as was her habit. Rai's mood had been a bit off, and though the girl might be odd, even knowing her for just a few days, it wasn't normal for her temper to turn cross. Getting lost must have upset her, even though she'd played it off as a funny mistake.

Somnu spoke. "How long has Rai been in the Sept with you?"

"She's been here a few days with me at the Waystation. There was another week or two before during her adoption and transport here by Stoi and Laan. Why?"

"It will help me to have a rough timeline while I'm rooting around for information. Not that we can know how long Rai was in the Temple, but the more detail, the better." His eyes were unfocused, staring off into the crowd. "Has she acted oddly in any way?"

"How do you mean?" Jesse debated how much to share. She'd known him since her childhood, and yet he wasn't Sept.

"Oh you know, emotional outbursts, bizarre comments, violent behavior, or unexplained reactions, that sort of thing."

Jesse bit her tongue. She didn't want to have to explain any details, including Rai's dream-inspired attack on her brother. She'd prefer including Rai in this conversation, and yet, Jesse was her senior, and the choice fell on her. "She's had some odd nightmares, but that's about it."

"Nightmares? About what?"

"She has these terrifying dreams where she's being chased through a forest. It's unlike any forest I've seen, with gigantic trees and sparse undergrowth. I've assumed it's a dream metaphor for fear of the unknown, but you should ask her about them next time you talk, she can describe them better."

"I'll do that, but I'm not sure it'll do much good, considering they're not memories but merely some fantasy world. Still, perhaps talking through Rai's fears will help the memories resurface." Somnu sat back in his chair, chewing his lip and knitting his brows. For a moment, his face darkened, and a brief frown passed across his face.

"What are you debating over there?" Jesse asked. She prided herself on figuring people out, but Somnu always surprised her.

"I'm not sure you want to know what I'm thinking. It's just a stab in the darkness, and I don't wish to offend you." His voice filled with hesitation and his eyes didn't even meet her own but instead played over the crowd.

"You never need to worry about offending me. I'm as tough as Kait, you know, so get to it." His attitude disturbed her. Somnu never acted this way, and it unsettled her deeply.

Somnu shrugged, giving in to her request. "You need to consider that Rai is perhaps not all she appears to be. I know she's part of the Durmah Sept now, and I would never doubt a Durmah's integrity." He took her hand and held it firmly. "You know this. Yet without knowing her past, you never know what she's capable of." His eyes held hers intently, and Jesse couldn't look away.

Jesse stared back in shock. She'd asked for his thoughts but hadn't expected anything like this. "You don't know her. You've only spoken with her for a few moments. She has a good heart, and Rai is devoted to our Sept. That can't be faked."

Somnu raised his hands and shook his head, begging off her temper. "I'm not saying she's faking anything or you should doubt her motives. I'm sure she's a lovely girl, but you can't predict how she will change when those memories surface. There's an element here I don't think even she can predict. The past brings with it allegiances, promises, and debts this girl hasn't had a chance to resolve."

This truth stirred a fear within Jesse, one she hadn't wanted to admit to herself. Rai's past might bring with it a variety of dilemmas. Jesse hoped Rai's memories remained lost, and Somnu's comments strengthened that belief.

Jesse shrugged. "I think you worry too much. Sure, those things may happen, but chances are her past isn't even worth talking about. She can't be more than seventeen years old. What troubles can she have acquired in such a short time?" Jesse refrained from pointing out her own share of problems at her own not so advanced age of nineteen.

For a moment haunted shadows passed over Somnu's eyes, but then the moment passed. Did she imagine it?

"You're right, Jesse. I guess I'm just too used to hunting down conspiracies--I even look for them in young girls now."

They shared a hearty laugh, and then sipped their wine and watched the crowd. Although Somnu looked as relaxed as ever, a growing apprehension now ate away at Jesse. She was tempted to ignore his arguments, but Somnu's concerns were valid. Jesse trusted the Rai she'd grown to know. The idea of a different person emerging when Rai's memories surfaced troubled Jesse. However, could Rai be content to let the past sleep?

CHAPTER 23

Matriarch Bauleel arrived at the private meeting chambers of the Elder's Council and found all of the other members already in attendance. A few already sat waiting, while others chatted softly in small groups. They'd forgive her tardiness, but being late to your own meeting was poor form. Next to each of the doors was a Temple Novitiate. They bowed to her as she entered. Bauleel tried to remember being that young, that innocent. It was a very long time ago.

Beneath the tall, domed ceiling sat a large V-shaped table, where the Temple Elders comprising the Elder's Council heard the concerns and requests of the people of Raven's Call. They also mediated disagreements among their constituents and handed down judiciary mandates. Tall, thin windows ran from ceiling to floor, letting in slivers of warm light, though it wasn't enough to illuminate the room.

Journeywoman Camille, who had followed her in silence from Bauleel's office, closed the towering doors behind them, which produced a muted clang upon lock-ing. All those not seated moved toward the remaining available seats as Bauleel took hers. The Matriarch's reserved chair stood neither higher nor more ornate than the other chairs, but a glittering silver fabric draped over the simple wooden form, lending it all the prestige she needed.

There were fourteen Elder Priestesses, and the number of remaining chairs reflected this. Age alone didn't qualify a Temple woman for Elder status. All of these women had elevated through the Apprentice and Journeywoman levels and attained full Priestess status. Only those with Priestess status retired to the position of Elder as their age caught up with them. This retirement brought two expectations; to serve as advisers to the lower level Priestesses and hold a council at the Petition-er's Chamber as their health allowed.

The room had quieted, the Matriarch moved to her seat and sat. Camille stayed by the door, dutifully prepared to turn away anyone not expressly invited to the Council. Bauleel doubted Camille capable of forcibly preventing anyone from entering if they got past the heavy locked doors, but the likelihood she'd have to do this was highly unlikely. The Elders waited for the Matriarch to open council.

"I am here today to share some disturbing news with you," Matriarch Bauleel said. "I'm afraid some of our shipments of luna berries have been tainted." Distraught gasps and groans met this news, but Bauleel knew some already had their own sources within the Temple. This didn't worry her; rumors within the Temple weren't too disruptive--it was when they moved into the city that things got dangerous.

"I want to assure you all necessary precautions are being taken. A few poor souls succumbed to an eczema treatment, but that has been contained. All luna berry shipments in all of the Temple Formulary storehouses on Az'Un are undergoing testing for contamination. The Formulary Priestesses have used the utmost care to limit the impact on the populace. Research is also being done to pinpoint the source of the taint, in hopes that we can resolve the problem before anyone else is injured." Bauleel thought it best to not to imply a human hand in the taint to the Elders. Most of the Priestesses sought mentorship with the Elders, and Bauleel knew information tended to flow both ways. Having people hunting for conspiracies within the Temple would be disastrous. "I hope you can under-stand my desire to keep this quiet from the populace. The people complain about the occasional side effects of the plague treatment. I fear any rumor might feed into their concerns over further ills, and we'd have more deaths on our hands. You can understand this is a deli-cate situation," Bauleel paused, waiting to see if any wanted to share their reactions.

"We will honor your request to keep this quiet, Matriarch," Elder Kaiya replied. Bauleel recognized her by voice and tone, known for her ability to remain level-headed and calm in any situation. "None of us wish to witness more deaths from the plague, whatever the cause. I am concerned, however, that the families of those affected by the contaminated eczema treatments will speak out. How are we to handle any rumors from that direction?"

Elder Kaiya's question led the discussion correctly. "The Temple's official stance on the contaminated eczema treatment is that it was a single contaminated batch, and the errors happened during production. They've been told steps have been taken to prevent future similar mishaps," Bauleel answered.

"I don't wish to question your decision, and I want to affirm that I support the chosen angle, but I have a concern I feel obliged to share," Elder Kaiya replied. "Rumors are circulating that the Temples are no longer equipped to handle our fight against the plague. I've heard talk of bringing in off-world help to assist in the search for a cure." Bauleel heard others shift uncomfortably at this suggestion.

"Thank you for voicing that opinion, unpopular as it must be," Bauleel acknowledged. "I am aware of the doubts our people have in us right now, and I empathize with their desire to seek out other aid. We need to remind our people that we have tried outside help in the past, without much success, and at significant cost. I know it has been some time since we hired the Erinin healers, so people may not remember that it cost us years of ore mining to pay them off for the few months of work they did. Considering that all their aid netted us was an elimination of possible treatments, it simply wasn't worth the price."

Elder Rebea spoke up this time. "And yet, my Esteemed Matriarch, it has been some time since we have sought outside help. Three generations, if I remember correctly." Apparently, the Elders shared this desire, as none spoke out contradicting her comment.

"I understand your concerns, and I will talk with the other Matriarchs about this possibility. It has indeed been some time since we evaluated outside options, and new technologies might be available to aid us at this critical juncture. We must take care to act in unity, for any price will affect all the Az'Un and not just our city," Bauleel replied.

"We must also keep in mind the Hegemony still holds a medical quarantine over the Az'Un people due to the research conclusions of the Erinin healers. It is possible that any outside species won't be able to encounter us without earning the Hegemony's wrath. Those that might be willing, for instance, races outside of the Hegemony's purview, might be rogue species. Are we ready to deal with that kind to find a treatment for us in this world?"

"I don't think anyone's suggesting we deal with scoundrels or thieves to achieve our goals." Elder Natre replied. "Do remember that we are not yet accepted as a protected species under the Hegemony." Natre had a history of being confrontational, and this only reaffirmed Bauleel's understanding of her character. Natre was also a member of the Anemoi, which lead to a whole other power dynamic between them.

"I do remember, Elder Natre. In fact, I remember all too well. How, exactly, do you think our petition requesting Acceptance of Sentience will fare if they knew we consorted with unaffiliated species to achieve our goals?" Bauleel pointed out, a hard edge in her voice.

"With all due respect, Matriarch, I don't think a simple query qualifies as 'consorting.' We are reaching a point of desperation, where exorbitant costs are acceptable if it allows our colony to survive," Elder Natre replied. Other Elders shifted and coughed, uncomfortable with the Elder's candid tone.

"When we speak of the Hegemony, realize that what we're actually speaking of is the Juggernaut. Although the Hegemony is comprised of many species, the Juggernaut are by far the largest and strongest. None can compare to their might. They are an ancient species. They view humanity's actions on a very long continuum. We might as well not even exist in their timelines. I warn you not to underestimate the range of their overview. They have the resources to monitor every interstellar action and communication of all human colonies without even breaking a sweat. I can assure you that any such discussion would draw immediate and negative attention, even if they chose to wait to act upon it. I remind you all that even our most advanced technology doesn't even begin to compare to theirs."

"I also resent your implication that I somehow am unaware of the status of our people, Elder Natre," Bauleel warned. "I am well aware of our declining birth rates. I know about the failing effectiveness of our plague treatments against an endlessly mutating and adapting infection. I am mindful of the fact that we are mere generations away from a hopeless situation. The problem has been and will continue to be, how do we save ourselves without also destroying our future?"

"We can't simply run away from our problems. Our

technology prohibits it and our population size, although small for a colonized world, is too large to transport. Remember that we came here on a one-way trip in the first place, hoping the planetary surveys would bear out. By and large, they did. Az'Unda has a variety of natural resources, a breathable atmosphere, and temperate regions we find habitable. The plague is the only problem holding us back. We will overcome this obstacle, and when we do, we must be able to leave it behind us. Gifting future generations with our debts only creates additional problems." Bauleel thought the history lesson a bit heavy-handed but wanted to drive the point home.

Elder Natre sat quietly. This time Elder Kaiya spoke up in support of the Matriarch. "We are all aware of these straightforward if sometimes discouraging facts, my Sisters. I agree with the Matriarch in that we should not act rashly or without appropriate consideration. Adding to our problems will not make our current issues easier to bear." Bauleel thought she heard Natre sniff in reply, but she couldn't be sure.

"Still," Elder Kaiya continued, "there is the issue of reassuring the populace that the Temples are still the best hope for a cure."

"We are of the same mind on this, Elder Kaiya," Bauleel agreed. "I want to reiterate that the other Matriarchs and I will discuss the possibility of off-world assistance and research thoroughly any options." Bauleel took a deep breath before continuing.

"There is something I will share with you now, a ray of hope. I've been debating bringing false hope, but I think the desperation voiced here today warrants the risk. The Technicians have found a subject who appears immune to the plague in its advanced stage. It has been over two weeks now, and the subject shows no signs of cellular degradation." A hush of awe fell through the room. Even Camille stopped taking notes for a moment to stare openly in wonder at the news. Bauleel hadn't mentioned the boy's mental instability, thinking it wouldn't lend to the mood of hope she hoped to build.

"I know this is no cure, but his immunity might lead us to a vaccine. Besides, the vaccine would apply to newborns only, but it's hope for future generations. It's almost too overwhelming, but imagine all children growing up without the burden of the plague hanging over them."

"The subject's health might fade any day. There are no guarantees in what I'm sharing with you. Yet, it's a ray of hope, and an opportunity we haven't had in some time. If negative rumors are to circulate, perhaps also rumors of a possible vaccine should also."

"Do not discount the joy this news brings to us, Matriarch," Elder Rebea said. "Hope is not to be ignored on Az'Unda. I am sure a few slips of this rumor in the proper places will improve the Temple's standing amongst the people."

"How long before the Technicians share their progress with you? Something definite is determined, do you suppose?" Elder Kaiya asked.

"I'm not sure, but I have been in close contact with them, and I will continue to do so where this research is concerned. I will also keep you informed of their progress," Bauleel replied. The Matriarch rose, signaling an end to the meeting. This quarreling drained her more than she cared to admit. The Elders all rose in deference to her office.

"We thank you for your dedication and devotion to our people, Esteemed Matriarch," Elder Kaiya intoned formally.

"As always, it is my great pleasure to be of service to the Temple and the Az'Un people of Raven's Call," Bauleel replied with equal formality. Bauleel rose and left the room, with Journeywoman Camille barely managing to unlock and open the door quickly enough for her to pass through. She was glad to have the briefing over with, but not happy of the headache it had bestowed upon her. True to her word, Bauleel headed toward the Technician's wing to obtain a status update on Terem. Would his health hold the hope she'd promised to the Elder's Council?

CHAPTER 24

Rai sat in the back of Headmaster John's planetary history class and tried to focus on what she considered a boring lecture on local geology as it related to traditional Az'Un trade routes. Her eyes strayed out the window, and her mind kept dwelling on her commitments back at the Waystation. Jesse hadn't been enthusiastic over her interest in attending classes at the school, but she'd allowed it.

They'd had a long discussion, and Rai'd argued exposure to historical information might trigger more memories. Rai got the impression from her scent cues that Jesse might want her to give up the hunt to discover her hidden knowledge, but she never came out and said as much. Jesse allowed her to attend the school three days a week during midday and early afternoon, saying the knowledge would round out her education. Rai had to return home to cover her evening shifts, lest it appear she wasn't doing her part.

There was another reason Rai found being away

from the Waystation desirable: Somnu. During the days, he always hovered in the background. Rai'd shifted from not trusting toward harboring a genuine animosity toward him. His penetrating gaze tracked her every move. Jesse had encouraged her to give Somnu a chance, reminding her that he was an old friend of the Durmah, and thus deserved her friendship as well. Rai had responded by being polite and helpful, but wouldn't truly open up to Somnu. Being at the school during the days helped her avoid him without slighting him. During the evenings Somnu entertained the Waystation patrons with songs and tales, which Rai felt kept a comfortable distance between them.

Focusing back on the Headmaster's lecture, Rai found him discussing the various mountainous spines on their continent. She'd remembered passing over the Baris spine, but otherwise, the discussion held little interest for her. The class was relatively small, having about two dozen total students. Almost all of them were male and in their late teens. Rai assumed most of the other females her age would still be fulfilling their terms of Temple service. Those not actively pregnant would be in Temple schools and not here with the other students.

The Headmaster referenced a large map on goat vellum he'd hung at the front of the class, and Rai now took a moment to study it. The map was too far away to read the names of given features, but the color-coded topography was easy enough to follow. The wisps of charcoal gray depicted the spines, with the tallest peaks and most advantageous passes marked with firm strokes. Predictably, the colors of the plains, forests, and grasslands had been drawn in greens, the roads in beige, and the oceans and bays in blue. The swamp areas were marked in a blue-green mixture, and cave complexes had simple gray outlines on top of whatever type of land they laid beneath.

The continental map reminded Rai of the map Stoi had shown her. It was a similar shape and color, except that Stoi's map didn't have the cave complex details upon it. From studying this map, it became apparent to Rai that the caves ran from the bases of the spines out into the lowlands. In some cases, the caves extended all the way to the shoreline, for instance at the Resounding Cliffs where the Northern spine peaked very high and wide.

Rai's mind released a tantalizing tendril of fragrant imagery and opened like a flower. A mental flash of great, hollowed out cliffs, standing hundreds of feet in height, their rocky spurs cut into the crashing surf, whipping foam from the peaks of the tall waves. To her left an expanse of black sand widened, drawing a broad line between the water and cliff walls. She looked out upon the waves, dizzy in her mind and yet her feet and body were solid, with sand between her toes as she walked on the beach of her memories. A name arose within her: Jeweled Cove.

Without thinking, Rai stood and cried out triumphantly, "Jeweled Cove!" She'd been hoping for this breakthrough! Not the sign of some unusual gift or talent, but instead a real memory.

The class turned as one to look at her. Rai wondered if she'd managed to awaken some of the bleary-eyed students from their naps. Headmaster John appeared quite startled at the rude interruption.

He crossed his arms and raised an eyebrow at her, even taking a few steps in her direction in response to her outburst. "Do you have something to share with the class, Mistress Durmah? What information concerning the Jeweled Cove near Resounding Cliffs do you wish to enlighten us with?"

Rai hesitated. All she had, at least right now, were images of the cliffs and surf, vivid though they may be. Rai was glad he'd recognized the name, confirming her memory was real. However, she had no idea what else the Cove represented. The class and Headmaster stared at her, and Rai's cheeks burned with embarrassment.

The Headmaster walked back to the map and touched a spot just up the coast from the Resounding Cliffs city. "This Jeweled Cove, Mistress Durmah?"

Rai looked at the point on the map and noticed the cave markings near to the Cove location he'd just pointed to. "Well yes and the caves as well, Headmaster." She tried to act confident and calmly met his gaze.

Headmaster John stared at her for a moment, brows knitting as he sought to work out her puzzle. All at once, his face relaxed, and he gave her a curious smile. "Did you mean to direct my lecture to the cave complexes at Jeweled Cove?"

Rai hesitated yet again. He didn't know about her amnesia, and thus wasn't testing her memory. Instead, she rolled the dice. "If you could, yes. I understand that they're quite remarkable?" she asked, hoping to draw the attention back toward the Headmaster.

"Indeed they are, but I wouldn't have expected you to have heard of them," he replied. Curiosity soon gave way to his desire to teach. "Please sit, Mistress Durmah, and I will address the geography of that area."

Rai sat, and the Headmaster continued with his lecture, covering the unique formations of caves meeting up with the ocean at Jeweled Cove. Here Az'Unda's deep cave complexes reached the briny ocean air, exposed to the sea at Jewel Cove, which rarely happened on the planet. He explained that this was a very difficult to reach location, and was only safe during the low tides. Unfortunately, the tides were under the influence of three moons, making for complex and somewhat unpredictable tidal schedules. The caves were in a state of partial collapse at the Cove, because of the relentless forces of the ocean tides constantly ripping them apart.

In the early years of the settlement, people tried to explore the caves and often disappeared. The area had been marked off-limits after repeated rescue efforts cost the young colony more lives. The Az'Un believed that the cave complexes ran deep, perhaps even merging with other cave systems further inland. They'd never identified hints of such an extensive network.

Rai gorged herself on these details--the first substantial link she had to her pre-amnesia memories. The possibility the amnesia was lifting filled her with hope, and she felt the flush on her cheeks fading and giving way to a rush of weightlessness in her chest.

The school bell rang, signaling the end of the afternoon session. A quick glance out the window confirmed the late hour--she should return to the Waystation before much longer. All of the students were jumping up and moving toward the door, eager to go back to their homes. The door was near the front of the class, so Rai had to wait until the other students filed out as she had sat in the rear.

"Have a good evening, students," the Headmaster spoke. "Remember tomorrow we cover the unique flora and fauna you can only find in the spines." The students streamed past him, not paying much heed on their way out.

"Mistress Durmah, could I have a word with you?" the Headmaster directed at Rai. By his tone, it was evident to Rai the following discussion was not optional. The other students shot her wide-eyed glances, happy to not be in her shoes.

Rai waited until most of the other students had cleared out and then approached his desk at the front of the classroom. Why she cared what the other students thought, she didn't know. Rai hadn't even bothered to talk to any of them yet.

"Yes, Headmaster John. Your lecture today was quite good. I really enjoyed it." Flattery didn't appease the Headmaster. She sensed his suspicion and impatience growing, so she quieted in hopes of not irritating him further.

"Mistress Rai, I am considering enrolling you in etiquette and eloquence training." Rai got the distinct impression that he was trying to figure her out, despite his vexation with her earlier behavior.

"This school offers classes in etiquette and eloquence?" Rai replied, surprised at the suggestion.

Headmaster John laughed in response. "Sadly, we do not. I'd argue you'd benefit greatly from such training, were it offered. Tell me, what school did you attend in your pre-Service years that allowed outbursts like the one you shared with my class today?"

Rai got the impression he was goading her, so she shifted her weight, unsure of how to respond without revealing her amnesia. "I can't remember a time my teachers ever encouraged my exuberance."

"Well, I'm sure they didn't, and neither do I." He held up his hands in a gentle plea. "Don't misunderstand me, I prefer my students to take an interest in their lessons. I must say, however, you spent most of the lecture staring out the window as if you'd rather be somewhere else. Then out of the blue, you disturbed the class with your comment."

"I'm quite sorry, Headmaster. I just thought they'd enjoy hearing about the history of the Jeweled Cove, given your discussion of cave geology."

"And I'm sure they did, but you could do us all the favor of making your future queries using the appropriate protocol in the future. You know, raise your hand and wait your turn. Asking your question in complete sentences would also be an enhancement to your communication style."

"I will keep that in mind, Headmaster. Again, I'm sorry that I offended you and that I disrupted your class."

"That's alright, Mistress Durmah. I just wanted to make sure you understood the expectations I have of my students. I must say I'm pleased you're devoting yourself to your schooling. I know it must be hard to get away from the Waystation, and your attendance is a testament to your desire to learn. I do wonder, however, if you might consider studying other subjects. Planetary history doesn't seem to captivate your attention. The discussion on Jeweled Cove was the first time I've seen you engaged in the debate."

Rai had signed up for the Headmaster's classes because she'd already met him. Getting to know other teachers would just expose her to more questions about herself. Usually, the Headmaster was too busy to speak with her one-on-one like this. She took Jesse's warnings about not sharing her amnesia seriously.

"Oh, I may appear bored, but I do like planetary history." She guessed telling the Headmaster she took his classes, in part at least, to avoid spending time with the Tinker Somnu wouldn't go over well.

Headmaster John gathered his things in preparation to leave for the day. Apparently, her argument wasn't terribly convincing in light of her disinterest during his lectures. "Well, you enjoyed hearing about the Cove. Did you grow up near Resounding Cliff's city?" He nonchalantly asked this, although her senses told her he was digging for more information on her.

"I'm afraid it wouldn't be proper to talk about that time. It precedes my life with the Durmah," Rai responded, pulling protocol on him this time.

The Headmaster now took a turn to apologize, a surprised look on his face. "Oh, I'm very sorry. I'd forgotten you're new to the Durmah Sept. I didn't mean to question you on a forbidden subject."

Rai doubted he forgot much. Still, he now knew she

wouldn't entertain questions about her past. Hopefully, that excuse would keep her from having to answer any further questions that might lead to suspicion of her amnesia.

Rai shrugged it off. "That's alright. I'm afraid I don't have enough of a history yet with the Durmah. I find it doesn't leave me with a lot to talk about sometimes."

"That will change in time."

Rai was tempted to like this man, despite his earlier chastisement. Not that she could trust him. So far, Jesse was the one she trusted most, and even she didn't know all of what was going on inside of Rai.

"I'm sure you're right. It's all just a matter of time," Rai replied, also thinking of her memories returning. Headmaster John nodded in agreement.

Rai stared at the map again, looking at the words 'Jeweled Cove' imprinted just north of the Resounding Cliffs city. Looking anew at the map, it struck her there was no ocean line drawn above the Great Northern spine. Was everything beyond that landmark merely wasteland?

"What's north of the Great Northern spine?" Rai asked without thinking. Someone who'd grown up there should know, after all.

She smelled curiosity swell anew within him. Someday she'd learn to think before she spoke. Someday.

"Oh, I'm sure I can find one of the old surveying maps for you if you're curious." A glint in his eye shone as he tried to comprehend the source of her interest. "There are no cities or settlements up there, so there's no point in adding it to the maps."

"Why haven't we settled that area?" Rai asked, not addressing his offer of full city maps.

"It's all highland area. The air's too thin for comfort for us up there."

"Oh, that explains it. Why have maps for a place you never go?" Rai said.

"Exactly. Shouldn't you be heading home? I don't mean to keep you beyond your appointed hour."

Looking out the window, Rai realized it was getting late. The Waystation was only a few minutes away from the school so she wouldn't get back too late.

"I'd better be going. Thanks for humoring my questions," Rai replied.

"We'll see you tomorrow?" Headmaster John asked.

"If I can get away," Rai promised half-heartedly while walking out the door. After staying so late today, it wasn't likely Jesse would let her attend tomorrow as well. Still, if the Headmaster found more accurate maps, it could be worth the trip. Rai bounded out the door, eager to share her news with Jesse.

The Headmaster looked at her. Rai feared she'd not only risen to the level of high-maintenance student but also one with a mysterious history. At least her past was a little less mysterious to her today, with the newfound memory of the Cove. This brought a smile to her face while she jogged home.

CHAPTER 25

RAI RETURNED TO A QUIET WAYSTATION, AT LEAST compared to the prior few nights of singing and storytelling. For the first night in days, Tinker Somnu wasn't entertaining the crowd, and because of this, the Waystation's patronage had dwindled to near-normal amounts, with only about half of the tables full. Rai breathed a sigh of relief, happy for the return to normalcy. Jesse stood behind the bar and motioned her over. Somnu sat over in the far alcove, talking one-on-one with a patron.

"Good day at school?" Jesse greeted her as she cleaned off the spigots on the beer barrels.

Rai leaned against the bar. "Yes. You might say it's beginning to have the desired effect."

Jesse tilted her head, looking back over her shoulder at her while she worked. "Is that so? How about we talk about what you learned today over an early dinner?" Jesse called over one of the staff to tend the bar for her and to bring over some food, and then she and Rai sauntered toward Jesse's preferred alcove.

Somnu waved at them, and Jesse motioned for him to come over and join them. Rai gritted her teeth, not wanting to share this newfound information with him. However, it was evident to her that excluding him now wasn't an option, not with Jesse inviting him to join them. Through a series of discussions over the past week, Jesse had made it clear to Rai that Somnu was a trusted and reliable resource. What about him bothered her enough to continue defying her sister?

"Does this explain why you're back later than normal?" Jesse asked as they sat down at the table.

"Yeah, it does. I'm sorry about that. You know I don't want to make things harder on you," Rai explained.

"Ah, don't worry. Today's been quiet, what with Somnu just finishing his business here. I doubt it will get busy until a bit later, after the dinner crowd."

Rai hoped that meant he'd be leaving soon. The sooner, the better, she thought. "What business is that?"

"Tinker business." The waiter arrived, and they paused in the conversation a moment while he placed the food on the table.

All Rai had observed Somnu do was sing, craft stories, drink, and chat it up with the patrons. "What's his business, besides singing and storytelling?"

Jesse opened her mouth to answer, but was cut off by the arrival of Somnu to their table. He appeared a bit pensive, in contrast to his usual jovial attitude. Rai wondered if something in his business was troubling him, but what that might be?

"Good afternoon ladies." Somnu greeted them, taking a seat across from them both. "What's on your minds?"

"Well, my sister here had a productive day at school, and I thought you'd enjoy hearing about it as well," Jesse said.

"Is that so?" he asked. He leaned on the table, his attention focused on the conversation. "Did you get the whole puzzle or just a piece?"

With their joint attention so focused, Rai brushed off her reticence and decided to share, despite Somnu's presence.

"Just a piece, I'm afraid, but at least it's something." She paused, debating how to tell the tale, but both Jesse and Somnu waited. "It was during Headmaster John's lecture on Az'Un geology. He described how the cave complexes run along the feet of the spines, and a memory just opened to me."

Rai closed her eyes, letting the image permeate her mind completely. "I stood on a beach. There was black sand underneath my bare feet, chill, and damp. On both sides, the beach ended at the rising walls of craggy cliffs. The tide rolled in around me, beating against the cliff walls in a deafening thunder. The damp wind whipped at the waves. The sun hid behind the clouds; I think a storm was forming. Behind me, a large gaping mouth in the cliff wall stood. It wasn't bright enough out to see far into the cave."

"And you were alone?" Somnu asked his voice quiet. Rai sensed the concern in his voice.

Rai opened her eyes, still in the daze of her memory. It was so clear to her; she smelled the ocean even now. Considering Somnu's question, Rai frowned. "I'm not sure. I don't see anyone else in this memory, just myself."

"What else was on the beach? Wreckage from a ship or a boat, tied off?" Somnu asked.

"No, the beach was clear. Just rocks, shells, and sand. Nothing else."

"Do you remember your emotions at that moment? Upset? Afraid? Alone?" Somnu asked.

Was this how he honed his stories? By delving into other people's minds?

"I'm not sure. It's not clear to me what was going on. I think I was afraid, but not alone. I do know I knew the name of the place: Jeweled Cove."

Somnu leaned back in his chair and let out a low whistle. Jesse's face mirrored Rai's frown. This was also new territory for her.

"Is that Cove still declared off-limits?" Jesse asked Somnu.

"Oh yeah." He nodded. "It has been for the past few hundred years. Still, that doesn't stop some of the locals around there from trying to explore it anyway, despite the risks. Is that all you remember?" he directed at Rai.

"I'm afraid so. It creates a larger puzzle than it solves. Still, it's nice to remember something. Anything."

"That it is, my girl, that it is. This memory might also yield more useful information than you'd at first think." Somnu sat and pondered.

"What do you mean?" Rai asked.

Somnu looked around first; ensuring no one was near enough to overhear him or her. "First off, that Cove is about a day north of the city by wagon, and about a half-day by boat. It just makes sense, as there are no other towns along that coastline, and not many safe harbors there either. Resounding Cliffs has a large, open bowl of a bay that shelters the city. Therefore, I'd say we should consider that you grew up in Resounding Cliffs."

"Secondly, your birth family must be fishers. Not just river fishers either, but likely bay anglers. Boating down south here or at Raven's Call is just too dangerous, what with the unpredictable ocean tides. Further north the ocean waves improve, and some brave folks are willing to take the risk. That narrows down the search to a small handful of Septs in Resounding Cliffs."

Jesse and Rai exchanged looks and shrugs. This conjecture of Somnu's might help them to understand Rai's past, so they awaited his conclusion.

"Now we can't confirm any of this yet," Somnu continued after a brief pause, "but consider this possible scenario. Some time ago, your birth Sept set out for a day of boating and fishing with you. We can't know exactly when, as we don't know how long your stay of service at the Temple took. That could have been months or years in length."

"Anyway, as you were out boating, either by chance or by choice, you came upon the cove. A storm might have caused the ship to sink, and then you swam ashore. A deliberate choice to go there may have netted the same effect. Any Sept that's willing to defy the quarantine on that Cove isn't too fond of the Temples and their edicts, that's for sure."

"Why would anyone want to go there?" Jesse asked. "I mean, it's off-limits because it's dangerous, right?"

"True enough. Still, there are tales of the cave walls

lined with precious stones. Thus, the name 'Jeweled Cove,' Somnu informed them.

"Well, I don't remember anything about that," Rai jumped in. "Just the beach."

"I doubt you would," Somnu interjected. "Those are just ancient tales, from the early days of settlement when we were still exploring and not yet accustomed to this world. The most probable scenario, with the memory you rediscovered today, is that you beached there after a storm."

"Perhaps the Matriarch of Raven's Call was telling the truth," Jesse added, bringing dubious looks from both of them. "I mean, she told Stoi and Meik you'd been injured before being brought to the Temple. She believed your amnesia occurred under the care of your birth Sept. Perhaps that moment you remember, on the beach, is your first memory after your injury," Jesse explained.

"Right, so maybe I'm recovering the post-injury memories? So, in theory, the Temple's medicinal or crèche-induced amnesia is finally wearing off, allowing me to know what happened before that?" Rai asked. The thought that this could be just a small step to regaining her full memory disheartened her. Still, it was the first of many such steps, she hoped.

"Sure, that's possible," Somnu agreed. "Still, until more of your memories surface or we're able to locate your birth Sept, we can't know for sure. Have you had any more of your nightmares?"

With her caution toward him, Rai wasn't sure she'd tell him the truth if she'd had more of them. She hadn't, however, so the choice was simple.

"No," Rai replied, "I haven't." Jesse gave her a probing look, seeking to confirm her honesty. Rai merely shrugged in return.

"Well, my girl, I know you don't want to have any more of those nightmares. But if you do, they may provide valuable information, so try to write down as much detail as you can. You never know what may solve the mystery," Somnu replied. He appeared so earnest, Rai wanted to trust him. Almost.

"I'm headed out of town in the morning, to Resounding Cliffs where I can try and figure out this mystery. I'll be discreet, but I owe it to the Durmah to do what I can to help out." Somnu respectfully inclined his head toward Jesse.

"You don't have to go all the way there just for me," Rai replied, shocked that he'd go so far out of his way.

Somnu chuckled. "Nah girl, I needed to get out that way again regardless. It's been a few months, and people are starting to ask for me again."

"What do you do, traveling around as you do?" Rai asked, finally comfortable enough to ask him.

"Tinker things!" Somnu replied, his attitude bringing a laugh from Jesse. He turned serious, leaning forward conspiratorially. "In all seriousness, besides the odd jobs fixing tech things I also do a bit of research on the side for folks. People make sure it's worth my time, and every-one's happy."

"So investigating my past is right up your alley?" Rai asked, and Somnu inclined his head in response. "I'd better start thinking up a way to repay you," Rai replied, not at all liking the idea of being indebted to this man; a man she still did not trust.

"Oh, I already said, I owe it to the Durmah. That and more," he replied. Still, as his eyes met hers, Rai got the distinct impression that he did this as a favor to the Durmah, but not necessarily to her. Rai also wondered what he owed the Durmah for, but decided not to ask.

"Oh! I'd almost forgot," Jesse said. "A temple healer came by today for you Rai, wanting to make sure those 'special' medicinals were working out for you. She was kind enough to leave another batch. She also asked that you stop by and get tested to make sure the treatment level is sufficient." Jesse shared all of this in a rather tongue-in-cheek fashion, clearly not pleased by the visit.

That mention of the medicinals made Rai's skin crawl, reminding her of the numbing effects they'd induced. "Do you think I have to go to the hospice now? If they test me they'll know I'm only taking the conventional plague treatments," Rai said, scared of what they'd do if they found out. It hadn't occurred to her that they'd follow up and check on her. Somnu eyed her carefully, and Rai realized that she hadn't shared that particular moment at the Temple with him. It didn't surprise him, however, and Rai suspected that Jesse told him about it when she wasn't there.

"No," Jesse stated. "You do everything you can to avoid them. I told the Healer that I'd supervised you taking the special medicinal myself. I also told her that we'd send you by if anything unusual came up, but that we've just been too busy to spare the time right now, and it would distress our business to do without you.

She wasn't willing to challenge me, or my honor, beyond that. She said she'd be by in another couple weeks to deliver the next batch, and then she left in a huff."

"What did you do with it?" Rai asked.

"Out in the storehouse. Why, you thinking of taking it?"

"Never," Rai replied. "I just wanted to know where it was."

"If you two will excuse me, I'd better get back to business before someone gets curious and comes over here," Somnu explained, standing and turning away from the alcove. "Do let me know if you remember anything else before I leave in the morning, all right Rai?"

"Thanks again for your efforts. I sincerely appreciate it," Rai replied, smiling at him for perhaps the first time since they'd met. She still didn't trust him, but Rai found fewer and fewer reasons to treat him poorly. Jesse also took note of her shift in attitude, and smiled warmly at both of them. Rai considered that it was often easier to go with the flow than stand your ground.

Somnu walked over to her and leaned close. "Don't lose hope, my girl. It's all bound to become known. Nothing stays hidden in the mists of memory forever," he replied. He clapped her gently on the arm and walking off toward the far alcove.

Although his flesh hadn't touched hers--he'd merely felt the fabric of her shirtsleeve--his presence lingered. Although Rai'd sworn to herself she'd stop using her gifts lest she be caught in the act, she'd picked up scents from that brief moment and couldn't help but focus on them.

Somnu held suspicion and distrust toward her, which didn't mesh with his otherwise sweet demeanor.

Continuing to stare at his back, those emotions became more intense. For a second Rai was certain Somnu viewed her as a threat, and one he was determined to expose. At that moment, almost in response to her probe, Somnu turned back and met her gaze. His icy eyes met hers, and Rai sensed a deep hatred in him. Still, he donned an affable demeanor and took a seat in the far alcove, his eyes bright with interest. Rai got the distinct impression that Somnu would stop at nothing to know her past, and he suspected something he hadn't yet shared with her. What he'd do once he knew, she had no idea. Rai shivered from the chill creeping up her spine.

"Are you alright? Is it another flashback?" Jesse asked, noting Rai's expression.

"Oh sorry. I'm all right," Rai replied, trying to pretend she hadn't just sensed Somnu's dark side. Rai chastised herself for opening up to him. You never knew what someone would do with information, and she didn't like the idea of him knowing what Jeweled Cove meant to her. Now more than ever, Rai doubted he had her best interests at heart. Although why he should think of her as some sort of threat, she couldn't begin to fathom.

"It's just a lot to think about," Rai replied.

"You don't do things the easy way, do you, sis?"

"Oh wait, there's an easy way?" Rai joked back at her, feigning ignorance.

"I'm sure there is, but I don't think I can tell you how to find it." Jesse laughed. "What I can say is that the pantry needs restocking and the linens need an inventory. Think you can handle that tonight?"

Rai was grateful for something simple to worry about. "That sounds grand, Jess. I'll get right on it." She was even more grateful about Somnu's imminent departure in the morning.

CHAPTER 26

#BEGIN TRANSMISSION#
#ROUTING CODE: GUARDIAN
GRAEBER, GUARDIAN SEPT,
ROAMING COM H3-29Y TO
MATRIARCH BAULEEL,
RAVEN'S CALL TEMPLE,
RAVEN'S CALL#
#ENCRYPTION: HIGH#
GRAEBER: Regrettably, my concerns
over latent physical memories were
entirely justified. It's clear the girl has
ceased taking the sensory inhibiting
medicinals.

Today in the local market, I observed her
blithely reading others, without
concern for the possible
consequences. If she tries to harness
her skills, especially without the
memory of how to master them, she

can't help but draw undue attention.
We must ensure that does not happen
or all that we have worked for will be
lost. Act quickly to get her back on the
treatments before I run out of options.

BAULEEL: This is distressing news. I've
ordered a visit to the girl by the
Temple healers, so soon she'll be back
on the special inhibiting treatment. I
share your concern over her latent
memories resurfacing despite our
precautions but do realize this may
happen regardless of whether or not
she's taking the treatment. It's only an
added layer of protection, not a
guarantee.

GRAEBER: I hope that visit will be early
enough. She could quickly become a
danger in this state, and I fear our
efforts may have been doomed from
the start.

BAULEEL: I don't believe that if the girl
regains her, shall we call them 'gifts,'
that they will necessarily cause
problems. As long as she integrates
into her new Sept for a few years,
what does it matter? Watch how she
utilizes the abilities first before taking
action. I bet she'll sense they're
abnormal and do her best to hide
them.

You must decide for yourself how far you're willing to allow this trial to progress. I trust your judgment. I know you won't allow things to deteriorate past a reasonable level.

The best outcome is for the girl to blend in and accept her new home. I still wish the cold-sleep crèche had been a viable option, but those were too obvious, and well watched by the others. Regardless, we must endeavor to keep her hidden. Every day that passes increases the likelihood the Anemoi won't discover her and what we've done to hide her.

GRAEBER: This girl has never done well at keeping a low profile. Add to that her abilities, and thus you have my concerns.

BAULEEL: I understand, but we have few other options. Please continue as planned.

I've been spending lots of time with the Techs of late. The Zebio boy you found may have a natural immunity to the plague. Can you imagine? A boy with innate immunity. Why it took nearly six hundred years to manifest vexes me.

I'll let you know what develops, but I'm hopeful. It's been far too long.

#END TRANSMISSION#

Bᴀᴜʟᴇᴇʟ ᴡᴀɪᴛᴇᴅ ꜰᴏʀ ᴛʜᴇ sᴇᴄᴜʀɪᴛʏ ᴅᴏᴏʀ ᴛᴏ ᴛʜᴇ Technician's wing to open, hoping Journeyman Rilte would have additional news on the Zebio boy's status. She'd visited once since her initial meeting with Terem, and at that time, his lucid and articulate mental state had impressed her. Bauleel estimated he'd been three weeks into living with the virus by now, a first for any of the Techs' subjects to date. Finished with the analysis on her blood sample, the security door beeped and slid open.

The Matriarch stepped into the research facility's arboretum and found it unusually sparse for the hour. It was post-dinnertime for the Temple folk, but Bauleel doubted the Techs had all gone to bed already. She headed for the testing labs and heard muted voices coming from behind the doors. If she didn't know the Tech's better, Bauleel would have sworn the discussion was not just a heated debate but also an argument.

Outside of her usual style, and to return their tempers to a level more appropriate to scientific debate, Bauleel opened the heavy door and stepped into a very crowded room with a bit of flourish. Bauleel counted heads--almost the entire group stood assembled here tonight. Whatever this was--her timing was impeccable. However, no one took notice of Bauleel's grand entrance and this in itself was unexpected. Although the Tech's didn't grant the Matriarch the same deference as the other Temple folk or general populace, Bauleel thought it somewhat surprising when they ignored her completely.

She observed a lively debate taking place across the room, but it was so animated Bauleel was at first unable to grasp the heart of the problem. Overcoming her initial irritation, Bauleel realized that this was the first time she'd been able to watch a Tech discussion without them noticing. The novelty of seeing one of their private conversations kept Bauleel quiet for a few moments longer.

"Look, let's review the progressions again, as there's still a bit of disagreement," the grey-templed Chief Girand spoke. His deep voice filled the room, drowning out everyone else. He stood in front of a projection whiteboard, which displayed a set of test results. She couldn't make out the details but realized that they'd surely notice her if she moved toward the front. The room was simply too packed, and she too short and apparent in her attire.

"With all due respect, Girand, I don't think any further review will cause us to change our minds!" Bauleel didn't recognize the speaker but was amazed the woman didn't address Girand by his title. The lady must have been almost thirty and had long blonde hair.

"The facts are simple. So simple, in fact, that I can restate them for everyone's benefit in less than a minute," she continued her argument, pacing back and forth in front of the group.

"A young, male subject develops a resistance to the plague treatments. Shortly after that, the subjects' system succumbs to the plague, and we monitor him here under lockdown. His state slowly deteriorates over a period of three weeks. Disregarding the lengthened timeframe of his decline, this case is no different from any of the others we've witnessed over the past few decades. There is a great danger in thinking this situation is different from what we've all seen before. We need to end this study before one, or more of us is endangered by the fruitless nature of the observations." She stressed this last point, a grave look on her face.

Whispers erupted all around. Clearly, she was not the only one concerned with the possible dangers of keeping a plague-ridden boy under observation long-term.

"Don't be ridiculous, Selna!" rebutted Journeyman Rilte. Bauleel once again noted the lack of title being used and wondered if this was just because of the heated debate, or if this was standard within this isolated Sept. "Yes, his state has deteriorated, but markedly slower than any other subjects to date. That alone is something deserving further study!"

Bauleel despaired internally. The Techs were debating terminating Terem. How could that be? He must have immunity!

"I share your interest in the boy, Rilte, and everything research into his progress can mean for Az'Unda!" Selna replied. "And I'd back an extended study of this subject if I agreed it prudent. However, the boy's experienced two full-blown psychotic episodes in the past three days!" Selna's raised voice and manic pacing grated on Bauleel's nerves.

"We can't yet know if those episodes are indicative of

dementia due to disease progression or the result of his confinement and loneliness," Chief Girand said in what Bauleel considered more levelheaded tones. She also noted that his reasoned tones seemed to demand more respect from the group, as most quieted their murmurs as he'd begun to talk.

"Have you watched the recordings of his episodes? Do you believe those rants of his were uninfluenced by the sickness within him?" she asked. Bauleel made a mental note to acquire a copy and watch it herself.

"I was present during one of them," Chief Girand replied. "Although it was disconcerting, I can't say whether it marked a progression of the plague into his mental state or not."

"Let's assume it isn't from the sickness itself, but instead his mental state. Look at the numbers on the sedation dosages required since he was brought here, including those two episodes."

Selna keyed the control panel and brought up a new graph. The first part of the curve showed moderate amounts but then consistently rose on the next dose. There'd been two significant jumps in dosage, and Bauleel assumed spikes corresponded to the dates of Terem's psychotic episodes. The chart was clear, each dose built upon the level of the last one, with the levels practically quadrupling over the last three days. Bauleel wondered at what level the dosage became toxic.

"Is it normal for individuals to build up a tolerance to the sedation medicinals?" asked a teenage boy. Bauleel didn't recognize the young Apprentice, but assumed at his age that he was quite new to the Technician Sept.

"Yes, Bente, that is indeed normal. However, this subject's tolerance to the sedation medicinals has risen much more quickly than normal," Selna replied.

"So, besides the boy requiring more of the medicinals that average, what's the primary concern?" Bente asked.

"The concern, at least to some of us here, is that the sedating medicinal is also used in much larger amounts for terminations," Selna replied. Girand frowned in response to Selna's explanation. "What do we do if the boy becomes immune to the treatment and we're unable to find a suitable replacement method when the time comes to euthanize? He will become resistant to the medicinal eventually--particularly at these dosage levels. What happens when his system succumbs to the plague, and we're left searching for a humane method of destruction?"

With this question, the murmurs in the room grew again in volume. Selna wasn't the only one wondering what would happen, and Bauleel heard fearful comments close to herself. It was a reasonable consideration, but Bauleel's larger worry centered on Terem not offering the solutions she'd hoped for.

Girand moved to the whiteboard and keyed up a different graph, one showing a much more gradual curve. He turned back to the group, and all quieted in anticipation of his next words.

"This graph charts the progressions I mentioned earlier. According to this, we will most likely have some additional weeks--perhaps even months' worth of study on this subject. We cannot predict the depth of value that we may reap from patience in this case. We've only begun studying the samples taken from the boy. Imagine what may be possible in the next few weeks!"

"I'm not the oldest Tech here, but I doubt that any of you older than me remember having the opportunity to conduct experiments with a live subject. Our modus operandi has forever been to collect samples while the subject wastes away, and analyze the data and compile our reports after the fact. This subject represents an opportunity to test out treatments on a live, infected subject. None of us may have a chance like this again in our lifetimes." Girand paused a moment, letting his diatribe sink in on the assembled ears.

"In my opinion, the unique nature of this case merits taking a few risks," Girand said. Bauleel had the clear impression he did not intend to bend from his stance. If he did, she would step in and over rule his orders. This case was indeed a unique opportunity.

Selna stood her ground. "All of that may be true, but you didn't address my question, Girand. What happens when his system does fail? If he doesn't die naturally, we will have to euthanize him. How can we do that if the standard medicinals fail?"

Rilte broke into the conversation, voice angry. "Last time I checked, Selna, it was our job to develop new treatments for the plague. This boy's survival extends our ability to test those on a live subject."

At Selna's surprised look at Rilte's response to her question, Bauleel wondered if Selna even realized that she was coming across as abrasive.

"And what about the risk to ourselves? The boy's

state will degenerate over time, and in all likelihood, he will become dangerous during this process."

"Isn't it our job to take risks?" Rilte replied. "After all, how is this danger any larger than the one each and every Az'Un takes every day when they hope our medicinals will protect them, or the risk the Guardians take defending us from Terrors every day, or the risk new mothers take serving our colony with birth after birth? We all take our own risks."

"The Guardians have toxins which are lethal to the plague. It's how they kill the Terrors. Surely one of those will be sufficient to terminate the boy when it becomes necessary," Bauleel said, choosing to end her silent watching and the mounting quarrel.

For well over a minute, everyone turned to stare at her, adjusting not only to the presence of the Matriarch but his or her previous lack of acknowledging her arrival. Selna was unable to close her mouth. Rilte appeared surprised but amused with this turn of events. He at least gave her a slight, brief nod. She'd managed to quiet the room even more efficiently than Chief Girand.

With the attention of the entire room, Bauleel walked up to the whiteboard and studied the progression chart up close. She hoped that if she acted like her attendance was an entirely reasonable thing that no one would dare ask how long she'd been listening. More importantly, Bauleel wanted the conversation to continue, anxious to hear more of the debate.

Girand bowed at her approach. "I wasn't aware, Esteemed Matriarch, that the Guardian's also developed medicinals to combat the plague?"

"Oh, well, they don't research cures as you do. You find treatments to forestall the progress of the disease, inhibit viral replication, and safeguard the populace. They, instead, seek out that which will kill not only the virus but also its host. They strive to eliminate their threats, not give them a nap, or keep them dormant."

"Hmm," Girand replied. "Still, perhaps you could arrange for an information exchange between our Septs? It'd be nice to have additional termination options on hand when the need arises. Besides, it's possible that they've discovered something we could use, in diluted or cut form, to treat the virus."

"I'd be happy to arrange a visit for you," Bauleel replied, pleased to have shifted the tone of the conversation. "I'll even make sure they bring plenty of samples in case you have an immediate need. Chieftess Raza will be most accommodating."

"We are most grateful for your assistance." Chief Girand inclined his head slightly. Bauleel heard uncomfortable shifting through the hush in the room.

"I'm sorry for disturbing your meeting, Chief Girand. I came to have another look at the boy and catch up on his progress."

"Your visits are never an inconvenience, Matriarch," Girard replied.

"I can escort you in to see him now if you'd like," offered Rilte.

"Thank you, Journeyman Rilte," Bauleel replied.

Rilte gestured for her to follow, and they walked down the room toward the door leading to the holding cells. Techs moved out of their way. Rilte opened the door without unlocking it or even using the doorplate. Was this outer door ever locked? With all of the attention Terem drew, the traffic must keep them from securing it regularly.

Passing into the room, Rilte closed the door behind them.

"Would you prefer privacy, Matriarch?"

"Yes, please," Bauleel replied. He keyed in a security code, and the light on the door lock switched from green to red. "My thanks."

Bauleel walked to Terem's cell and noted the dimmed light. She raised her veil and tucked it back behind her ears. She'd gotten in the habit of removing her veil while she talked with Terem, as it appeared to calm him.

Terem lay on the cot, sleeping peacefully. Looking at his face, Bauleel was amazed at the serene expression. His skin didn't look as pallid as before, and Bauleel could swear he was improving. However, the room was disorderly, with stacks of the promised books laid haphazardly around the room. His half-buttoned shirt also lent to his state of disarray.

"He looks better."

"I agree, even his mental state has improved overall, except for the episodes. Do you want me to wake him, Matriarch?"

"Oh no, don't do that. He looks so relaxed. Please, call me Bauleel."

"If you prefer, Bauleel." It was odd, yet comforting, to hear someone call her by her actual name. Someone who wasn't Anemoi.

"What was all that about, anyway?"

Rilte leaned down toward her. "How much did you hear?"

"Enough, but I missed what initiated the disagreement."

"Ah, well Terem, I suppose." Rilte stared at the boy.

"Was it the psychotic episodes?" Bauleel asked. Rilte's gaze fixed on her, and by the confused look on his face, Bauleel suspected he had witnessed at least one of the episodes.

"Yes, the last happened early this morning, and it was pronounced. They're odd because his health and mental states have improved otherwise. Everyone is worried what it means. Those like Selna don't want to wait to find out."

"Can you describe to me what happened?" Bauleel asked.

"I'd rather not."

"When can I get the recording?" Bauleel asked, not wanting to push him into recounting the tale.

"They'll want to review the data and include an official interpretation and summary before handing one over to you. I'm afraid you'll have to wait a day or two."

"Typical. Well, I can't ask a Tech to do a fair job, can I? Wouldn't be proper, after all."

Rilte shook his head at her humor, but the confused look didn't leave his eyes. "Terem ranted, Bauleel. He talked about bizarre things."

Terem's sleeping form again drew her attention. "Such as?"

"He threatened us. Said he'd kill every Tech for

'bringing him pain.' He said he finally understood that we are the evil on this planet, and he wouldn't stop until he'd destroyed us all."

"Bizarre delusions, indeed. He can't be the first to blame the Techs and not the plague for his illnesses."

"No. However, you didn't see his eyes, his face. I'd swear it wasn't even him talking, he looked so disturbed. This malevolent hatred somehow just took voice within him. It didn't even sound like his voice."

"Have you asked him about the rants afterward, when he's more lucid?"

"Yes, we have, and he doesn't remember a thing. It's not as if he's embarrassed and won't admit to it. He truly doesn't remember."

"How long do they last?"

"The first one lasted for only a few minutes, and Terem spoke little. He merely paced and glared at us. The second episode rambled on for nearly twenty minutes, during which he talked about our coming destruction. During each episode, we sedated him. The second time it took a couple of doses to bring him down."

"I want you to alert me the next time it happens. While it's going on," Bauleel said.

"You want to watch it in person?" Rilte replied. "You're going to drop what you're doing and come running?"

"Yes," Bauleel stated.

"Why?" Rilte asked. "Why would you want to subject yourself to his madness?"

"Because, Rilte, this psychotic boy is the best hope we have right now of finding a cure. My presence calms and reassures him. If I'm here when it happens again, perhaps it will make a difference."

"I hope you're right, Bauleel. If it doesn't, and his state worsens, the Techs will vote to terminate."

Bauleel couldn't very well return to the Elders with news that the boy had died without yielding more hope of overcoming the plague.

"I can't allow that to happen. I will supersede Chief Girard and the other Techs on this. Terem must live, until the very end. All attempts to harvest data are worth the risks involved."

Rilte sucked in a breath. "That won't make you very popular with Selna and the others."

"I know, Rilte, but I have to do what I feel best."

Rilte met her gaze, the concern he held blatantly evident. "I understand. You're the Matriarch."

Bauleel turned back to Terem's holding cell and reached up to the glass, grasping onto the tenuous state of her own hope. "Yes, I am the Matriarch."

CHAPTER 27

PONAR ARRIVED AT THE DURMAH SEPT HOUSE IN Raven's Call city full of anxiety over reuniting with his mother, Kait. The last time they'd talked, Kait had made it abundantly clear there would be no more delays choosing a wife from the available candidates she'd approved. It wasn't that he didn't want to marry; just that he had no interest in any of the choices at hand. Ponar had watched Stoi and Chirey together, and he knew they loved each other deeply. They had definite chemistry going for them, in spite of the occasional argument. Conversely, Ponar had noted a complete lack of chemistry with all of the girls Kait had selected for him.

Ponar pulled into the stable yard and spotted Meik's unhitched travel wagon. Another wave of anxiety rippled through Ponar. Now he knew he'd get Kait, Stoi, and likely Meik pressuring him to marry. After observing how unhappy Meik had been with his wife, it always confused Ponar why he'd be so pro-marriage for others. Ponar mused that perhaps Meik just didn't want anyone else escaping from his consigned fate. Regardless, Ponar foresaw many matrimonious debates this evening around the hearth.

Stable hand Matieus emerged from the main hall. "Master Ponar! It's good to see you again!"

"Matieus, well met. Have things been busy today?" Ponar stepped down off the wagon and unhitched the horse on the left.

Matieus helped unhitch the other horse. "No Sir, it's been a slow day today. Master Meik returned yesterday, so there was the usual business getting everything unloaded, delivered, stored and then reloaded."

Despite Ponar's extended absence, the horses' whinnied welcomes to Matieus, which he rewarded with a quick pat and chunks of red fruit pulled from his pocket while they walked them to the stables. Ponar shook his head at his indulgence. The man spoilt the horses as a matter of course.

"Is Meik leaving again tomorrow?" Ponar asked.

"Oh, I'd suspect so, Master Ponar. You'll be turning things around pretty quick too, as you usually do?"

"Likely so, Matieus. You know how busy Barrow's Grove and the swamplands keep me," Ponar replied.

"Oh, I know sir. Quite busy indeed!"

As it was late in the afternoon already, Ponar figured most of the family would be preparing for dinner or already eating. "Do you mind finishing up with the horses while I unload the wagon?" Ponar asked.

"Not a problem Sir," Matieus replied and set himself entirely to the task.

Ponar began unloading his wagon's contents into the

storehouse, glad for the mindless pure physical labor. He might have asked another steward to help him unload, but doing this alone allowed him to delay the inevitable marriage questions and demands yet another few moments. Every moment counted.

During the entire trip back to Raven's Call, his mind drifted between thoughts of his mother's expectations of him and the time he'd spent with Rai in Kiya's Grace. It was no different now. In fact, the closer he came to confronting Kait, the more his time with Rai flooded his mind. He didn't know why Rai captivated him, but against his better judgment and Jesse's advice, he'd been unable to get Rai out of his mind. He'd experienced the spark with her, powerfully and intensely. Their night-long conversation had brought him closer to her than Ponar had been to any member of his Sept for years. The irony wasn't lost on him that the one woman he wanted was also untouchable. Ponar knew Jesse and the others all thought he was quite the ladies' man, quickly flirting with any attractive woman he ran into. Just because he'd fall into conversations with people he'd just met didn't make that so.

Ponar remembered waking up next to Rai. The image of her short, curly hair framing the pale, milky skin of her face like a cloud had never left him. She'd been so vulnerable to him at that moment. He wished he could do something to quiet the inner demons he sensed haunted her. Perhaps it was her amnesia, but he sensed there was a deep, brooding, longing in her, and he feared she was searching for something she'd never find. He'd laid there beside her for the greater part of an hour, watching her breathe and wondering how things might have been different if she'd been marriageable.

Rai had let out a soft groan and shifted fetchingly in the bed. Ponar remembered reaching out, softly running his hand down her face to soothe her. That had triggered an incredible response. At the moment his flesh touched hers, she'd awoken and attacked him. Her hands found easy purchase around his neck. He'd been stunned and angry at the time, wondering what sort of a person laid with a man one moment, and tried to strangle him the next. Now he regretted yelling at her because it had quickly become clear that she'd acted defensively to some veiled threat from her dreams. The utter bewilderment on her face had convinced him of that.

After their discussion that afternoon with Jesse, Ponar had wanted to pull Rai into his arms and comfort her, but it hadn't been the time or the place, and he feared to have only upset her and Jesse. She'd been so distraught to find out they were Septmates, he hadn't known what to say or do to make it better. He'd been upset too, but he'd known by her tattoo she was barren, and therefore not someone of marriageable status anyway, so he'd already accepted the doomed nature of their encounter. He accepted he couldn't publicly admit to their attraction, but that didn't mean he would or could let go of his desire for her. Time would bring them together again, and opportunities would arise.

Ponar finished unloading the wagon and emerged from the storehouse. Meik's appearance startled him out of his reverie about Rai.

"You planning to work all night, or are you going to

come in and eat something while the food's still hot?" Meik bellowed out to him across the stable yard.

"I wanted to get unloaded before dark," Ponar replied. Ponar grabbed a towel out of the wagon to mop up his sweat.

"Never a bad plan, but you could have had the stewards do it!" Meik replied. "You should know your mother's aware you've arrived, and she just can't wait to catch up with you."

"I'm sure she can't."

Meik laughed. "Don't worry; she'd got bigger things bothering her tonight than bugging you again about choosing a wife."

"I don't think Mom ever gets too busy to not nag me! I'm in need of a change before dinner, however."

"Nonsense, stop worrying about how you look and get on inside before she comes out here looking for you."

"Good point," Ponar agreed. "I guess it's a bit late to delay at this juncture."

Meik shrugged at his comment. "You got to eat too."

"Oh yeah, food would be nice," Ponar replied.

They headed inside to the dining hall and the associated familial pressures. The happy screeches of children greeted him, and they crowded around, hugging greedily at his legs. Their hubbub effectively drew the attention of everyone in the hall, and he greeted many in the crowd while he returned the children's affections. Just as quickly as they'd run to him, the novelty of his arrival passed, and the small horde ran off toward the secondary hearth, and to the post-dinner games they'd been playing.

Kait, Nele, and Laan sat at the oval table nearest the

original hearth. Kait waved them both over. Steeling himself, he walked over to join them, Meik at his side. Were the tense looks on their faces due to his arrival or something else?

Ponar approached Kait, leaned over her and placed a kiss on her forehead. "Good evening, Mother." He took the chair next to her. Meik sat across from them, next to Laan. Nele sat at the end of the table. Did Kait invite Nele into the conversation or had she just helped herself to a seat? Nodding at Nele and Laan, he said sincerely, "Good to see you all. It's been too long."

"That it has," replied Laan. "Welcome home. Help yourself to some food while it's still hot."

"My, son, at long last, welcome home," Kait replied. "Did you come here on the road from Kiya's Grace?"

"Yes, Mother," Ponar replied. "I took the high road along the Baris Spine because of travel advisories along the coastal route." He heaped sausages from a serving platter onto an available plate.

"I trust your trip here was uneventful?" Kait asked, her pinched brow indicated she expected some form of trouble. Laan, Meik, and Nele all waited expectantly for his response.

"Quite. What's going on?"

"Stoi and I had some trouble on our last trip to Kiya's Grace," Laan explained. "Iron wolves," he said as if that explained everything.

"Yes, I'd heard about that. I'm grateful everyone made it through all right," Ponar replied.

"So you've met our newest addition?" Kait asked.

"I have," Ponar replied, keeping his voice and expression neutral. "I spent a night at Jesse's Waystation on my way here. I barely had time to drop off supplies and pick up new cargo before moving along." Ponar focused on the food in front of him, hoping he appeared nonchalant about his visit.

"Hah, I bet Jesse kicked you out!" Laan laughed.

Ponar inclined his head. "Jesse insisted I come directly home. She implied my presence was desired here." Ponar finished, his shoulders hunched, dreading his mother's reply.

Kait chuckled ruefully. "I'm glad you heeded her advice, son. As things stand right now, I need you to help out with Stoi's routes for the time being."

Ponar realized that the tension he'd picked up from the group wasn't due to his extended absence, but instead to his uncle, Stoi.

"Is Stoi alright?" Ponar asked. He chastised himself for not noticing Stoi's absence sooner. After all, he and Laan always traveled together. Stoi missing dinner with his family should have sent up a red flag. He'd definitely been out of touch for too long.

"Stoi's fine," Meik replied, pulling himself away from his tankard to join in the conversation. "Chirey's birth brother got sick off of the Temple's most recent mistake." Meik looked away and drank a large gulp of his ale.

This pronouncement quieted the group, and Ponar was wise enough to wait it out. After a few quiet moments, Laan spoke up to clarify.

"It's some sort of nerve damage from a botched batch of medicinals. It's so bad; he can't even take care of himself. He won't recover. It's only a matter of time, they say. Chirey's a mess over it, and needless to say, Stoi hasn't left her side in days."

"Understandably," Ponar replied. This news hit Ponar hard, remembering how close Stoi and Chirey were, and how much they loved each other. It must be unbearable for him to see her so upset. "Is there anything we can do for her?"

Kait sighed. "Stoi is the only one she will even talk to right now. She's even refusing to eat." Ponar got the impression Kait wanted to give Chirey support but guessed this was not the easiest time for her to open up to the Sept Chieftess. "But you can help out Stoi if you're up to the task?"

"How could I not?" Ponar replied, taken aback at her questioning his loyalty.

Kait looked at him squarely. "Well, son, it's not like you've been very reliable. You've been away from the Sept halls almost four months now."

Ponar assumed a good deal of her ire stemmed from his lack of choosing a wife and not his absence.

"I've been trying to save time by not taking unneeded trips. There's quite a bit of product to be moved between Barrow's Grove and Kiya's Grace before it ever gets here. The swamplands are vast, and they take more effort and time to cross. It's not fair to say I haven't been contributing to our family's growth and success!"

Ponar ended his tirade, noticing his voice had risen to where he drew looks from people at other tables. Many had retired to their rooms for the evening, but the room was nowhere near empty yet.

Kait waited a moment to respond, giving him plenty

of time to regain his composure. "I don't want to imply you haven't been keeping Durmah's best interests at heart. It's just that with all the travel, it's harder to keep everyone connected. I know you're doing a great job. Otherwise, I'd have demanded your return. While you've been working the western coast, our exports have dramatically increased. However, since you've been away so long, sometimes people forget you're off working for us. Visibility is often just as important as getting the job done!"

Kait's praise surprised and elated Ponar. Perhaps she was right. He'd been gone so long that he didn't even realize the impact of his work on the family. While he'd been off worrying about Kait's mandate for him to marry, he'd also missed her praise for his accomplishments.

"I'm sorry, I have been gone too long," Ponar replied.

Kait took his hand. "Don't worry about that, son. Just make sure to drop by every so often. Regular reports to Jesse wouldn't hurt either."

"I can do that, Mom," Ponar agreed, happy that he no longer sensed the strain between them. He remembered that she'd had another request. "Now, how can I help out Stoi?"

"I need you to start running his routes in addition to your own. I know it won't be easy, and you won't be as productive up in Barrow's Grove in the meantime. This is just short-term until Chirey is better and Stoi is comfortable leaving her in our capable hands."

"Ok. Will Laan and I be running the routes together?" Ponar asked.

"I think it's best we keep the full loops separate for

now," Laan answered. "You can run the loop from Raven's Call to Barrow's Grove and back while I concentrate on the shorter loops from Raven's Call to Kiya's Grace. Meik is busy enough with the Northern Pass trails already."

"How soon do you head out again?" Ponar asked Laan.

"Tomorrow by midday, I'm afraid," Laan replied. "I've just been waiting to talk to Stoi before I head out again. Now we can travel from here to Kiya's Grace together and discuss those regular shipments which will bring you up to speed. I know you haven't had to run those recently."

Ponar admired Laan's practicality. Most probably, his arrival today was the only thing keeping Laan from having to take on Stoi's entire load.

"True enough," Ponar agreed. "Is there anyone else available who could pitch in?" Ponar asked Kait.

"I'm afraid not. We've been stretched thin over the past few years setting up the Waystations in Kiya's Grace and Resounding Cliffs. Blethe and Marra will marry once they emerge from Temple service, and then their husbands will join our lineage. However, that will hopefully be years away from now, after they've had a few more children."

"True, but aren't any of my cousins of age to help out?" Ponar asked.

It was Nele's turn to speak up, as Ponar was referring to her children now. "I'm afraid all of your able-bodied older cousins are already busy at the Resounding Cliffs Waystation or have duties here at the Sept house. There's the possibility that the Temples may grant us another adoptee, but that will also take time." She held her chin high, pride gleaming in her eyes.

"Yes, it will. It always takes lots of time to negotiate with the Temples," Kait said. Everyone at the table shared her irritation, evidenced by their snorts and sarcastic comments.

"For now, although I'd prefer to keep my wayward son up and grill him for information on trade in Barrow's Grove, I think it's best if we all eat well and catch up on sleep," Kait announced. "I believe that we've all got plenty to tackle tomorrow. I wouldn't want you three hitting the roads without getting a full night's sleep under your belt."

"Agreed," Laan replied. "My wagon is packed, and I'll make sure the staff gets Ponar's packed by mid-morning." Ponar nodded his consent, the realization this visit wouldn't even last a full day finally hit home.

"We should catch up with Stoi in the morning," Meik said. Ponar got the impression that Meik had something specific that he wanted to discuss with them but perhaps didn't want to talk about in front of Nele.

Kait nodded in response. "Why don't you three meet me at Stoi's quarters after breakfast? Chirey often sleeps late, so we shouldn't disturb her. Knowing Ponar will be filling in for him should reduce his stress."

Everyone but Nele stood, a good night's sleep foremost on their minds.

"I'll go and get Matieus organizing the packing of Ponar's wagon," Laan said. "Until tomorrow."

"I'd better go catch up with my wife," Meik said. "She

retired early as she's been overseeing the brood in the mornings." He motioned to the few children still playing in front of the far hearth. "Good evening all." He headed upstairs.

Kait frowned. "Speaking of the children, Nele, why don't you get them off to bed?"

"Dearest sister, I'd be happy to," Nele replied. Nele rose and sauntered over to the children.

Ponar found himself alone with his mother for the first time in months. Thinking of this moment had brought him great angst while he'd been away, but now that he stood next to her that anxiety didn't surface.

Once Nele had moved out of earshot, Ponar leaned in close to Kait. "Have Blethe or Marra borne any female children yet?"

Kait gaze narrowed. "Sept business, I knew you cared about. Politics, I didn't think you paid much attention to, son."

"How can I not? You're not simply my mother, but Sept Chieftess. Nele's your younger sister, and next in line to inherit the title if your daughters don't bear girls themselves. Even I can figure direct matrilineal descent on a graph. So, have they, or haven't they?"

Kait bit her upper lip and then shook her head. "No, not yet. I have three new grandsons, all healthy. Both girls are fertile, and they're still early in Service. There's time yet."

Ponar ran a hand through his hair, casting a nervous glance over at Nele. "Let's hope so. She may hunger for your position, but Nele doesn't have the fortitude for it, if I may be so bold."

"You can always be open with me. Please don't worry about speaking ill of Nele to me, there's no tenderness between us, trust me." Kait looked up, studying his face, her weariness and joy apparent to him. "How about I walk you to your room?"

"That'd be nice." He offered her his arm to lean on, and she quickly took advantage of his support.

"It's good being with you again. I don't like thinking I've lost track of my only boy!"

"I've missed everyone here too. There are times I'm negotiating, and I have to wonder if I know enough to make the best bargains. Not to mention falling behind with Sept news."

"Well, our ancestors decided to eschew technology for a simpler, more family-oriented way of life. I doubt they ever considered the needs of an extended and traveling family like ours when they set down the colony's by-laws," Kait replied.

"I wonder if they'd approve of how we live today. I mean, our family doesn't prioritize the familial bond over business. We're generally close and loving, but we don't spend all that much time as a unit."

"I think they'd be happy enough we're still alive. After all, most of the trade we do wouldn't be necessary if we didn't have to supply rare medicinal ingredients across the continent. The founders never foresaw the plague, or the effects it would have on the culture they wanted to foster."

Kait stopped in front of his door and opened it, revealing a very comfortable room. The large bed, filled with pillows and warm blankets, practically called to him. Considering Ponar had lived out of his wagon for the past few months, this looked downright blissful to him.

Ponar sighed. "I'll sleep well tonight."

"See, I'm not beyond bribery to help convince you to visit more often." Kait chuckled back.

Ponar walked over to the dresser, hoping Kait had arranged for a fresh change of clothing.

"As you'll be leaving tomorrow, I don't want to add to your stress by pushing you on a decision about a wife. Yet I want you to know it's still on my mind."

"Oh, I didn't figure you'd forgotten about that," Ponar replied, unsure of how to address the issue. Opening the dresser, he pulled out what he thought was a linen shirt. Unfolding it and holding it up, he realized it was a woman's nightshift.

Kait's face was confused for a moment. "How did that get in there?"

"Well, it's not mine."

"Oh, that must be your new sister's, Rai's clothing," Kait said. "She must have left it here."

"Rai stayed here?" he answered, a bit too brusquely. He focused on refolding the night shift and avoiding looking up at Kait until he regained more control over his emotions.

Kait laughed at him. "Really darling, do you think we keep the room reserved for you when you're gone?"

"Well, no," Ponar replied, happy she'd mistaken his surprise for entitlement. "I'd just hoped to find some clean things. I won't have time to launder what I have before I leave tomorrow."

"Ah, that won't be a problem, dear. I'll have Nimma get you something new first thing."

"I'll take these back to Kiya's Grace for Rai, if you'd like," Ponar offered.

"I'm sure Jesse has given her plenty to wear," Kait replied. "Still, she might want these things too. It's not as if we're poor and can't afford to spare them, so please pack them up and give them to her."

"Whatever you'd like, Mother," Ponar replied. He removed the small stack of shirts, shifts and pants from the drawer and placed them on top of the dresser. "So I don't forget them," he explained.

"I'm sure your future wife will admire your thoughtfulness and generosity. Perhaps the next time we talk you can tell me whom you've picked. Just think how much simpler things will be once you're married. After all, I'll have to stop needling you over your choice."

"Yes, I can look forward to trading your needling for a nagging wife," Ponar quipped. He realized he was straightening and picking at the pile of Rai's clothes, and quickly restrained himself by clasping his hands behind his back and turning full toward his mother.

"Nagging, sure you'll get that. There are benefits, however, to you and to the Sept. Along with your added contentment and happiness; the Sept will gain extra hands. With your sizable dowry she'll be able to bring a few of her children along into the fold."

"I'm well aware of the potential benefits to Durmah," Ponar replied. "I've just not settled on the right one yet."

"Our Sept may not be the largest, but because of our financial success you have the attention of many. As my only son, you can't help but draw their notice. If you can manage to choose one of the many contestants for your affection, I guarantee the stress on you will pass. Besides, a favorable match can mean permanent favors from the Sept we align with, from permanently reduced par on their goods to an annual early pick of the best they produce."

Something in his demeanor must have warned her off because Kait's mood turned apologetic. "I'm sorry, I said I wouldn't push you about this tonight. There's plenty else to worry about now."

Ponar shook his head in disagreement, walked over, and hugged her. Releasing her, he took a deep breath. "No, you're right. Deciding on a wife will be good for me, and help me focus on the important things." Like not obsessing over an impossible relationship with Rai.

Kait's wan smile beamed up at him. "I'm so glad to hear that. Should I get you a current list of eligible candidates?"

"Yes. I can review it and get you an answer the next time I'm in town. Please mark the ones you feel would be the most advantageous allies for our Sept. I want to follow your counsel in this. It shouldn't take more than four to five weeks to complete the circuit to Barrow's Grove and back."

"Your wisdom has matured these past few months, son. I'll leave you detailed notes, and trust you to make the best decision for the Sept. Not all of the girls are out of Service yet, but it doesn't mean you can't lay a claim to one of them, assuming they've produced children. Now, get some sleep, and I'll make sure Nimma gets you up in time to meet with us in the morning." Kait moved toward the door.

"Thanks, Mom. Sleep well."

"Goodnight son," Kait said, closing the door.

Hearing the door close solidified the verbal commitments to Kait, and they reverberated through his mind. He walked back to the dresser, picked up Rai's shift, and brought it to his face. Inhaling deeply, he caught the smell of her still in the garment, rousing memories of his time alone with her. Gripping the fabric, he forced himself to set it down and let go of it, placing the crumpled nightshift back on the pile. Shifting his attention to undressing and preparing for sleep, Ponar knew choosing a wife from Kait's list would be the best for everyone involved.

CHAPTER 28

Ponar hadn't slept well. Knowing Rai had shared his bed just a few weeks earlier, even before he'd met her, added to his obsession. He was anxious for the morning's meeting with Stoi as well. After Nimma had brought the replacement clothes and he'd packed, he wasn't surprised to discover Laan already in the dining hall. At his approach, Laan looked up and nodded in acknowledgment. Various travel papers and maps covered the table along with a small stack of bags piled at the end.

"You're up early," Laan said.

"At least I slept a little. By the look of this, I'm tempted to think you didn't sleep at all." Ponar placed his bag near the others and joined Laan in reviewing the documents.

"Oh, I haven't been up very long," Laan replied. "Just long enough to pack my bags, fill out and review the travel papers for accuracy, have the stable hands load your wagon, and order food and supplies from the kitchen." Laan's nonchalant manner belied his flurry of activity.

"Yes, it appears you've just climbed out of bed. Is everything in order?" Ponar asked, motioning toward the paperwork.

"Yup just finished it. I'm thinking of sending one of the kitchen staff to the permits office to drop these off. It's that or wait until we're on our way out of town, and I'd prefer to give the Guardians more lead time than that."

"Good idea. When did you want to talk to Stoi?"

"Now. Meik and Kait are supposed to meet us up there." Laan rolled up the maps and stuck them into his travel bag. Picking up the travel permits, Laan walked toward the kitchen, with Ponar following close behind.

Upon entering the kitchen, the sumptuous smells of meat roasting over the fire and bread baking in the oven greeted them. Ponar's stomach responded, and his mouth watered. The Head Chef, Serille, walked around, busily supervising her three scullery boys.

"It'll be another thirty to forty minutes until breakfast, I'm afraid," Serille said.

"Yes, thank you, Serille," Laan replied. "I was wondering if one of your boys could run these over to the Travel Permits office."

Serille frowned in response. "I suppose this needs to be done immediately?" she asked. Ponar noticed that more than one of the boys redoubled their efforts, most likely wanting to look busier than before so they wouldn't get the undesired task.

"If things are too busy here I can always check with Nimma instead."

"No, no, it's not a problem. The butlers are always busy this time of day anyway. Jaren here can run those over right quick, can't he?" she replied, patting the boy on the back.

"Yes ma'am," Jaren replied with a pout, playing the part of the harassed errand boy. Ponar considered it a measure of the mutual dislike of all Guardians that the boy preferred to toil in the kitchen rather than take a walk through the city and briefly encounter them. Setting aside the paring knife he used to slice potatoes, Jaren wiped off his hands and approached Laan.

Laan handed him the paperwork. "Go to the western gate, boy. That's the one we'll be traveling through."

"Yes sir," he replied. Jaren quickly ran out of the kitchen, documents in hand.

"Thanks, Serille, I appreciate this," Laan said. Serille shrugged in return, having taken up the task of slicing the potatoes.

Laan looked at Ponar and gestured for them to head upstairs. Ponar let Laan lead the way. In familial order, Ponar outranked Laan, as he was the Chieftess' son, while Laan was her nephew. As Laan was his elder, Ponar deferred to him.

On the second floor, they ran into Meik and Kait rounding the corner. The group of all four of them ambled down the hall as they shared the obligatory morning greetings. Perhaps it was just because the day was yet young and she hadn't had a chance to tire out yet, but he hoped that she was improving. The last time he'd been in town Kait had been so exhausted that he'd hardly seen her.

When they arrived at the door to Stoi and Chirey's room, Kait took the lead and tapped upon the door with her knuckles. After a few moments, the sounds of a rustling could be heard within, followed by soft footfalls. The door latch clicked in retreat, and the door opened a few mere inches, revealing an irritated and scruffy looking Stoi.

His gruff demeanor quickly dissipated. "I take it this isn't a social call?"

"Can we come in for a few moments?" Kait replied.

Stoi nodded and backed up, swinging the door wide for their entrance. When they entered the suite, the lack of light in the sitting room struck Ponar as peculiar. Somehow, he felt that little light just couldn't be healthy. Stoi closed and locked the door behind them. Perhaps simply out of habit, but it appeared almost paranoid behavior.

"What's all this about?" Stoi asked. "Has something else gone wrong?"

"Why don't we sit?" Kait replied, still leaning on Meik's arm. "There are a couple of items we need to fill you in on, and I'd be more comfortable on the couch."

Despite Kait's robust appearance, her comments had the desired effect. They walked over and sat on the couches near the currently unlit hearth. No one wanted to tax the Chieftess' strength, but Ponar guessed this was a ploy to help Stoi relax. Stoi sat next to Kait and Meik, while Ponar and Laan sat across from them on the opposite couch.

Ponar found himself looking eye to eye with Stoi. "Hey there stranger," Stoi said. "Get lost?"

Ponar tried his best to hold his irritation in check. He deserved the comment and considering the stress Stoi was under Ponar didn't want to take the bait.

"I'm back now," Ponar replied. Stoi raised an eyebrow in confusion, surprised at the simplicity of his answer.

"Ponar has offered to help Laan with your trade routes for as long as you need," Kait said, shifting Stoi's attention.

Relief erased the furrows in his brow. "That's good, but I don't want to stop the shipments from his routes in the swamplands altogether either." His attention drawn away from the sleeping Chirey in the next room, Stoi appeared to be calculating something. "Meik, could you alternate routes with him? Go from here to Resounding Cliffs, and then turn around and go to Kiya's Grace on the next loop? That way Ponar can run big circuits from here through Kiya's Grace to Barrow's Grove and back. I think we'd lose less business that way." Stoi wiped his brow with his hand.

Meik and Ponar both nodded in response. "It will mean fewer days off between trips, and I'll have to use your narrower wagon to make the Northern pass on the Baris Spine, but whatever you think is best." Meik agreed. Ponar suspected he wasn't the only one who found Meik's unusually pleasant attitude refreshing.

"That's fine, Meik," Stoi replied, gratitude tangible in his voice. "It means a lot to me that I can rely on all of you." His comment received reassuring smiles all around. His eyes strayed to the bedroom door and Chirey's presence beyond.

"You know you can. Always," Laan replied.

Stoi looked at them and cocked his head. "I get the impression that isn't all you dropped by to discuss. Did you discover something new about Rai's amnesia?" He directed this at Kait, who looked a bit surprised at the question. Ponar's curiosity piqued at Stoi's mention of Rai.

Kait shook her head. "Not yet, but I'm still waiting to hear back from some of my associates on that one. The only new rumors leaking out of the Temples recently have been whispers of a possible vaccine. Now mind you, I don't give those any credence. After all, these are the same folks who can't keep the simpler treatments safe!" Kait said. She skipped the obvious connection; that Chirey's birth brother wouldn't be dying if the Temple healers were indeed competent.

"Well, what did you all want to talk about?" Stoi asked.

"I overheard something in the Formulary at Resounding Cliffs," answered Meik. "And I don't think you're going to like it."

"We've talked about this amongst ourselves," Laan jumped in. "As Ponar and I are heading out today, we wanted to bring you into the discussion."

"What did you hear?" Stoi asked Meik.

"One of the Formulary Priestesses told Journeywoman Teirna to have our medicinals tested. Not all of them, mind you, just the luna berries. They had me separate out the bags into a different piles and everything," Meik said.

Stoi looked confused. "Don't they always test some of the herbs?"

"Yes, they always set aside a bag or two for testing," Meik replied. "But I overheard them talking, and they were specifically waiting for the luna berry shipment from Sept Durmah. All of our bags were to be tested. They're looking to stick the blame on us!"

"They did just have problems with the eczema treatments ... what if they added new purity testing to help prevent future contamination-related illness?" Stoi asked.

"That's possible," Meik answered. "But you didn't see the looks on their faces. Journeywoman Teirna was quite cheery until she saw the luna berries. She was afraid of them."

Ponar's mind flashed back to his last conversation with Rai in the storehouse. "You're sure it was luna berries, Meik?"

"Yes," Meik replied. "Why?"

"Because the day I left Kiya's Grace I reviewed with Rai our procedures for warehousing product. She smelled the piles of luna berry bags ... I guess out of curiosity ... and said one of the bags stunk; like it wasn't luna berries at all. Neither Jesse nor I smelled the difference, and the bags were all tagged the same. Everything appeared normal to me, but now I'm wondering: did she somehow pick up on some off smell?" Ponar asked.

"Our little Rai's full of tricks, isn't she?" Meik said. With the harsh glances he got, Meik realized that no one else appreciated his joke and sought to defend his stance. "What I mean is you've told me about her shooting skills, and now this scent thing ... I just can't wait until her memory returns, and we get to know where she learned all this stuff."

Stoi redirected the conversation. "So Ponar, the bags Rai thought smelled off, did you bring those here on this trip?"

"No, I'm afraid not. I'd assumed you and Laan would transport them on the next loop," Ponar replied.

"What do you have in mind?" Kait asked Stoi.

"I wouldn't think this if Ponar hadn't shared that bit about Rai getting an odd smell off of the berries, but frankly I believe that we should be on the lookout. If the Temples are testing for contamination of those same berries ..." Stoi looked at Kait, his voice fading.

"This is a serious cause for concern," Kait replied. "If they trace any befouled product back to Durmah, they may also blame us for the illnesses. The contamination may not be in any berries Durmah shipped, but I want to track down the producers of that bag Rai hit on. We're better off finding the cause before the Temple does. If another Sept is responsible for the contamination, then we're just cautious. The farmers may not even be aware there's a problem so we might be able to stop it at the source. Above all, we don't want to draw the Temple's attention or ire down upon Durmah."

"Agreed. Do you remember which Sept that bag came from?" Stoi asked Ponar.

"No. It was a busy morning," Ponar replied. That's something of an understatement. "I'm positive that with Rai's help I can locate it when Laan and I arrive back at Kiya's Grace."

"Review the logs and determine what farm or vendor the bag came from. I know they're not always very specific, but do your best," Kait directed. "Meik, travel with them to Kiya's Grace to help out. I'd like all our resources on this one. Ponar, once you know which farm or swamp we're dealing with, I want you to head up into Barrow's Grove and the swamplands, wherever the source of the affected bag is, and find out what you can."

"I'll need to take Rai with me," Ponar replied. His motives weren't the purest, but he kept this to himself. "To help identify the off scent she smelled."

"That's an excellent idea," Laan agreed. "Perhaps Meik or I should go along too, in case the farmer doesn't cooperate. There's always a possibility they know about the taint because they put it there in the first place. Perhaps they're trying a new fertilizer or made a mistake, and don't want anyone to know."

"It's a less than ideal situation," Kait replied. "If you even suspect that's the case, involve the Guardians. Either way, Durmah will not take the blame for this. If I find out someone is setting us up ... they will pay, and pay dearly."

CHAPTER 29

Rᴀɪ ꜰᴇʟʟ ɪɴᴛᴏ ᴛʜᴇ ᴅʀᴇᴀᴍ ᴀɢᴀɪɴ, ʙᴜᴛ ᴛʜɪꜱ ᴛɪᴍᴇ she recognized it as the dream. It was ever the same: a tall forest of gigantic trees and widely fanned ferns, the distant melodies of a stream, and shafts of light landing in dappled puddles along the fog-laced earth. Her feet were sore and muddy from running barefoot, and her short, chin length hair was peppered with bits of fern leaves and moss. Her tunic and cape were black this time, and Rai wondered if this reflected her mood or her more recent clothing choices. Everything was so bright and vivid, for a moment Rai didn't believe this was a dream-- and yet she knew without a doubt that it was.

The echoing voices came again, malicious in pitch and pressing down on her from all sides. They accused her of violations, of crimes, of murder. They called for her death.

However, this time she wasn't scared. Rai was angry. This dream had made her injure people on previous occurrences. Perhaps because of her lucidity, knowing it was indeed just a dream, she wouldn't take the threats the voices uttered seriously. Remembering the direction she'd taken running through the forest on previous iterations of the vision, Rai deliberately sought out a new path. Turning uphill, she walked toward the voices and fog and entered a wall of mist.

She ambled along, unsure of her footing in the mist. The whispers became roars, but Rai steadily moved forward, undaunted by their threats. The light grew and pierced the fog, and Rai stepped into a bright, quiet glen. The voices didn't follow her here. The glen was framed by the ancient forest she'd become so familiar with, but the fog dissipated, yielding to a dazzling, midday sun.

At the far end of the glen, Rai spied a pond, dotted by giant ferns. She jogged toward it, hoping to find some new landmark in this expanding landscape. Rai wasn't disappointed. With the pond to her right, she saw a small hillock nestled amongst tree trunks, covered with ferns and fallen leaves. Rai might have thought it just a large mound of earth, but a shiny glint caught her eye, and in turn drew her attention and footsteps.

She reached the hill and inspected it. If it hadn't been for the glittering brightness reflecting the sun, Rai doubted she'd have noticed the metal door lock hidden under some leaves and soil. She brushed away the debris covering the panel. It appeared a standard lock, simply located a third of the way from the bottom of the somewhat steep-sided mound, located at chest height. Inspecting the moss and fern covered mound, Rai found no outline of a doorway, but that didn't mean anything. Why have a door lock, without a door?

Rai looked around, yet was still alone. The only motion in this beautiful, quiet place was a slight wind upon the ferns and pond upon the brilliant foliage. This place felt familiar to Rai, comfortable. She should be able to name it, but she couldn't quite put her finger on it. Delaying no longer, Rai placed her left hand firmly upon the door lock.

The cool metal at once became smoldering hot, glowing red at the contact. Pain seared up Rai's arm, blinding her with the overwhelming shock of the sensation. Blood-curdling screaming filled her ears. Pulling her hand quickly away, Rai ran the few dozen steps to the pond and jumped in, submerging her pain in the meager relief of the cold water. Only as the pain subsided and her vision returned to normal, did Rai realize that the screaming hadn't yet stopped. Placing her right hand over her lips, she discovered them closed and knew then the screaming issued from the mound itself.

The serene landscape belied the hideous, high-pitched shriek. The screaming continued and grew in volume, filling Rai's ears and mind until she thought her eardrums might burst. To avoid the noise, Rai submerged again under the water.

The screaming disappeared, replaced by the sensation of the water moving around her, pulling her back and forth. Rai knew she'd jumped into a pond that shouldn't have waves or tides, so she opened her eyes and pushed herself up out of the waist-high water, and into an altogether different location.

Gone were the forest, mound, and pond. Instead, Rai stood in the freezing ocean looking up at Jeweled Cove.

Rai walked toward the dry ground, not wishing to remain in the chill ocean any longer than necessary. The bright sun hid behind dark, roiling clouds, portending a thunderstorm. Everything seemed dark here: the caves were black, the sky was dark and angry, and the ocean turned foreboding.

The chill wind blowing in off the surf made Rai's fingers ache, and she rubbed them together to warm them. Realizing that this didn't hurt, Rai looked down and discovered her left hand recovered. She also now wore a simple, dry white shift that offered little protection from the cold. Emerging onto the sand, Rai gazed down the beach and spotted a form lying motionless in the distance. Rai ran toward it, the cold air biting into her skin.

When she reached the body, which was lying face-down in the damp sand, Rai fell to her knees beside it. The tide must have been shifting, as the surf now rhythmically crept toward them, soaking them within the swirling waters. She turned over the body and came face to face with a woman of strikingly beautiful features and long, jet black hair. Rai studied her pale, cold, face and was startled when the woman opened her eyes.

She gasped for air, coughed up briny seawater, and then gasped again. Looking up at Rai, terror and confusion filled her eyes. "You can't be here!" she croaked at Rai. "You weren't ever supposed to come here!"

"Why? Why can't I be here?" Rai asked, cradling her close.

The sky abruptly darkened, and the flapping sound of a large, winged creature moved overhead. Looking up,

Rai couldn't see the beast, but instead, the clouds appeared to reach down toward them.

"What is it?" Rai asked.

Dark, angry tendrils of cloud met with the ocean offshore, closing in the landscape. Rai heard wings beating against the mists. A sharp screech echoed off the craggy cove walls and reverberated through Rai, impossibly loud.

"What is it? Rai yelled over the sound. Rai searched the sky, trying to sight the creature, but all hid within the rapidly approaching clouds and fog.

"Retribution," the woman answered. Rai looked down at her and was shocked as arterial red blood soaked through the white shift the lady wore. The woman's face paled further, and when the surf rolled in the water was blood red. Looking out into what she could still see of the ocean, all was crimson. The fog and clouds picked up the scarlet tones and now surged forward again. Soon the blood mists would envelop them both.

"What did I do to deserve all this?" Rai cried out in frustration.

The woman looked up at her, eyes full of loathing. "More than enough." The beast screeched again, the sound now directly overhead. Blood oozed out of the woman's mouth, and she sneered at Rai.

The quiet blood fog rolled over them. The silence lasted but a moment, and then a shrill cry from the winged beast shattered her thoughts. The sound was in front of her, and the creature's hot breath was upon her face, but Rai could only see the blood-red haze all around.

Razor-sharp claws sliced into and across her right shoulder. Screaming with the pain of her now useless arm, Rai blocked with her left arm, only to have the beast grab and bite into her left hand.

Flailing against the brute's bloody vice grip, it forced Rai on her back flat onto the sand. Its weight pressed against her belly, claws digging into her flesh and viscera. It's weight pressed against her, and Rai screamed as she sank further and further into the sand. The crimson tide washed over her, and she inhaled in shock as it burned in her wounds. Bloody seawater filled her nose and throat as the beast's claws ripped out her intestines.

Rai woke screaming and drenched with sweat, her arms beating against the boards above her. Someone pounded on her bedroom door, calling out her name, demanding to know if she was all right. Was she? Becoming more conscious of her surroundings, Rai realized she lay naked under her bed, with no idea how she'd gotten there. Crawling out from under the bed, scratches and cuts covered Rai's hands, arms, and knees--probably the result of thrashing against the rough wooden slats under the bed.

Standing up, Rai found her legs shaky from the dream fight and her hair around her face damp with sweat. She took a deep breath to steady herself and puzzled over her present naked state. Jesse's voice called from the other side of the door, and then the jingle of keys. Panicked, and not wishing others to find her naked,

Rai grabbed a blanket off the bed and wrapped it around herself just as the key turned in the lock. The door swung open, Jesse and the maid Kasha hot on her heels.

"Is everything okay?" Jesse asked.

Still, in a daze from the dream trauma, it was all Rai could manage to stare back at Jesse. Things were nowhere near all right. Not only had she experienced another instance of the recurring nightmare, but she'd woken up naked under the bed, with no idea how she'd gotten there. Where had her clothes gone? The thought that her terrifying dreams now had her sleepwalking made Rai lightheaded and shaky. It was now obvious to Rai the effects from the post-waking episodes were escalating or deteriorating, depending on how you looked at it. Rai searched the room with her eyes, looking for something out of place but found all else was as she'd remembered.

"Begging your pardon, Mistress Rai. I heard screaming, so I fetched Mistress Jesse," Kasha explained.

Jesse walked cautiously toward her. "You're bleeding." She pointed to Rai's scratched hands. "Kasha, fetch a towel, a warm basin of water, some salve and bandages, quickly!" Kasha ran out of the room.

"Why don't you sit down, Sis?" Jesse, now standing next to Rai, reached out and took hold of her shoulders, pulling her to sit at the end of the bed.

Rai avoided touching them in case one of them could pick up on her reading them. She also wanted to insulate herself from often overwhelming emotional experience. This time, however, the deliberate and focused essence of Jesse came to Rai's aid. Through Jesse's touch, and thus perception, Rai grounded her consciousness and brought herself into focus--because that's how Jesse felt right now. Immediately calmer, Rai allowed Jesse to guide her to the bed.

"It was the nightmare again," Rai explained. Rai soaked up Jesse's emanating clarity and solidity. Jesse sensed her contact was a comfort to Rai, so she kept a hand on Rai's shoulder when she sat down next to her on the bed.

"I assumed so. How did you scratch yourself up?"

Kasha returned, bearing a tray with items Jesse asked for. "I'll take that," Jesse told her. Jesse placed it on the bed between them. Rai noticed the loss of their physical connection, but the support she'd gained from those brief moments had calmed her trembling.

"Why don't you shut the door on your way out, Kasha? Thanks," Jesse said. Kasha bowed and left, not one to question her Mistress' orders.

Alone again, Jesse wet the towel and cleaned Rai's scratched hands and forearms.

"I got them beating against the wooden slats under the bed," Rai replied.

Jesse paused, brows furrowing in confusion. "Why were you under the bed?"

"Don't know. What's really confusing me is that I have no idea what happened to my nightshirt."

Both sisters looked around the room, searching for the elusive garment. Everything laid in place in her tidy, simple room.

"Well, at least I now know why you're wearing a blanket." Jesse laughed. "I'll make sure and have Hilse check the entire second floor for your missing night-clothes."

Rai blushed deeply at the thought of sleepwalking naked through the halls of the Waystation. "My door was locked, so it must be in here," Rai said, flustered.

"Don't worry about it. I'm sure it'll surface sooner or later." Rai winced as Jesse cleaned a deep gouge on the palm of her right hand. "You got yourself pretty good. I wonder how you got under the bed?"

Rai shrugged. "I must have crawled under there trying to escape from this huge bird with razor-sharp claws in my sleep. I even scraped up my knees kicking at the bed." Rai pulled the blanket up to show Jesse.

"Wow, when you're fighting off beds you really put everything you got into it, don't you?" Jesse snickered and then tended to those cuts as well. "The giant bird sounds new. Or am I mistaken? I don't remember you mentioning a bird from the previous dreams."

"The bird was new. The dream started off the same, but this time I walked away from the figures in the mist." Rai continued describing the dream while Jesse salved and bandaged her wounds.

"Did you recognize the woman on the beach?" Jesse asked.

"No ... I don't know. There was something familiar about her, and I feel like I should know her ... but I just can't place her."

"Perhaps her identity will come to you in time if she is someone from your past." Finished bandaging, Jesse gathered the items back onto the tray. "What's interesting about these dreams is your recurring theme of guilt: guilt for trespassing in the forest, punishment for trying to open the door, being blamed by the woman for going to the Cove where you weren't welcome. It makes me wonder if maybe your amnesia is a result of some disobedience to your old Sept, or if your subconscious guilt somehow keeps the amnesia from lifting."

"You may be right, but it's hard to know what I regret precisely because of the amnesia."

"I'd have to disagree with that, Sis. Even though you have the amnesia, your dreams keep offering up more clues to your past. It's just a matter of time before it all comes out." Jesse picked up the tray and walked toward the door. Something about the phrase 'all coming out' gave Rai a sinking feeling in the pit of her stomach. Rai caught the scent of anxiety on Jesse too. Rai wasn't the only one worried about what might surface.

"I'm not sure how much more of this I can take, Jesse," Rai said, lifting her hands up to make the point. "What's next, me breaking the furniture or my bones? I'm sure our guests aren't too pleased with me screaming my head off either!"

"Oh, I don't worry about that, darling! It's a little after midday, so most everyone is out in the town now. However, I can't have you serving our guests food and drink through the night with your hands all cut up and bandaged."

"I'm sorry, Jesse. You know I'd never try and hurt business."

"I know you wouldn't. No sane person attacks a bed. I have some errands around town that need doing, and I think you'd benefit from the walk and the fresh air those require. Hilse can fill in for you tonight."

"'That sounds great." Being cooped up inside was particularly unappealing after waking up in a confined space. "I'll be right down."

"No rush. Take your time finding your clothes. You know, 'cause that's a little bit of a challenge for you today!" Jesse said with a chuckle as she exited the room, closing the door behind her. Rai knew by now Jesse always had the last laugh, but this time the bewilderment at not knowing what she'd done with her nightshift curdled her humor.

Alone again, Rai stood and unwrapped the blanket from around her body, laying it back on the bed. Walking to her dresser, Rai opened it and selected her preferred garb; dark blue leather pants and a matching loose, flowing soft flaxen tunic. Pulling these items on with some difficulty due to her cuts and scrapes, Rai sighed with disappointment when she hadn't managed to find her nightshift in the dresser.

Pulling on socks and her calf-high black boots, Rai scanned the room for possible nightshift-hiding locations while lacing up her boots. She'd only been in the Waystation for a couple of weeks, so her room was still relatively bare. In her visual inventory, Rai counted a bed, a dresser, a desk and chair, a couch, a couple of floor rugs, and some curtains. Having already inspected the rather obvious choice, the dresser, Rai looked in the desk drawers, behind the couch cushions and drapes and under the floor rugs, all to no avail.

Perhaps in her rush to leave the confines under the

bed, she'd missed spotting the night shift. Rai crouched down onto her knees to check. Placing weight on her bandaged scrapes stung and burned, but Rai endured it and peeked, half expecting to encounter a sharp-taloned bird. The only thing under the bed was dust; no evidence of the nightmares or night shift remained.

Picking herself up off the floor, Rai sat upon the bed and tried to reason out other possible locations for the night shift. She knew the last time she'd seen it when awake; she'd had it on in the bed. Perhaps she'd pulled it off and left it under the covers? Standing up, Rai looked afresh at the bed, but this time the simple act of looking at the bed raised the hair on the back of her neck.

The covers and beige sheets met the beige pillow-cases along a sharp line near the top of the bed. However, somewhere near the center of that line Rai's eye caught on a tiny fringe of white. Her white nightshift. Hesi-tantly she reached out and grasped the sheet at the corner of the bed, although it hurt her hand to do so. Rai's breathing grew shallow and fast as she pulled back the covers. Tears clouded her vision and streamed down her face as she retreated in shock from the unbelievable sight in front of her. The covers continued to peel off the bed as Rai shrunk away, unable to release the sheet and thus pulling it and the blankets onto the floor in a mound at the base of the bed.

Rai ran into the desk and leaned on it for moral support while staring at the bed, unable to avert her gaze. There, benignly lying flat on the bed was her nightshift. Its existence in the bed wasn't surprising, but its state was utterly unnerving. It lay neither crumpled in a ball nor heaped into a pile. Rai remembered sleeping curled up on her left side in the bed, and there the nightshift still mirrored that pose--except now it proclaimed a disturbing caricature of form: torso flattened to the left, left sleeve folded up at the elbow, right sleeve angled down and across the skirt.

Rai knew she hadn't taken off the night shift. It would have been impossible to lay it out like this and replace the covers while sleepwalking. No, she hadn't taken it off. She'd left it. Exited it.

One question encompassed Rai's being: not who, but what, was she?

CHAPTER 30

Rai's day of errand running passed by in a blur. She returned to the Waystation with the last item from Jesse's impromptu list--a selection of her favorite specialty jams--and entered the storehouse via the stable yard. She stored the tiny jars with the other kitchen pantry items.

None of Jesse's tasks had been challenging, but her internal self-doubts made each item a strain. Exiting the storehouse, Rai looked up into the fading sunlight. With the coming of nightfall, weariness rolled over her, but she had no inclination to return to her bedroom.

Her inward battle to make sense of her dreams and the impossible events from earlier had driven her to the point of numbness. Keeping busy throughout the afternoon had helped, but nothing removed the image of her nightgown laid out in her own sleeping shape upon the bed from her mind. No rationalization she tried even came close to explaining the phenomenon. Yet there it was, still vivid within her mind even though she'd torn all of the sheets off her bed that morning.

"Good evening, Mistress Rai," Hilse said, appearing from the doorway leading to the main dining hall. "Were you able to get all of Mistress Jesse's shopping done?"

"Good evening, Hilse," Rai replied. "Yes, I got back with the final item just now. Did you come to get something out of the storehouse? I can help you carry it back inside if needed."

"Oh, don't you bother yourself, Mistress. I'm just running out for some salt, and I assume I can carry that back on my own! How are your bandages holding up?"

"Fine, no problems there, Hilse," Rai replied. Rai only wished her problems were as simple as dirty bandages. "I think I'll head up to bed now ... get some extra rest and all. You'll let me know if you need any help, won't you?"

"Don't you worry yourself one bit, Mistress. Hilse will keep things running just fine down here. You concentrate on getting some decent sleep!" Hilse continued toward the storehouse.

Although Rai doubted trying harder might offer her a better night's sleep, she appreciated Hilse's good-intentions. "Thanks, Hilse, I'll go hit the hay right now!" Rai lied.

"Good to hear it, Mistress. I'll see you in the morning." Hilse disappeared into the storehouse.

Knowing Hilse would tell anyone who asked she'd gone to bed; Rai took the opportunity to slip out of the Waystation unnoticed after tucking a dagger into her belt. More walking might not help, but Rai was convinced sitting and staring at her bed for the next few hours might just drive her insane. Besides, something was calming in the act of walking. Even though Rai couldn't solve the puzzle of whom she was or what had happened while she'd slept, she could still put one foot in front of another and at least make that--albeit simple act--happen.

No longer having one of Jesse's tasks to distract her, Rai thought of her situation as the sun set on the streets of Kiya's Grace. After today's events, Rai realized she could no longer hide from her talents and avoid the questions of her past. These issues weren't something Rai could ignore and hope got better. The guilt she'd experienced in the dream was overwhelming. Even now, the dread ate at her belly. Apparently, her subconscious felt she deserved punishment, and it wasn't about to give up without making its point. However, how could she atone for a transgression she didn't even remember?

Her recurring nightmares were, well ... continuing to recur. She'd awoken violently on each of the three occasions, each time trying to fight off unseen attackers. Although Rai considered taking some of Jesse's much-touted faown to force a profound and dreamless sleep, becoming addicted to a medicinal meant for animals didn't strike her as a good alternative. Yet it wasn't simply the dreams. Her other skills kept surfacing, and she needed to understand how they defined her.

The largest part of Rai's resentment was that avoiding using her talents hadn't kept the nightmares at bay. Rai'd hoped to bury her oddities: both from herself and from her Sept. The fact that the deal hadn't worked was a betrayal of her mind against her. It just wasn't fair!

The happiness and peace she wanted with the Durmah was slipping away between her fingers.

The night surrounded her with a profound darkness, as none of Az'Unda's three moons had yet risen. Looking up, Rai saw the stars above her, serene and deaf to her fears. She wound through the dimly lit city streets, debating what path would be safest for her to pursue. Rai could continue suppressing and ignoring her talents or try learning about them and accept whatever risks accompanied that knowledge. After all, if she did nothing, there was still the possibility that she'd hurt others or attack more furniture. Exploring her gifts might also bring an enhanced level of control. That would keep everyone safer.

Rai located a trash bin on a corner and stopped, pulling at her bandages. She unwound them and tossed them into the bin. Inspecting her hands, Rai saw the scratches didn't need another wrapping. Digging into a pouch in her belt, Rai located the salve Hilse had given her earlier and rubbed some more into her wounds to speed what was left of the healing.

Turning down another street, Rai wandered her way to the park in front of Headmaster John's school. The tranquility of this vast, empty space broken only by occasional trees or boulders called to her. The soft, grassy turf was a comfort to Rai's feet after the stone and cobble streets she'd walked all day long. Deep in the center of the park, there was a large, thick tree whose branches rose into the stars above her. Looking around, the empty park faded off into the darkness. This reminded her of the beautiful rolling hillsides north of the Baris Spine.

This calmed her raging mind and brought her emotions into long lost focus.

The time had come to cease hiding the truth and take action. Quiet action, but action nonetheless. Pacing under the tree, Rai first decided that keeping her adoptive Sept unaware of her hidden endowments was still priority number one. The Durmah's were uncomfortable with the affect Rai's amnesia and nightmares had on her ability to function within the Sept. If they found out Rai believed she could read people's emotions, including their own, they'd think she was insane or plague-ridden. Such a revelation was not something you'd expect to win other's confidence with.

She didn't know of anyone whom she could trust, inside or outside of the Durmah Sept. Somnu and Matriarch Bauleel she distrusted on instinct alone. Rai supposed that Jesse was the person she could trust most, but she didn't know if Jesse would protect her if she deemed Rai a threat to Durmah. Ponar had a good heart and felt trustworthy, but Rai somehow doubted that bringing him into her confidence would be a reasonable option. After all, how do you get past an attempted strangling and inappropriate intimacy with someone? It was just too much to ask.

Rai decided to use her senses to their fullest in hopes she'd gain better control over them and perhaps learn more about herself. Yes, there was always the risk someone might realize she displayed unusual talents. For instance, that man in the market. Looking back at that brief encounter, Rai regretted not finding out who he was, as it would have helped her to understand herself.

At the time, she'd assumed that the man was a threat, but there was no real evidence to that point, just her own paranoia warning her to keep her identity hidden. Either way, Rai felt that she had to push herself forward and discover the true range of her abilities.

Walking in a circle around the tree, Rai breathed deeply in hopes of picking up a stray scent. Aromas of tree sap, grass, moss, and moist dirt filled her senses, but nothing relating to a human presence came to mind. Considering she stood in an empty park at night, the lack of human scent wasn't surprising. Rai resolved to refine her skill in the Waystation and market, where human interaction was commonplace.

Closing her eyes, Rai listened to the world around her. The insects chirruped, the wind rustled through the leaves, and a bird cooed softly in the distance, possibly quieting its young. Focusing harder, she could just make out the sound of footsteps on the street at the far end of the park, about a thousand feet away. She recognized two distinct sets of footfalls, one heavy, and one light. Opening her eyes, Rai turned and squinted in the direction of the sound. The trees obscured their movements, frustrating her attempt to locate them.

Behind her, an unexpected popping noise startled her. Spinning around, Rai scanned the area for movement, but nothing caught her eye. Was she still alone? Rai walked in the direction the noise originated, carefully studying every nuance of the landscape around her. After placing this intense focus on visually seeking out the source of the sound, something new and odd happened to her vision.

Although no moon in the dark night sky, everything brightened and clarified in her vision. Lines gained distinction and shadows gained form. Colors remained flat in the darkness, but the granular detail allowed her to see as well as in the daylight. Rai ran her hands through her hair, pulling it away from her face. This talent will definitely come in handy. It seemed bizarre to Rai that she hadn't noticed the enhanced night vision before today. I can change how my eyes perceive light. Cool. Thinking back over the past couple of weeks, Rai realized she couldn't remember a time she'd been alone in the dark without a candle or lantern. She hadn't had cause to push herself.

Well, well. I guess I don't need candles anymore.

Entranced by her new night vision, Rai had almost forgotten about the popping noise. A slight movement, something she'd never have noticed without her altered vision, caught her eye. Rai spotted a rock she didn't remember being there. She approached within ten feet of the stone, and what at first glance had appeared a short, roundish rock between three and four feet in height was clearly a form shrouded in a large, draping cloak. A slight movement of the wind pulled at the folds of the fabric, breaking the illusion of hardened stone.

Rai wanted to sit on the pseudo-rock or kick it, purely for entertainment value. However, her gut warned whatever motivation a person might have for pretending to be a rock; they might not take well being ridiculed for the pretense. She might have walked away, but after discovering the trick, she needed to let this person know she wouldn't be snuck up upon unobserved again.

"May I help you?" Rai addressed the stone that was not stone. Rai's hand reached for and grasped the dagger sheathed at the small of her back, hidden under the billowing folds of her shirt.

Her words met with no response. The rock chose to call her bluff. Rai took another few steps toward the enshrouded form, stopping two arms lengths away. The dagger now rested hidden in her palm, warmed from its proximity to her flesh.

"By 'you,' I mean the 'you' not so successfully attempting to personify rockiness."

A baritone, snide laugh answered Rai's jeer. The rock lost shape and shifted as the form within arose. The man stood and threw back his Guardians hood, glaring at her. Rai took a step backward, recoiling from the venom in his gaze. She knew this man. He'd accompanied the Durmah's from Raven's Call, and he'd forced Jesse into the overnight stay at the hospice. The strength conveyed by his stance gave Rai pause. This man, in the name of safeguarding the city, could eliminate any threat per his discretion. Rai wondered if her talents were some form of plague-related sickness. Had this Guardian been following her to assess her for illness? Did he know she was different?

"Have you been following me?" Rai asked, trying to figure out why she'd seen this same Guardian three times in as many weeks. It couldn't be coincidental.

"I was transferred just recently to Kiya's Grace from Raven's Call. I patrol this sector of town. You happen to live in it."

His voice grated against her ears. She hadn't seen

him every day, but then again, how would she know for sure? If it hadn't been for her enhanced night vision, she'd never have noticed him. "How long have you been following me?"

"I noticed you when you entered the park." His eyes studied her. "I don't often find anyone here at this hour. Never alone." He alluded to the question but never asked it.

Rai laughed at the absurdity. "What? You think I came here to consummate an affair? How ridiculous! Is that how you entertain yourself? Viewing illicit couplings here in the seclusion of the park?" Rai giggled at the thought of the big bad Guardian watching couples make out in the park late at night.

"Well, if you did, I'd say by now it's safe to assume you've been stood up." The corner of his lip lifted ever so slightly.

Rai bit her tongue, itching to slap the smirk off his face. "Why are you here again? I can't be that interesting to follow, alone and healthy as I am. Don't you have anything better to do?"

A breeze picked up behind her, blowing her hair into her face, and she wondered how long the Guardian had watched her. Had she talked aloud to herself at all? The possibility sent a chill down her spine.

"Not at the moment, no." He reached into his coat and pulled out a med scanner, which Rai remembered seeing used in the Temples. Holding it up, he activated the med scanner and keyed the controls. He'd done this at the Waystation, right before he took Jesse off to the

Temple healers. Light from the screen illuminated his face, casting his chiseled features in a harsh glow.

"It is unusual to find someone wandering about, alone, in the middle of the night. It makes me wonder if they're feeling well." His eyes looked up, challenging her. "How are you feeling, Rai Durmah?"

Rai wanted to snarl. What about this Guardian brought out her claws? She imagined the feel of her fist connecting with the hard line of his jaw and curled her fingers in anticipation. "I wanted some air, a quiet walk in the park." How did he know her name? Perhaps he read it off the scanner. "I'm well, I can assure you."

"So it appears." The Guardian turned off the device and slipped it back into his pocket. "Aren't you worried about being alone out here in the dark?"

"I'm not alone now. You're here after all." The Guardian frowned. "Besides, what do I have to fear in the middle of the city, protected by Guardians like you who go around imitating rocks? Ooh, scary rocks ..." Yeah, she wanted to punch that scowl right off his face, and then kick him hard in the ribs for good measure.

At that moment, the popping sound came again, but now off to the right of them both. It hadn't come from the Guardian after all.

"Well, you should be. You might want a better grip on that dagger." He turned and tracked the noise, moving silently away from her.

Rai was surprised he'd noticed the dagger in the dark. Perhaps he'd caught sight of it when she was gesturing or laughing. Taking his advice, she allowed the blade to slip down into her right hand, the comfortable grip of the hilt light in her palm. Rai followed, not wishing to be alone with whatever the Guardian deemed dangerous.

"Could it be another Guardian, or some couple wandering the park?" Rai whispered, scanning the park with her newly discovered night vision, but saw nothing.

"Quiet," he ordered, also at a whisper, moving slowly forward. Despite his authority, his tone offended Rai.

The Guardian approached an open area and stood still as the stone he'd imitated. Rai stopped a few feet behind him and scanned the small glen. A flicker of movement caught Rai's eye, bringing her attention to a lone breacat walking awkwardly across the open space. She'd seen a few of the animals around town. People kept them to kill off the unwanted vermin. Something about the stilted way it shambled across the grass made the hair on the back of Rai's neck stand on end in warning.

The breeze picked up again, coming now from across the glen toward them, and Rai wondered if the Guardian had chosen their position as it was downwind from the breacat. Somehow, she sensed a warrior of his caliber considered such things. The breeze grew stronger, and a sudden rank, putrid scent filled Rai's nostrils. She almost gagged from the shock. This was no longer a breacat. It continued to amble with its strange gait and looking closer, Rai counted three legs on the rear instead of the usual two.

"That isn't a breacat," Rai whispered, unsure of what he'd seen in the dark. The animal displayed no visible reaction to her voice. The breacats head wobbled loosely while it stumbled forward, reinforcing its unbelievable nature upon Rai.

The Guardian cast a glance back at her and rolled his eyes. "Terrors never remain in their original forms for long."

Rai gaped for a moment, knowing that the breacat wasn't what it appeared, but also not believing such a creature of nightmares would look so inept and unintimidating. The Guardian turned his attention back to the now revealed Terror, and his body grew tense with anticipation of the inevitable confrontation.

"I should go home," Rai whispered. The Guardian ignored her. Could she outrun a Terror? If she lived through the evening, taking up regular running stints would be an exercise for another day.

Being this close to the Guardian and with the air current, for once, blowing from him to her, Rai took in his scent. The previous physical distance and inopportune breezes had kept her from catching a glimpse into his psyche to date. Now, with his mind entirely focused on the creature, what Rai sensed was clear and unambiguous. He wasn't afraid, he simply waited for some interpretive sign, some move from the Terror, before queuing his attack. The thrill of anticipation rolled through him, along with a yearning for the hunt.

There was something peculiar to the scent. Something that struck Rai as profoundly out of the ordinary-- so she breathed it in more deeply. There was his palpable desire to kill--directed at the Terror, but also unexpectedly at Rai herself. Against her own will, a grisly sequence of images flashed across Rai's mind. An image of a stiletto blade sliced across her bared neck. Her blood flowing out while she stared emotionless back at him, color slowly draining out and blanching her face as her eyes glazed over. An image of her own body, crumpled to the ground, an empty corpse.

Gasping for air, Rai recoiled from the visions that resounded with her nightmares and knocked into a low branch on the tree behind her. Shaking her head, she tried to clear away the cold and calculating picture of her own death as her now empty hands gripped the tree trunk. In her disorientation, she'd dropped her dagger, and the Guardian had disappeared.

The Terror let out a rasping whimper. Rai looked up and met its unfortunate gaze. This freak of nature hadn't overlooked her movement. Its head had ceased the previous bobbling, and it took a tentative step in her direction. Briefly frozen against the tree, Rai wondered how much of a threat this two-foot tall, awkward monster could be.

In answer to her question, the creature stretched and moaned. Its eyes never left Rai's, and its mouth widened impossibly into a caricature of a smile gone horribly wrong. The beast's teeth grew wider and longer. The impossibility of what she witnessed made Rai question reality. It gnashed and bit its teeth in her direction, and Rai wondered morbidly if it was attempting to open its maw large enough to swallow her whole. The breacats limbs lengthened and widened as it continued to march a slow but steady pace in Rai's direction. A deep and resonating growl issued from the Terror's throat. Although it appeared an impossible creature, it unquestionably held her attention.

Rai looked around, but even with her enhanced night

vision, it was evident the Guardian hadn't returned. In his thoughts, he'd envisioned her corpse. Perhaps he'd left her to the Terror, a more grisly but just as sure death. Panicking, Rai fell to her knees and searched the ankle-high grass for her discarded dagger, unable to take her eyes off the approaching fiend.

Her fingers grazed metal, and Rai clutched the knife in her hand. Still on her knees and now armed, however inadequately, Rai raised her blade to defend herself. Standing slowly, Rai figured the monster was now within fifteen feet of her and at least three times her size. If it was steady enough to jump, Rai feared the weight alone should crush her. With her luck, such an impact wouldn't kill her quickly, giving the beast time to sink those glistening, sharp teeth into her flesh.

Unable to just stand and await the monster's arrival and knowing that she couldn't stand up to its assault, Rai found her feet and dashed under the trees behind her, hoping to elude the Terror for at least a few precious minutes. A horrible wail answered her temporary escape, and soon she heard it crashing through the trees, furiously growling and mewling in pursuit.

Breaking out from the copse of trees, Rai ran into the open and toward a large rock formation. Just as she reached it, the Terror crashed beyond the last of the trees, howling triumphantly. An arm shot out from around the rocks and pulled Rai roughly around, pressing her back against the rock with a hard thud, knocking the wind out of her lungs. A Guardian Rai hadn't noticed pressed a gloved hand over her mouth.

"Stay here and be quiet, and you'll most likely be safe."

Rai nodded. The Guardian moved confidently, released her grip, and ran toward the approaching noise of the wailing and yapping Terror. Panting for air, Rai checked to make sure she still held her dagger and gripped it ever more tightly. It astonished Rai to see the female Guardian chase after such a dangerous beast. How could she alone defeat it?

Much to Rai's surprise, the Terror soon let out a feral scream, as if in great pain. The beast continued to howl angrily, and Rai inched around the rock, curious to watch the battle despite her fears. Peeking around, Rai saw the limping animal surrounded by five Guardians. The female who'd aided Rai joined her allies in their attack. The beast screeched and collapsed after one Guardian flitted quickly past the still strong rear leg, efficiently hamstringing and further disabling its ability to attack. From this relatively safe distance, the beast looked smaller than Rai remembered when it had chased after her.

Watching the Guardians adeptly dispatching the beast, Rai sheathed her dagger and let out a low whistle.

"Impressive, aren't they?" a familiar voice came from behind her. Spinning around, Rai faced the Guardian she'd been talking with earlier.

Rage flared within her belly. "You left me alone with that thing. It might have killed me!" If she knew his name she would have cursed him by it. Multiple times.

"Oh, they'd never get a chance to learn if I handled

everything myself. A newly-formed terror shouldn't give my trainees much of a challenge."

His flippant attitude did nothing to assuage Rai's anger. "Are you implying you used me as bait?" Rai realized the Guardians must have been present while the Terror had transformed and chased her down.

For once, he didn't snipe at her or otherwise respond. Rai found this lack of a reply even more infuriating. Without questioning the reasonableness of her action, Rai fluidly unsheathed her dagger and lunged at him in a single motion, aiming for his throat. He made no move to stop her attack.

Rai's arm crumpled, struck down hard from above by a third party. Spun around and pushed to her knees in a move that jarred her spine, her blade fell to the ground from her hand, her wrist twisted painfully from the position behind her back. After a few deep breaths to clear her head, Rai looked up and saw the female Guardian who'd previously pulled her out of harm's way now had her securely pinned.

The familiar male Guardian walked around in front of her, and he leaned down and spoke into her ear. "If I did use you 'as bait,' it would have been completely within my rights. A word of caution. Don't ever attack me again. My patience with you wears thin. Much more stretching and the wire will snap."

He turned to the female Guardian. "Escort the girl to the Durmah Waystation. Make sure she enters and does not leave again until morning. Don't bother to wake the house. I'm sure she's learned her lesson." He walked off toward what was left of the melee. The beast no longer struggled to defend itself.

The female Guardian lifted Rai to her feet by her upper arms, then slid Rai's dagger back into its sheath. The message was clear to Rai: she was no threat to them, with or without the blade. Motioning in the direction of the Waystation, this Guardian left no room for debate. Not that Rai was arguing. She'd had plenty of air and walking about for the evening. Exploring her talents in the comfort and safety of the Waystation was suddenly much more attractive to Rai.

Rai picked up her pace, not looking back while the Terror uttered its final squeals in the distance. Back on cobbled streets signaling the edge of the park, Rai realized the female Guardian was laughing.

"What's so funny?" Rai asked, sure the joke was on her.

"You!" the Guardian replied, falling into step beside Rai. "I've never seen someone outside of my Sept attack a Guardian, let alone a Senior Trainer."

"He used me as bait, and I got angry about it," Rai replied. The Guardian's question drove home, however. When she'd gone for his throat with the blade, Rai hadn't even considered the fact that he was a trained fighter and she just a simple girl of a Trader Sept. Her attack had been an incredibly stupid thing to do.

"Bait? I can assure you, that's not possible. We got the call a couple of minutes ago that there was a Terror loose in the park," the Guardian replied. Rai wondered if, when the Guardian had pulled out his scanner to assess her health, he'd instead been signaling for aid. Still, if he'd known about the imminent danger of the Terror, he should have warned her about it.

"Besides, we Guardians protect--not try and get people killed." She shook her head again.

When they reached the Waystation, Rai debated which entrance might bring the least amount of notice to whoever was working the night shift. She bet on the locked side door that the staff seldom used. Hopefully, she'd sneak inside and get upstairs without attracting any notice.

The Guardian stepped in front of Rai and stopped her motion with a hand firmly placed on Rai's shoulder. It wasn't lost on Rai that the Guardian picked her right shoulder, the one still sore from their encounter earlier.

"You do realize he could have killed you for attacking him? A simple report citing your 'unstable mental state' is all it would have taken to him to have you locked up." Rai wondered if all Guardians talked this much, and decided that the lady's curiosity must be getting the better of her. She withdrew her hand, crossing both arms in front of her chest. "You're such a young thing. Did you honestly think you could injure him?"

Clearly, the Guardian was unwilling to let Rai enter the Waystation until she was satisfied.

"No. I'd kill him," Rai answered. By the look in the lady's eyes and her scent, Rai knew she found her answer neither repellent nor humorous. Instead, Rai could tell that the Guardian was fascinated. Rai pulled out her keys and elbowed the Guardian aside.

"I'll be sure to give him your regards." The Guardian disappeared into the shadows across the street.

"Please do so," Rai replied. Certain she'd repeat every word, verbatim.

Rai entered the Waystation without further incident, locking the door behind her. Heading up the back stairway to her quarters, Rai wondered how she'd been so convinced she'd be able to kill the Guardian. She mused it must have been the product of her temper at the time. There couldn't be any other feasible possibility.

CHAPTER 31

Ponar walked behind Laan, lugging a now full water sack back to camp under the shady canopy of the forest. Both he and Laan had taken quick dips in the stream after filling their water bags. Baths were rare on the road, so they'd jumped at the opportunity--regardless of the icy nature of the water. Now water dripped from his hair onto his shoulders and back, dampening his shirt and cooling him from the day's earlier heat.

Ponar hoped Meik would have dinner ready for them once they got back. He was starving. They were still too far from camp to smell Meik's stew in the air, but that didn't stop Ponar from taking a couple deep, anticipatory breaths. Suddenly, Laan stopped short, motioning for Ponar to be quiet. Startled out of his reverie, Ponar shot a questioning look at Laan and stopped beside him. Laan pointed into the forest, back toward the stream, with an amused look on his face.

Ponar looked where Laan directed and saw their female escort greeted by a new male Guardian, and knew at once that another traveler must have joined their camp. For a moment Ponar thought this was all Laan found of interest, but as he watched the two Guardians interact, he realized there was more to the situation than just two Septmates sharing information from the road. The new Guardian stood rigidly in front of their escort, hands clasped behind his back and head bent forward--his eyes focused on the ground.

"You ever see them do that?" Laan asked him. "Is the new guy saluting or bowing to our escort?"

"Yeah, he must be. I guess it makes sense they have some system of rank--I mean they are a large Sept."

"Leave it to the Guardians to keep their internal ranking secret from everyone," Laan said.

Their Guardian made a dismissive gesture at the newcomer, and then she relaxed and began talking. Soon the two were in deep conversation, and Ponar got the impression that the newcomer was now reporting to their Guardian.

"I suppose I'm happy we've got the senior ranking escort. That's never a bad thing, right?" Ponar asked.

"One hopes," Laan replied. "Let's get back to camp before one of them notices us."

Ponar nodded his agreement, and they tiptoed away from the escorts. Within a few minutes, they returned to camp, finding Meik and Tinker Somnu sharing a bottle of wine. Ponar was glad to see the Tinker if a bit surprised at the coincidence of running into him on the road.

"Well, isn't this fortuitous!" Ponar said. "Greetings to you, Tinker Somnu."

"It's genuinely good to meet up with you again, old friend," Laan said earnestly, reaching out and heartily clasping the Tinker's outstretched hand.

The Tinker's sharp gaze lingered on the new arrivals, at odds with his relaxed posture. "And greetings to you as well, friend Durmahs!" Somnu replied.

Ponar and Laan hefted their water sacks into their own wagons, and pulled up chairs around the small campfire Meik had setup for cooking.

"I hear from Meik you're finally going to settle down and make the family proud, young Ponar," Somnu said. "My congratulations on your pending engagement! Who's the lucky girl?"

Ponar shot Meik an irritated glance, not happy over the announcement when he hadn't yet settled on the bride to be. "I'm afraid that hasn't been finalized yet."

Somnu peered back and forth at the three Durmah's, looking for the answer in their expressions. "I'm sure the lucky girl will accept your offer soon. She'd be a fool to refuse an opportunity to join lineage with the Durmah Sept."

"Yes, yes, I'm sure you're right," Meik replied. "And I'm sure the lucky gal will, once our Ponar sends her an offer." Laan chuckled behind his tankard.

"Now wait a minute," Ponar said, his voice rising in tone and force. "Enough of your jibes! I told Kait I'd have a final decision once we return home from this trip, and I'll keep my word to her. Until then, no more grief from you!" All three met his gaze with bewildered looks, unused to the hot temper from the usually mild-mannered Ponar they all knew so well.

Somnu's teeth glinted in response as he smiled, but his eyes lacked any sense of warmth. "Ah well, that's quite sensible, dear boy. Far be it for me to question a pact between Chieftess Durmah and her firstborn son. If she is pleased with the arrangement, then so it stands. I can imagine the petals raining inside Sept Durmah already. Make sure I get an invitation to the wedding feast!" He raised his cup toward Ponar.

Ponar respected Somnu leaving family business well enough alone. He raised his tankard to Somnu's and clapped the two together. Meik and Laan joined theirs a moment later, wisely avoiding further commentary on the subject. All drank deeply of the Tinker's wine.

"What brings you this way?" Ponar asked the Tinker. "It seems like I just saw you at Jesse's Waystation last week."

Somnu pursed his lips together as if he had a bitter taste in his mouth. "Durmah interests. You might say I'm on an errand for Chieftess Durmah herself."

"What?" asked Meik. "I don't remember hearing from Kait about any requests of you or the Tinker Sept." Ponar thought for a moment that Meik looked downright upset and offended by the possibility of not being within Kait's confidence.

"No worries, my dear friend," Somnu replied. "I'm referring to your Chieftess' request, as relayed to me through Jesse. The request concerning your new adoptee, Rai." The mention of Rai's name sparked Ponar's curiosity.

The Durmahs nodded, confirming to Somnu their knowledge of Kait's request to the friends of Durmah to aid in finding clues about Rai's past. Aware the Guardians were nearby, even if they weren't present now, no one spoke the details of Kait's request aloud. Everyone knew that the Guardians were lapdogs to the Temples--thus anything they spoke in earshot might work its way back to a Matriarch's ears.

"We'll let our Chieftess know that you're generously helping us out, friend Tinker. Where does your road lead today? Raven's Call?" Laan asked.

"To Raven's Call? Yes, but just a short stop on my way to the Resounding Cliffs. Rai mentioned the fishing's quite plentiful north of Jeweled Cove this time of year, so I thought I'd check it out," Somnu replied.

The Durmah shared confused glances at the mention of Jeweled Cove.

"What kind of fish do you think you'll catch up there?" Ponar asked. Ponar knew that Jeweled Cove was a dangerous place, the bay proper off limits to fishing. He worried what a past involving the Cove might mean for Rai.

"Hmm, see I'm not entirely sure. I figure I'll speak with the local deep-sea fishermen, and see what they think. I doubt I'll stay long, as I've meant to spend some time in Raven's Call also," Somnu replied.

"Have Rai and Jesse been doing fine otherwise?" Meik asked. "It's been a few months since I've spent time with Jesse. It'll be good to catch up with her again."

"Well, Jesse looks in good health, and--as always--has things at the Waystation in tip-top shape. From what Jesse's said, Rai is doing quite well with adapting to her new duties, although the girl's still confused at times.

Anyway, you'll be there in another three days now, so you can all make your own conclusions." Somnu refilled his tankard and offered more to the Durmah. Only Meik took him up on the offer.

"True enough," Laan replied. "You were there with them for the better part of a week, right?" Laan asked, and received a quick nod of agreement from Somnu. "Do you think the girls are getting along?"

"Oh, well enough. I wasn't worried about that so much as ... well, I suppose it wouldn't be proper for me to say." Somnu wore an uncharacteristically embarrassed look on his face, and Ponar wondered if his wine had gotten the better of him.

"Now Somnu, you've always been a loyal friend of Durmah. If there's something concerning you, please know that you can share it without worrying about offending us," Laan said.

"I just don't want you thinking I disrespect the Durmah," Somnu said. "I wouldn't want to cause trouble for your esteemed family."

The three Durmah men shared guarded looks in the uneasy silence. The Tinker's words hung in the air and a knot of anxiety formed in Ponar's gut. Somehow, he knew Somnu was referring to Rai. He took another drink, hoping she hadn't accidentally, or otherwise, attacked anyone else.

"Don't be ridiculous, dear friend," Meik replied. "We've known you long enough not to suspect you of troublemaking. If something is troubling you about Jesse and Rai, you must share it with us. We will hear your words and decide for ourselves what to make of them."

"Truly Somnu," Laan said. "You're practically obligated to share your fears with us."

"All right, all right, I will give in to your pleas. Although I must emphasize this is against my better judgment! However, I do trust you can evaluate my words for yourselves, and act upon them as you deem appropriate." He paused, hesitating yet another moment.

"During my days at Jesse's Waystation I had a goodly amount of time to get to know your new adoptee, Rai," Somnu continued. Ponar took another drink of the wine, trying to mute out his growing anxiety over Rai--and what Somnu might expose about her. "She's a very capable girl and a fast learner. She gives her all to the task at hand, and I never saw her shirk her duties or do less than her fair share."

"So far, friend, I do not hear anything to be concerned about," Laan interjected.

"I'm endeavoring to give an even-handed account, Laan. Despite my concerns, the girl is a great help to your niece, and I don't wish to discount that."

"Fair enough," Meik said, nodding overenthusiastically from the wine. "Continue!"

"What concerns me is her obsessive curiosity with her past," Somnu replied.

"Wouldn't you be curious yourself, if you were in her shoes?" Ponar spoke up, perhaps a touch too defensively. Yet he was glad Somnu hadn't spoken of Rai acting violently.

"Oh yes, I would," Somnu replied. "But this is different. I think her compulsion to regain her memories is affecting her ability, at times, to reason with a clear head.

There are moments she remembers things--or otherwise lost in some place in her mind--when it's impossible to get a simple response from her because she's so detached from the world around her. I'm concerned she's pushing herself so hard to remember her past that she's losing touch with the present-day world." Somnu paused, looking a bit lost himself.

"If you're so concerned with Rai's obsession about her amnesia, why are you helping hunt down information about it for us?" Laan asked.

"Two reasons," Somnu replied. "First, I hope if Rai is able to remember her past her unhealthy obsession can stop and then she can get on with her life. Second, with the unstable way she's been acting, I think Chieftess Durmah deserves to know about Rai's past--and if there's anything to worry about."

"What do you mean by 'unstable' and 'something to worry about'?" Ponar asked.

"There are times Rai acts--oddly. You can look into her eyes in those moments she's lost in the past, and it's as if she's not even there. Like some hollow, empty shell--I fear the girl may be losing her mind. It's terrifying. Don't just take my word for it, ask Jesse. She and I have discussed this, and I know she shares my fears."

Ponar couldn't picture any of what Somnu was describing. He'd only been around Rai for less than a day, but during that time she'd been levelheaded and sane. Yes, she'd attempted to strangle him, but her nightmares had been to blame, not her mental state. He didn't want to consider the possibility that she might be unstable. He'd always thought of himself as good at reading people, and he couldn't bear to view her in this light.

"I can't bear to believe Rai is so far gone, but if Jesse sees it too, well ... that's something we all need to take into account," Laan replied. "And I understand why you wouldn't want to bring it up with us, but it's good you did."

"I agree wholeheartedly, Somnu," Meik said, the drink slurring his words slightly. "We'll have a chance to see for ourselves here, and it'll be good to have your concerns on our minds. After all, if the girl's obsession has made her unstable, Kait needs to know."

"Thanks for being so understanding," Somnu replied. "You know I'm only saying these things because I'm concerned about your Sept's welfare. The Durmah have helped me out in the past, and--what can I say--but I owe it to you to do the same." Meik and Laan nodded in agreement with Somnu's words, as Ponar took a long drink and emptied his tankard.

"Enough of this dour mood!" Meik declared. "Let's eat dinner."

"Yes, and while we eat, I can atone for my dull conversation with a lighthearted tale of mirth I recently picked up on a trip to Barrow's Grove," Somnu replied.

"That sounds fantastic!" Laan replied, smiling again.

Ponar hoped Meik and Laan wouldn't bring up Somnu's concerns during the rest of the trip. He'd heard enough tonight to sour his stomach. Ponar doubted that his uncles worried what this newest revelation meant for Rai. The best interests of Durmah always came first, and rightly so. However, he also knew Rai needed an advocate and friend about now, and he'd step into that role if she'd let him. If Somnu was correct ... if Rai was losing herself to her amnesiac obsessions, then she'd need a lot more than just his friendship. The threat of mental evaluation by the Temples caused his throat to constrict. Could she escape if they narrowed their focus on her wisps of memories?

Bauleel waited while the security door to the Technician's Wing analyzed her blood sample. Journeyman Rilte had sent her a message earlier in the morning informing her Terem Zebio was having another of his rants, but she hadn't caught it until she'd checked her queue at lunchtime. Bauleel had asked for an alert the next time Terem had a fit and had been surprised when she hadn't heard from Rilte sooner. It'd been almost two weeks since she'd last been to the labs, and she'd hoped beyond hope Terem was recovering due to the apparent lack of ranting episodes. Sadly now that appeared not to be the case, yet Bauleel held out hope for some progress toward a cure. Soon the Elders would continue pressing for more details on the Technician's progress with this new variant. The Matriarch had to have satisfactory answers for them, or they'd keep pushing for off-world help.

The security door beeped and slid open. Bauleel stepped into the Technician facility's arboretum and headed for the holding cells in the containment area where Terem was confined. Such was her determination that it took a dozen or so steps for the sight and stench of the room to sink in, bringing her feet to a standstill. Not caring about the consequences, Bauleel pulled off her veil in disbelief of the somewhat dim view from behind it. She took in the ruined arboretum as she gagged on the rank smell of freshly spilled blood. The Technician's Guild was a veritable slaughterhouse.

Blood covered everything; dripping from a leaf here, a stream of droplets sprayed over an overturned couch there. Almost artful arcs of crimson wound their way across the floor, around chair legs and scattered dishes, up walls and over pictures ... even crisscrossing the ceiling overhead. In her dismay, Bauleel lost hold of her veil. The sheer fabric poured into a pile on the ground-- the brilliant white fabric shimmering red as it sucked up the viscous blood underneath her feet. Growing fingers of crimson tainted the hem of her long robes, and Bauleel gathered her skirts in her hands, picking them up off the blood-soaked ground. It was too late; the damage was done.

Bauleel walked deeper into the facility and yet spied no bodies. There was plenty of blood everywhere, how hard could it be to find its source? Yet there were no bloody footprints or blood trails from removed bodies to lead her search to the dead. It was almost as if the bodies had disappeared. This disturbed her more than the deaths of many Technicians. It hinted at a method of killing Bauleel couldn't yet begin to understand.

For the first time in her long memory, Bauleel felt

fear. This wasn't mere concern over how the Elders would react when they discovered her promises of a cure had once again fallen apart. Nor her nagging fear that the Anemoi would discover her treachery and she'd have to face their inevitable deadly wrath.

This was an immediate visceral fear for her life. Bauleel was aware that whatever had caused this blood-bath was still nearby--and likely looking for more victims.

She knew the smart thing to do would be to leave and call in the Guardian Sept to clean up this mess. Bauleel hesitated, scanning the pools of blood staining the arbore-tum. Was it callous to go without first searching for survivors? She shrugged off this guilt and turned back toward the security door leading to the main Temple complex. She needed to alert others to this atrocity rather than remain and put herself in further jeopardy.

Halfway to the door, Bauleel paused as the muted sound of someone crying reached her ears. Leaving a place empty of apparent survivors was an entirely different matter than abandoning someone to an appar-ently gory fate. Compassion overcame her fears and Bauleel ran toward the laboratory doors--the direction the sound originated.

Opening the doors to the lab, Bauleel found it surprisingly bloodless, and yet completely ruined: computer displays were smashed, upended stools and tables punctuated the landscape, broken beakers and test tubes covered the counters and floor, chemicals oozed from a toppled supply cabinet, and torn papers laid haphazardly throughout the room. It reminded her of a toddler's temper tantrum--magnified about a thousand fold. Bauleel choked and coughed as the smell of the spilled chemicals permeated the room. She found no bodies here either, and the few upended tables and benches afforded little hiding space. Where was everyone?

The only sign of life was the occasional far-away sound of punctuated sobs, coming from the direction of the containment area. The echoing cries sounded like a lost, wounded animal, beyond all hope. Bauleel walked to the containment area's door, all the while scanning the room for any signs of survivors or corpses--and found none. The doorlocks display indicated someone had locked it from the inside. Another wretched sob broke from the lone survivor of this massacre, and at this proximity, it was clear the person was indeed behind the door.

"It's going to be ok," Bauleel said. "Whatever happened here is over now. I'm going to open this door, and then we can leave. Together." Sure, she had no proof the cause of the carnage was gone. Bauleel just wanted to calm this person so they could leave quickly and quietly.

Sniffling sounds met her ears. "You can do that? You can open the door?" asked Terem Zebio.

Bauleel wondered how he was out of his containment cell. It sounded like he was just on the other side of the door. Perhaps someone attempted to evacuate him earlier. She could understand the Techs sacrificing themselves trying to protect Terem. His innate ability to withstand the plague was priceless. She had ordered his protection.

"Yes Terem, this is Matriarch Bauleel. I can open any

door we need. Hold on just a moment while I get this one unlocked."

Bauleel keyed the door lock, overriding the security on the door by displaying her palm print and waiting for verification. There was no door in the entire Temple complex that wouldn't open at her command. Moments later the door slid open, revealing a tearstained and miserable Terem. He was the only one she saw in the containment area. Again, there were no bodies. Bauleel swore he'd been trying to tear his hair out; it was mussed and sticking out all over.

Seeing Bauleel, a glow of hope lit Terem's face. "Without your veil, I know for sure that it's really you. You're so beautiful, Matriarch." Terem's voice wavered so Bauleel was afraid he might burst into sobs. What could he have seen to make him so scared? Bauleel decided she didn't want to wait around and find out!

"Yes, Terem, it truly is me," Bauleel assured him, hoping to keep their conversation as quiet as possible. "But we should go now. Are you ready to leave this place?"

"Oh yes. That's all I've wanted to do since all this started."

Bauleel held out her still gloved hand, which he grasped tightly. "Now let's stay quiet while we move to the exit, ok?" Bauleel pulled him out of containment area and walked quickly through the laboratory.

"Can I go home now, Matriarch?" The strain of today's terror was unquestionably wearing at him.

Bauleel tensed as they walked hand in hand. She hadn't planned this out. There was no way he could go back home. In fact, until the Technicians' area had been decontaminated there wasn't a secure place to keep him considering his infection. The only option Bauleel had was to put him in a coldsleep stasis crèche for a time until the containment area was functional again.

They passed through the arboretum, and the reek of blood filled her nose again. At least whatever caused this destruction hadn't yet returned.

"I think we'd best stop by the Healer's Ward first," Bauleel said, unwilling to disappoint the boy. "They can make sure nothing hurt you during this fiasco."

Terem's hand abruptly pulled out of hers. She turned back, wondering what was wrong. "Terem, we need to leave now."

"But I want to go home. Now," Terem replied. There was a dark, depressed look in his eyes.

"Like I said, we can worry about that later. Right now we just need to get out of here."

"But you said! You said if I lived long enough I could go home!" Terem kicked his bare foot against a blood-covered fern and knocked it out of its pot.

"That's right Terem, I did." Bauleel hoped to set an example by keeping her voice calm and soft. "But right now all I can worry about is getting us safely out of here. Does that make sense?"

Terem's anger flared, and his face reddened with the heat of his wrath. He clenched and unclenched his fists angrily as he kicked the poor displaced fern to bits.

"You gave your word, my Lady, but you're just like all the others, aren't you? All of you lie and use people however you want! You're filthy and disgusting just like the rest of them."

Bauleel feared she was about to witness one of Terem's rages, without the protection of the containment cell.

"No Terem, I'm not. I meant what I said. It just hasn't been quite long enough is all. Please just stay calm, and let's deal with the crisis at hand."

Terem looked up at her, eyes blazing with fury. "How much longer, exactly, will be enough for you, Matriarch?" He slowly took a few steps toward her. Stopping at arm's reach, he glared down at her.

It suddenly occurred to Bauleel that she didn't remember Terem being quite this tall when she'd last been with him. If her memory served her, as it always did, he'd been a three to four inches shorter the last time they spoke. He had been barely taller than her height. She remembered the floor of the containment area--was lower than the surrounding hallway? No, it wasn't.

Bitterness etched across his face. He reached forward and gripped Bauleel's shoulders with his hands. "See, O Revered One ... you don't even know for sure, do you?"

Bauleel held Terem's gaze and realized that she'd made a horrible mistake. Terem wasn't himself anymore; all that remained was the plague. She knew what happened when the disease ran rampant, whether the host was alive or dead--it didn't matter. The plague trans- formed what had once been a human or other creature, into a Terror--a bestial animal intent on one thing only: consuming and destroying life. Until this moment, Bauleel had never seen a Terror act so rational and sentient. She wasn't stupid enough to think the danger was any less just because the beast controlled itself so well.

With great horror and the realization struck: Bauleel hadn't told Camille where she was going. No one knew she was here, and neither did anyone know of the deaths in the Technicians' ward. She stood alone with no weapons and completely unprepared. She'd lived too long to be so idiotic.

In her panic, she fumbled a step back to break Terem's grip on her shoulders. He only gripped harder, his fingers boring into her flesh. Sensing her fear his expression turned to one of disgust.

"You were going to leave me here to rot, weren't you? Am I some sort of caged animal to you?" As he said this, he grew taller and thicker, his weight bearing down on her shoulders.

"I wouldn't have done that to you," Bauleel replied, almost forgetting that this thing couldn't properly reason. It just played out the prior memories of its host's body.

A searing flash of pain ripped through her shoulders when the Terror morphed, extending ragged claws through her skin and gripping tighter, scraping against the bones. Her left collarbone shattered under the pressure, and she almost vomited from the sensation. Her blood oozed out between his fingers, a stark contrast against the brilliant white fabric of her robes.

The Terror brought his face down to hers. "How fascinating, my dear Matriarch. You think that you would have let me go--had I proven my health to the Technicians?"

Bauleel tried to maintain clarity and eye contact with him through the pain. She knew Terror's read emotions through contact with bodily fluids--but it was more impressive to witness than she'd imagined.

"Yes. I want life and freedom from the plague for all the Az'Un," she replied, trying to convince herself that her argument might matter to this monster.

The Terror growled deep within its throat. "I believe you. None of that matters now, does it? I'm going home. You're going to open the door, and then I'm going to leave this wretched place."

He released his grip on her right shoulder, which was undeniably just as painful going out as it had been going in, and then half walked--half-dragged Bauleel to the security door.

"Open it. You said you can open all the doors," it demanded.

Bauleel panicked yet again, wanting at all costs to avoid sending the Terror straight through the heart of the Temple complex. He'd kill dozens in the few moments before an alert reached the Guardians, and even more in the ensuing fight. She couldn't let him out this door, but she also knew if she lied, he'd know immediately.

"You won't make it out that way, Terem. The Guardians will hunt you down before you even see the sky. You need to use the other exit."

The Terror brought his face very close to hers, digging his clawed fingers around in her shoulder. Bauleel cried out once again with the pain of bone shards rubbing and tendons tearing.

"Again, you tell the truth. I don't want them coming

after me. You think they can hurt me, don't you?" Bauleel nodded. Terem laughed at her, his emotions gargling through his thickened throat. "Where is this other exit?"

"It's ... on the far end ... of the cafeteria," Bauleel replied between agonized breaths. "A loading dock ... where supplies are delivered. No one tracks it, so you'd get out unnoticed. It's through the door on the left." Even through her pain, she wondered at his degree of focus, which was unusually intense for having lost himself to the disease. Too bad no one had survived to study him-- surely they'd gain new insights from his actions today.

"You're a very good girl."

The Terror loosened his grip, but never extracted his grating, sharp claws. He walked to the door she'd indi- cated, dragging her along after him. It was all Bauleel could manage to keep upright under the force of his pulling on her torn and bleeding shoulder. Bauleel considered the trail of blood she left upon the floor a blessing. At least when someone came looking they'd find some evidence she'd passed this way.

"You're different from the others, aren't you? Do they know you're different, your Eminence?"

Bauleel knew what he was hinting at, but not how he'd come to the conclusion. There were constituents in her blood he definitely wouldn't have picked up in any of the Technicians. "No, they don't know, Terem. I can't ever tell them."

This brought a deep, rumbling laughter from him. "Would they lock you in a cage for it too?"

"No Terem. They'd kill me instead."

He looked at her intently, studying her face. "So you

already live in a cage." Insane as he was, he'd summarized her life concisely.

Before Bauleel knew it, they'd passed through the cafeteria and stood at the wide delivery dock doors.

"Open them. I know you can open them." He thrust her toward the door lock unit.

"Even if you go home, Terem, they'll be afraid of you because they think you're dead. They'll call for the Guardians, and then you'll have to fight them." Although she'd stopped him from waging havoc in the Temple compound, Bauleel also wanted to keep him out of the city and away from the Zebio Sept.

The Terror made a half-roaring, half-screeching noise. Bauleel feared the worst and closed her eyes against the impending onslaught of his rage.

"You may be right, Matriarch. Perhaps I can learn from you. Learn to hide right in front of everyone." She looked back at him and once again, he appeared as she'd first met him. A young teenage boy, except for the claw-like hand which remained embedded in her shoulder.

"Now open the door!" he screamed, his rage barely contained under the docile facade.

Bauleel raised her right hand to comply, pain from her pierced shoulder searing anew down her arm and across her chest. Her palm made a bloody print upon the door lock, but that didn't keep it from scanning her. The doors beeped and slid open, revealing a bright sun in a slightly cloudy, mid-afternoon sky. This entrance opened out and away from the city proper, so the view was of cultivated plains crisscrossed by irrigation ditches. Per her expectations, this passage was vacant. The Technicians only received supplies once a month, via the Guardian Sept, so very few knew of this entry.

For a brief moment, Bauleel tried to lose herself in the beauty of the view, trying to forget her present dire circumstances. The heated emotion in the Terror's face transformed as muscles relaxed, leaving his face calm within seconds. He extracted his claws roughly from her left shoulder and took a few steps outside, reveling in the fresh air and sunshine. Bauleel fell to her knees, aware that a fresh rivulet of blood poured down her chest. Bauleel wondered how much blood she'd lost, and how much more she could lose before she fell unconscious. Did she still have the strength to make her way back through the compound?

A shadow moved over Bauleel's face, and she looked up to see the Terror looking down upon her, its face unreadable. She'd assumed he'd leave once the door was open, yet he lingered.

"Thank you. Freedom is a good thing."

"I understand, Terem."

"I want you to be free too." A perverse, twisted smile widened across its face.

"That's all right, Terem. I'd prefer to stay here." He can't mean to take me with him, can he?

It nodded agreement and came down onto its knees, so they were face to face. "I agree. It's best you stay here."

"Yes Terem," Bauleel replied, hoping he'd leave before she bled out onto the cafeteria floor.

The Terror reached out his hands and closed them ever so gently around her throat. It had such a kind, compassionate look in its eyes it took Bauleel a moment to realize his intention as the gentle grip turned into a vice. This Terem-looking Terror pushed her back onto the ground, its face still kind and calm as she suffocated.

Bauleel pulled away and tried to fight it off with her right arm. Her legs were bent underneath her, and thus useless in this battle, but she knew she was no match for the strength of this Terror--legs or no legs. This was no ordinary Terror, but one mutated over many weeks. One she'd forced the Technicians to protect and harbor. Pinpoints of color flashed before her eyes, and her vision became fuzzy, losing the crisp details of edges.

"Just another moment and you'll be free too. It's the least I can do," the Terror who had been Terem said.

Tears ran down Bauleel's cheeks, as she lay helpless under this monster. Her lungs would surely either explode or collapse. Even her ears were hot and about to burst. Had the doors shut again? The sunlight was gone.

In that last moment, everything became weightless.

CHAPTER 33

RAI AWOKE TO A SOFT BUT INSISTENT KNOCKING ON her bedroom door. A sliver of light snuck through a gap in the thick drapes, bathing the room in its soft glow. From the angle it cast on the floor, Rai knew it must be mid-morning, much earlier than her usual rising time. Slightly annoyed at the early hour, Rai rose and pulled a robe on over her nightshift. Her hair and face were damp with sweat, so she presumed she'd had another night-mare--although she couldn't remember any details about it now.

"Just a moment," Rai called out. The knocking stopped at the sound of her voice.

Rai opened the door to an apologetic Hilse.

"Very sorry, Mistress Rai. I know it's early for you, but Mistress Jesse has requested your presence in the private family dining quarters."

"What's going on?" Rai asked, thinking that they hadn't eaten in that dining room since the last time Stoi and Laan had been in town.

"Meik, Laan, and Ponar arrived this morning. There's to be a family meeting as soon as possible."

"Do you know what about?" Rai asked, attempting to stifle a yawn.

"I don't know, Mistress. I do know we're already packing the wagons. They're leaving again in the morning."

Rai knew that a quick turnaround wasn't unusual for the Durmah. Trade was more lucrative when you didn't take days off. Still, what would they need to discuss with her that Jesse wouldn't be able to tell her about later?

"Thanks, Hilse. Tell them I'll be right down."

"Yes Ma'am." Hilse hurried off down the hallway.

Rai closed the door and threw on some fresh clothes. Rai glanced in the mirror and ran a brush through her mop of hair, not that it did any good. The sweat from her nightmares had left it damp, and now small ringlets broke away and framed her face.

Rai hoped that Jesse would assume she'd gotten her hair wet--not that she was having nightmares all of the time. However, she guessed the dark circles under her eyes spoke for themselves. Sighing, Rai wished she didn't look upset, but wishing wouldn't change a thing.

Rai headed downstairs to the private family dining room. She paused at the closed door, trying to listen to the tone of the conversation, but heard nothing through the thick, heavy door. Rai knocked two short staccato raps.

"Come on in!" Jesse yelled.

Rai opened the door and saw Jesse, Meik, Laan, and Ponar sitting around the table. It didn't require Rai's enhanced senses to tell they'd been arguing--or at least in a heated debate. Meik was eating, fixedly staring at his plate. Laan looked up at her and shot her a brief, half-hearted smile between bites of his own breakfast. Jesse sat back in her chair, arms crossed, with a sour look on her face. Jesse's eyes fixed a pointed glare on Meik, and Rai got the distinct impression Jesse was waiting for him to answer a question. Jesse also held a crumpled letter in her hand. This was delivered to her by the Durmah Sept upon arrival this morning, and the focus of the argument.

Ponar's eyes met hers, and the genuine depth of concern surprised her. At least there was no lingering tension in the air there.

"Have a seat, Sis," Jesse said. The sinking feeling in Rai's gut told her she was involved in some direct way.

Rai took a seat between Meik and Jesse, not wanting to sit on Jesse's other side because then she'd be sitting right next to Ponar. It was best not to appear chummy with him, especially in front of their uncles.

"Have a hard night?" Meik asked her, flashing a critical look. "It doesn't appear you slept too well." He watched her. Rai sensed he was curious about her mental state. Rai tensed, wondering what Meik was hinting at.

"I'm fine. It's just a bit early for me," Rai replied.

"You'll remember Rai covers night shifts at the Waystation, Meik," Jesse said. Rai didn't miss the territorial nature of Jesse's statement.

"I remember that Jesse and I'm happy it works out so well for both of you. I know Kait's very pleased Rai has settled in here, and that the two of you are already so close. Please try to remember, Rai's absence would only be temporary--at most just a few weeks until we get things sorted out."

"Wait--my absence? Where am I going?" Rai asked, confused both by her lack of sleep and coming into the conversation mid-stream.

"You're coming with us," Laan explained. "Up to Barrow's Grove."

"Remember how you smelled something different on those bags of luna berries?" Ponar asked.

"Sure, but you said that didn't mean anything, and they were normal."

"Well, Ponar here's smart, but he's no Healer," Meik replied. "It appears there was something wrong with the berries."

Meik caught up with Rai and Jesse about his interactions at the Temple in Resounding Cliffs, and how they'd treated the luna berry shipment. He then filled them in on the unusual health issues Chirey's birth brother had been afflicted with. "Kait wants us to check out our suppliers in the hopes we can identify the problem at the source. She won't have Durmah blamed for the bad berries."

"That makes sense, but how do you know that what I smelled on the berries was the corruption the Temples have pinpointed?" Rai asked.

"Well, we don't," Meik admitted with a frown. "However, if the Durmah have been transporting corrupted product, you can guarantee it won't go well for us with the Temples."

"But there's no guarantee Rai will even be able to

help you out!" Jesse replied. "Whereas I can warrant that her presence here will help the Durmah cause."

Rai couldn't blame Jesse for wanting to keep her at the Waystation. With the nightmares and the bizarre episode where she'd awoken underneath the bed, Jesse might also be wondering if Rai wasn't mentally up to a long trip through marshlands.

"I disagree, Jesse," replied Laan. "Even if Rai can't identify anything odd in the berries smell, the mere fact that four Durmah tried to research the problem will let the Temples know we're not the problem. Our top priority is that we won't be blamed for the contamination, right?"

Jesse shrugged. "I suppose you've got a point."

"So that's our plan? We travel up through the swamplands, talk with the luna berry farmers, I smell some bags, and if anything smells bad to me we report it, and then return here?" Rai asked.

"Exactly," Meik replied, his placating smile confirming she'd understood. "You never know, a farmer might be able to identify a change in harvesting or fertilization procedure that might explain the bad batches. Either way, we can report what we find to the Temples immediately. That will keep them from placing blame on us, and possibly even improve our Sept's standing. However it works out, Durmah looks good."

"But you have no idea how long you'll be gone, do you?" Jesse asked, arms still crossed even though her expression had softened somewhat. "Ponar sometimes spends weeks in the swamplands!"

"Well, that all depends on travel conditions, Jess,"

Ponar replied. "We'll only visit a few of the farms, and we're headed into winter--so the roads won't be too soft that far north. I doubt we'd keep Rai from the Waystation for more than three or four weeks."

"When do we leave?" Rai asked, still trying to wrap her head around this sudden shift in her life.

"Within the hour. Perhaps two? The travel papers have already been filed," Meik replied.

"Wow, that's short notice." Rai's head spun at this turn of events.

"It is, but Kait wanted us to investigate our suppliers as soon as possible," Laan replied.

"And what my mother wants, she gets," Jesse replied. She rose and stormed out of the room, slamming the door behind her. Jesse's reaction left everyone in varying states of surprise.

"Let me go talk to her, try and calm her down," Ponar said.

"If you think it will help," Meik replied. "I'm not sure why she's so upset. This is just the best for Durmah, after all."

"She's upset Kait didn't give her a choice in the matter, and I can't blame her for that." Ponar headed out the door.

"I'd better go too." Rai rose to leave.

"Good luck with calming her down. That girl's got quite the temper!" Meik shook his head.

Rai was glad to shut the door to the family dining room behind her and on Meik's callous attitude. Too bad she'd now have weeks of conversations with him.

RAI FOLLOWED PONAR TOWARD THE STOREHOUSE AT a distance while she tried to make sense of her conversation with the Durmah. She understood Chieftess Kait's desire to have Rai help the Durmah in this matter; she also knew Jesse's irritation over losing her help around the Waystation.

Although Rai wasn't sure what she'd smelled on the luna berry bags was necessarily a contaminant, it was a definite possibility. One the Durmah couldn't ignore-- especially if it could keep them safe from unwarranted blame. It dawned on Rai that, in this circumstance, her enhanced senses would be of direct use to Durmah. This positive spin brought a smile to Rai's lips. Perhaps she'd be an asset to Durmah after all, instead of just the questionable burden Somnu had hinted at.

Rai entered the storehouse a few moments after Ponar. She hesitated at the door, not sure whether her presence would help calm Jesse or not. She watched Jesse pacing back and forth, muttering angrily to herself. Ponar quietly approached, reaching out a hand toward her shoulder in an attempt to comfort her. She shrugged his hand away, lip half-curled into a snarl.

"Don't. Just don't!" Jesse thrust her hands onto her hips and planted her feet on the floor. Although Ponar was a good head taller than her, her intimidating presence couldn't be denied.

Ponar stood his ground. "Now, Jess. You know this is a good move for Durmah, even if it does inconvenience you for a few weeks."

"But there's no guarantee, is there?" Jesse asked. "Kait can change her mind and give Rai a wagon of her own, can't she?"

"Sure, I suppose, but I doubt that," Ponar reasoned. "I was there when Kait made her decision. There's no intention on Kait's part for Rai to leave the Waystation and work trade routes on her own."

"Yes, fine. For now!" Jesse threw her up hands in the air. "What happens next year, or the year after? I have no say in things! I'm not even there to give an opinion. By the time I hear about Kait's edicts, it was decided weeks ago!" A lone tear slid down her cheek.

"That's what this is about, sis?" Ponar asked. "That you'll never have any say in Durmah politics? That you'll never be our Chieftess?"

Jesse covered her face with her hands, and Rai heard her sob quietly behind them. Ponar reached out and brought Jesse into his arms, comforting her.

"You don't know how hard it is, Ponar. To grow up your whole life, groomed for something every day, just to have it taken away. Kait sent me out here to hide my shame so my failure wouldn't be a constant reminder to the family. I'm abandoned out here."

Ponar held his sister at a loss for words. What could you possibly say to comfort such a wound?

Rai snuck away to her room. She had a trip to pack for and knew she couldn't help Jesse now. At least she could do something to help the Durmah.

CHAPTER 34

Rai walked through the mists of her dream world. However this time the diffuse light was bright and devoid of color. None of the haunting voices joined her, everything was quiet. There a noxious but familiar scent in the air, but Rai couldn't quite place it.

The mists slowly cleared as the light brightened around her, revealing a stark white hallway ending at a flat, metal door. Rai looked behind herself and saw the other end of the corridor ended with a matching metal door. No other distinguishing features stood out in the hallway beside the recessed lights in the ceiling, which were mounted in such a manner Rai hadn't remembered ever encountering previously.

Rai reached the door and stopped to examine it. It was gray, polished, and seamless, with no markings or standard doorknobs upon it. It gleamed brightly, reflecting Rai's silver jumpsuit. There was a metal door lock to the right of the door, and this one had an outline of a hand marked in black on it.

Rai lifted her hand to the plate, but paused, unsure of the wisdom of her choice. The last time she'd activated one of these metal plates, it had caused excruciating pain, and she had no wish to relive that experience. However, what else was there to do? This dream environment offered another door at the other end of the hall, and who was to say it was any safer? Rai resolutely reached her hand out, placed it on the metal plate within the handprint, and waited, wincing in anticipation.

A red light flashed under the plate, almost in time with her pulse. Rai was about to withdraw her hand when the flashing light turned a solid green. She removed her hand and letters appeared to the right of the green light, in corresponding green characters. Rai tried to read the words, but they were too fuzzy to be legible, except for the three letters 'RAI' in the middle. She knew this must be her name, but even her dream self wasn't able or willing to read the entire name on the display. This puzzled her, but she didn't have long to ponder on it as the door clicked, hissed and opened.

Rai hesitated and then stepped into the dark, wary of what she'd discover. Her footsteps triggered an automated lighting system that illuminated the area adjacent to her. The air sighed as it circulated through the extensive chamber. It was chilly for her preference. The floor and ceiling were composed of a metallic mesh grid, through which Rai saw additional levels both above and below. In front of her stood a single pedestal with a screen on top. Behind the pedestal were stacks of rows upon rows of mysterious black boxes, which reminded

Rai of closed shelves. Could this be some sort of massive storehouse?

Rai approached the pedestal, and the screen activated. She couldn't read the words and symbols on the screen but watched as the colors and shapes flickered until they settled on an image of a powder. An arrow appeared on the screen, pointing to the left. How am I supposed to locate anything in this huge place? A series of white indicator lights inset within the mesh floor turned on, answering her question.

Rai followed the lights though the storehouse down countless rows, and up three flights of stairs. Eerily the ceiling lights tracked her movements, turning on as Rai moved into a new section, and turning off as she left one. Just when she thought the dream was leading her on a wild breacat chase, Rai came to the end of the indicator lights. Looking up at the black containers around her, she saw a flashing green indicator on one. Not sure of what else to do, Rai touched the light, and a brief beep rewarded her initiative, and the drawer slid out of the unit.

The drawer had a clear cover with the following text imprinted:

Thallium
Sample derived from cadmium ore
Atomic mass - 204.38
Atomic number - 81

WARNING - DO NOT HANDLE WITHOUT PROTECTIVE GEAR

Please seek treatment immediately if any of these symptoms present after exposure: abdominal pain, vomiting, bloody diarrhea, tremor, delirium or alopecia.

RAI DIDN'T UNDERSTAND WHAT ALL OF THAT MEANT but guessed from the severe warning the substance was some sort of poison. Underneath the drawer cover, Rai saw bluish-white chunks of rock surrounded by broken flakes and dust from the sample.

She began lifting the cover up to get a better view of the rocks and wondered if it was safe to do so. How silly, Rai chided herself; it's not as if a substance from her dreams could make her sick in reality. She slid the cover back, and an unusual, acrid smell greeted her. It was all too familiar. It was much more potent than what she'd smelled on the luna berries, but it was unmistakably the same smell.

An alarm sounded; the blaring tones driving all thought from Rai's mind. Red lights flashed everywhere, and Rai could barely focus her eyes. She looked for the cause of the alarm, but couldn't see anything besides row upon row of storage units. Abandoning the still open drawer, Rai ran back toward the door--at least insofar as she remembered its location.

Just as quickly as they'd started, the lights dimmed into darkness, and the alarm stopped. Rai continued on, stumbling forward in the pitch black of the room, unsure of what else to do. Her enhanced night vision was of little use, as it was now pitch black.

Out of the silence came a distant, muffled voice. "Raaaaaaaiiiii?" it called out her name in a mock song.

Rai felt she should recognize the voice, but she couldn't quite place a name to it.

Again the rough, grainy voice sounded, but now much closer. "Raaaaaaaiiiii?"

Rai tried to move away from it, fearing this unknown yet familiar visitor but managed only to crash back into one of the storage units.

Rai walked forward, wondering how long it would take the stranger to find her. At just that instant, a hand found her neck and gripped her, pushing her back into the storage unit.

"Now, what do you think you're doing," the man asked, tightening his grip. Rai struggled to breathe; shocked breathing in the dream was still required. The acrid odor of the thallium filled her nostrils, even though it must have been aisles away.

"You know you're not allowed here, don't you? I'm afraid I'm asking you to leave."

Pain seared through Rai's belly. She reached down and felt a blade protruding from her stomach. She felt the blood ooze out and run past her fingers, down her legs. She tried to hold in the precious, sticky fluid, but it was of no use.

"After all, traitors aren't allowed to come back," he said. He twisted the knife deeper into her belly. Rai screamed as more than just blood poured out of her abdomen.

RAI WOKE SCREAMING, DRENCHED IN HER OWN sweat. The sound of someone pounding on the wagon door reminded her she wasn't in some remote warehouse but instead safe in the back of Laan's wagon. Rai sat up and checked under her tunic, half-expecting to see the scar of some old wound on her belly, but found nothing. When was this going to end? Such was the realism of her dream that the smell of the thallium salts still lingered.

"Hey Rai, everything all right in there?" Laan asked.

"Yes, yes. Everything's fine." Irritated that yet another nightmare had disturbed her sleep, Rai wondered how far her scream had carried while she donned a dry outfit. "I'll be out in just a moment. Can I assume we've arrived?"

"Yeah, we're at the, uh, fourth farm on Ponar's list. He and Meik are talking to the Chieftess right now, but this farm looks just like all the rest."

"I know what you mean. We've been on the road not

even a full two weeks now, but it's beginning to feel like forever."

It'd taken them five days to reach the first farm on Ponar's list, and then another day to visit the second and third farms. Rai hadn't picked up anything peculiar-smelling at any of those locations, so they'd kept traveling up the swamplands toward Barrow's Grove, after alerting each farm to make sure they followed safe harvesting procedures and to keep an eye out for anything unusual. Rai, remembering Jesse's concern over this being a fool's journey, kept wondering if she'd indeed prove herself useful.

Yesterday Meik's wagon bogged down in the muck wasting an entire day's travel while they worked it free. Rai calculated it had been eight days since they'd left Kiya's Grace. At this pace, she doubted she'd make it back to the Waystation in the three-week time span that Meik had promised Jesse. Rai hoped Jesse wouldn't get too upset, but she also doubted Jesse would be able to help herself.

"I've never worked this route before, so I didn't realize it took so long to navigate these swamps. I think I understand why it takes Ponar months during the rainy season to hit all of these farms," Laan explained. "Stoi's been pushing him too hard."

Rai finished tugging on her boots and opened the door, blinking back the bright midday sun. Used to sleeping in the mornings from her night schedule at the Waystation, Rai had continued sleeping in late while they traveled northward. "That's possible. Will you suggest Stoi take it a bit easier on him?" Rai stepped out of the wagon.

"I'll do that," Laan replied. "Say, it's nice you get along so well with Jesse and Ponar."

"Thanks." Rai hoped Laan didn't suspect she got along too well with Ponar. She'd been careful not to be alone with him during the trip. "Do you think it's about time for lunch?"

"We can always ask. Let's check in with Meik and Ponar, and find out how the discussions are going."

"Lead on!"

They walked through the courtyard and Rai surveyed this farm's layout. Compared to the prior three, nothing looked odd or out of the ordinary. There was the large main farmhouse, an adjacent stable, dormitories for the hired staff, and a processing and storage building for the produce. Rai recognized these buildings from tours of the former three farms.

As they neared the farmhouse, Rai spied a cart full of freshly harvested pale white luna berries sitting outside the processing building at the far end of the courtyard. Rai took advantage of this proximity and strolled over to the cart, curious if the telltale scent was evident on these berries. Rai scooped up a handful of the berries and smelled them.

They smelled just like the thallium salts from her dream.

A chill ran up her spine. Until this moment she hadn't believed they would find anything, and in fact, she'd almost convinced herself what she'd smelled on that bag of luna berries in Kiya's Grace had been a mistake.

Rai focused harder on the berries, trying to determine if anything else was different besides the scent. A dizzying array of sensations entered Rai's mind while her enhanced senses spiraled open. Rai could taste the metallic tang of thallium on the berries. She crushed one of the berries between her index finger and thumb, and in some way, she knew the thallium had penetrated the interior of the berry instead of only coating the outer husk.

"Well?" Laan asked.

"These berries have thallium within them."

Rai realized the acrid odor of the poison not only clung to the berries themselves but also hung in the air. The faint scent must have triggered her dream as they'd approached the farm. After all, the dream's timing and her discovery of more tainted berries wasn't merely coincidental. However, whether the dream's storehouse was literal or metaphorical--that she might never know.

"What's thallium?" Laan asked.

It must not be something taught at school, otherwise, Laan might have recognized the name. *Then where did I learn it?* Did the storehouse from Rai's dreams actually exist, and if so, where?

Rai was about to explain when Meik and Ponar appeared, exiting the main farmhouse. They were accompanied by an older woman clad in a simple brown dress and a tan scarf wrapped down the length of her long, braided hair. Rai dropped her handful of berries back into the cart and wiped the mashed berry from her hand.

"Laan and Rai, this is Chieftess Therji of the Stime Sept," Meik introduced the frowning woman.

"From the looks on your faces, I take it you found something?" Ponar asked.

"I did," Rai confirmed. "These berries are poisoned." To her astonishment, Ponar didn't look at all surprised.

"As I suspected," Ponar replied.

"But how?" Rai asked.

"Remember the bag you thought smelled funny?" Rai nodded. "The tags identified it as coming from this particular farm," Ponar explained. Rai looked to Meik and Laan, noting this also wasn't news to either of them.

"So, why exactly have we been running around on a wild trendar chase if you knew this farm had the tainted berries?" Rai asked.

Ponar's face flushed red with irritation. "First of all, the other luna berry farms were on our way here, so no time was, in fact, lost. Secondly, we needed to check the other farms and make sure they didn't have a problem and to warn them to watch for anything unusual."

"Well, you might have told me that was your plan," Rai replied. She felt hurt that he'd keep such detail from her, but then it's not as if she'd given him any chances in private either.

"What, don't like having that nose of yours tested?" Meik asked. "Look, we wanted to check and see if what you'd picked up on that first time was for real. Now that this poison has been confirmed, the Stime Sept can report the problem to the Temples."

"Wait, if I understand you right, Rai can somehow smell this supposed poison?" Chieftess Therji asked.

"Yes. Rai detected thallium on these here luna berries." Laan replied.

Rai watched their faces to see if anyone recognized the poison's name, but confused expressions stared back at her. How had she learned of such a substance when none of them had?

"What in Ence's name is that?" Meik asked.

"It's a water soluble metal that's poisonous when ingested or absorbed through the skin," Rai explained, surprised to hear such a scientific explanation from her own lips.

"Let's say I believe you. What types of symptoms would someone exposed to this supposed thallium experience?" Chieftess Therji asked.

"It would depend on their exposure level. You'd have vomiting, tremor and hair loss," Rai said, remembering the information printed on the container's lid in her dream. How had she known the medical term alopecia meant hair loss?

Meik, Laan, and Ponar were too taken aback to ask. They stood by and watched this exchange with astonished expressions.

The look on Chieftess Therji's face, however, shifted from doubt to recognition. "My nephew Jonnet died last month, after experiencing many of the symptoms you've just described. We'd attributed it to a probable insect bite. Pests are hard to control in these swamplands. He'd always been fond of swimming out in the bogs, but I'd never imagined it would be the death of him. Do you really think this thallium is to blame?" she asked Rai.

"I'm sure of it." The acrid odor of the poison hung in the air, giving Rai an idea. "Chieftess Therji, is there a particular bog your nephew preferred?"

"It's at the southern corner of our property. It's unique because sweet lilies are growing there."

"Sweet lilies?" Rai asked.

"Yes, Jonnet was quite fond of their fruits. Despite the name, they're powerfully tart and I've never liked them. Just not to my taste, and no one ever wants to buy them. We consider them something of an infestation as they quickly spread through bogs, crowding out the luna berries we can farm," Chieftess Therji explained."

"The lilies grow in the water, right?" Rai asked, fearing she'd guessed how young Jonnet had met his end.

"Yes. That's how the lilies crowd out our luna berry crops," Chieftess Therji replied.

"Can you take us to this bog?" Rai asked. "I'd like to have a look."

"Sure, just let me get someone to help us with the boats. Please, wait here." The Chieftess disappeared back into the main farmhouse, and Rai heard her barking out names. Rai was once again grateful to be a part of Durmah under the loving hand of Chieftess Kait.

"What do you think we'll find out there?" Meik asked, pointing a finger squarely at Rai.

"I'm not sure, but I want to see the place for myself."

"Do you remember where you learned about this thallium stuff?" Laan asked.

"No, but I guess it wasn't at the regular city schools, or you'd all know about it too."

"Perhaps you heard about it at a Temple school? I'm sure they pride themselves on teaching lots of obscure facts," Ponar said.

"Well, I don't remember it." Rai shrugged.

"Whatever the case, if it keeps Durmah from being implicated in this poisoning, we're lucky you knew about it," Ponar replied.

"Thanks." Rai tapped Ponar on the shoulder with her fist, appreciating his support. She looked back to their wagons in the stable yard and saw the Guardian who'd been accompanying them tending to her mount. Suddenly, Rai knew how to prove beyond a doubt whether thallium was to blame in Jonnet's death and the luna berry poisoning.

"Just a moment." Rai walked over to the Guardian.

This Guardian was as tall as a man, red-haired and willowy-framed. Rai read a challenge in her piercing brown eyes at her approach.

"Excuse me, Guardian. Could you please assist me with something?" Rai wondered if asking for her support was too bold a move, but she couldn't see how it would cause any harm.

If the Guardian was surprised, Rai couldn't tell. "What do you require, Mistress Durmah?"

"We're about to head out to one of the Stime Sept's bogs. I have reason to believe that there is a contaminant in the water. Can your scanning device be calibrated to detect such a thing?"

"What are you looking for? What makes you think there's a contaminant?"

"Just a guess," Rai replied, unwilling to divulge any details. "Will you help us?"

The Guardian's nose twitched like a breacat after a bowl of milk. "Sure, it's not as if I was doing anything important. Lead on."

Rai rejoined her Sept-mates, and Chieftess Therji reappeared with two men. All eyed the Guardian cautiously.

"You're not thinking we'll find a Terror out there, are you?" Laan joked.

"Oh no," Rai answered. "I'm just looking for definitive proof. Are we ready?" Rai asked the Chieftess.

"Indeed. May I introduce my sons, Liren and Prane. They'll be helping us with the boats."

"This way," Liren said, motioning them toward a well-used path into the swamp.

Within a few hundred feet, they came upon a dock with a half-dozen boats tethered to it. Some Stime farmhands were unloading freshly harvested luna berries from two of the ships. How many of these berries contain the taint?

Chieftess Therji invited Meik and Laan to join her on Liren's boat, while Rai, Ponar and the Guardian climbed aboard Prane's. Rai took a seat at the prow of the long, thin boat, eager for the view. Ponar sat down beside her, shoulders and hips touching hers on the narrow seat.

"Sorry I didn't tell you we knew which farm the tainted bag came from," Ponar apologized, speaking in hushed tones.

Rai raised an eyebrow. "It was Meik's idea?"

"Yeah."

"How am I not surprised?"

Ponar laughed. "Well, he did prove your nose was right on the money."

"Yeah, I suppose so."

"Where did you learn about this thallium stuff, anyway?" Ponar asked.

"My dreams." Ponar gave her a sideways glance. "There was even a label in the dream, with a full description."

"But how do you know what you dreamed was real? I mean, your subconscious could have just made it up to explain the smell."

"Well, I don't know for certain. That's why I invited her." Rai motioned toward the Guardian, who sat alone in the middle of the boat. "I'm hoping she'll be able to detect the poison or prove its absence."

"Good plan. I'm hoping you're right, that the poison is here. At least then the Temples can figure out a way to remove it, and they won't find Durmah accountable as we helped to find it. If that's not the case, it would mean what you've smelled isn't the problem the Priestess at Resounding Cliffs mentioned to Meik."

"Trust me, I know how important this is to Durmah."

His lips scrunched into a frown. "I don't think anyone doubts your intentions. Even if you can't find out what's going on with this weird smell, you're not at fault for the contamination."

"I'm not sure Meik would agree with you," Rai said. "I don't get the impression he favors me."

"Don't worry about him, he's harmless. Are you okay? You've been a bit on edge since we've arrived."

He reached out and touched her hand, overwhelming Rai with the intimate knowledge of his emotions. It was as if, having previously found the path to her innermost self, he could return in a moment through a simple touch. His desire for her beat steady with tones of curiosity and concern laced through the flow of feelings. Rai knew she'd been right to keep her distance, as she sensed the strong attraction Ponar still held for her.

Rai pulled her hand away. "Oh, I'm all right. I just wish I knew what these dreams are trying to tell me."

"You appear to be doing a good job figuring them out so far."

"I suppose we'll know that soon enough, won't we? Otherwise, everyone will wonder if I've gone round the bend."

Ponar laughed. "I doubt that. I'm betting you're right on target."

"Thanks."

They sat in silence for a few minutes, just watching the swamp drift by. Rai didn't know the names for the local flora but found it beautiful despite the somewhat rank smell of moldy decomposition in the air.

"You know, I can't quite shake this impression that you've been avoiding me," Ponar said.

Rai cringed. Her efforts had been noticed. "Everything's fine, I just didn't want Meik or Laan getting the wrong idea by seeing us spending time together."

"And you don't think they'll wonder why you're avoiding me?"

He had a point. "Sorry, I guess I've been a bit obvious."

"Yes, you have." They shared a laugh. "Besides, I'm dying to know if you've had any memories return yet. You haven't mentioned anything to Laan or Meik."

"That's because there's been nothing to tell, except for these horrible dreams."

"I'm sorry to hear that. It sounds like they've gotten worse?"

Rai thought back to her dream with the beach and the flying monster. She shuddered, remembering how the beast's talons had ripped into her belly, and how she'd awoken naked and scraped up under the bed. "You could say that."

Ponar laid his hand on hers. "Sooner or later, you'll pull the pieces together and they'll cease haunting you."

"I can hope, can't I?" Rai covered his hand with hers and squeezed, smiling at his sincerity even though she doubted the truth to his words.

"Looks like we've arrived," Ponar said. Liren's boat had ground ashore on a nearby bank.

Shortly after that Prane directed his boat alongside the first, and everyone disembarked, taking care not to become entrenched in the sticky mud of the bog.

Liren lead the group in silence into the swamp along a raised trail of packed, dried mud, which twisted and turned every few steps. Rai wondered how anyone kept his or her bearing in such a dense, overgrown area. Rai found her hearing sharpening, focusing on the muted footfalls of those ahead of and behind her. This focusing somehow also helped her realize the smell of the thallium was indeed stronger here.

Around another few turns, the group emerged into a clearing, and the sun shone across the lake in front of them. Iridescent white flowers rode gracefully on thick, bare stalks a few feet above the water. Their green, fern-like fronds danced just below the water's hazy surface, revealing a slow but present current within the lake.

"They're so beautiful," Rai said.

"They're so irritating, you mean," Prane spat. "Those sweet lilies grow so wild and so fast, nothing else even stands a chance."

"Well, it's good we're not here for the scenery," Meik stated. "What now?" he asked Rai.

"Guardian, could you set your device to scan for thallium sulfate?" Rai asked. The scent was strong here, such that Rai could barely smell anything besides its acrid bite because she was so attuned to its noxious odor.

The Guardian raised an eyebrow, curiosity filling her eyes. She nodded and began adjusting her scanner.

"Must we resort to such gadgets to solve this problem?" Chieftess Therji asked.

Rai felt a knot form in her belly. "Please excuse this temporary reliance on machines, Chieftess. I'm afraid I knew of no other way to quickly identify the source of the contamination."

The Chieftess frowned. "Our ancestors knew the dangers of using such tools as crutches."

"I can assure you I will complete this task as quickly as possible, Chieftess Stime," the Guardian replied.

After a few moments, the Guardian stiffened, as if readying for battle. "I have an active detection in the water and plants for the substance." She walked as she talked, passing the device back and forth in front of her as she walked. "It's much higher than expected for trace environmental patterns. Checking density patterns ... challenging with the currents." the Guardian muttered that last bit under her breath.

Rai breathed a sigh of relief. She expected to be right about the smell, but the Guardian's confirmation amazed her. Somehow her dreams were revealing her suppressed memories. If only she could separate the memories from the subconscious ramblings!

"You've got a nose like a bloodhound!" Laan exclaimed, clapping Rai on the back.

"See, I told you it wasn't just a coincidence," Ponar said.

The Guardian walked along the path to their right, continuing to monitor readings via the scanner. Rai followed close behind, and soon the entire group trailed the Guardian clockwise around the rim of the lake.

"Why did you suspect increased thallium levels in this area?" the Guardian asked Rai.

Rai related the story of the tainted luna berries to the Guardian. Chieftess Therji also took a keen interest.

"Very smart of you all, connecting things together like that. Not what I'd expect from merchants." Rai couldn't tell whether that was an insult or a compliment. The Guardian came upon a widening in the path and stopped, continuing to scan the area. "What interests me more is how you even know about thallium. Where did you learn about it?"

"I'm not sure, must have been in something I read somewhere," Rai replied, not wanting to trust this Guardian with details of her personal life.

"That's curious. Do you read a lot of chemistry texts?" Her sarcasm made it clear to Rai that she didn't believe her explanation.

"Occasionally," Rai replied. "They aren't as dry as you might suppose."

"Last I checked, only Technicians have access to such information," the Guardian replied. "Oh, and how did you learn a smell from a book?"

Rai flushed, unsure of what to say. Did she come from the Technicians' Sept? That might explain her dream with the storehouse. Rai had no idea if the Techs even had such storehouses, assuming the dream was real at all.

"What does it matter?" Ponar asked. "Shouldn't your concern be the source of the thallium contamination?"

"It matters because it's impossible to smell thallium. Although there's enough in this water to poison anyone who consumes it, or I suspect anything that has grown within the bog."

Rai had been so overwhelmed with her perception of the acrid stench and her nightmare she's forgotten that no one else smelled it as she did. Rai had revealed her unusual ability to perceive odors, and in this case scents of things that didn't even normally have them, and to a Guardian no less. How could she have been so careless?

"Who cares about the stupid smell?" Chieftess Therji

yelled. "What I want to know is, what's caused this poisoning, and are my other swamps affected?"

"As I've already stated, the poisoning is due by the presence of thallium deposits within your swamp. I can't say until a thorough scan is done of all of your lands, but I'd make an educated guess that because of the currents I'm picking up, all areas downstream of this spot contain some lesser degree of the poison. As to what's causing the build-up ..." she continued walking forward, and then much to everyone's surprise jumped down into the water.

The Guardian sloshed through the plants and chest-deep muck, oblivious to its stench. She waded out a good thirty feet, now partially hidden from their view by the thick stalks of sweet lily flowers.

"I wonder what she's looking for," Meik asked.

"Did she just go underwater?" Liren asked. "Those Guardians are crazier than I thought."

"You'd better hope she is underwater, saying that within her earshot!" Chieftess Therji. Liren blushed.

The Guardian reappeared, soaking wet, with a few tendrils of swamp grass caught in her hair. She held a black cylinder above the water's surface and wore a grim expression on her face. The cylinder was over three feet in length and must have been at least four inches in diameter as the Guardian barely managed to get her hands halfway around the tube.

Laan whistled a long, low note. "What is that?"

Rai stared at it, a nagging familiarity stirring at the back of her mind. "It's an aqueous dispersal unit," she answered, knowing it was true the moment the words tumbled out of her mouth.

Everyone turned to look at her as if she'd spoken complete gibberish.

"Huh?" Meik said. Everyone waited expectantly for her response.

The Guardian answered. "She's correct, although, again, I'm quite amazed at the quality of your schooling." Her eyes fixed on Rai, curiosity now overcast with suspicion. She set the cylinder down upon the bank and then clambered up and out of the water.

"What does that ... thing ... do?" Chieftess Therji asked.

The Guardian picked grass and roots from her hair and clothing. "Aqueous dispersal units were used by the original colonists to terraform Az'Unda. They release mineral and bacterial environmental modifications over an extended period. One of these could seed an area the size of your property for, say, a decade or so, depending on the degree of modification required."

She rotated the cylinder, quickly locating and then pressed a button. A panel slid open on the device, revealing a touchpad and screen. The Guardian keyed in a sequence, and the screen lit up.

"So, in other words, it's an abandoned, ancient artifact?" Meik asked.

"Ancient, yes. Abandoned, no," the Guardian answered.

"It's still active? Wouldn't that mean it's been running for well over 600 years, since the colonization?" Ponar asked.

"According to this, it's been active for less than two years," the Guardian answered.

"But how can that be?" asked the Chieftess.

"Someone must have placed it here and activated it to release thallium salts."

"But who would deliberately set up a device to fill our swamp with poison?" asked Chieftess Therji.

"Unfortunately, the device isn't programmed with that information," the Guardian replied as she continued to investigate the device.

"More importantly, why would anyone want to poison a plant essential to the anti-plague regimen?" Rai asked.

"And who'd have the know-how to use one of those things?" Meik asked.

The Guardian picked up the device and walked back toward the boats. "We're leaving now. I must report my findings to my superiors."

"But what are we to do?" asked the Chieftess, as she sprinted to catch up with the Guardian. "We're already midway through this harvest!"

The Guardian stopped and turned to face the Chieftess. Although Rai was at the rear of the group, she heard the Guardian's edict through the dense overgrowth along the twisted path.

"As of this moment, the Stime Sept will cease all farming and production efforts. All goods located on the premises will be quarantined until the Matriarch of Barrow's Grove Temple deems them safe. This is just my guess, you'll be destroying them, because they aren't."

"You can't be serious!" The Chieftess squealed. "How long will it take before we can sell our goods again?"

The group moved forward again at a fast pace. "That

depends," answered the Guardian. "A cleanup crew will be sent out to further evaluate the situation and develop a plan to deal with the contamination. Any affected product will be destroyed. I'd guess it might take years before the bog or any affected areas downstream have the quarantine removed. In the meantime, we must do anything and everything possible to alleviate the threat to the populace."

"But how can we manage to feed ourselves if we can't sell our product?" Chieftess Therji asked. "They're the only thing we make any profit on!"

"The Temple won't let you starve," answered the Guardian. "Surely they will recognize the sacrifice you're making. Assuming no one in your Sept is found responsible for the poisoning."

The group emerged from the thick canopy to where they'd left the boats. The Guardian urged everyone to board quickly, leaving little time for discussion.

"I can assure you, Guardian, no Stime was involved in this!" Chieftess Therji replied.

"If that is the case, I'm sure the investigation's findings will support your claim," she replied. Chieftess Therji didn't appear at all comforted by her sentiment.

"Don't forget to mention how Durmah Sept helped point you in the right direction," Meik said.

"Have no worries, Sir Durmah. The Temples will receive a full accounting of your actions in my report. I'm sure they will be very interested in your involvement."

The boats pulled away from the bank, Liren, and Prane expertly turning them around in the cramped quarters.

Rai leaned in close to Ponar and whispered, "That's what I'm afraid of. How do I explain how I learned of this poison?"

"Well, perhaps we need to keep you busy and away from the city until they finish sorting this out," he whispered back.

"What are you thinking?"

"Well, we're just two, maybe three days from Harper's Sorrow. I bet Jesse can spare you for another week, don't you think?" he winked conspiratorially.

"How ... wait, did Jesse tell you about that?"

"She mentioned your nightmares might have been about Harper's Sorrow. When we spoke in the storehouse, she said that since we were coming up into the Barrow's Grove swamplands, we might as well check out the forest if it wasn't too inconvenient."

Rai hadn't dared hope there'd be the time or cause to visit Harper's Sorrow and compare it to the one from her dreams. Leave it to Jesse to plant the idea and give her a chance to visit the place for herself. The timing was perfect. What better way to avoid questions from the Temple than to disappear for a few days?

"Thank you, Ponar," Rai beamed up at him.

"Now we just convince Meik to go along with our little plan."

If her luck held, Rai thought, finding the source of the luna berry poisoning had Meik in an amiable mood. Agreeable enough to grant her this one favor. She reckoned she was due one favor and a late lunch.

CHAPTER 36

"I'll make you a deal, Ponar. If you can convince the Guardian to approve this side trip to Harper's Sorrow, we'll go," Meik said.

Rai hated Meik in these moods. His confident tone of voice berated Ponar for even trying, and Rai didn't want to jump to her ex-lover's defense, not when she knew the men could work it out on their own. Yet she hated biting her tongue.

The four Durmah stood next to their wagons in the Stime Sept's stable yard. Chieftess Stime had been cordial enough after the discovery of her poisoned bogs to feed them a late lunch once they'd returned to the farmhouse, but afterward, she wasn't interested in chatting about news from the city. She'd already had more news than she could bear in a day. Instead, she'd offered them her hospitality for the night, bid them well, and retired to private discussions with her Sept-mates, without even bartering for a fee. A few credits made no difference after the reality of having her farm shut down.

After lunch, the Durmah ventured outside and prepared their wagons and horses for the next day's journey.

"Since we're in the area, I don't see why we don't go ahead and head up the road to Harper's Sorrow and fish out Rai's little dream forest mystery while we're at it," Ponar threw out as if it were the most natural consideration on the planet.

Meik heaved a heavy sigh. "I think we've had enough adventure for one trip, don't you?"

Laan busied himself with currying his horse, Rai noticed. She bit her lip and checked over his wagon for loose fittings and bolts.

"We won't get into any adventures, it's just another route back. Besides, you remember the mud on the roads we were bogged down in. I'd prefer to take another route myself."

"There's no guarantee the higher road will be any smoother--and then we'd have to cut back through Raven's Call and the Baris Spine. We'd waste a nearly a good week or more!"

"Since when is time on the road 'waste' to merchants?" Ponar laughed. "The more we move around, the more we trade. At least this way we'd make the trip worthwhile if we find something rare to sell. You never know what new farms have set up along the Northern Road--it's been a good year since I've run the route."

"In backcountry?" Meik's eyes widened. "Yes, I know there are a few rugged souls who brave life outside city walls, but they are far and few between. I'm sorry, but we must resume our regular schedules. Rai's needed back at the Waystation. Do you know how Jesse would react to hear you going on like this?"

Ponar hung his horse's tack on the side of his wagon from some strategically placed hooks and then ran a hand through his hair in frustration. "Yeah, I can imagine how Jesse would react. She'd want us to check it out and for Rai to know if she'd ever been to Harper's Sorrow before. What it could have meant to her. Jesse would want this matter laid to rest once and for all."

Meik, Ponar, and Laan all turned to Rai, and she stared right back at them. They knew what she wanted. She wasn't going to beg. Listening to Ponar and Meik talking about her as if she wasn't even there had already made her more than a little uneasy.

"It's pointless, and the Guardians will never approve the course change," Meik replied, throwing cleaning gear into one of the open side panels of his wagon.

"We'll see about that, won't we?" Ponar answered.

From the dubious look on Meik's face, Rai doubted he thought Ponar could get approval from the Guardian. He hoped to end the discussion. Perhaps he thought Ponar wouldn't be willing to debate the itinerary with the Guardian. That he'd be too intimidated by the Sept to risk their ire. Meik was wrong.

Rai followed Ponar toward the group of Guardians at the far end of the stable yard. "Thanks for taking a stand for me," Rai said. "If you weren't fighting for this trip, I know it wouldn't happen."

"Oh, don't underestimate Meik's curiosity." Ponar shot a frustrated glance back in Meik's direction. "I think a large part of his argument was geared at getting me to ask the Guardian so he wouldn't have to."

"Ah. What do you think she'll say?"

"I have no idea. I've never tried changing destinations mid-trip before." He winked, and Rai chuckled.

Both grew serious when they came within earshot of the Guardians. The Guardians also stopped their discussion, awaiting the pair's arrival.

"What do you need, Durmah? We are busy right now." Their Guardian appeared, in Rai's estimation, on the edge of an emotional outburst of the weapons variety.

"Sorry to disturb you, but I thought it prudent to update our itinerary with you before we head out tomorrow."

The Guardian nodded and pulled out one of her many devices. "I assume you'll be heading back to Kiya's Grace, or do you plan to continue visiting swamp farmers?" she asked.

"Actually, we intend to travel on to Resounding Cliffs, via the Northern Road," Ponar spoke nonchalantly as if this were a perfectly reasonable request.

Their Guardian raised an eyebrow. The other two looked at them both, curiosity evident.

"Why?" She asked.

"We have business there." He shrugged. "But I don't want to bore you with the details while you're so busy. Meik thought it'd save us time over the southern route since we'd have to travel back through these swamplands southwards. After all, we're just within a day or so of the Northern Pass, right?" Ponar was cool as ice with the Guardians, but his anxiety was plain to Rai.

"Yes, but it's rare for anyone to travel the Northern road." The Guardian keyed information into her device. Rai wondered what variety of uses her machine served. They had so many devices, she mused they were almost a natural extension of the Sept itself.

As Rai watched the Guardian's movements, something made her think that this machine was a communications device, but she couldn't quite tell why.

A few moments passed. "So that route's fine? We don't need to fill out any paperwork or anything?" Ponar asked.

The Guardian looked up from her device. "I have submitted your request, and am now awaiting approval."

"How long until you hear back?"

"An hour, perhaps more. I'll find you ..." The machine beeped, and she studied the device. The Guardian's nose wrinkled in confusion for a second, but the moment passed quickly.

"You're in luck. My replacement will be accompanying you along the Northern Road," she informed them.

"Replacement?" Ponar asked.

She looked at Rai and frowned. "Yes, since I discovered this poisoned swamp I've been appointed to lead the cleanup task force. In all likelihood, I'll be here for the next few months." She didn't appear very happy at the prospect.

"I bet Meik will love to hear the good news," Rai said to Ponar, eager to change the subject.

"I'm sure. Thanks for your help," Ponar said to the Guardian.

She glared in response and stalked off.

They walked back to their wagons and Rai sensed unease from Ponar. "Did that go well?" Rai asked him.

"Yes, much easier than I've come to expect from a Guardian." He looked puzzled.

"But you're acting like this was bad news?" Rai asked.

"It's just a bit weird she got an answer so quickly. I mean, whoever wrote that response replied immediately. I've always had to wait at least a couple of hours to get itinerary changes approved along regular trade routes."

"That is weird," Rai replied. "Maybe, since she's coordinating the cleanup effort her messages are being read more often?"

"Could be. Oh well, it's not as if I've ever been able to understand their Sept before. Why should the Guardians start making sense now?"

"True enough. I wonder how Meik will take the news."

Ponar barked out a short laugh. "Yeah, he was counting on the Guardian winning the argument for him. Now he's committed to the detour, whether or not he likes it."

"They approved?" Meik asked. Laan attempted to hide his laughter over Meik's reaction.

"Indeed. I just explained we had business in Resounding Cliffs and didn't want to muck back south through the swamplands," Ponar replied.

"Business! What business?" Meik demanded as his

face turned red. "This is just another of your wild trendar chases!"

"Well, I picked up some knit shawls from the cotton root farm we passed on the way up here. Personally, I think there might be a market for them at the Cliffs, what with the cooler, windy nights up there," Ponar explained.

Rai remembered his purchase, how odd it had been at the time. She wondered if Ponar had been planning this detour all along. He must have. Rai again felt bad for keeping him at arm's length while he'd been going out of his way to help her.

"Hmm, you might be right," Meik replied, beginning to cool off at the promise of profit. "Still, no one goes that way! We have no idea what we might run into!"

"I doubt the Guardians would allow us to travel into danger," Laan interjected, always the mellow voice of reason. "I'm sure the road's reasonably safe. Besides, we'll get to look at this Harper's Sorrow Grove, and we'll find some clues into Rai's past. Far as I can tell, it sure beats mucking southward through these swamps."

"Well, I won't miss that either," Meik replied. "Let's just hope our Chieftess finds our course agreeable too, or we'll all be answering for it!"

THE FOLLOWING MORNING USHERED IN A BRIGHT and clear day, a welcome change from the hazy, humid norm of the swamplands. Rai stretched her legs, reveling in the sunny warmth of the morning while the men secured their wagons for the trip. None of the Stime Sept bothered to see them off. They had their hands full with a few dozen Guardians who had arrived during the night. However, true to her word, the Chieftess had shared her rooms, baths and a hearty breakfast with her guests without asking for so much as a credit.

"You ready for this?" Ponar asked her.

Rai felt uncertain. "I guess so. It's hard, I mean, even if we find the place from my dreams, that's no guarantee it'll answer my questions."

"True, but it might help stop the nightmares. I've found facing your fears can make them go away."

"Is that so? I wonder if that holds true if you can't remember what the fears are about." Rai chewed her lip. "What's the use of feeling guilty when I don't even know what I feel guilty for?"

"I can't help you there. All we can do is hope and find what we find."

"You're right. Thanks again," Rai said, smiling.

"Hey, that's what brothers are for, right?"

Rai flashed back to their interlude at the Waystation in Kiya's Grace and almost blushed. "Is everything ready to go?"

"We're just waiting for our escort, then we'll get going. Meanwhile, Meik and Laan are debating the asking price for a cotton root shawl."

Rai looked around and spotted the two walking down the path from the swamp boat pier, discussing, Rai assumed, the price of shawls. Ponar flashed them a thumbs-up, signaling he was ready to leave. They waved and started back toward the wagons.

"Now all we need is our Guardian escort ...," Rai said.

"Who is here," answered a familiar voice.

Rai turned, coming face to face with not just any Guardian, but one she'd come to dread. One she'd most recently tried to gut with a knife. How did he sneak up on me? She'd turned away from the road for only a moment.

"What are you doing here?" Rai asked, irritation straining her voice. The Guardian raised an eyebrow.

Ponar shot Rai a quizzical look. "You know him?"

"Not really. I mean, I've run into this Guardian around Kiya's Grace a few times."

"I was recently posted there and was on my way to a posting in Barrow's Grove when I received this reassignment. As you can imagine," he gestured to the other Guardians walking around, "we're a little short-staffed in the swamplands at the moment."

Meik and Laan reached them in time to hear his last sentence. "I'm sure we'd understand if this trip is too much of an inconvenience to the Guardian Sept," Meik replied, seeking an opportunity to avoid the unfamiliar northern passage.

"Whichever way you travel, it's no difference to us," he replied.

"Then perhaps we should be off?" Ponar redirected the conversation.

"The sooner, the better," replied the Guardian. "With any luck, we'll make the Northern pass by sunset."

"We'll get the teams hitched up," Laan replied. Meik followed him, looking slightly disgruntled.

"How long will it take to reach the Cliffs?" Ponar asked the Guardian.

"I can't say for certain because this isn't my usual route." Rai wondered what his normal way was, besides doggedly trailing her, time after time. "According to the maps, we're about a full day's travel to the upland pass. After that it'll take us seven or eight days to reach the eastern coast, assuming the weather is fair."

Ponar sighed. "Well, that's still shorter than heading south and then east from Kiya's Grace. Thanks. I better get my team hitched up too." Ponar walked away, intent on the task.

Rai stared up at the Guardian, wondering if his showing up could be a coincidence after all. "How long before we reach Harper's Sorrow?" she asked. Was it just her imagination, or did his look stiffen in response to her question? Between the acrid odor of the thallium in the air and the few feet separating them, Rai couldn't begin to get a reading from him.

"That grove is relatively close. Once we hit the Northern Road, I'd guess about two days. Why do you ask?"

"They have giant trees, where they're so tall you can't even see the tops. Will we get a chance to stop and take a look around when we get there?"

His expression was grave. "What exactly do you think you'll find amongst a bunch of trees?" Rai detected none of the sarcasm in his voice she'd come to expect during their prior encounters. This, together with the seriousness of his gaze, made Rai feel distinctly uncomfortable. Although she couldn't sense his emotions, her common sense told her she was treading on dangerous ground.

Rai considered trivializing her interest in Harper's Sorrow but thought better of it. "A bit of history?" Rai dared to speak honestly, if vaguely. "Isn't that what old growth forests are good for? Learning about the past?"

"I suppose if you go for that sort of thing. I'd say the past is history, and best left alone." She knew he was waiting for some sign from her, but she had no idea what that might be, or what consequences such a signal might bring.

"It's not always that easy," Rai replied.

"No, no it's not," he agreed.

Rai couldn't shake the impression they were discussing more than an ancient grove of gigantic trees. Did this man know something about her past? Is that why he kept showing up? Watching and waiting to see if she remembered anything? No, surely she just being paranoid, looking for subterfuge where there was none? Rai resolved to try to satisfy her curiosity during this trip by finding out all she could about this mysterious Guardian, including his name.

With the teams hitched, Ponar's wagon pulled forward to where Rai and the Guardian stood. Meik and Laan's wagons followed close behind.

"We're ready," Ponar announced. Rai stepped up onto Ponar's wagon and took the seat next to him.

"Let's go," replied the Guardian. He mounted his horse in a single, fluid motion, and turned to lead the way.

CHAPTER 37

Journeywoman Camille looked up from her desk in the Matriarch's offices at Raven's Call Temple to face an Elder standing in front of her. She couldn't tell which Elder, as her brown veil and robes totally obscured her form. Had she fallen asleep for a moment, or had she been too engrossed with paperwork to notice the woman's entrance?

"Excuse the wait, Elder. How may I be of service?"

"No worries, child." Camille instantly recognized Elder Natre's voice due to its grating quality. "I know these past few days have been challenging for you, to say the least. Actually, it is I who is here to help you." Elder Natre handed her a scroll.

Camille took the scroll and paused a moment to reflect. She knew what this meant, and knew her world would change forever upon the reading of it. Why did it have to be Elder Natre?

Resolutely Camille unfurled the scroll and read. She

scanned through the text, quickly locating the critical information.

... This document confirms the appointment of
Elder Natre

as

Matriarch-elect of Raven's Call Temple,
until Matriarch Bauleel can be located.
The Matriarch-elect is granted all rights and privileges
accorded to her station from this point forward. She has
the full faith and goodwill of the Elder's Council of
Raven's Call Temple ...

THE SIGNATURES OF EVERY ELDER WITHIN RAVEN'S Call Temple followed this.

Camille stood and genuflected. "It appears congratulations are in order, my Esteemed Matriarch," Camille said, surprised how smoothly it rolled off her tongue.

"Oh now, let's not dawdle on pleasantries and chit-chat. Up, up! I have not only the job of running this facility, but I must also solve the mystery of Matriarch Bauleel's disappearance."

"Indeed. How can I be of assistance?" Camille wondered if tendering her resignation on the spot might come across as overly helpful under these circumstances.

"I'll start by searching Matriarch Bauleel's quarters and reviewing her recent letters and personal notes."

The idea of Elder, no Matriarch, Natre violating

Matriarch Bauleel's privacy made Camille's skin crawl. Matriarch Bauleel's sudden, unexplained disappearance had done nothing to shake her steadfast loyalty. Camille was sure the Matriarch had a good reason for her absence if she'd had any control in the matter, of course.

"I've already been through her files and her quarters. I can assure you I found nothing."

"Yes, my child, I'm sure you didn't."

"I was thorough! If there were anything to report, I'd have immediately brought it to the Elder's Council."

"Yes, I'm quite sure you would have. However, you do not have access to Matriarch Bauleel's protected files or secured areas within her quarters. Gratefully I was able to persuade the Matriarch's of Barrow's Grove, Resounding Cliff's and Kiya's Grace to grant me that level of access this morning. The system was updated with my codes shortly after that." She held out another piece of paper, no doubt confirming her words.

Camille took the paper and placed it upon her desk, not even bothering to read it. What was the point? It's not as if you could lie about your access codes. Either they'd work, or they wouldn't.

"Where would you like to begin?" Camille replied.

"With her private files. Can you show me where she keeps her message terminal?"

Camille hesitated only a moment. "Of course."

"This must be very hard on you. I'm sure you loved Matriarch Bauleel dearly," Matriarch Natre said. Camille nodded and opened the Matriarch's desk. "If you'd rather I choose another assistant, I'd completely understand."

Camille considered for a moment, tempted to accept any excuse to avoid working with this woman, but who'd protect Matriarch Bauleel's interests if she was gone? "It'd be an honor to continue serving the Matriarch. This is the drawer she keeps it in, but I don't have the access code for the lock."

"It's settled then. I'm sure I'll find your assistance as valuable to me as Matriarch Bauleel did."

Matriarch Natre sat down in Matriarch Bauleel's chair and punched in a code on the drawer's lock keypad. A green light next to the keypad flashed briefly, then the drawer yielded to Matriarch Natre's pull. She reached in and pulled out the message terminal, placing it flat on the desk.

Matriarch Natre, although elderly, was obviously no stranger to technology. She navigated the console expertly, quickly bringing up all of the most recently edited files and transmissions. They dated from the day of Bauleel's disappearance before the Matriarch had bidden Camille a cheerful good night on her way to bed. So Camille had thought until she checked in the next day and found the Matriarch's quarters vacant and the bed not slept in.

Matriarch Natre read a number of the notes and files. Nothing appeared out of the ordinary to Camille. Then Matriarch Natre tried to open one of the transmissions, and an error popped up, "Access Restricted." How odd, wouldn't Matriarchs have complete access to all files, regardless of the file's access level?

"I desire a moment of privacy."

"Of course, Matriarch," Camille replied, averting her eyes. She walked back over to her desk and sat down.

Camille picked up the order for some bolts of blue broadcloth needed to make new Apprentice robes. Camille signed off on the order and marked it for delivery to the Rask Sept, one of the premier weavers Septs within Raven's Call.

Many minutes passed, while Camille observed Matriarch Natre's constant activity over the message terminal. "Well, this certainly changes everything," Matriarch Natre said softly. Camille wondered if she'd forgotten the Journeywoman was still within earshot.

"Did you find something that will help us locate Matriarch Bauleel?" Camille asked.

Matriarch Natre stood up. "Unfortunately, no." She placed the message terminal back in the drawer and slammed it shut. "Matriarch Bauleel made some choices I do not agree with, and I'd love the opportunity to review her reasoning with her."

"Perhaps it's something I can assist you with? Matriarch Bauleel always kept me up to date with her projects."

Matriarch Natre let out a short, derisive laugh. "Somehow, I seriously doubt Matriarch Bauleel discussed this particular issue with you. Although it might explain her sudden disappearance."

How was that possible? The Matriarch relied on her so heavily and had asked Camille to annotate documents in her name. Surely, Matriarch Natre was mistaken.

"Let's go inspect her quarters." Matriarch strode

towards the door. Camille reflexively picked up her notepad and dutifully followed behind.

The trip passed in silence. Within minutes, they reached Matriarch Bauleel's quarters, and Matriarch Natre didn't hesitate in activating the door lock. Camille was surprised she hadn't attempted to announce herself, so ingrained was the habit.

Matriarch Natre strode purposefully into the sitting room, and Journeywoman Camille followed.

"In your prior checks of Matriarch Bauleel's quarters, did you notice anything amiss?" Matriarch Natre asked.

"No," Camille answered. "I inventoried her closet and found it lacking one set of Matriarch's robes. Presumably, she wore it at the time of her disappearance."

"You're telling me you kept an accounting of how many sets of robes she had?" She walked through the Matriarch's private office, across the bedroom, and into the closet, turning on the lights as she whisked through the space.

"Of course. I always made sure she had six full sets of white linen Matriarch robes available at all times. I had her maids alert me whenever a tear or blemish marred an outfit, and I'd have another one created to replace it."

"That's very efficient of you."

"Thank you, Matriarch," Camille replied.

"That reminds me, could you order me six sets of Matriarch's robes?"

"Of course, Matriarch. I'll schedule a fitting for later today," Camille jotted down a quick reminder on her notepad.

"Thank you, Camille. It does appear that Matriarch

Bauleel kept a supply of other clothing here as well. Are you sure none of it's missing?"

"I am," Camille responded confidently.

Matriarch Natre continued her inspection, looking through the bathroom, the bedside drawers, and cabinets, and again in the closet before walking back into the private office. She sat down at Matriarch Bauleel's desk and rifled through the stacks of paper and drawers.

"Perhaps if I knew what you were looking for, I could be of more assistance?" Camille offered, hoping to stem Matriarch Natre's indiscriminate investigation.

Matriarch Natre sat back in the chair and folded her arms. "I take it you've been through all of this as well?"

Camille blushed. "I thought it prudent at the time."

"And so it was, my child. I suppose you found nothing of interest?"

"Nothing unexpected."

"You knew the issues facing Matriarch Bauleel. Can you think of anywhere she might have run off to?"

"The entire Temple has been gone over with a fine-tooth comb, Matriarch. If she were here, we'd have located her. I personally inspected the Medicinal Vaults and Formulary three times, just in case she'd been crushed under a falling pile of medicinal bags. You know how high those can get!"

Matriarch Natre snorted out a laugh. "Oh, what a morbid thought, my dear! I doubt such a fate has befallen our beloved Matriarch Bauleel. But why should you think she'd be spending time there?"

"She was concerned over the tainted luna berries."

"And did she not trust Priestess Parthe to handle the matter on her own?"

"I'm sure you're right, Esteemed Matriarch. Matriarch Bauleel stated no concern over Priestess Parthe's abilities."

"Well then, Camille, is there anywhere else you think she might have gone? Somewhere away from the Temple grounds, perhaps?"

Camille considered. "Sometimes Matriarch Bauleel would travel around the city, dressed simply as a Temple Elder. But if that were the case we'd be missing a different set of clothing, or there would have been some reports of people encountering Matriarch Bauleel in her white robes in the city."

"Very true."

"The only other place she's been going recently is the Technician's wing, but I'm sure we'd have heard from them via transmission if the Matriarch had fallen ill during a visit."

"True, and there were no such communications from them on her terminal," Matriarch Natre replied. "Still, I know the other Elders are curious to get an update on that poor child the Technicians are holding, so perhaps I will visit them now regardless."

"I'd have checked with them myself ...," Camille said.

"Except that you couldn't, my child," Matriarch Natre stood. "Well, now that I've been granted access I can confer with them and eliminate their wing as a possibility for Matriarch Bauleel's location as well. Will you walk with me there?"

During the five-minute walk from Matriarch

Bauleel's quarters to the Technician's wing, Matriarch Natre asked Journeywoman Camille to fill her in on all items she'd been keeping track of for Matriarch Bauleel. Camille complied, reciting the litany of events and minutiae, just as she'd have done for Matriarch Bauleel during their usual morning catch-up sessions. Matriarch Natre didn't ask her to go into detail on anything, but instead quietly listened until they reached the Technician's wing.

"Excuse me, my child. Could you wait here for a bit while I check on things?" Matriarch Natre asked, and then activated the door lock.

"Of course, Esteemed Matriarch," Journeywoman Camille replied. After the Matriarch-elect had stepped through the doorway, Camille pulled out some paperwork for review from the back of her notepad. She was never one to waste time standing around, and thus always planned to have work on hand.

Almost an hour later the door opened, startling Camille out of a half-doze as she leaned against the wall. Matriarch Natre emerged, silent. The door closed behind her, and they both stood in silence for a moment.

"Is everything alright, Matriarch Natre?" Camille asked softly, sensing something had gone horribly wrong.

"I'm afraid a great tragedy has occurred here, Camille. I regret to inform you the plague-ridden Zebio child broke free and killed a number of Technicians, and escaped," Matriarch Natre explained. "Due to the damage to their facility, the few survivors were unable to alert us to the situation."

"By the moons," Camille whispered. "How many died?"

Sorrow filled her voice. "Of the six dozen or so stationed here, only eight survived."

"No!" Camille replied, distraught. "Wait, you said the Zebio child escaped, but that's impossible! The technician facility safeguards prevent unauthorized access. No one without proper clearance can open either of the exits." As the words left her lips, a sinking sensation settled into her chest.

"Matriarch Bauleel chose to visit at a very inopportune time. The Zebio child killed her too, after using her palm to activate the Technician's supply door to the outside."

Tears ran down Journeywoman Camille's face. "What a wretched way to die."

"Try not to think about it, my child. In this dire hour, we must do what we can to prevent what hardship we may. We must rouse the Guardians to find and destroy the Zebio child, and alert the city to the danger. We must contact the Technician's Guild at Resounding Cliffs and ask them to send reinforcements. Send our finest healers, so the remaining eight have what care they need. We must assess our storehouses for supplies to refurbish our Technician's tools, lost in the attack."

Journeywoman Camille tried to pull herself together, jotting down the Matriarch's requests within her notebook. She'd do Matriarch Bauleel proud. "You can count on me, Matriarch."

"I know I can, Camille." Matriarch Natre placing a

hand on Camille's arm. "We must also plan Matriarch Bauleel's funeral. She will be sorely missed."

"Indeed, she shall be," replied Camille. "But we also have a celebration to plan, in honor of our newest Matriarch. The people will find joy in this news."

"The celebration will have to wait a short time, my child. Out of respect. There is much to do now."

"As you wish, my Esteemed Matriarch. There is another message terminal in Matriarch Bauleel's quarters. It's the quickest way to alert the Guardians."

"Let's go at once."

CHAPTER 38

Rai spent the first three days of the journey riding with Ponar, making up for her previous avoidance of his company. His lighthearted banter helped the time pass quickly, and had the added benefit of keeping Rai from thinking too hard about her nightmares of the forest--the same forest they might soon enter at Harper's Sorrow. She doubted the chase and tormentors from her dream had been real. It's not as if any of the angry hordes would come after her again, had they ever been real, which they just couldn't be. The images continued to tug at the back of her mind as they neared the grove, building into a quiet, anxious tension.

The Guardian pushed them hard along the road, from dusk until dawn, and they reached the base of the Northern Pass the first evening despite the muck-racked roads of the swamplands. The next morning they tackled the steep, narrow pass up the side of a dizzyingly sheer cliff, which Rai found both breathtaking and nerve-wracking. Along the ill-kempt Northern Road, the

Guardian allowed almost no breaks, pushing the horses hard. He'd appeared so driven, Rai wondered if they'd have any time to have a look around the grove once they reached it, or for that matter, if he'd even bother to point it out when they passed by.

During this leg of their journey, the trees had transformed from the sprawling mangroves of the swamplands to the tall, thin highland pines she'd become familiar with during her trip to Kiya's Grace. Although these trees had a similar structure to those of her nightmares, they lacked their girth and height. However, Rai did spot the occasional fern in the forest's undergrowth, but they were small and spindly in contrast to the broad-leafed giant ferns in her dreams.

Rai sighed in frustration.

"Still nothing recognizable?" Ponar asked, bringing up the familiar topic of conversation.

Rai nodded. "I'm afraid Meik's right--this route is a complete waste of time."

"Well, there's always the shawls." He arched a brow.

She laughed. "Somehow I doubt Chieftess Kait will consider those reason enough for this detour. Do we even know how much farther it is to Harper's Sorrow?"

Ponar shrugged. Rai knew he wasn't sure either. This route was new to all of them, except the Guardian--who had been everywhere. At least Rai assumed the Guardian knew the road well. Surely Guardians had to be familiar with a route before leading travelers down it? However, considering the overgrowth along the sides of the road, it didn't appear well maintained or well traveled.

"Perhaps you could ask him," Ponar suggested, motioning to the Guardian who had stopped just ahead. "Looks like we're stopping for lunch."

"Isn't it a bit early to eat again?" Rai asked, noting that the sun hadn't yet reached its zenith.

"Yeah, but we stop when he says, regardless of the time. You never know what he might be trying to avoid out there," Ponar said. Rai shivered as an image of a pack of Iron Wolves came to mind. "Why don't you just ask him when we reach the grove?"

"I don't want Meik to see me talking with him. You know how he dislikes them. I can do without a lecture on the dangers of getting too 'comfortable' with Guardians." Rai rolled her eyes.

"It's up to you," Ponar replied.

"Whether I ask or not, we'll still get there at the same time. I might as well not rock the boat and be patient."

"Hmm, and you call asking 'how much farther' every few miles being patient? Nice to know," Ponar ribbed. Rai good-naturedly punched him in the arm.

Ponar pulled his wagon to a stop behind the Guardian, who was studying one of his various devices while still astride his horse. Rai heard Meik's and Laan's wagons come to a stop behind them. Ponar and Rai dismounted, eager to stretch their legs.

A few seconds later Meik appeared and walked up to the Guardian. Laan wasn't far behind. "Is everything okay?" Meik asked nervously.

The Guardian didn't even look up at Meik. "There's a troupe of sclern up ahead."

"Why should we be afraid of them? I thought they

were harmless," Meik asked. Rai remembered a picture of one from a biology textbook at the school: petite, gray-furred beasts that you could almost mistake for a stone, assuming they weren't moving.

"Because there are tens of thousands of them, and it's mating season." The Guardian's was once again speaking in his usual condescending tone. "The individuals tend to be quite tame, but they can become very territorial and vicious when mating. Our entry into their territory will most likely be deemed as a threat, and they have been known to swarm."

"So what can you do?" Meik asked.

"I can try to convince them to move out of the way while we run the wagons past them. How have your horses tolerated smokescreens in the past?"

"Fine," Meik answered. Laan and Ponar nodded in agreement.

"Wait, you're going to set fire to the forest?" Rai asked, alarmed at the rising costs of this detour.

The Guardian let out a derisive snort. "No, I won't. I have smoke sticks which usually scare off wildlife."

"And what if the smoke doesn't scare them off?" Ponar asked.

"Then we run as fast as we can." He answered, seemingly unconcerned with that possibility.

Rai noticed all of the Durmah shift uncomfortably, including herself.

"Perhaps we should turn back and avoid them?" Meik offered.

"I'm afraid we can't," he replied. "My scans show a pack of Iron Wolves about a day behind us, to the west.

From what I can tell, they aren't pursuing us now, but we wouldn't want to aim right for them either. The best option is to push on ahead."

"Talk about being stuck between a rock and a hard place, except this is between lots of slow, little teeth and some very fast, big teeth," Laan said, frowning. Rai held back a laugh.

"How much of the road do they cover up ahead?" Rai asked.

The Guardian rechecked his scanner. "At the moment, the troupe intersects with about a half-mile stretch of this road. With our present pace, we'll start encountering them in about an hour, hour and a quarter. The terrain's flat along that stretch, but it does run steadily uphill. I'm guessing it will take us about ten minutes to traverse the troupe, assuming their position remains the same."

"Ten minutes? That doesn't sound too bad," Ponar replied.

"Hopefully it won't be," replied the Guardian. "Let's get moving. I'll ride out ahead and plant the smokescreen, then ride back in time to escort you through the troupe. Keep a steady pace for now, and then when I give the signal speed up to match my pace. Remember, don't stop." The Guardian waited for nods of understanding from the Durmah. "Then, once we've cleared the troupe, I'll want to keep up our pace for a good hour or so afterward, just to get a good distance between us and the sclern. Any questions?"

"Won't that exhaust the horses?" Meik asked.

"Yes. That's why we'll stop early tonight, to give them

a chance to rest up. There's a large river up ahead, Harper's Channel, which should serve as a natural barrier to the sclern. Once we're past that we should be safe," the Guardian explained.

"Harper's Channel? Would I be correct to assume that it's close to Harper's Sorrow?" Rai asked eagerly.

The Guardian raised an eyebrow. "Yes, it serves as the western boundary to that grove."

"So then we'll be setting up camp in Harper's Sorrow for the night?" Ponar asked.

"Yes, but I'd advise you to worry about where we'll camp later after we've managed to navigate the sclern threat. Go ahead and put blinders on the horses and then head out at a reasonable pace. I'll be back within the hour," he advised. The Guardian then urged his mount forward into a gallop eastward. Soon the clouds of dust kicked up by his steed obscured his departure.

THE DURMAH FOLLOWED THE GUARDIAN'S directions, taking only a few extra moments to retrieve their lunches before continuing eastward along the Northern Road.

"How long has it been since he left?" Rai asked Ponar.

"Three-quarters of an hour?" Ponar guessed. "Sorry, I'm afraid I left my watch stored in the back."

"I suppose it doesn't matter anyway." Rai scanned the horizon, trying to see a hint of anything different or unusual. "Shouldn't we be able to see smoke by now?"

"Here I thought all you'd talk about would be your chance to see Harper's Sorrow tonight."

"Oh don't get me wrong, I'm thrilled we're going to camp in my nightmare forest this evening. I suppose I'm just a little concerned about this matter of thousands of little angry furballs with teeth," Rai replied.

"Technically, it's tens of thousands of little angry furballs with teeth," Ponar corrected.

"Thanks, that really helps." Rai rolled her eyes.

"I just think you might be taking all this too seriously. I mean, if it were too dangerous then the Guardian would have found an alternate route."

"Yeah, you have a point," Rai replied.

"And didn't Laan mention how this guy took on Iron Wolves during your escort from Raven's Call to Kiya's Grace? How can these furballs compare to a pack of those beasts?"

"I think we're about to find out," Rai replied, pointing to a plume of smoke rising from the road ahead. "That's odd; I don't I see any sclern yet."

"Well, isn't the smoke supposed to frighten them off?" Ponar replied. "Perhaps they've already cleared out?"

Just then, the Guardian rode out of the smoke at breakneck speed. He continued at a gallop until he passed them.

"Where's he going?" Rai asked.

"I'd guess he's giving Meik and Laan a head's up that we're about to encounter the troupe. Can you stow this in my bag?" he asked, handing her the remains of his sandwich and his water flask. "Somehow I doubt I'll have time to finish it."

Rai did as he asked, taking the opportunity to store away her own flask. A few seconds later, the Guardian reappeared. Rai noticed a sheen of sweat on his horse, indicating he'd been riding hard and fast.

"Follow my pace," he ordered, wiping the sweat off his face with a gloved hand. "Stop for nothing." Then he was off, not waiting for their response.

The pace the Guardian set was a fast trot, which caused the wagon's seat to bounce uncomfortably. Rai watched the line of smoke fast approaching.

"Hold your cape up to your face, so that it covers your mouth and nose, and use it to breathe through. It'll make dealing with the smoke easier." Ponar advised, and then demonstrated with his own cape.

Obviously, he'd had to do this on multiple occasions, thought Rai. She tried to copy his wrapping technique, which allowed him to keep both of his hands-free for the reins, but couldn't quite get it right in time. Instead, she used a hand to keep the cape in place as they slipped into the smoky haze.

Although the smoke had appeared thick and dense from the outside, Rai was surprised to find it easy to see through. She could see the Guardian up ahead and about twenty to thirty feet in each direction, depending on rolling nature of the smoke's obscuring thickness around them. The ground was slightly harder to see, the smoke seemed thicker closer to the ground. To Rai's sensitive ears the sounds of the horse's hooves and the wagon wheels appeared to be somewhat amplified, as they were reflected back at them by walls of haze.

"Isn't it scary to travel this quickly when you can't see

very far ahead?" Rai asked; her words muffled by the cape.

"It's a little daunting," he shrugged. "You really just have to trust your escort at times like these."

The minutes dragged by, and, unable to see the scenery passing by, Rai began to wonder if they were moving forward at all. She kept scanning the road for any sign of the sclern. Although Rai didn't see any, her nose began picking up a new scent. It reminded her of the time she'd found a breacat nest in the back of the storehouse at the Waystation in Kiya's Grace. The smell was musky with a trace of what could be urine.

After the scent had grown to almost overpowering, Rai began to hear them. The sounds of thousands of sharp claws, scratching their way across rocks and stones reached her ears. Shrill cries, although muted by the smoke, still held a sense of the creatures' irritation, whether at the intruders to their realm or at each other, Rai had no way of knowing. She could sense their movement, aware of an undulating mass just beyond the smoke's boundaries.

Rai found that she could see more clearly. "Is the smoke clearing?" she asked Ponar.

"No, it looks the same to me," he frowned. "Don't worry, I'm sure we'll be through it soon."

Confused, Rai looked around again, noticing how she could see the Guardian, his horse, the trees, bushes, and the road, all with greater clarity. It was as if they radiated a phosphorescent glow, which by some means was visible through the haze. How was this possible, Rai wondered? Could this be some newly rediscovered forgotten ability, like her ability to smell beyond the normal human range? Or rather was it just some trick her mind was playing with her, and she imagined it?

Through the smoke, Rai saw something peculiar with the ground. A shimmering mass, which she hadn't noticed before, appeared to undulate and shift to their left. It reminded her of water rippling. Could it be they were near a lake or river? However, the wave of glowing movement was coming closer and closer to the road, which for some reason made Rai nervous.

"Can you see the water off to our left?" Rai asked.

"What are you talking about?" Ponar replied. "I still can't see anything."

"Well, it seems to be getting awful close to the road." In fact, from the movement of the shimmer, Rai could swear the water was now on the road up ahead, but that couldn't be right, could it?

Ponar looked at her as if she'd gone crazy. Perhaps she had. Rai saw the Guardian's horse trot through the shimmer, apparently without incident. Seconds later, their horses reached the glow, which Rai could now distinguish as separate, round ... things.

"Oh no," Rai said. She closed her eyes, wincing.

Crunch ... crunch crunch crunch ...

Came the sounds as the horses' hooves landed upon the sclern. A mere second later the wagon wheels cut through their tiny bodies, creating a cacophony of breaking bones, squishing organs and shrill cries. The smell of blood and urine filled the air as spraying fluid painted the horses' legs and the wagon's underbelly.

"How did you know?" Ponar demanded, yelling over the screeching, angry sclern.

Rai looked at him, meeting his gaze. She didn't want to lie to him; he had earned her trust, and thus warranted her confidence. "I can see them. They glow."

Rai could see the confusion and disbelief in his eyes. "I don't know why, and it's never happened before today."

"At least as far as you can remember," he countered.

He was right. For all Rai knew this could have been something she used to use on a daily basis, before her temple service and subsequent amnesia.

"Hey, can you also see how much farther before we're clear?" Ponar asked.

Rai watched the shimmering ripples of the sclern moving around them and found the boundary where the glowing ceased up ahead. "Not far, perhaps another minute or two?"

"Good to hear," he answered.

They rode on in relative silence, with the sound of angry, broken, and dying sclern filling their ears.

CHAPTER 39

THEY EMERGED FROM THE SMOKE, WITH ONLY THE blood on the horses and wagons as evidence of their encounter with the sclern. The Guardian slowed their pace, checking to make sure all was well with them before riding back to check on Meik and Laan.

Rai looked around to see if she could see any sclern in the distance, and observed no evidence of the troupe. The road ahead sloped downwards, leading to a bridge over a broad and placid river. On the far side of the river, the woods appeared denser, seeming to swallow the road beneath its dark, thick canopy.

Rai felt a chill go down her spine. Was this the place of her nightmares? What ghosts from her past might linger there, ready to pounce?

"I can't get over what you did back there," Ponar said. He unwrapped his cape and then laid it on the seat between them. "Do you still see a glow around anything?"

Rai placed her cloak over his. "The shimmers disappeared along with the smoke."

"I wonder why?" Ponar asked.

"Perhaps because I can see more than a few feet in front of my face again?" Rai replied.

"That would make sense. Do you think this is something you can just turn off and on as you might need it?" Ponar suggested.

"That'd be nice, wouldn't it?" Rai replied. "But shouldn't I have noticed it happening at night, like when I needed to use the bathroom and didn't want to stub my toe on that stupid chair leg like I've done dozens of times?"

"Why not move the chair?" Ponar asked, the glimmer of curiosity unmistakable in his gaze.

Rai shrugged. "Guess I figured I should know the room better than that."

"Have you had anything else like this happen before?"

"Well, there's my strong sense of smell," Rai replied.

"Did that come on slowly, increasing over time?" Ponar asked.

The Durmah knew she could smell the poison on the luna berries, but she'd never told them about her ability to notice emotions and random thoughts, which Rai felt stemmed from that faculty.

"It has, yes," Rai replied, honest but unwilling to go into further detail.

"Then perhaps this will do the same, whatever 'this' is," Ponar said. "You know, it's as if instead of your memories coming back from the amnesia, it's your abilities returning, bit by bit as you are in need of them."

"What a bright idea," Rai replied. "But wouldn't it be easier for me to recover my memories, and thus remember how to use my abilities, and what they mean?"

"Last time I checked, life is rarely easy," Ponar replied. "Still, it's progress."

"It's only progress if it can keep me from bumping into things at night," Rai said, and they both laughed.

They reached the bridge without further incident. They reached a large bridge, wide enough to accommodate wagons passing in opposite directions with room to spare. The horses' hooves rang against the broad wooden planks as they crossed, announcing their arrival.

"I wonder why they built such a big bridge here, on a road no one uses," Rai asked.

"Not sure. It's the older, colonization-period style too. Perhaps the founding colonists thought this road would get more travelers than it does?" Ponar replied.

"That's funny, I never figured you were a history buff."

"I'm not, but with all the traveling I do, you see a lot of roads and a lot of bridges."

The Guardian reappeared, slowing his mount to match their speed. "After we enter the Grove, the road winds down through a series of switchbacks, and you'll need to take it slowly with the wagons. We'll set up camp about two miles in, after the road levels off. I'll ride ahead and scope out the territory." Without waiting for a response, he urged his mount into a gallop toward the forest.

"Such a chatter, that one," Ponar said. Rai chuckled.

They continued along the road, and Rai watched the forest line near with an increasing sense of apprehension. Within minutes, they entered the woods. The smells and sounds of the grove embraced her with familiarity. The trees looked similar to those of her dreams, with broad, flat, needle-like leaves and black-tinged bark, but they weren't the behemoths she expected. She recognized the ferns dotting the landscape. They were similar to the boulder-sized ferns she'd dreamed of, but these were much, much smaller. Surely, this wasn't the place.

"Well, here we go." Ponar pointed ahead to the first turn in the road.

Rai nodded, mesmerized by the smells of the grove. The scent of the rich, earthy soil overlaid with a hint of musky vanilla Rai immediately associated with the trees themselves. A wet, almost moldy odor inferred hidden pockets of stagnant, standing water laden with algae. The fragrance combination was potent and matched her dream forest. Rai was convinced she actually remembered the smell.

"See anything you remember yet?" Ponar asked.

Rai shrugged. "Frankly, it smells more familiar than it looks."

"I guess that makes sense, with your nose."

While they descended, Rai realized the canopy above remained level at the same height, and the trees grew taller and thicker to reach it. With each switchback, the road dropped another thirty to forty feet, and it wasn't long before it was tough to make out the tops of the trees. There was no longer any direct sunlight on the forest floor. Instead, the Grove captured all of it so thoroughly that the remaining light at this depth remained muted and diffuse.

Time passed, soon they had finished their descent, and the road leveled off, revealing the Grove in all its glory from the forest floor. Their Guardian escort awaited them at the base as promised. Without a word, he led them deeper into the woods.

This grove was exactly as it had been in her dreams. Exactly. The ancient trees were impossibly tall and wide, their crowns lost within the canopy far above. A thin mist clung to the forest floor, winding its way around boulder-sized ferns and through sections of fallen trees and branches. Over the sounds of the horses and wagons, Rai made out the occasional trill of a bird echoing down from above and the melodious trickle of a nearby stream.

A wind ran through the tall trees high above, and they shuddered and shifted. Rogue flickers of light escaped through the net of leaves, dancing on the tree trunks and valley floor. A muted creaking echoed while their trunks pulled and twisted, reminding Rai of a whispered conversation passing amongst the stand. Rai had the oddest impression that they were now in the belly of some giant creature, witnessing its breath, digestion, and circulation.

A turn in the road revealed a small, relatively flat clearing, dotted with ferns and bounded by a brook at the far side.

The Guardian stopped and dismounted. Ponar reined in their horses, bringing the wagon to a slow stop.

Laan and Meik brought their wagons alongside Ponar's, as there was plenty of space available. The Durmah climbed down off their wagons, in quiet awe of their surroundings.

"We'll camp here tonight," announced the Guardian.

"We have the afternoon to take a look around?" Rai asked.

"Only with me as your guide, and only after you clean the blood off of the wagons and horses." The Guardian pointed to the underbelly of Ponar's wagon.

Blood spatter covered the underside of all three wagons, a gruesome token of their encounter with the sclern. Rai beheld bits of brown fur and white bone sticking to a nearby wheel but decided not to investigate further.

"Ugh, what a mess!" Meik wailed.

"We're safe here at the moment, but I don't want us to travel any further with the wagon's in this condition," the Guardian replied.

"Oh, right," Meik replied. "We'll get this cleaned up."

"The water from the brook is fresh and will aid your efforts," the Guardian advised. He then led his horse over to the water and began his own cleaning efforts.

The Durmah assessed the damages. "This might make me sick," Laan warned.

"You're not the only one," Ponar replied, obviously disgusted. "We should have brought Markel along."

"Why, just because he's a Sept-less stable hand?" Rai asked, offended.

"Oh no, it's not that. It's just he's got an iron constitution. Nothing, and I mean nothing, makes him retch." Ponar explained.

Everyone laughed, and then they all got down to work.

THREE HOURS LATER THEY'D WASHED, CURRIED, watered, and fed the horses and then cleaned the wagons. Numerous items of soiled clothing hung to dry from impromptu clotheslines strung between the wagons. An early dinner and tending to the tack and gear occupied the travelers.

After consuming a late lunch, everyone appeared exhausted from the day's events even though the sun had yet to set. The Guardian approached the Durmah, who all sat in a circle on their travel-chairs. From the concerned expressions of the others, Rai knew she wasn't the only one wondering what was up.

"You did a good job," he announced. "You've just missed one thing."

"What are you talking about?" Meik replied.

The Guardian's lip curled, surly as always. "You four stink of a midden heap." Was it Rai's imagination, or did he like getting a rise out of Meik?

"Now look here, that trickle of a stream's too filthy and tiny for us to get properly washed up," Meik replied.

"Very true, this is why I'm taking you to a nearby lake. It's about a ten-minute hike from here."

"Will it be safe to leave our horses and wagons unattended, or should we go in shifts?" Ponar asked.

"I've scanned the area, and there's nothing close enough to worry about," the Guardian replied. "But we need to leave now, so we can be back before it gets dark."

It didn't take any further encouragement to rally the group into action. In less than two minutes, they'd grabbed their towels and soap and were walking up a dry riverbed toward the lake.

"Well, what do you think?" Ponar asked Rai. They were the last in line, and far enough back that Meik and Laan couldn't overhear them.

"Uh, I think it's great we won't be stinking of horse dung soon?" Rai replied.

Ponar rolled his eyes. "No, I mean about this forest. Is it the one from your dreams?"

Rai nodded. "I'm certain it is. The only problem is it's a vast forest, so I have no idea how to find the mound from my dreams or even the lake it's next to."

"Perhaps you'll get lucky and find out. The Guardian's leading us to a lake after all ..."

"I somehow doubt there's just one lake in this entire forest."

"Yeah, but how many are close to the favored camping spot just inside the forest's boundary?"

That hadn't occurred to Rai, but he had a point. How many lakes were there be within the grove and within easy distance from the road? "Well, we'll find out soon enough."

They walked on, listening to the birdsong and insect chirrups accompany their footfalls. Every step on the thick, damp forest floor sounded like a sigh to Rai, intensifying her surety that this grove was a sleeping giant behemoth.

Rai spotted brightness ahead, and it grew bit by bit until they emerged into a small glen ringed by the forest on all sides. Rai stopped, almost not believing her own eyes. A small, placid lake lay to their right in the glen, it's banks dotted with rare giant ferns and boulders. Rai looked to her left and spied a low hillock at the far side of the valley. A pair of trees partially obscured the mound, yet she recognized this as the same exact place from her dreams.

"This is it, isn't it?" Ponar asked. Her reaction hadn't been lost on him. Rai couldn't manage to speak. "We should keep walking, or the Guardian's going to wonder what's wrong," he advised.

Rai nodded, and they walked again. A mixture of excitement and anxiety ran through her veins. "Do you realize what this means?"

"The place you dreamed of was ... is real?" he replied.

"It's more than that. It's also my past."

"I'm afraid you just lost me."

"It's just that, if this is real I must have been here, at least once. Yet the Guardian admitted that it's very unusual for anyone to take this road except other Guardians. There are no cities in either direction for days. How can I have been a simple girl from Raven's Call and get all the way out here?" Rai asked, knowing he didn't have the answer.

It was Ponar's turn to stop. "Wait a second, are you saying you think that you were a Guardian?"

This time Laan, who admired the view, noticed them

lagging behind and frowned. He gestured for them to catch up. Rai grabbed Ponar's arm and gently pulled him into a brisk walk toward the others.

"I mean it, do you think you were a Guardian?" he asked again.

"I don't remember, Ponar. I suppose it'd make sense, wouldn't it? What if I was a Guardian and I worked this Northern Road at some point before my Temple service. Perhaps when I was found barren, they kicked me out, rather than allow me back into the Sept in disgrace?"

"But aren't the Guardian's different with how they manage their Sept? I mean, it's not as if they're just in one family bloodline, there are too many for that. What would it matter?"

"Since when do Guardian's do anything the easy way?" Rai replied.

"Sure. But, why waste all of that training by sending you on to another Sept?"

"Perhaps no dishonor can stand. Maybe because the Guardians have such large numbers it allows them to disassociate with disgraced members. Hey, they could even have arranged for the administration of some amnesia medicinals to ensure that I wouldn't reveal any of their special Guardian secrets ..."

"Now you're scaring me."

"What, you think I'm wrong?" Rai asked.

"No, I think what you're saying makes lots of sense. It's a lot of assumptions, but that scenario covers a good deal of the questions you've been grappling with."

"But there's still no way to know for sure unless my memory returns."

"Not necessarily," Ponar replied. "Wasn't there some-thing special about this glen from your dreams?"

"In the dream that hillock over there had a door lock on the side."

"And it opened some hidden room beneath the ground?" he asked. Rai shrugged. "Then let's search for the door lock after we bathe."

"I'm not sure that's a good idea. When I tried to open it in the dream, it burned my hand."

"Ouch!" Ponar replied.

"Besides, the Guardian will be keeping an eye on us. You think he's going to let us open up some secret stash right under his nose?"

"Why would he think we'd be looking? If any of this is true, it's not likely that out of all the Guardians on the planet he'd remember you from your pre-Temple service days," Ponar said.

Rai agreed that yes, out of all the Guardians in the world that it was highly unlikely she'd ever known this one personally, assuming she was once a Guardian. Still, she'd encountered this particular escort many times since she'd awoken with the amnesia, and it wasn't the first time she'd wondered if that was coincidence or if he was tracking her for some reason. If her theory was correct, it explained them keeping an eye on her to make sure the amnesia remained. However, this all seemed farfetched; why waste the energy and labor?

"I'm just not sure ..." Rai began. A chill ran down her spine as she wondered what the Guardian Sept would do if she did regain memories of being one of their members.

"Hey, I have an idea!" Ponar blurted out. "Tell the

Guardian you're unwilling to bathe with the men. Say you're too shy or something. While you're alone, take advantage of the situation to look around."

"I'll do it!" This way she'd decide what to share with the others--assuming she found anything. Not that she was planning to hide her findings from Ponar, but she was less than enthusiastic on letting Meik and Laan in on her past.

"I can't wait to hear what you find," Ponar said. "Bring it back with you, if it's small enough. You'll want to have something to show Meik and Laan, and the Chieftess too."

Oh yeah, find hard evidence that proved she was once a Guardian, wouldn't that just make everyone all warm and fuzzy toward her? Rai nodded, as they'd finally neared the lake's edge.

Taking Ponar's advice, she walked over to the Guardian. Ponar mouthed a soundless "good luck" and walked off. The Guardian and the others were undressing down to their underclothes, wasting no time.

"Excuse me sir, but could I bathe separately from the men?" Rai asked. She still couldn't get a reading off the Guardian. Was it a part of the Guardian's training?

The Guardian eyed her. "Just head over there a little way."

Rai frowned and shook her head. "No, by separate, I meant I'd prefer a bit more privacy."

He raised an eyebrow. "I wouldn't have taken you for the prudish type."

Rai knew he was trying to bait her, and wouldn't fall for it. "You don't know me very well, do you?"

The Guardian glowered at her. Rai wondered if she'd disappointed him by not playing his little game.

"Once the men are done I'll escort them back to camp, and you can bathe here, alone. I'll come back and retrieve you afterward. Will that give you enough private time?"

Again with the surly attitude? This guy needs some time off! "That'd be wonderful, thanks," Rai replied, forcing a cheerful smile.

"You sure you won't be scared, here all by yourself?"

"You said the area was safe. I trust you."

"Oh, now you trust me," the Guardian replied. Rai did her best to keep smiling, and again, not take the bait.

Rai walked away and looked out onto the lake. Meik was slowly wading in, complaining the whole time of the water's frigid temperature. He took another cautious step, slipped, and was suddenly standing in water up to his ears, and bellowed. Laan ventured out to help him, but that only added to his ire.

Ponar dove into the lake, dressed only in his underwear. Rai watched his tanned, muscular body glide through the water while he swam, and sighed in appreciation.

"Yes well, I wouldn't want your tender sensibilities affronted," the Guardian said in his usual sarcastic tone as he passed by her on his way to the water.

For a brief moment, his bare arm brushed hers, and Rai got the distinct impression of ice-cold water pouring down over her body. The sensation was so crystalline clear it raised goose bumps on her entire body. Was he thinking of how cold the lake is? It was a rare moment for her to sense anything from this man, who was normally a blank slate to her.

Could he be sending me a message? An implied awareness on his part of her ability to read others? Rai remembered that day in the market when a stranger had warned her not to read others, lest she alert another gifted like herself to her presence. Could that have been this Guardian?

Then there was the time she'd run into the Guardian at the park in Kiya's Grace at night and had sensed a malevolent image of a blade cutting her throat. The combination made her consider him in a different light. Was the vision of cold water meant as a threat, humor, or mere happenstance? Rai doubted the wisdom of her plan to bathe after the others. Now she'd be alone with the Guardian.

While Rai waited for the men to finish, she sat and sunned herself on a nearby boulder. After the stress, their encounter with the sclern troupe it was nice to see her adoptive relatives happy, carefree and laughing, if only for the moment.

A half hour later the Guardian emerged from the water, and yelled, "We should head back now," to the men. As they emerged from the lake, Rai saw the Guardian's skin was free from scars, and this surprised her. Wouldn't a protector of the people have some scars as evidence of his defensive efforts? Her gaze met the Guardian's eye, who marked her silent examination, and she quickly looked away.

The men dried off and walked back to camp ahead of the Guardian. "Do try and finish up quickly. It'll be dark soon, and we don't want to be out for long after dark."

"I thought you said this area was safe?" Rai asked.

"Safety is never guaranteed." He turned and left, following the Durmah men.

Within moments, Rai was alone. Truly and utterly alone for the first time she remembered. Instead of fear, Rai felt liberated. Although she'd had a room all to herself at the Waystation, it was common for Hilse or Jesse to come knocking at any hour when they needed help.

She removed all of her clothing and jumped naked into the lake head first. The icy water hit her like a thousand tiny needles driving and biting into her skin, but within seconds, the sensation passed, leaving her refreshed and rejuvenated. Rai cleaned up, exiting the lake a few minutes later. She pulled on the clean blue pants and matching cotton tunic she'd brought along in her knapsack. She blotted her wet hair with her towel and stowed it, her soap, and the clothes she'd worn earlier in the bag. Rai didn't want to waste precious time drying her hair. She had a mystery to solve.

Rai threw her knapsack over her shoulder and walked over to the mound. No door lock was visible, and so she thought back to the dreams and tried to remember its location. Rai got down on her knees and felt around the side of the hillock with her hands.

"Moons, if I can't find something I swear I'll accept I've gone insane. Well, at least no one is here watching me act like an idiot ... oh my ..." There, right underneath her left hand, Rai found it. A hard, flat piece of cool metal. A shiver ran up her spine while she searched and subsequently found the edges of what was, indeed, a door lock. Moss covered most of the metal, but it yielded, and Rai lifted it up, revealing the door lock in its dull, grimy entirety.

At least in this, the dreams had been real. It wasn't quite as nice as regaining her memories, and yet this was undeniable proof of her past. Somehow, sometime, she'd been here. This wasn't very helpful, but it was one more piece of her past's puzzle.

Rai took out her still damp towel and wiped the dirt and dead plant matter from the door lock. Rai reached out and placed her right hand flat on the metal plate. In her nightmare, the door lock had burned her flesh, but this metal remained cool to the touch. Seconds passed, and Rai wondered if the mechanism had broken over time. Worse, was this a secured door, and she didn't have the authority to pass? Rai cringed. Did unauthorized access attempts get logged and reported? The Guardians? Temple Matriarchs?

A high-pitched affirmative beep sounded, and Rai pulled back her hand and stood up. It was too late to debate the issue now. A rumbling sounded deep within the ground, and Rai took a couple of precautionary steps backward. Clicks, whirrs, and a hiss sounded as a door-sized arched section of the mound to the right of the door lock lifted outwards, encouraging dirt to fly about, and then slid upwards.

"What the ... ?" Rai said as she looked into the cavern. Recessed lighting provided a soft glow, illuminating a small rock-walled room giving access to a descending staircase. She hesitated only a moment before stepping into the chamber. The door did not close behind her. The air inside smelled stale yet sterile as if some cleaning agent still lingered from a recent cleaning. There were no adornments on the walls, save the lights on the ceiling and a door lock to the right of the opening. A simple wooden railing assisted her descent down a long staircase.

Rai took in the well-hewn steps and walls, running a hand along their smooth surface. They appeared reminiscent of the style she'd seen within the caverns of the Raven's Call Temple. Did this structure date back to Az'Unda's early colonization? She remembered Headmaster John describing the laser-rock cutters used to create the first safe houses and Temples. Who would build all the way out here?

Rai remembered Ponar speculating about the bridge on the Northern Road, and how it might have been constructed during the initial colonization of Az'Unda. Perhaps this structure was intended as the basement to some great house or Temple, for later expansion, once the population called for more cities. Then the plague had hit, and the Az'Un inability to increase their population because of it, had all become a harsh reality. Maybe, one day, people would use this building for its intended purpose. Now it just smelled barren and deserted.

After descending about three dozen steps, Rai reached the bottom and found herself in another small room, identical to the one at the top of the stairs. Except this door was closed. Rai held up her hand and placed it on the door lock, this one responded within seconds with the usual affirmative beep. The door slid open, and Rai took her first step into the dark room.

Before she even got a good look, someone spun her body around and moved her backward, out of the new space and back into the outer room. She heard and felt her head crack the wall behind her.

"Oof!" The sound issued from Rai's throat as someone knocked the wind out of her. Confused and irritated, she tried to see beyond the bright spots in her vision and failed. Rai reached up--the pressure on her neck and chest demanding relief, only then realizing another held her forcibly against the wall.

Her vision cleared enough to understand her situation. Their Guardian escort had caught up with her little adventure. He didn't appear very pleased with it.

He swore vehemently. "What do you think you're playing at here?"

He was livid. It wasn't simply the reddening of his face, the subtle shaking of his shoulders, or glowering of his eyes. She sensed his emotions as palpably as the wall cutting into her back.

It took Rai a few moments to catch her breath after hitting the wall, and a few more to clear her head from the overpowering musk of his fury.

"I needed to come here, to see this place again." Rai knew she had to be honest, and knew that wasn't what he wanted to hear. He wanted details, and she didn't have any.

She sensed his anger build. Rai wondered what shape his wrath would take when he exploded in the inevitable frenzy.

He released her and backed away a few steps. Rai knew better than expect this meant a change in his mood.

"And what, exactly, Kilawren, did you hope to accomplish with this little visit to your past? Are you trying to get yourself killed?"

Rai stared at him in shock, having heard her birth name for the first time in her albeit short memory.

CHAPTER 40

JOURNEYMAN RILTE STOOD AT THE DOOR TO THE main Temple complex with the other seven Technician survivors, perplexed and uneasy. Elder Natre, no--she'd insisted he call her Matriarch--despite the dark brown robes she'd worn, had just left. Although Rilte had been thrilled to have a visitor from the outside arrive, the presumptive Matriarch wasn't at all what he'd expected. According to the new Matriarch, if Bauleel's Journey-woman Camille hadn't informed her of the Zebio boy's case and Bauleel's frequent trips to the Technician's wing, they'd still be awaiting discovery.

"Well, at least someone came. I was beginning to wonder if Terem had destroyed the entire Temple complex," Apprentice Nance said, running a hand wearily through her long, dark hair.

"I'm also relieved he didn't wreak havoc in the Temple. That would have been devastating. Where did he go?" Priest Youne asked.

"Well, if he hasn't been seen in the Temple or city,

then He must have headed out into the forest. All that matters is he doesn't come back here," Apprentice Nance replied.

"What would be the point?" Journeywoman Appene asked. "He's already paid us back for his imagined slights."

"Indeed," replied Priest Youne. "Elder Natre's visit ensures we'll receive visitors and supplies, probably within the hour."

"She said to call her Matriarch," Journeyman Rilte said. Everyone shifted quietly.

"Temple politics are not your concern, Journeyman Rilte," replied Priest Youne. "If the Elder's Council appointed her Matriarch, so be it."

"Yeah, well, the last time I checked, Matriarch Bauleel isn't dead yet! Just because she's spent the past two weeks recuperating in a stasis crèche doesn't mean she won't be able to resume her rightful position once she's recovered."

Priest Youne met his heated glare. "That's not our decision."

Rilte reflected that Priest Youne was the only surviving Technician who outranked him, and he should, therefore, treat him with respect due to his age and rank. Rilte remembered position had never stopped him from doing what he thought was right and needful.

"No, no, you're right. It's not our decision at all. It's up to the Matriarch to choose her successor," Rilte replied. He traversed the arboretum and burst through the door into the Triage Ward, with Priest Youne close behind him.

"You cannot reawaken the Matriarch now," Priest Youne advised. "Matriarch Natre expressly forbade us."

"And why, exactly, do you think she did that, Youne? She's not a healer, so I doubt it's in the Matriarch Bauleel's best interest."

"You will win her ire," warned Youne.

"I'll wear it as a badge of honor."

Once at the sealed triage stasis crèche Rilte engaged the console by placing his hand in a slight depression at the foot of the crèche. The crèche's console lit up, and a soft, pinkish light illuminated the interior. Rilte looked down at Matriarch Bauleel. Black and blue bruises mottled her skin--they'd barely begun to fade despite the intensive treatment. Had it really only been two weeks ago when Rilte had placed her broken and bloody body into this crèche, hoping against all hope there might be a chance in a thousand she'd survive?

Rilte reviewed her status via the console. "Look, Youne. All of her internal bleeding is contained, and her organs are now functioning within normal levels."

"Barely," Youne conceded after reviewing the data. "But I'm sure the healers Matriarch Natre would send along would more accurately assess Matriarch Bauleel's condition. It's not as if you have years of training with this device."

"This is Juggernaut technology, and therefore it's automated. Her bones have responded well to the accelerated knitting treatment regime, that's good news too." Rilte pointed to the display. Because Youne observed his every move, Rilte deliberately avoided checking the immunology statistics.

"I'm sure Matriarch Natre has her reasons for wanting her healers to review Matriarch Bauleel's health. She could still be critically ill in some way you aren't able to identify. You might not be reading all of the information correctly. I remember how badly injured she was when you found her, and I still consider it remarkable she didn't die that day. You've done an excellent job, but don't you think it's time to turn her care over to the professionals?" Youne pleaded.

"I'm sure Matriarch Natre has her reasons for her request, and I also have mine," Rilte replied. During her recovery, Rilte discovered certain things about the Matriarch, things he knew would get her into big trouble. He'd managed to keep her secrets from the other Technicians, and he wasn't about to allow some power-grabbing Elder access to that information either. Besides, otherwise, he might never have a chance to have Matriarch Bauleel confirm his findings, and explain how her survival was possible. The scientist in him just couldn't abide that possibility.

"Well, I can't dissuade you, is there anything I can do to assist?" Priest Youne offered.

"Can you fetch some clean clothes for the Matriarch? I'm sure she'd prefer something fresh and comfortable to wear once she awakens."

"I'll be right back. Perhaps I'll also fetch a cup of warm broth. No doubt she'll find it comforting after her ordeal." Priest Youne walked away, paused just a moment at the Triage Ward's doors, but then exited, his thought unspoken.

Journeyman Rilte activated the shutdown routine. A

message flashed up, warning the patient had not yet returned to optimum fitness and did he still want to end the healing process? Rilte responded yes, and the crèche interior lights brightened, and the touch screen display switched over to monitoring the Matriarch's signs of wakefulness. Alerts flashed on the screen as painkillers, sedatives and nutritional support were deactivated. Needles withdrew from her arms, legs, and abdomen. Rilte hoped the medicinals didn't take long to flush from her system. He had no idea when Matriarch Natre's people were due to return.

Rilte switched over to the immunology display. The gauges and dials on the screen showed nothing below the eighty-fifth percentile, despite the fact the Matriarch was nowhere near fully healed. A select few items displayed a current capacity at one hundred and sixty percent, with a peak at an unbelievable two hundred and fifteen percent of normal human levels. Rilte let out a low whistle, remembering none of her regenerative factors had been above a mere twenty percent when he'd first laid her in the crèche.

When he'd first viewed those results, he'd thought the device was flawed. Yet all of the other values were within a more reasonable range. He had no idea how the crèche calculated a particular person's maximum potential for any given metric, but he did know Juggernaut technology was accurate.

Since the attack, Rilte had checked in on the Matriarch multiple times each day, and all of the gauges had slowly crept higher and higher as she'd healed. Her other vital statistics were also greater than average, but generally not above the one hundred and twentieth percentile potentiality mark. Any sufficiently technical and complete scan would reveal this data. Rilte thought he knew how this was possible. Now, if only the Matriarch would awaken and confirm it for him!

Priest Youne returned, carrying a set of wonderfully soft purple pajamas and a mug of steaming broth. "How much longer?"

Rilte quickly switched the display back to monitoring the Matriarch's awakening. "She's progressing quickly. It shouldn't be long now."

Priest Youne snorted derisively. "You'd better hope she agrees with your reasons and not Matriarch Natre's. Otherwise, you're going to have one pissed off and hurting Matriarch upset with you."

As if on cue, Matriarch Bauleel's eyes fluttered open, and she reached out, placing her hands on the transparent, plasticine crèche cover. Panic and fear filled her eyes. Rilte laid a hand atop hers on the outside of the lid, and she looked right at him.

"It's all right," Rilte said. "Everything's okay now."

Although Matriarch Bauleel couldn't possibly hear Rilte through the sealed crèche, she relaxed. A moment later the crèche uttered a bing, rather reminding Rilte of an oven timer going off, and with a hiss of escaping antiseptic-laden air the crèche's clamshell lid hinged upwards.

Matriarch Bauleel tried to sit up, only to stop in discomfort.

"Gently, Matriarch. I'm afraid you're not yet recovered." Rilte helped her sit up the rest of the way.

"Here's some warm broth for you, Esteemed Matriarch," Priest Youne said.

She took the cup and sipped slowly. "Please forgive me, but I don't remember your name," Matriarch Bauleel replied, her voice hoarse from lack of use.

"Priest Youne, Matriarch. Here are the most comfortable clothes we have available." He placed the pajamas in the crèche next to her. "It's not your usual garb, but I think you'll find them a comfort to your skin."

"Many thanks, to you both." She stood with a little difficulty, and unselfconsciously pulled on the pajamas over her bare and thin frame. "I had feared we'd all die."

"Most of the Technician's stationed here did," Priest Youne replied. "Only eight of us survived. You would have died as well if Journeyman Rilte hadn't gotten you into the triage crèche when he did."

"I am deeply indebted to you, Journeyman Rilte. Thank you for choosing to place me into the crèche instead of one of your brethren. You would have had every right to do so."

"Matriarch, those of us who survived had already locked ourselves in a secured room during the attack. You are the only one who faced Terem Zebio and lived."

She sighed, rubbing her aching temples. "I'm very sorry to hear that. What a tremendous loss for your Sept and the people of Az'Unda." The Matriarch finished the broth and handed the mug back to Priest Youne. "Could I bother you to fetch me another?"

"I'd be happy to, Matriarch. I'll be just a moment." Priest Youne left them alone on his errand.

Matriarch Bauleel's tone shifted. "You're the one who placed me in the crèche, Rilte?"

Rilte took note of her using his name without the title and followed suit. "I did, Bauleel. I found you, barely breathing, in a pool of your own blood in the cafeteria. Many broken bones, a sucking chest wound, numerous lacerations, internal bleeding from more organs than I can count, and some swelling of the brain due to being beaten." He paused, allowing a moment for the list to sink in. She held his gaze, waiting for him to continue.

"That you're standing here now, as healthy as you are, is almost beyond my comprehension. You're the only survivor we found who Terem met. I carried you here and activated the crèche. You know what it advised?"

"What?" She asked softly, her brows furrowing.

"It assessed your condition and recommended against treatment, estimating successful recovery at less than five percent."

"Yet you didn't heed its advice."

He shook his head. "Just as I ignored its advice and woke you before the healing process completed. That's why you're not quite back to normal yet."

Bauleel nodded. "I wondered about that. Why the early waking? Why by you? Shouldn't I have been moved to the Healers Hall by now?" The Matriarch slowly lifted her left arm. Rilte imagined it was still excruciating. Her left shoulder had been ripped to pieces.

"Unfortunately Terem destroyed our computers and communications equipment before he left. Until this morning, no one outside the Technician's unit knew what had happened."

She stared at him in shock. "I ... I'd just assumed you'd been able to alert the Temple and Guardian's Sept about the attack. Wait, how much time has passed?"

"Just over two weeks."

For the first time, Matriarch Bauleel appeared totally and completely awake and aware of the world around her. "What changed this morning that convinced you to awaken me?"

"Because of your extended absence, The Elder's Council appointed Elder Natre Matriarch-elect. This allowed her to access the Technician's wing, and she discovered the current state of affairs here, so to speak."

"That wouldn't be the only thing she'd have access to." Matriarch Bauleel now looked on the verge of panic. "How long ago was she here?"

"A little over half an hour ago. Natre ordered us to leave the crèche untouched. She said she'd send someone to transfer you to the Healer's Hall within the hour."

Bauleel took his hand in hers. "I am doubly indebted you to, Rilte. Both for saving my life and for saving me from being handed over to Natre. Now, I know why I don't trust her, but why did you risk her wrath by awakening me?"

"First, because she wasn't happy you were alive, and that didn't seem right to me. Second, because even knowing you'd survived she still insisted that I call her Matriarch."

"You have fantastic instincts, Rilte."

Priest Youne returned with another mug of broth for the Matriarch. "Sorry that took so long, Revered Matriarch. The others wanted to know how you were doing, and are very happy to hear of your recovery."

"Thank you, Priest Youne." Matriarch Bauleel took the mug from him and sipped gingerly. "Journeyman Rilte has been kind enough to agree to escort me to the Healer's Hall. We'll be leaving presently."

Rilte hid his surprise with a nod of agreement. Priest Youne looked confused. "Wouldn't it be better to wait for a Healer to escort you? We Technician's aren't that familiar with the Temple compound, after all."

"Not to worry. I remember the way, and all I need is an arm to lean on." Matriarch Bauleel attempted a smile despite her deeply bruised face. "I do thank you for all of your assistance. I am indebted to your Sept."

Bauleel handed the mug back to Priest Youne and reached out for Rilte's arm, which he offered for support. They ambled at first as Rilte allowed Bauleel to set the pace. He'd expected Priest Youne might raise more objections, but instead, he escorted them to the door to the Temple complex. The other survivors observed this curious procession with some amount of awe. None of them had seen an unveiled Matriarch before now. Rilte thought that the sight of her beaten face contrasted by the purple pajamas must have added an additional bizarre quality to the experience for them.

Matriarch Bauleel activated the door with her palm and turned to address the group. "Thank you for saving my life, and I am very sorry for the tragic loss you have suffered. I'll leave this door unlocked when I leave so you won't have to wait for the Guardians or Natre to return to access the outside. Be assured, I will do everything I can to assist in the rebuilding process, and in the destruction of Terem Zebio." The door opened behind her, and Bauleel walked through it without another word, practically pulling Rilte along after her.

Matriarch Bauleel walked resolutely down the corridor, gaining strength with every step.

"Why is it I doubt we're headed to the Healer's Hall?"

"Because we're not. I must ask you, were you the only one who attended to the crèche during my healing?"

"Yes. I also instructed the device to delete the record of your treatment upon shutdown."

Bauleel paused in her stride, the impact of his words driving deep. "You're a truer friend than I deserve, Rilte. May I also assume you shared none of your medical findings with the other Technicians?"

"Just the basics. Nothing of any further ... interest." They came to an intersection, and Bauleel directed them down an empty hallway.

"I'm not sure what I've done to earn your confidence, Rilte, but I'll make you a deal."

"You name it."

"If you help me escape, I'll repay your kindness by explaining the crèche's findings to you. Once we're well away from here."

"You need to escape?" Rilte asked, somewhat alarmed, but also intrigued by her offer. "I thought you'd want to go and put Elder Natre in her place and assume your rightful place as Matriarch?"

"I'm afraid it's too late for that now. No doubt Natre has already announced my death and has the funeral arrangements well under way."

"She'd go that far?" he searched her face for doubt and found none.

"Further than you'd know. If you hadn't awoken me from the crèche, she'd have ended me immediately, blaming it on Terem. She'd have told all of you there were unforeseen complications, despite my short-term improvements. Will you help me?"

Rilte blew out a low whistle. "Well, I can't have you hobbling off on your own alone, now can I?"

Bauleel rolled her eyes. "Well, I'm not an invalid, yet I'm very grateful for your help."

"Before we leave, I need you to answer one thing for me."

Bauleel sighed. "Perhaps I can."

"I've lost my family, the colleagues I worked with day in and day out, due to what Terem Zebio became, and your push to keep him alive longer than our Sept thought wise. If you have answers to my questions, I'd appreciate them."

Her eyes dropped to the floor, but not before he caught a hint of glistening sheen welling at the corners. Dammit, he hadn't meant to upset her, but he needed to know.

"Go ahead," her voice held the slightest hint of a tremble.

"Did you get the Methuselah treatments here on Az'Unda or off-world?"

She held her tongue, and Rilte wondered if he'd

come to the wrong assumptions from the crèche's data. "Perhaps I misinterpreted the data. It's just with your enhanced immune capabilities ... well, I've only ever heard of that discussed in the scientific literature in association with ..."

"Off-world," Bauleel answered in a whisper, such that he barely caught it. She stared straight ahead, her face a blank, unemotional mask. "But not here. Not now."

Rilte nodded. "What now?" Rilte tried to get his mind off the implications of her answer. The Hegemony forbade all life extension treatments within their accepted sentient species, and candidate species, such as humans. Just how long had Bauleel been alive, and what was worth the risk to possible inclusion in the Hegemony? She was right. Not here. Not now. "I'm eager to learn how a Matriarch escapes from her own Temple."

"Oh, the building's easy. Avoiding the inhabitants-- that's the tricky part. That's why we aren't going out the front door." Bauleel stopped abruptly along the hallway.

"Forget something?"

"Not at all. Now, where is that ..." Bauleel said. She reached out her hand to the flat wall, which was devoid of any ornamentation. Rilte wondered for a moment if the Matriarch wasn't thinking clearly.

"Ah, here we go," Bauleel said. She pressed her palm against an area of the wall that appeared no different from the rest, but a small section yielded slightly to the pressure of her hand. "I bet you wondered if I'd gone a bit feeble." A segment of the wall swung inward, and Bauleel motioned Rilte to walk into the dark room beyond.

"Oh, never," Rilte lied. "I've just never seen a door lock look like that, without the metal plate, I mean." As he entered, Rilte noted that the door was comprised of a foot-thick section of rock. The room beyond was simple, composed of a couch, dresser, mirror, and desk. A doorway opposite the one they entered led to a second chamber.

"Oh, that's not a door lock, it's a simple lever." She followed him into the room. She flicked a switch just inside the door, which illuminated the room, and shut the heavy door behind them. It appeared to glide closed via some unknown mechanism. "Any door lock I touch will alert the system to my presence, sending all sorts of helpful folk rushing along to assist their wayward Matriarch."

"But, we exited the Technician's wing via a door lock. Shouldn't that alert Matriarch Natre?" Rilte asked.

"I'm sure it did. I'm just hoping Natre is so busy organizing things for cleanup she hasn't had time to check her message terminals. We got here without running into anyone, and no one who works here knows this place exists."

"What, you had the craftsmen who built it shipped in from out of town?" Rilte asked.

"No, but I shipped them out after completing this addition, and they're no longer alive to tell tales."

"That's a bit ridiculous, don't you think?" Rilte asked.

"All for the safety of the Temple, my dear Journeyman." Bauleel winked. "Now let's see, it's been some time since I've visited this room ..."

The Matriarch ransacked the dresser, pulling out

various articles of clothing. "We can't leave here with you in that Technician-style pantsuit. Will this fit you?"

Rilte looked at the mottled brown tunic and leather pants she offered him. "They should."

"I'm afraid I don't keep men's shoes on hand, however. So your everyday black shoes will have to do." Bauleel pulled out some clothing for herself constructed of the same mottled brown material.

Rilte turned away from her and changed into the clothes. The cloth changed colors from brown to green to gray depending on how the light hit it.

"There's something familiar about this fabric. Yet I can't quite place it."

"I expect you will," Bauleel replied. "Can you help me with these boots?"

Rilte turned and looked at Bauleel struggling with a boot while seated upon the couch. She wore a matching set of the tunic and pants she'd given him. Seeing the clothes on her, he knew immediately. "Wait a moment; these are Guardian's clothes!"

"Yes, they are. Now, are you going to help me with this boot or just stand there and watch me fumble with this clasp?"

Rilte knelt down and helped her with the boots, which were of the same colors but made of thick leather. "I don't understand. Why are we dressing as Guardians?"

"Because no one questions the movements of Guardians. Not even other Guardians," Bauleel explained with a wink.

Rilte stood back up. "I get the impression you've been planning this escape for some time."

"Well, not today's, in particular. I am known for the occasional excursion." She stood slowly, walked over to the mirror and braided her hair.

"Where do you tell your staff you've gone?"

"It's easy. I say I need to spend a day or two in quiet reflection, and they leave me alone. No one questions me."

Bauleel tied her braid off with a leather band, and then walked over and sat down at the desk. She slid out an unlocked drawer and pulled out a backpack. She loaded a scanner, a small style message terminal, a gun, and a small first-aid kit into the bag along with some other items he didn't recognize.

"You're really going to just walk away, and never come back?" Rilte asked.

Bauleel met his gaze unflinchingly. "Never is a long time. Perhaps I will return if I can manage to get some things straightened out, but I doubt it. I'm tired of playing the Matriarch. It's exhausting and not without risks." She zipped up the backpack and hefted it over her shoulder.

Rilte shook his head, not understanding the Matriarch's reasoning. If she wasn't coming back, would he be able to return to the Technician's wing? Then again, there wasn't much left to come back to now.

"Let me carry that for you."

"Oh no, you get to take the canteens and cloaks. They're located in the bottom dresser drawer."

Rilte scratched the nape of his neck. "Is there anything you're not prepared for?"

"Just your endless questions," Bauleel replied. She

pulled a flashlight out of the backpack. "C'mon, we'd better get climbing."

Rilte located the two full canteens and slung them over his back. He found a spare backpack, placed two of the Guardian cloaks into it, and then slid it over his shoulder.

"Climbing?"

Bauleel turned on the flashlight and lit up the far room with it, revealing a set of rising stairs cut directly into the rock.

"How far?" he asked.

"For how horrid I feel, way too far. Just hope you don't have to carry me," Bauleel said, and perhaps he would if her body didn't cooperate. "Don't worry though, once we're at the top we can wait in the Temple orchards until nightfall, then we can leave without being seen. Besides, I need to write a few messages."

"To your staff?"

"Sadly, no. I worry about Camille, she has a kind heart, and I'm guessing she's too dedicated and loyal to quit, which means Natre will work her to the bone. No one should have to put up with Natre's moods!"

"I'm sure she will quit, if necessary. You trained her. She's got to have a good head on her shoulders."

"That's kind of you, Rilte. Anyway, I have a few friends outside of the Temples who will expect to hear from me." Bauleel started climbing up the stairs. "I bet they're wondering what in the world I've been up to these past two weeks."

"I don't doubt that," Rilte replied, following her. "Especially if they know you half as well as I do."

#BEGIN TRANSMISSION#
#ROUTING CODE: ALL ANEMOI
    IDS, VARIOUS COM
    LOCATIONS, OUTBOUND
    ONLY#
#ENCRYPTION: HIGH#
#PRIORITY: HIGH#

Greetings to the Anemoi,

In case you haven't already heard through other channels, we've had a recent incident at the Technician's Guild here at Raven's Call. After Matriarch Bauleel was incommunicado for two weeks, I stepped in and assumed her post, and thus discovered the ruined condition of the Technician Guild halls.

I have already written to Chieftess Raza considering the escape of one Terem Zebio. I will trust in her to relay all necessary details.

Most importantly, only seven Technicians remain at Raven's Call after this tragedy, so my first priority is to restore the Technician Guild as quickly as possible. I am scouring the rosters of our local schools to find the brightest minds, but I'm afraid that I must make an unusual request if the

Guild here is to not only survive but
also in fact thrive.
I humbly request Matriarch Heilen of
Resounding Cliffs Temple discuss
with her local Guild the possibility of
permanently relocating a segment of
their seasoned members here to assist
with the rebuilding and direct future
research efforts. Also, if Chieftess
Raza could spare a few Guardians to
help with their relocation efforts, I'd
be much obliged.
Please know your efforts will assist not
only myself but also the entirety of the
Az'Un during this most difficult of
times.
Respectfully,
Matriarch Natre
P.S. Bauleel dearest, if you're out there
listening, could you please let us all
know you're doing all right?
#END TRANSMISSION#

#BEGIN TRANSMISSION#
#ROUTING CODE: GUARDIAN
SEPT, ALL OUTPOST &
ROAMING COM IDS,
OUTBOUND ONLY #
#ENCRYPTION: HIGH#

#PRIORITY: ALERT#

Guardians,

Approximately two weeks ago the Technicians Sept at Raven's Call Temple suffered a containment breach. A stable mutation escaped and decimated the Sept and then escaped from the compound. Over five dozen lives were lost.

City and outpost managers are to allocate all available resources and perform an extensive audit of all persons within their zones within the next three days. All Guardians are to search in pairs and report their locations back to headquarters at dawn and dusk.

No exceptions.

If these scheduling changes mean travelers are inconvenienced and have to wait a few days, so be it. This is now everyone's top priority.

All Guardians on ranger operations will perform ongoing level three sweeps of their assigned regions from now forward until the threat is found and eliminated. For those who serve at an outpost, please enable your personal locator beacons to immediately signal in the case of your death.

Pictures and data files on the suspect are

attached. His name was Terem Zebio, of the Zebio Sept in Raven's Call. It is possible he is hiding out in the surrounding forest, or he may have traveled some distance already. Guardians stationed at Raven's Call should take extra care in case he attempts to contact the Zebio Sept.

Most importantly, once you acquire the target, do not engage without backup. Assume once identified he will attack.

Chieftess Raza
#END TRANSMISSION#

CHAPTER 41

"Well?" the Guardian asked. "Don't just stand there. I deserve an answer, and I want it now."

Before she had a chance to answer Rai was distracted by a prickly sensation ran up her back and neck. He's trying to read me! "Hey, stop that!" Rai demanded, sure the Guardian was the cause.

The sensation abated. "Explain yourself. Otherwise, I'll get what I need to know, one way or the other."

Had anyone she'd read been aware of that similar prickly sensation? She considered returning the favor but worried he'd know immediately if she tried.

"I'll explain, you just knocked the wind out of me." Rai rubbed the back of her head.

"Oh please. You're made of tougher mettle than that."

Such familiarity. "Why don't we go in and sit down?" Rai said, unaware of what lay in the room beyond. The Guardian couldn't know how much she knew, and Rai'd play that card as far as it would take her.

The Guardian stared, and for a moment, Rai thought

she'd lost the gambit. "Whatever. I can always make up an excuse to the Durmah if we run late."

He walked into the room and flicked on a switch. Rai followed, amazed by what she saw. This was not simply some ordinary supply warehouse, which would have had boxes and bags of supplies orderly stacked in piles and heaps. Instead, it was evident to Rai that this was, at least at some point in time, someone's living space.

In the middle of the room, two semi-circular indigo couches framed a short green marble table. A large, white, translucent, sphere-shaped fixture hung from the ceiling, illuminating the entire room with soft light. Subtle sky blue tones and wisps of clouds filled the painted domed ceiling. The overall effect was visually striking. No expense had been spared.

Off to the right was a small kitchen, including a table, sink, stove, small refrigeration unit, and storage cabinets were hewn from what appeared to be local lumber. How could this place exist out here in the middle of nowhere? What was it used for, and by whom?

At the far left of the room stood a large computer terminal, similar to the old-style ones Rai had seen pictures of in the history schoolbooks at Kiya's Grace. A large black padded chair sat in front of a u-shaped black console. A high transparent display screen rimmed the edge of the console, giving it a somewhat fishbowl-like appearance. The terminal wasn't active, and Rai noticed a starburst-shaped crack in the center of the screen as if a human fist had damaged it.

Two doors on the opposite side of the room and a dark hallway beyond the kitchenette beckoned Rai to explore further, but she doubted the Guardian's humor extended that far.

He sat down on one of the couches. "Are you going to sit or just stand there admiring your decor?"

My decor? This place was once mine. She took a seat on the couch across from him, somehow hoping space and table might provide protection. From him, or her past? Rai wasn't so sure anymore. How did she know him? How well? Was it possible for your body to explode from the internal pressure in your mind? None of this made any sense. How could she, at only sixteen years of age, have had this life?

"I'm on the verge of losing my patience with you, Kilawren."

"Where should I start?"

"Start by explaining how much you remember, when you shouldn't be able to recall anything from your past."

"Well, I remember everything after waking up in the crèche at the Temple in Raven's Call, clear as a bell."

He glowered at her for a moment. She was altogether too familiar with that expression on his face. "And before that?" He leaned forward and rested his elbows on his knees.

"It depends."

"On?" The dangerous edge to his mood focused wholly on her, daring her to retreat.

"Will you kill me if I'm honest?"

The tension in his shoulders softened. "I've been keeping you alive so far."

Rai took a leap of faith. None of this made sense, and yet there he was, staring her down. He knew her, was it too much to hope they'd once been friends and that he was willing to help her? He wasn't acting like someone out to hurt her. She'd have to trust he'd help her, and be honest with him. Rai wished she could remember his name.

"Most of what I've remembered has come through my dreams. Or, more accurately, my nightmares."

"You're saying it's through the dreamland of your subconscious that you've come this far?" Rai nodded. "That's amazing. Yet you've made it here," he gestured to the room, "and to this forest, managing to drag your adoptive family along with you. Honestly, that's a bit hard for me to swallow."

Rai shrugged. "It's the truth. Between the dreams and the ... unusual ... senses I have, I guess you can say I've had a hard time taking things at face value."

"I told Bau you were too smart and resourceful for your own good, not that she listened."

Bau? Who's that? "Thanks, I think."

"Describe these dreams to me." Rai didn't get the impression he'd settle for less than accurate accounts. What did she have to lose?

Rai described the dreams, in the order she'd experienced them. She recounted hooded figures chasing her through the glens of Harper's Sorrow--and how they'd called her a traitor. The Guardian listened in silence with a tormented expression on his face. She described dreaming of finding thallium salts in the storehouse and waking to that exact smell on the air at the Stime Sept's farm. She also described remembering the name of Jeweled Cove in Headmaster John's history class and dreaming about how a large bird had attacked and eviscerated her on the shore. That particular story, especially when she talked about the lady dying on the beach, caused the Guardian to frown.

It was good to talk about her nightmares to someone who'd known her, and yet at the end, she felt exposed and vulnerable to a man who she still didn't remember. Again, Rai noticed the familiar prickling sensation and became irritated, wondering how long he'd been snooping in her thoughts.

"Pardon me. Force of habit." The sensation stopped at once. "My name's Graeber, by the way." He watched for her reaction.

"Thanks, Graeber." Rai shifted uncomfortably. The name struck a chord with her, but she couldn't quite place it. She tried to read him but got nothing. He didn't even react to her attempt. It appeared he was much better at this.

"I'm amazed at the detail of your dreams. It's an unfortunate complication, and one I'm afraid causes difficulties to our charade."

The hair on the back of her neck stood on end. "What do you mean, a charade? You mean my amnesia?"

He raked a hand through his hair, exposing his face. Exposing the raw emotion, he no longer tried to keep hidden. "I'm sorry. I know this hasn't been easy on you."

"That's an understatement. Look, if you know how to cure my amnesia, do it. Do it now."

"I'm afraid I can't do that."

"Can't, or won't?" He met her gaze, sorrow evident in

his eyes, and said nothing. "Don't I get a say in what happens to me?"

"You already have, you just don't remember it."

Once again, Rai felt like he'd knocked the wind out of her. "You're implying I chose to make myself an amnesiac?" He nodded. "What possible purpose does that serve?"

"It kept you hidden, and alive." Rai searched his expression for any sign of his typical insincerity and found none.

"That doesn't make any sense, Graeber!" Rai stood up and walked around the room. "How does forgetting my past hide me? None of this makes any sense! Not this place, not you, nothing!"

Graber stood and blocked her pacing. "Look, I don't have time to explain right now, but trust me, you made a choice to walk away from your past, and it has kept you safer."

"How in the world can you expect me to trust you?"

He made a low, growling noise. "What alternatives do you have? Right now, I'm the best chance you have of staying alive."

"The Durmah stand by me."

Graeber shook his head. "You don't understand the scope ..."

"Explain it to me!"

Graeber walked toward her as if he sensed she was about to bolt. "Stay calm, all right? I'm trying to figure a way to salvage this situation."

"Look, even if I did once decide to hide away, now I want to know why, and how."

"No, the less you know, the better." He held a finger to his lips, gesturing for her silence. "Understand this: without your memories, your personality has shifted, and thus your signature reads. The more you remember, the more you return to that previous you, and that past signature. It's absolutely imperative that not happen."

"Why?"

"Because, if any of those hooded figures from your dreams read the real you, are able to recognize you, they'll kill you without hesitation." He spoke in a whisper, commanding her attention.

"The dreams were real?" Rai asked.

Graeber nodded agreement.

An icy shiver ran up her spine. "Why did they want me dead?"

"You were a part of their group, our group, and you broke the rules. They wanted to stop you and to make sure that no one else followed your example. So they ordered your death, to ensure you'd never be a problem for them ever again."

Rai remembered the voices in her nightmare calling her traitor. "Does this group have a name?"

He hesitated a moment. "The Anemoi."

This meant nothing to Rai, and yet it was good to have a name for one's enemies. "Why aren't I dead? In my dream, I remember them catching me, and then I wake up."

"They did catch you. They beat you nearly to death. When the time came, your sister and I asked if we could cremate your body ourselves, and thus finish the job."

I have a sister? Rai wanted to ask more about her, but

it would have to wait. "Hold on, so you and my sister are also members of this 'Anemoi' group?"

"Yes. We're all three members."

"So how does the Anemoi relate to the Septs and everything?"

"It doesn't, and I'm not going to explain any more about them to you. However, you should know all of the special abilities you have, like reading others and your enhanced eyesight and hearing, every member of the Anemoi has those as well. This is why you must be very careful not to read others or otherwise display any signs of your gifts. If they catch you doing it, they'll know you're one of them."

"But when they encounter me, why wouldn't they just look at me and say, 'hey, there's that girl we wanted dead and dusted'?"

"Because, when we took you away we healed you, shifted your appearance, and removed your memories. The process took many months, but it has kept your appearance and your signature from revealing your true identity."

No wonder my own reflection looks foreign to me. "So I bet you thought using my keener than average nose to find the thallium salts in the Stime's swamplands wasn't the best idea?"

He shook his head, his frustration was palpable. "I spoke to the Guardian you were with and explained she was to note in her reports I found the contamination, not you. Your name and the Durmah Sept name will be excluded from all of her reports."

"Thanks."

"No problem."

"Although you're vague, this is all beginning to come together. So after you healed me and altered my appearance, I assume you handed me over to the Temples for placement with the Durmah?" He nodded. "Wait. There was no miscarriage either, right? That was all part of the sham too?"

"Correct. We used your supposedly barren state as part of your cover story to allow for your adoption by the Durmah."

"Have I borne children?"

"You haven't, but I doubt you're truly barren. You've never tried to conceive."

"That doesn't make any sense. Are you saying I never performed my Temple service like every other female on Az'Unda?"

"You never did. Your duties to the Anemoi took precedence over serving as a breeder for our colony."

"What did I do for them that was so important?"

The enigmatic sadness in his eyes drew her closer, but he kept distance between them. "You expect me to answer that?"

"No, I suppose not. So, that's why the unique plague medicinal formula they gave me after my supposed miscarriage dulled my senses? It was an attempt to prevent me from noticing and subsequently using my enhanced senses?"

"Yes. Why'd you stop taking it, anyway?"

"It numbed my tongue as well as my nose. It was annoying. Everything I ate tasted about as exciting as dirt, so I took the regular stuff instead."

"Too bad. We should have thought that one through further."

"Did you even test it before giving it to me?"

A shadow passed over his face, and he was serious again. "I wasn't in charge of that part."

Rai thought it best to switch the subject. "Can I ask something else?"

He sighed. "Go ahead."

She walked over to the computer terminal and ran her hand over the broken part of the screen. "You mentioned I decorated this place. Did I once live here?"

He followed her across the room. "You noticed that slip?" Rai gave a curt nod, unsure how far she could push him. "Yes, you did."

"Weird. Yes, you're right. I do favor the decorating style. Now, how is it that I'm sixteen and yet somehow I used to live in this safe house in the middle of nowhere? What Sept would ever allow that?"

Graeber crossed his arms and leaned up against the plasticine screen. "You're not sixteen...you're quite a bit older, and you've never been in Sept before."

"See, just as I think you're about to solve this puzzle for me, you have to go and start in with the crazy talk. Will you explain either of those answers?"

"No."

"I didn't think so." Rai reflected on all of this new information, unsure of what to ask next.

"Have I at least managed to impress upon you the importance of staying hidden? Of not flaunting your abilities? Please try to at least appear to play the part of a Durmah Merchant?"

"Yeah, yeah, keep my nose down lest the big bad Anemoi tries to kill me again. I'll do that, but what's the next step?"

"Not just you. If it's discovered your sister and I kept you alive, they will sentence us to death as well. Your ability to play the part affects all three of us."

Rai was stunned. "What was my crime?"

"It's not important. You didn't deserve to die for it." His eyes smoldered banked rage.

"Tell me," Rai said softly.

"No. It reveals too much."

Rai swore. "If you want me to cooperate, you're going to explain to me why I agreed to remove my memories, and evade my death sentence."

"If only we could have removed your stubborn-headedness too." Graeber splayed his hands on the desk to his sides, his internal debate evident in the tension through his form. "You had a wild theory on the plague virus. You thought it was trying to communicate with us. You thought if you could crack the code, then perhaps that would be another way to put a stop to it."

"Okay. That's bizarre, but so what?"

Graeber's expression darkened. "You kept individuals without plague medicinal and recorded their delusional statements, in hopes you'd get messages from the virus itself."

The urge to vomit soured her throat, the pain flaring throughout her chest. "How many died from my experiments?" Graeber wouldn't meet her eyes, and she had to fight against a sudden buckling sensation in her knees. "How. Many."

"Over a hundred."

Rai bent over as the pain from her chest spread to her solar plexus. Breathing hurt. "You should have let them kill me. Let me stay dead," she whispered.

"Many unusual things have been tried to combat this plague. Your experiments did yield interesting results. You showed the virus might have some sort of driving force. However, they destroyed your research before it could be thoroughly analyzed."

The deadpan delivery in his voice didn't convince her of his sincerity. How could it, when he'd revealed her monstrous actions?

"Don't you hate me for what I did?" Rai looked up into his eyes, yet saw only compassion.

"This planet is a harsh mistress. Don't blame yourself for her extremes. No, I don't hate you for it, and neither does your sister. However, the Anemoi would not take kindly to finding out we'd saved you."

She blinked slowly, confused why Graeber and her sister would risk everything after what she'd done. They didn't hate her as the other Anemoi, but it didn't stop her from despising herself.

"I'll do my best to stay hidden. Whatever it takes, so you two don't pay for my mistakes. After that, what's the next step?" The words felt hollow falling from her lips--as empty as she felt inside.

"I don't have that answer for you yet. Honestly, I didn't think we'd make it this far."

"I suppose I'm glad to still be alive. One day you're going to unlock my memories, right?"

"It might be a long time from now, but yes, that

would be our goal. When it's safe to do so, I can unlock them for you. For now, we've got to find a way to curtail your dreams, or they'll go getting you into more trouble."

Knowing her memories still existed, and she'd recover them someday gave Rai a sense of peace. She finally had a measure of control in her life. It was small, but nonetheless, measurable.

"My sister Jesse mentioned some medicinal, faown. It brings on a deeper sleep and stops you from dreaming. I can try that."

He nodded and pulled a device out of his vest pocket. "That's not a bad idea. I'll do some research on my end and let you know if I find anything else that might help. We need to head back while there's still light. The sun's starting to set, and we don't want the Durmah suspecting anything unusual."

Rai walked to the door, and he followed behind her. "Will we be able to talk again? I know I'll have more questions for you after I have a chance to process all of this information."

"Yes, but we have to be discreet. You'd do well to go back to acting as you have toward me." He motioned for her to ascend the staircase ahead of him, and followed behind her while he intently accessed a series of menus on his hand-held device.

"What are you doing?"

"I'm erasing the records of your handprint accessing these doorlocks." He returned the device to his vest pocket. "There. Now if anyone checks the logs they'll be clean."

After they had reached the top, Rai watched the door

slide back down and into place, closing the opening in the mound and entirely concealing the entrance. Rai picked up her bag and slung it over her shoulder while admiring the russet, violet and golden tones of the beautiful sunset reflected in the still lake of Harper's Sorrow. Graeber led the way back to camp.

He'd revealed so many mysteries of her past, and yet everything would stay the same. She'd go back to the Waystation with Jesse and keep herself out of trouble. How hard could that be? The prospect of sitting around and hoping the Anemoi wouldn't find her wasn't exactly her cup of tea. Rai wanted to do something, not hide and cower.

"Look, I know it's not an exciting future, but it is the safest course at this time."

Rai stopped short. "Stop it, you rude bastard!" This time she hadn't even sensed him eavesdropping.

"I've been called worse, by you." He shrugged, his admission not surprising her. "You can't keep running around, trying to hunt down clues to your past and attempting to save the planet's problems anymore! You need to settle down and behave like an ordinary citizen!"

"I understand what you're saying, I do. What am I supposed to tell the Durmah? I mean, we've been checking into the tainted luna berries to make sure the Matriarchs don't think Durmah's involved. Wait, did you poison the berries?"

"No," he scowled. "I've been protecting the people of Az'Unda for longer than you can imagine. Why would I try to kill them off now?"

Rai shrugged her shoulders. "I didn't think so...not really. It's just, someone set those dispersal units."

"As hard as this is for you to hear: Let. It. Go. Others will figure it out from here."

"I'll try. The Durmah also know I've had dreams of my past that reminded me of this place. How do I explain those?"

"It's simple. Tell them you found nothing. Perhaps say I lectured you on the dangers of wandering off and outside of the protection of the Guardians. You're very creative, I'm sure you'll come up with something. You can leave the luna berry issue to me. I'll make it clear the Durmah name has been absolved so they can go back to business as normal."

Rai tried to imagine Ponar's reaction when she told him that she'd found nothing. She'd have to act disappointed if he was going to buy it. Perhaps Graeber was wrong. Why couldn't she trust Ponar, and for that matter Jesse as well, to keep her secrets?

"I'd advise against trusting them," he replied to her unspoken thoughts. "They're kind people, but it's best you share none of what we've talked about today with anyone. In fact, I have to recommend avoiding physical contact with them too."

Rai flashed back to earlier that afternoon, and how she'd watched Ponar's tanned and muscular frame. She thought fleetingly of when she'd first met him at the Waystation in Kiya's Grace, and then deliberately suppressed all imagery of Ponar. "What do you mean?" she asked, unable to contain a slight blush.

If he'd been reading Rai, Graeber gave no outward

sign of it. "Physical contact makes reading another much easier, but it also creates a false intimacy with the other person. If you're not used to it, such as in your case when you don't have a full grip on your abilities, it can be diffi- cult to control your reaction and differentiate your thoughts and emotions from the other person's."

Rai blushed from her head to her toes. "Well, that explains a few things. I'll be cautious and follow your advice in the future."

"You do that," he replied, his face blank of emotions. "The camp is just down the hill. We should be going."

"One final thing. You said you and my sister, was her name 'Bo'? You mentioned the name earlier, saved me from the fate the Anemoi had in store for me?"

Graeber hesitated, and Rai wondered if he'd rather she'd not have remembered the name. "Bau. We need to go." He turned and walked away.

"One more moment won't change anything." He stopped but didn't turn to face her. "I can understand how my sister, Bau, wanted to save me. Why you?"

Graeber turned and walked back toward Rai, measuring every step as he stalked his prey. He walked right up to her until they almost touched. The look in his eyes was feral, beast-like, and panic shot through her. His scent was hungry, deadly, and she knew this hunter never lost his quarry. Irrationally, she didn't want to escape Graeber's intense focus--but instead wondered what would happen if he caught her.

He leaned in and, taking great care not to let their skin come into contact, whispered into her ear. "Ah, Kilawren. It's a shame. You were so bright once. I'd help you out, but I'm quite sure you can figure this one out all on your own."

Graeber turned on his heel and walked away, leaving Rai alone on the hill in the twilight.

Rai stood there, gasping, with tears running down her face. Graeber was right. She could have--no, should have--figured it out all on her own.

Meik watched Rai and the Guardian standing there talking, apparently unaware of his presence. Meik prided himself, amongst many things, on his ability to interpret other's body language. All it took was paying a little attention to detail, after all. Besides being a fun sport, Meik was always amazed at how much information you could gather when others weren't aware you were watching them.

As he leaned into the bark of the large tree, Meik strained to hear what they were discussing, but he couldn't quite make it out. The Guardian looked and sounded very serious, he had that what Meik had come to think of as his serious face on as he stood with his arms crossed and kept shaking his head with every response. Did he practice that in front of a mirror, or did it just come naturally for someone with such an over-inflated ego?

Rai kept asking the Guardian questions. Meik could tell they were questions because of the way she kept shrugging her shoulders and tilting her head to the side looking all confused like; Rai did that all the time. The

Guardian kept shaking his head no and looked to be stonewalling her. Nothing new there, Meik thought. That girl was a bit silly at times. She said and asked things no one should talk about aloud, and never in front of a Guardian.

Meik wondered if he should intervene before she angered the Guardian. Now he was smiling at her as she blushed and looked even more confused. Poor girl, that Guardian was making her feel like an idiot.

Then the Guardian took a few steps down toward the camp, but it looked like Rai didn't want to give up her argument. She just kept talking and talking. The Guardian's irritation rolled off his powerful form as his muscles bunched and hands clenched. Suddenly the Guardian turned and stomped right back up to the girl, looking darned angry. Meik half expected the Guardian to slap Rai, but instead, he was, what? Whispering in her ear? Next thing he knew, the Guardian walked away from Rai, leaving her alone in the dark. But why did she stand there crying?

Meik didn't know what to make of it, other than it made him uncomfortable. What in the moons was going on here? Rai stood there for a few minutes, which made Meik worry that she was injured. He almost moseyed up to check on her, but he didn't want her knowing he'd been watching their exchange. Rai then walked down the hill toward the camp, so he didn't have to intervene.

He wanted to know what the Guardian had said to Rai. It looked like they'd talked quite a lot, to get into arguments that heated and emotional and all. Meik knew he'd know soon enough though. Rai was a Durmah, and she'd be sure to share any interesting details at the next available opportunity.

Meik couldn't wait to find out.

#BEGIN TRANSMISSION#
#ROUTING CODE: ANEMOI
BAULEEL, ROAMING COM W9-
62B TO GUARDIAN GRAEBER,
GUARDIAN SEPT, ROAMING
COM H3-29Y#
#ENCRYPTION: HIGH#
#PRIORITY: HIGH#

BAULEEL: Sorry I've been incommunicado these last two weeks. If you haven't already heard, there was an incident at the Raven's Call Technician's Guild.

GRAEBER: I tried to reach you via com, but you never answered. What's happened? Are you all right?

BAULEEL: Terem Zebio, that plague-ridden child you brought in a few months ago, not only maintained a stable mutation, but also managed to escape the confines of his cell and destroy most of the facility two weeks ago. I came upon him in his rampage in the Technician's wing, and then was taken by surprise and almost killed. Worse, he used my handprint to activate the supply door. When he kills again, that blood will be on my hands.

I was a fool. Doubly so because I barred them from terminating him when it was still a viable option.

From what Matriarch/Anemoi Natre (elected this very morning by the Elder's Council -- and I'm sure manipulated into position by the Anemoi) told the surviving Technicians today, it appears although he escaped, he hasn't attacked anyone within the city or surrounding farms. I can't imagine why he's stopped, but we're lucky he hasn't yet.

GRAEBER: *I don't have to tell you, but that is extremely unusual behavior for a Terror. Something I've never heard of before.*

BAULEEL: *I've left the Temple and plan on staying off the grid. I have no idea*

*where he is, but I'm going to find out.
Then I'm going to kill him. That little
project of ours which you've been
attending to doesn't need your
watchful eye anymore.*

*I forgot to mention I have a Technician
with me. I made him a deal to explain
the scans from the triage crèche with
him in exchange for helping me get
away from the Temple safely, but I'm
not sure how I'll keep my bargain. We
Anemoi keep so many, many secrets.
How do I explain the Methuselah
treatments without dragging him
deeper into our web?*

*GRAEBER: I'm afraid the timing of your
request is a challenge for me. My
project is at a critical stage. I'll get
back with you in a few days. Will the
Technician be an aid or hindrance? I
doubt he can protect you.*

*BAULEEL: He saved my life once, and he
has my trust, as far as I'll give it. Don't
take too long stabilizing your current
situation or you'll miss out on the
hunt.*

Send replies only to this roaming comm.

Please keep in mind Natre now has access to my old terminal and therefore must know we've been corresponding. I doubt she's cracked my access codes for personal items, so she hasn't read the content of those messages, but the frequency would give her pause.

We must assume she will at the least suspect something is going on, and we've not been altogether truthful. Perhaps she'll believe we plot some future conspiracy.

GRAEBER: We can't do anything about Natre now, but this changes our long-term plans. I'll do what I can with my project, and then join up with you after.

We can discuss further then. It may be time for plan B.

BAULEEL: Plan B isn't an option.

GRAEBER: Considering the circumstances, we may not have a choice.

#END TRANSMISSION#

CHAPTER 42

TEREM WAITED IN THE SHADOWS OF THE FOREST hills while the sun slowly rose and cast its light into the valley. He watched the farm come to life. First, the roosters welcomed the day, and then the farmhands, roused from their beds at this early hour, began their chores.

He liked the look of the place. A peaceful place, surrounded by green fields and acres of cultivated crops. The people here were happy, at least from a distance.

"Jonquin Sept, farmers of cotton and yellow-wort. Yellow-wort roots are prized for the brilliant orange, yellow and brown fabric dyes they produce," the whispers shared, unasked.

"Shut UP!" Terem yelled aloud. Why wouldn't they go away! Only silence and the calls of an aggravated bird answered.

Terem continued to wait until a large, burly brown-haired man emerged from the central Sept hall.

"Treus, the eldest son of Chieftess Ozzat Jonquin," offered the whispers. "He oversees all of the hired help."

Terem walked down the road leading to the Jonquin farmland. It took only a few minutes along the pleasant path lined with wildflowers to reach the main complex, surrounded by a high fence. A man feeding the goats took note of his arrival and brought it to Treus' attention, pointing up at Terem on the road.

When Terem reached the compound and knocked at the gate, Treus opened it.

"What's your business on this beautiful day, son?"

"May I please speak to Treus Jonquin?" Terem asked.

"That'd be me. How can I help you?" he asked, raising a curious eyebrow.

"The work placement office at Raven's Call Temple said you were looking to bring on some help. Told me you might be seeking to expand a bit." At least, that's what they'd said, and they'd better be right.

"You came all the way out here on your own?" Treus asked, looking back up the road.

"No sir," Terem replied. "I hitched a ride with a supply wagon to the Guardian's outpost to the south. I walked here this morning after the sun rose."

"Mighty brave of you, kid, coming out here without an escort. What's your name?"

"Thad. Do you still need help, sir?"

"We sure do. Have you ever worked on a farm before?"

"No, I've lived in the city my whole life, crafting pottery. When the last Sept I worked for had to cut back on their hired hands, I figured why not see another part of the world for a change?" Terem replied. You've practiced that line so often these past few days, it almost sounds like you believe it.

"Well, we can't offer you the safety you might be used to back in the city, Thad, but you will get your chance to see our fields and the beautiful countryside around here. My terms are simple, you work an honest day's work, every day, and we feed, clothe, and give you your own room and bed to sleep in. Once your job is done, you'll have your afternoons and evenings to yourself. When our harvests are quite large, everyone gets a bonus. Does that sound acceptable to you?" Treus asked.

"Sure does!" Terem replied, both to Treus and to the voices.

"Now, you've got to understand one other thing: if you're not safe in the main house by nightfall, you're on your own for the night. The entire night. I'm not given to searching around in the dark for stragglers."

"I can handle myself," Terem replied, bristling inwardly at his tone. Who does he think he is? He'd be dead in seconds if we just ... "You won't have to worry about me at all," Terem continued over the hateful internal dialog he'd been becoming used to, forcing a pleasant smile for Treus' benefit.

Treus nodded down at him, oblivious to the voices Terem heard regularly. "Somehow, I believe you, kid." He extended a hand, which a smiling Terem accepted, and they shook on it.

"Welcome to Jonquin Sept's farms, Thad. Come on in, and I'll introduce you around." He stepped aside, motioning Terem into the compound.

"Thanks, Treus. I'm indebted to you for your kind-ness." Terem walked in through the open gate. He embraced his new identity as Thad and imagined the nightmares from the past slipping away into the dark where they belonged.

"Sure, you're safe enough for now; but they won't stop coming, will they?" asked the whispers. "What then?"

"Then I'll kill them. All of them."

Terem decided to start ignoring the whispers. After all this beautiful place promised a fresh start.

END OF BOOK ONE

Thank you so much for reading The Dream Sifter! It would mean a lot to me if you could leave a review. A single line or two makes a big difference for other people when deciding if a book is a good fit for them.

The next book in the series, Dreams Manifest, is out now.

Turn the page for a sneak peek of book two.

Read on for an exclusive excerpt from the next book in the series:

Dreams Manifest

Facing a new threat and the potential end of the colony, Rai Durmah just may be in over her head.

★★★★★ "I found this to be utterly engrossing, with a good mix of fantasy and sci-fi."

★★★★★ "This was a very fascinating storyline that kept me going and had so many twists and turns that I almost had whiplash. The storyline was so intricate that you could visualize just what was going on."

★★★★★ "The plot became very intricate and was a real page turner."

Caught between her adoptive family who doubts her loyalties, the alien Juggernaut, and a Guardian protector she fears, Rai unwittingly unearths the answers to solve or destroy Az'Unda's future.

When she stumbles upon an ancient power that could change everything, there is hope. Hope for Rai, hope for humanity, and hope for survival.

As long as she can manifest the strength to fight...

Turn the page to preview the first two chapters or click here to pick up your copy today!

Gazing into the mirror Brague surveyed the work of his colorist, ensuring all of the details were perfection. Brague had had his sigil improperly applied once before, and to his great embarrassment, it had taken almost a full season to grow out. He'd killed the colorist as soon as he'd seen the flaw to prevent anyone else from being scarred...no, *maimed* as he'd been. The offending colorist had gotten the yellow background swirl a whole tone darker than normal, throwing off the overall harmony of the design. Spending another few moments checking over the placement and color choices, Brague gave a perfunctory nod to the colorist, signaling his acceptance of the proposed work.

He held very still while the colorist activated the chemical heat-set, and felt the radiating warmth of it through his thick, insulating shell. At that inopportune moment, his communicator chimed. He waited impatiently for the process to finish, lest he mar the design. It took only another few moments, and then the colorist moved in to polish and shine the crisp new lines. Brague waited patiently, knowing that this step was necessary to seal in the colors. The colorist finished and then backed away, deferentially exposing the vulnerable cleft of his neck to Brague.

Brague raised himself to his full height and examined every detail of the finished work in the mirrored wall. It satisfied him to discover all elements met his exacting attention to detail. His communicator chimed again, reminding him that there was an urgent message awaiting his attention. The colorist waited, frozen, waiting for Brague's judgment.

"It is ... acceptable," Brague graciously intoned.

The colorist eased his submissive posture and bowed. "I am honored to please you. I will endeavor to exceed your expectations in the future."

Brague caught a quick, caustic whiff of emotion lacing the air, entirely at odds with the colorist's demeanor. He took another, deeper breath, but Brague no longer scented the affront. Brague chose to ignore the cheeky colorists moment of indiscretion and strode back toward his research facility. Keying the security algorithm into the communicator on his left arm, Brague accessed his systems. Bringing up the messaging relays, he found a communiqué from Princess Qwell awaiting his review. He'd heard she was working on a particular project, and this was her request to have *him*, Selector Brague, placed on this assignment. He keyed off a quick acceptance note, full of the requisite honorifics and gratitude. Brague had assumed he'd be chosen for the project and would have been greatly disappointed if his assumption had been proven incorrect. Still, this gratifying moment of acceptance was a unique thing to be savored.

Brague adored his job, but he had no cause to find it anything less than exceptional. His illustrious career as a Selector had earned him full autonomy over all aspects of his research, from the specimen labs to the computing systems. The Hegemony had endowed his recent projects with generous resource budgets, both monetary and material, much to the chagrin of lesser-ranked Selectors. Due to his proven and dependable results, Brague had been granted great freedoms with his Selection process and staff allocations. He had a reputation as one of the best available, with no errors in Selection and an Evaluation rate of over 96%. Accurate Selections avoided losses of resources and time for the Queens, allowing the territories of the Hegemony to expand at a calculated and consistently planned pace. His most recent assignment to Princess Qwell was surely a sign of the Hegemony's enduring faith in his abilities.

Entering his research quarters, Brague noted everything was precisely as he'd left it. He strode to the main terminal interface, not wanting to delay starting on his new assignment another moment. He reviewed all of his current projects and found none of them at the level of Princess Qwell's priority or status. Brague foisted the rest off onto lower rated Selectors, (He gave them) nothing above their abilities but quite beyond their prestige.

After taking care of reassigning his current project

load, Brague searched through the databases for candidate planets. His carapace hummed faintly in excitement, for this was no ordinary Selection.

Princess Qwell's directive was to create a new breed of Juggernaut that would be adapted to submerged, aqueous environments. With the resources required for proper growth margins, utilizing partially or wholly aqueous planets opened up a much wider range of options for future expansion. Presently specialized equipment was needed for their race to operate underwater. This raised the cost of extracting needed minerals and chemicals from the oceanic floors to prohibitive levels. Logistics wasn't the only problem. Such operations experienced a worker loss in the mid-fortieth percentile as well, which was wasteful and inefficient. This Selection might prove to be the most exciting, interesting, and hazardous challenge of Brague's entire career.

Failure to Select an appropriate planet would be a disgrace with the potential to ruin his career. Although he'd never botched a job, this assignment brought with it the highest risk of failure to date. Erroneously Selecting a planet that led to Princess Qwell's failure would, of course, mean his immediate extermination, a possible but highly improbable outcome in consideration of Brague's exemplary record.

There were plenty of water worlds out there, but as always, the trick was in Selecting the one that would allow for the best success for the future Queen's goals. All Selectors created their own search and filtering algorithms, and Brague had the utmost confidence in his methods. Selecting the right planet for this mission would ensure the highest of honors for Brague--the ability to contribute his genetic material to future generations.

Brague's first step was to compile a listing of possibilities for Evaluation. The needs of this particular case opened up an entirely new range of planets and criteria most often excluded from common searches. A humid, primarily oceanic world with some swampland would be ideal, to provide a transitioning zone for Princess Qwell to experiment with different genetic variations of Juggernaut pupae. Caves were also desirable for this type of work, as they lent shelter, safety, and privacy to the Queen's activities.

Brague was familiar with all steps in the Juggernaut life cycle and Juggernaut physiology. This extensive and exhaustive standard training was required of all Selectors and would play heavily into this assignment. The database filter netted a variety of initial possibilities, many of them inevitably inhabited by lower beings that were often more suited to such climates. Brague had noted over his many cycles of research that the less-than-sentient races often gravitated towards wetter climes, but he'd never cared enough about them to find out why. Upon brief reflection, he discovered he still didn't care.

Brague mused that when this initiative proved successful the expanded range of the Juggernaut's territory would mean fewer "safe" colonization options for such pathetic life forms, which was as it should be. Species who couldn't compete due to a lack of intelligence or hardiness should do the universe the favor of extinguishing themselves or at least cease their predictably incessant breeding.

Perhaps it would be preferable to Select a planet already colonized by one of the more disgusting races? Choosing an already inhabited world would send a message that their infestations on proper Juggernaut territory would no longer be tolerated. Expanding Juggernaut territory options in this manner would significantly limit colonization options for a variety of inferior species, especially the invasive species of primates. All affected lesser races would have no choice but to accept their subsequent reduction of position within the celestial hierarchy.

The idea of bringing home to the substandard races the gravity of their mistake in colonizing Juggernaut lands pleased Brague immensely.

Brague updated the database filters to include only planets colonized by lower beings. The enormity and significance of this project made good, solid supply lines (and frequency of transit within them) of paramount importance, so he added another filter, one that specified planets with proximity to military outposts and agricultural distribution points. Soon a preliminary list of a few hundred planets ranked in descending order of relevancy appeared in his result set.

At this point, his real work began. Just because the database listed a given world did not mean it still met the necessary qualifications. The experienced Selector knew that the real determinant of a planet's usefulness lay in one key factor above all others: toxicology. Especially with colonized worlds, frequently the new inhabitants had introduced toxins or chemicals into the ecosystem that were difficult or time-consuming to remove, and these potential hurdles didn't always get into the database promptly. Not all settlements were reported as required to the Hegemony, and some species of lower beings foolishly continued to ignore Hegemonic mandates.

To maximize the efficient use of scientific resources, inspections of distant planets didn't occur with any real frequency, at least not until they were needed. Thus was the need for skilled Selectors, to sniff out problems and challenges well in advance of any resource commitment.

For instance, the fourth planet on the list looked particularly promising. Topping the list were its extensive cave complexes, deep oceans, vast mineral deposits, sizable areas of swampland and a humid but mild climate. It fit all the major criteria perfectly. It also matched with Brague's secondary requirements, having a small colony of primates, who were clinging to a meager existence and plagued by disease.

Primates were still a relatively new species, and as such, hadn't won the Hegemony's formal Acceptance of Sentience ranking. Based on what he'd learned of the species, Brague doubted they ever would. Weak races that couldn't adapt to life off of their home world were doomed to failure in the goal of galactic expansion. The primate species current circumstances didn't bode well for their future. Primates should have taken the hint in the beginning and given up!

It was evident they weren't up to the task. After all,

the database showed primate numbers across all of their colonized worlds were in a slow, steady decline. How primates kept fighting without any discernible forward progress was beyond Brague, and he idly wondered what possessed such a lowly race to attempt seemingly impossible things beyond their means. It would be a charity to release them from their problems, and it genuinely pleased Brague that he might be the one to do so.

Brague sent a communiqué to Princess Qwell, presenting the current list of options. Even for a well-respected Selector like Brague, frequent demonstrations of progress were essential. He included a timeline for narrowing down the attached list to a few dozen for Evaluation, setting an aggressive goal of a mere three Latnes for this task. He also noted that comprehensive progress reports would be sent every sub-Latne. This was more detail than necessary, but Brague preferred to keep Princess Qwell as involved as possible. This meant assignment completion would occur in the Nithe Tor-Latne of the Sun Trine, always an auspicious time for accomplishments involving new growth and Juggernaut expansion. Of course, with the importance of this task and what was at stake, Brague would Evaluate each of the final options personally.

Brague swelled with pride over the Queens' enduring faith in his abilities. He only hoped to be rewarded with the highest of honors for success in this venture. The competition was brutal amongst his caste for the limited breeding rights available. Surely the enormity of this task would secure his privileges?

Quickly cross-checking his personal lab's roster of available specimens with the initial list of planets he'd forwarded to Princess Qwell, Brague was pleased to find some matches for initial testing and research. He found it quite remarkable what one could learn about a planet through its evolved fauna, especially when those creatures experienced certain ... *stressors*. Heading off to his lab, Brague considered that this part of his job was by far the most interesting and certainly the most entertaining.

Selector Brague Research Notes,
Princess Qwell Assignment,
Kacke Prime-Latne of the Dark Trine.

UPDATE FOR THE FIRST SUB-LATNE OF THE PROJECT. Initial re-screenings of the top 200 identified prime pre-Selection planets have been ordered and scheduled. While waiting to receive the re-screening reports, I have spent my time in my formidable lab researching flora and fauna specimens that correspond to planets on the pre-Selection list. Specimen research is always most gratifying, but I'm anxious to begin reviewing pre-Selection reports so a visitation schedule can be set. It's most important to keep up the pace! Princess Qwell will be expecting status reports soon.

Specimen research has proved educational, yet I cannot fully apply it until the present stage of the project is completed. I have placed orders for new sample retrievals from the top 25 planets on the list, as I found some of my stocks lacking. I expect these to arrive within days. It's frustrating to have to wait that long, yet I can't waste my time doing the scut work myself. Better to take full advantage of my status and staff by delegating such work to them.

Also of note for this log entry is that Princess Qwell's personal guard and assistants have supplemented my staff. Extra ships from her fleet have been placed at my disposal. Although I could, of course, have managed with current resources, it is a generous gift nonetheless. Resources are clearly not an issue for *this* Princess. She wants results and seems quite free with her assets to help make it happen.

I must have the final Selection listing for Princess Qwell's review by the next Latne as promised in the initial project plan, which would be Perith Prime-Latne. Although I'm not comfortable spending an entire full Latne just to narrow down the search and conduct specimen studies, with what's at stake for this project I consider it necessary. Failure to properly screen out planets not matching Princess Qwell's requirements would only add precious sub-Latnes to this project.

Best to keep myself busy in the lab while I await the re-screening results. Besides, I find lab work can be quite gratifying, second only to hands-on fieldwork. Experimentation sometimes yields the most surprising results, often giving clues to a creature's native environment and culture. Dealing with specimens during fieldwork in their natural habitat elicits more precise responses.

Although it is not related to the current project for Princess Qwell, I must note progress on one particular experiment I've had underway for some time. The species known as Taska of the Hunchen galaxy will continue to care for injured individuals within the breeding group, even when it is evident that the person's wounds are beyond all repair. They even allocated a portion of their already limited rations to the dying member! This demonstrates an inability of this species to think clearly in the face of crisis. No truly rational--and certainly never any true sentient being--would ever behave so foolishly!

THE LOUD SCRAPING OF THE BARN DOOR OPENING startled Terem, making him look up from oiling the saddle. Treus entered against a backdrop of fading sunset. How was it already dark outside? With the lanterns lit in the barn, Terem hadn't noticed the hour.

"Still hard at work, I see?" Treus smiled at him, leaning against the doorframe.

"I'll be in for dinner in just a moment, sir. I'm almost done getting the saddles cleaned."

"I doubt they've ever been cleaner, Thad. Still, you have to eat sometime, son."

Terem smiled at being called his pseudonym 'Thad,' a reminder of his success in recreating himself post Zebio Sept and after the horrors of the Temples. "Oh, I will. The cook always sets a little aside for me," Terem replied.

"I'm sure he does. Look, you should know that all the Jonquin have noticed how dedicated you are to your work, and how impressed everyone is with you because of that," Treus stated. "It's rare to find hired help with such dedication."

It was pure self-interest, although Treus didn't need to know that. The harder Terem worked, the less often he noticed the voices. They were the only reminders of the nightmares he'd suffered.

"Thank you, sir. That's very kind of you to say so," Terem replied.

Treus nodded. "It's a simple truth. There's just one problem."

Terem felt a sinking feeling inside. "What's that, sir?"

"It's just that you work so hard and such long hours, no one has had much of a chance to get to know you very well," Treus replied.

Which I have to do, Terem thought to himself, to protect the Jonquin and myself. "*You aren't kidding,*" whispered the unbidden voices. The weirdest ideas would come into his head when he was with people. He would feel with total and complete certainty that there was something wrong with them and that they needed to be eradicated permanently. Not engaging others, avoiding talking, and staying busy seemed to ameliorate the problem.

"I guess I'm a bit shy, is all," Terem offered, a pitiful excuse even to himself.

"I understand," Treus continued. "Just break for meals with everyone, that's all I ask, okay? You don't even have to say much, just be there, smile back at people, and make some small talk. It'll help you fit in better."

"I'll make an effort," Terem replied, unsure if he meant it.

"You'll do great," Treus smiled at him. "I'm gonna leave you to it. I still have to make sure we're locked up for the evening."

"Have a good night!" Terem replied.

Treus started to close the barn door and then stopped. "Oh, I almost forgot! A Guardian is inside the main hall, catching everyone at dinner for a quick scan. Should I tell her you'll be right in?"

Time's up. We told you it wouldn't last. "Is there a problem in the area?" Terem asked.

"No, no. Sorry, I didn't mean to alarm you. We have a Guardian stop by every few weeks and check up on us all, make sure everyone's healthy and what not. Do they do it differently in the cities?"

"Yeah. People are scanned on the street while they're going about their business. You'd never even notice unless you were watching the Guardians. Sometimes, when someone hasn't been logged with a scan for a few weeks, they'll come by your Sept Hall," Terem explained.

Not that you'd know anything about that, Terem, would you?

"Makes sense," Treus explained. "They visit us in the evening because we're all accounted for and in one spot, so it's easier and quicker for them."

Terem nodded understanding. *"You know, I'm going to be just a little bit longer on this. Do you think it'd be too much trouble to ask the Guardian to come out here?"* Terem felt one of the voices ask through his mouth.

"Sure, I can ask. Doubt it will be a problem. Just stay here until the Guardian comes and finds you, all right? I don't want her having a fit cause she has to hunt someone down."

"I'll wait right here," Terem replied. "Have a good night, sir."

"Good evening, Thad," Treus answered and then pulled the door shut behind him.

Terem waited, pacing back and forth in the barn.

"What am I going to do?" he asked himself. "I like it here. I don't want to have to hurt everyone."

There is another way. Trust us.

Minutes later the door scraped open again, revealing a short, blonde female Guardian, dressed in their standard green and gray multi-hued garb. Terem noted that she didn't have her scanner in her hand at the moment. Luck was with him.

He smiled broadly at her. "Thanks so much for stopping by out here. I just managed to get everything finished up."

She shrugged. "Makes no difference to me. This barn is on my way out."

Terem watched her pull out a device from her pocket. *That's a medical scanner. She'll know you're infected within three or four minutes of activation.* "So, you travel back to ... wherever ... from here?" he asked.

"I'm stationed out of an outpost to the south of here. It's a few hours by horse," she explained.

"You came on horseback?" he asked. "Why didn't you stable the mare for the day?"

"No bother. I don't ever stay long. I just let her graze a bit inside the front gate while I get things taken care of." She waited for the scanner's results.

No more time. "*I was wondering if you could do something for me?*" the voices asked.

"What?" asked the Guardian.

"*I need to get a message out to an old acquaintance.*"

The Guardian looked up at him, a confused expression on her face. "I don't usually handle mail, but as the Jonquin have always been nice to me, I'll see what I can do for you. Where's the message?"

"*Well, it's not something for them to read, per se. It's something they need to see an example of to understand.*"

Terem noticed a red light began flashing on the scanner's screen. The Guardian glanced down, and then back up at him. All of her lassitude was suddenly replaced by a keen, calculated stance.

"An example of what?" she asked, sliding the scanner back into her pocket. She started to slowly reach for her pulse weapon with her left hand.

He reached out and grabbed her by the throat, while also pinning her left arm to her side with his right hand. The thing that once was Terem acted, well beyond the reaction speed the Guardian possessed. She struggled but was unable to move or breathe as his digits elongated, encircling the Guardian's neck. She lost the ability to breathe as he crushed her windpipe. He smiled, watching her eyes fill with agonizing panic.

"Death. Would you like to help me?"

Click below to buy the full ebook, Dreams Manifest, now!

US

UK

CAN

The loud scraping of the barn door opening startled Terem, making him look up from oiling the saddle. Treus entered against a backdrop of fading sunset. How was it already dark outside? With the lanterns lit in the barn, Terem hadn't noticed the hour.

"Still hard at work, I see?" Treus smiled at him, leaning against the doorframe.

"I'll be in for dinner in just a moment, sir. I'm almost done getting the saddles cleaned."

"I doubt they've ever been cleaner, Thad. Still, you have to eat sometime, son."

Terem smiled at being called his pseudonym 'Thad,' a reminder of his success in recreating himself post Zebio Sept and after the horrors of the Temples. "Oh, I will. The cook always sets a little aside for me," Terem replied.

"I'm sure he does. Look, you should know that all the Jonquin have noticed how dedicated you are to your work, and how impressed everyone is with you because of that," Treus stated. "It's rare to find hired help with such dedication."

It was pure self-interest, although Treus didn't need to know that. The harder Terem worked, the less often he noticed the voices. They were the only reminders of the nightmares he'd suffered.

"Thank you, sir. That's very kind of you to say so," Terem replied.

Treus nodded. "It's a simple truth. There's just one problem."

Terem felt a sinking feeling inside. "What's that, sir?"

"It's just that you work so hard and such long hours, no one has had much of a chance to get to know you very well," Treus replied.

Which I have to do, Terem thought to himself, to protect the Jonquin and myself. *"You aren't kidding,"* whispered the unbidden voices. The weirdest ideas would come into his head when he was with people. He would feel with total and complete certainty that there was something wrong with them and that they needed to be eradicated permanently. Not engaging others, avoiding talking, and staying busy seemed to ameliorate the problem.

"I guess I'm a bit shy, is all," Terem offered, a pitiful excuse even to himself.

"I understand," Treus continued. "Just break for meals with everyone, that's all I ask, okay? You don't even have to say much, just be there, smile back at people, and make some small talk. It'll help you fit in better."

"I'll make an effort," Terem replied, unsure if he meant it.

"You'll do great," Treus smiled at him. "I'm gonna leave you to it. I still have to make sure we're locked up for the evening."

"Have a good night!" Terem replied.

Treus started to close the barn door and then stopped. "Oh, I almost forgot! A Guardian is inside the main hall, catching everyone at dinner for a quick scan. Should I tell her you'll be right in?"

Time's up. We told you it wouldn't last. "Is there a problem in the area?" Terem asked.

"No, no. Sorry, I didn't mean to alarm you. We have a Guardian stop by every few weeks and check up on us all, make sure everyone's healthy and what not. Do they do it differently in the cities?"

"Yeah. People are scanned on the street while they're going about their business. You'd never even notice unless you were watching the Guardians. Sometimes, when someone hasn't been logged with a scan for a few weeks, they'll come by your Sept Hall," Terem explained.

Not that you'd know anything about that, Terem, would you?

"Makes sense," Treus explained. "They visit us in the evening because we're all accounted for and in one spot, so it's easier and quicker for them."

Terem nodded understanding. *"You know, I'm going to be just a little bit longer on this. Do you think it'd be too much trouble to ask the Guardian to come out here?"* Terem felt one of the voices ask through his mouth.

"Sure, I can ask. Doubt it will be a problem. Just stay here until the Guardian comes and finds you, all right? I don't want her having a fit cause she has to hunt someone down."

"I'll wait right here," Terem replied. "Have a good night, sir."

"Good evening, Thad," Treus answered and then pulled the door shut behind him.

Terem waited, pacing back and forth in the barn.

"What am I going to do?" he asked himself. "I like it here. I don't want to have to hurt everyone."

There is another way. Trust us.

Minutes later the door scraped open again, revealing a short, blonde female Guardian, dressed in their standard green and gray multi-hued garb. Terem noted that she didn't have her scanner in her hand at the moment. Luck was with him.

He smiled broadly at her. "Thanks so much for stopping by out here. I just managed to get everything finished up."

She shrugged. "Makes no difference to me. This barn is on my way out."

Terem watched her pull out a device from her pocket. *That's a medical scanner. She'll know you're infected within three or four minutes of activation.* "So, you travel back to ... wherever ... from here?" he asked.

"I'm stationed out of an outpost to the south of here. It's a few hours by horse," she explained.

"You came on horseback?" he asked. "Why didn't you stable the mare for the day?"

"No bother. I don't ever stay long. I just let her graze a bit inside the front gate while I get things taken care of." She waited for the scanner's results.

No more time. "*I was wondering if you could do something for me?*" the voices asked.

"What?" asked the Guardian.

"*I need to get a message out to an old acquaintance.*"

The Guardian looked up at him, a confused expression on her face. "I don't usually handle mail, but as the Jonquin have always been nice to me, I'll see what I can do for you. Where's the message?"

"*Well, it's not something for them to read, per se. It's something they need to see an example of to understand.*"

Terem noticed a red light began flashing on the scanner's screen. The Guardian glanced down, and then back up at him. All of her lassitude was suddenly replaced by a keen, calculated stance.

"An example of what?" she asked, sliding the scanner back into her pocket. She started to slowly reach for her pulse weapon with her left hand.

He reached out and grabbed her by the throat, while also pinning her left arm to her side with his right hand. The thing that once was Terem acted, well beyond the reaction speed the Guardian possessed. She struggled but was unable to move or breathe as his digits elongated, encircling the Guardian's neck. She lost the ability to breathe as he crushed her windpipe. He smiled, watching her eyes fill with agonizing panic.

"*Death. Would you like to help me?*"

Get more Dreams Manifest now!

If you loved the book and have a minute to spare, I would really appreciate a short review on the page or site where you bought the book. Your help in spreading the word is greatly appreciated. Reviews from readers like you make a huge difference to helping new readers find similar stories.

Thank you so much for reading and supporting my work!

Candice

P.S. If you'd like to know when my next book comes out and want to receive occasional updates from me, then you can sign up for my newsletter at candicebundy.com. I promise I will never sell your email to the daemonic marketing hordes.

WRITING AS CR BUNDY

The Depths of Memory Series

The Dream Sifter

Dreams Manifest

For a list of my full catalog of available titles, visit my Amazon Author Central page.

ACKNOWLEDGMENTS

No book happens in a vacuum. I've been blessed with fabulous support by loving, smart, and talented people, and this made all the difference in completing my journey. I want to take a moment to mention these wonderful people, and I hope you'll take the time to appreciate them with me.

To Jen, Steven, Ket, Amber, Alan, Kiersten, and Keri for your advice, kind words, and kicks in the rear as needed. I'm much obliged and will continue to return the favor.

A special thanks to my writing posse, who thrive in a pool of support and instigation. Y'all rock.

Thanks to Zippy Wizard Redaction for their editing and proofreading services.

And lastly to my friends and family who've been a source of unending strength, laughter, and wine over the years: thank you for the inspiration.

ABOUT THE AUTHOR

Candice lives in Denver, Colorado with her son and their cat Newt. A professional hedonist, rabble-rouser, winemaker, and goat-herder, she adores archeology and mythology. Candice focuses on habit hacking to meet minimalist, health, productivity, and positive mojo goals, and sometimes even blogs about it. An unrepentant epicurean, she grows heirloom tomatoes and ferments a variety of sauerkraut, sourdough, kombucha, pickles, and water kefir.

If you would like to know when she has new books out, please sign up for her newsletter at candicebundy.com. Or, email her at candice@candicebundy.com if the mood strikes you.

Editor: Zippy Wizard Redaction

Identifiers: ISBN-10: 0-9854185-1-6 |
ISBN-13: 978-0-9854185-1-9

Published by Lusios Publishing, LLC, Centennial, CO. Second Edition,
2017.